A MAGICAL KISS

"Elinor," he said softly.

"What, my lord?"

"Just this."

His lips descended to hers. She closed her eyes and surrendered to their magic.

It might well be folly. It was most likely sin. She no longer cared.

Even if she had cared, could care, she was helpless to prevent it. At this moment, she wanted his kiss more than life itself.

She raised a hand and slipped it beneath the hair at the nape of his neck. With a sharp, indrawn breath, he pulled her still more tightly against him, deepening the kiss.

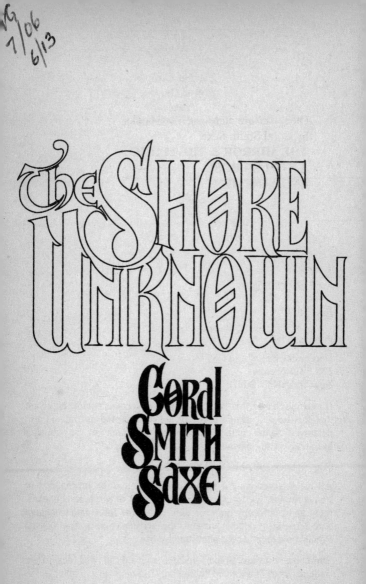

The Shore Unknown

Coral Smith Saxe

LEISURE BOOKS NEW YORK CITY

For Da Girlz:
Ingrid Durfee
and
Jane Kirschman

A LEISURE BOOK®

July 1997

Published by

Dorchester Publishing Co., Inc.
276 Fifth Avenue
New York, NY 10001

Printed in the United States of America.

"Let me dream that love goes with us
to the shore unknown."
—Felicia D. B. Hemans

Chapter One

England, 1420

Elinor turned the child toward her and placed her hands on her sister's slender shoulders. "Remember. That's all I ask of you. Now, speak the words again."

"But, Linnie—"

"Say them. Show me you remember."

"Oh, very well." The girl licked her lips and began to recite in a piping singsong. "I am the Lady Joanna DeCourtenay, daughter of the late Gerard, Baron Newborough, in, um, Oakfield, given to his four fathers in the year 1067 by a conqueror. Did I do it aright, Linnie?"

Elinor nodded and kissed Joanna's cheek, satisfied that her little sister's efforts would get her message across. Next, she turned to face the tall young boy who stood watching.

"Say them, Thomas."

The lad needed no prompting. Drawing himself up,

he spoke in the husky voice of a boy making a rapid transition into manhood.

"I am the Baron Thomas DeCourtenay, son of the late Gerard, Baron Newborough. I am master of Oakfield House, Oakfield on Trent, which land was given to my forefather in the year 1067 by the hand and seal of King William the Conqueror himself."

Elinor's impulse was to hug her brother, but she knew his adolescent dignity might be impaired by such a wanton act of sentiment. Instead, she clapped a hand on his shoulder and smiled.

"Well done," she said, her voice soft with fondness. "Never forget who you are, no matter what fortune befalls us. We are the DeCourtenays and that name shall not fail, save God Himself wills it so."

She made the sign of the cross and then grinned at her siblings. "And let us not forget the DeCourtenays are ever wont to argue their case, even with God."

"Amen," said Thomas, a small, wry smile passing briefly across his solemn features.

"That's true enough," Joanna said with a chuckle. "Remember when Mama told Father Leary that if God had meant her to be meek and submissive to men on earth, He wouldn't have given her a brain and left so many men begging?"

Elinor wanted to laugh but hid her amusement. Though not yet a nun proper, she was a resident of the Abbey of Wednesbury and her mother's plainspoken manner was not the model her superiors would wish for her.

"Mama, God rest her, was a challenge to Friar Leary, 'tis so. But the good friar was as peppery as his beard and could answer her back. In our circumstances, we must adopt a more moderate demeanor. Neither Mama nor Father are here to defend us should we trespass."

She turned and pulled up Joanna's hood, tucking the girl's wild, deep-red curls inside, out of the wind. The scent of spring flowers surrounded them, as sweet and poignant as the season of their blossoming, making Elinor's heart ache with tender memories of days when these fields had been her play-place and home. Only the future, and in particular, her actions this night, would determine if this land might ever hold the same place in the hearts of Thomas and Joanna.

Elinor waited as her brother mounted the large gray horse standing saddled and ready, then helped her little sister up before him. She touched Thomas's arm.

"The sun is near setting," she said. "Take the western road for Stafford. There's enough coin in your purse for a night's shelter there and a bite to eat, but mind you leave the town at dawn. Haste then to Alderbrydge House. If you cannot reach there by nightfall, ask for lodging at Lilleshall Abbey, then press on to Alder village the next day. The Carrowes will see that you are well cared for at Alderbrydge ere I come again."

She hesitated, looking away toward her destination, a dark and rugged castle whose tower spiked into the sky from its perch on a nearby hilltop.

"If, for some reason, I do not return, you must bid the Carrowes aid you in getting to London. Father and Mother had still some connections at court—you have the letter, Thomas—and those friends will perhaps offer help should you need to sue for your protection." She clasped her hands beneath her chin. "Pray God it doesn't come to that."

"It shall not," said Thomas. "You and I would carry our cause even unto the court of the angels."

In the late afternoon light, his eyes showed only a hint of his fears. He was his mother's son, Elinor thought, full of courage and eager to taste life's adventures. Fortunately, he also had some of his father's reserve to temper those impulses.

If anyone deserved his chance at noble manhood, it was young Thomas. As for the irrepressible Joanna, who was wriggling in her seat, eager to begin this adventure, she needed a home and a firm hand, lest she decide to try for a life as a jongleur or a pirate.

"All right, be off with you. And Godspeed."

Elinor gave the big horse a light slap on the rump and the steed started off at a ponderous, clopping walk, bearing away the last of her family.

She swallowed hard against the panic threatening to rise up and overwhelm her. The Carrowes of Alderbrydge House would see to everything Thomas and Joanna needed—they were among the two or three who had remained true and generous friends, despite all the DeCourtenays' troubles. But friendship had its limits, Elinor knew, and even the impoverished and humbled DeCourtenays had their pride, however tattered. So she must go and do what she could to secure her family's future. As the eldest, she must take responsibility. She only hoped she could settle this matter once and for all. Then she could return to the abbey and the life she had long since planned for herself.

A conflagration of red and orange flared out from the setting sun as Elinor crossed the sturdy stone bridge across the stream and made her way up the low hill to Castle Clarisdoune. She pulled her cloak and hood close about her against the chill edge of the early May wind. Shivering as much from fear as from cold, she strode on, head down, to the great gate. No one hailed her from the keep, no one stood there to admit her, so she admitted herself, using the small open door cut into the larger gate.

Utter quiet filled the great courtyard, with only the sounds of the winds whistling about, the chickens muttering in their roosts and the occasional nicker of a horse in the nearby stables. All the residents must still be at table, she thought, else surely someone would have challenged her. A good time to come, if she wanted to make her entrance public, and if she wanted to delay the inevitable.

Elinor devoutly wished for both.

She went up the steps of the main hall and banged the great iron ring against the massive oak door. No sounds came from within, no answering rattle at the latch. Had they moved on to another house? It was unlikely. Oakfield House, her family's home, was Clarisdoune's nearest neighbor. She or someone else at Oakfield would have seen an entire household, carts, horses and all, progressing down the only road connecting the two houses with the highway.

"Hello!" she called out. "Is anyone there?"

She waited, wondering if she was to be spared this last trial in her efforts to salvage her family's home and pride. But if she was spared, what else could she do, where else could she turn for help? She backed down the steps, searching for a light or some face in the upper windows.

"Who hails there?" a deep, rich voice called from above.

Elinor recognized the unmistakable voice of Roger Aston, master of Castle Clarisdoune. It was unmistakable for its sheer beauty and seductiveness, like a mellow horn. She also knew Aston could use that voice to work his will on the unwary. She peered up and saw him leaning on the narrow ledge of a window, high above her. When he saw her, his handsome mouth curled up in a sardonic smile.

"Elinor DeCourtenay," she called, though she knew full well he recognized her. She wished to make this whole event as formal and as impersonal as possible.

If she didn't, she feared she might go mad.

She reached up and threw back her cloak, revealing a light silken gown of palest blue. Her long hair caught on the winds whipping about her; it felt like ropes twining about her in the chill courtyard. She lifted her face to the window.

"I have come, my lord," she announced, "to pay your price."

*   *   *

13

". . . to pay your price . . . to pay . . . price, pay price, price, price . . ."

Her words rang around her head, an echoing, mad repetition, punctuated by peals of thunder. She staggered and almost tripped over a stone, feeling sick and dizzy with every motion. What had happened? Night had fallen and yet she had no recollection of time passing since she'd stood in Clarisdoune's courtyard.

She heard running water, felt herself falling onto a stony surface. She knew where she was; her groggy mind was able to scrabble together some weak sense, at least. Somehow, at some time, she had come back to the bridge over the Oakfield stream, and now she lay, crumpled and weak with nausea, on its chill, rough stones.

She'd been running hard; she could feel her heart slamming against her breast and a stitch knifing into her side. Some strange scent—or was it a taste?—filled her nose and throat, a bittersweet mixture of heavy roses and musty rue. She wanted to cough it out, but she lacked the strength to make the effort.

Then she heard them, the thundering hoofbeats. It had to be Roger's horse approaching, riding out of the solid wall of night. His roars of outrage, those peals of thunder, rose and gathered. She summoned the strength to stand, hauling herself up by the low stone wall that edged the bridge.

She sensed, deep within her, that she must face him, though her body and her mind screamed at her to cower in some dark corner, out of sight and sound of this oncoming horror.

The roaring built. That voice of his! she thought, wincing. It was more powerful than she had dreamed. She looked up and caught the flash of his eyes. Like his voice, they seemed to grow larger and they burned brighter and brighter until they blinded her with their fire. She held up her hand to shield herself from the hideous light as the roaring in her ears increased tenfold.

He was torturing her senses, her soul. That sickly scent, she thought, her other hand moving to her throat as if she could ease the discomfort there. The pain did not abate. There was more torment coming. The light, the sound, the fear, the sickness and pain— she could bear them no longer. She screamed her terror and let the dark madness swallow her.

Chapter Two

Sonoma County, California, Present Day

"What the hell!"

Against her will, Elinor roused once more as she heard the muffled curse above the buzzing and roaring in her ears. She sensed grave danger, but her legs had suddenly turned to water. A roiling sickness rose in her stomach as the beast thundered past her, blasting her with its terrible hot breath. She saw it circle at the end of the bridge and turn back toward her, its hideous light stabbing into her vision.

Her earlier determination deserted her. Let Roger take her, she thought, slumping down further against the bridge wall. She was past caring.

The roaring came to an abrupt halt, but the light remained, forcing her to close her eyes against its power. She heard footsteps pounding toward her. She cowered against the cold stones of the bridge, hiding her face from Roger's fury.

"Are you all right?"

The voice wasn't Roger's. It was rich and deep and male, but it held a slight, rusty edge to it and its tone held none of Roger's characteristic sarcasm, nor his rage. A peek out from the tangle of her hair caused her to gasp and hide her face again.

It was a devil!

She raised her hand and quickly made the sign of the cross, though the effort cost her. *Sweet Jesu*, she thought to herself, she knew she had sinned in her life, but she hadn't expected such punishment as this. Still, the hideously large head, the single shining black eye, the leathery skin—she'd seen enough pictures in church and in the books at the abbey to recognize a minion of Satan when she saw one. Was this the Black One himself? She shook doubly hard, fear and sickness washing over her body in waves.

Its hands touched her, causing her to choke back a scream. What hideous torture did it have in mind for her? Her back was to the wall—she could go no further.

To her surprise, the touch proved gentle. The creature's hands went lightly over the length of her arms and legs. Its—his?—leather skin and wings rustled as he settled back on his haunches. Cautiously, she ventured another peek at him.

"Nothing broken that I can find," he said in his eerie, muffled tones.

She shuddered, closed her eyes. The monster had no mouth yet he could speak. Demonic, for certain. Still, he'd made no move to harm her or glory in her fall to Lucifer's realm. Could she be mistaken? She ventured another look.

Most decidedly, it was a mistake to look. The moment she let her guard down, the creature reached up and yanked open a strip of his neck. Elinor screamed with all her might as the evil thing put both hands to his temples and ripped off his own head!

Coral Smith Saxe

"Whoa! Calm down. I'm not the Terminator." His voice sounded different, clearer.

She gulped and forced herself to look at him. Terminator? Surely as apt a name for the Evil One as any, she thought. "You are not?" she asked.

He shook his head in reply.

She gaped at the new head now seated on his shoulders. He had taken on the visage of an ordinary man. How mighty were the powers of darkness! She knew she must be on her guard, for, as the Bible said, the devil—and, most likely, his attendants—hath power to assume a pleasing shape.

In truth, she thought as she watched him reach into a hole in his chest, he had assumed quite a pleasing shape indeed, at least about the face. Pale, wheat-colored hair flowed to his shoulders, and his light blue eyes seemed filled with concern. A single white gemstone glittered in one earlobe, and she saw skin neither ink-black and glassy, as his first head had been, nor leathery and seamed as the rest of his body.

Now that the bright light of the steed's hideous eye had been doused, she saw by the moon's light that his face was tanned, yet fair, like many of the men she knew. It also included two eyes, a nose, a mouth, and two ears—all handsomely arranged in the features of a living son of Adam. Was this a trick of the Deceiver—the Terminator—or was he a man in truth?

He interrupted her contemplations by nudging her hand with something. She jerked back from him.

"Here," he said. His voice sounded calm, though she thought she heard a note of irritation in it. "Drink this," he urged. "You're probably in shock."

At the mere mention of drinking, Elinor's thirst returned, clawing at her throat like a briar. Without thinking, she reached out and took the odd, smooth flask from his massive black hands and put the thing to her lips. She took a taste, then choked and spat.

" 'Tis water!" she exclaimed. Did he mean to kill her?

18

"Spring water. Evian," he said with a frown. "It won't hurt you."

She gave him a narrow stare, but her parched lips and raspy throat, still tasting of bitter smoke, cried out for aid. She felt as if no drop to drink had passed her lips in a hundred years. Lord save her, she thought, but she needed something, even *water*, to quench this dreadful thirst. Gingerly, she lifted the flask to her lips once more.

To her complete relief and joy, the clearest, sweetest liquid she had ever tasted poured into her mouth. This Evy-Anne quenched a thirst far better than the most delicate ale. She drank deeply, in great gulps.

"Take it easy," he said, amusement edging his words.

She took the flask from her mouth, gained a breath, then tipped it up again. The cooling liquid coursed through her, restoring her as if it were an elixir of life. She drank until, at long last, she'd had enough.

"Many thanks, my lord," she whispered. She handed the flask back to him, wincing as his hands touched hers in the exchange. She felt unharmed by the drink, so far, only refreshed and calmed. Perhaps he wasn't going to harm her.

"I'm not a lord," he said, capping the flask. "The name's Drew. Can you walk?" he asked.

Elinor took stock of her limbs. They felt weak and weary, as if she had run many miles, yet she believed they might bear her. Bear her they must, she thought, because she didn't believe she could abide more contact with this confusing creature. She nodded and tried to stand.

He caught her as her knees began to buckle under her. Before she knew what was happening, he'd scooped her up into his arms and carried her to a broad-limbed oak. He set her down and went to retrieve his other head.

Elinor's very teeth seemed to rattle with her shaking. She'd survived his touch, yet she knew she couldn't run if she needed to escape this dark angel-creature. She would have to stay with him. But what did he have in mind for her? How was she to ascertain his intentions? If he was a minion of the Terminator, then he had both strength and supernatural powers. He could overwhelm her, mind, body and soul.

If he was a creature of honor, though, she thought, he might prove a gallant rescuer. The notion of being rescued by anyone did not ordinarily appeal to her, but she felt this occasion warranted an exception to her rule.

When the man-creature returned, he squatted down before her once again. He rubbed the back of his neck and sighed.

"I'd better take you to the ER. You've got a cut on your head that might need stitching."

Elinor raised her fingers to her forehead and winced. Her fingertips came away stained and sticky. She didn't recall hitting her head.

"The ER in Sebastopol's not too far," he told her. "Okay?"

"Eee Are. O-kay."

Elinor repeated the foreign sounds to herself. His words were near gibberish. Eee Are could be another name for his liege-lord, the Terminator. Was she to be taken before the throne of the Dark Angel himself?

"Okay." Man-monster Drew stood and reached out his thick black hand. "You'll have to ride."

"Ride?" she asked, coming to her feet with his assistance.

"My bike." He gestured to the shining silver and black beast standing statue-like by the side of the road.

Elinor scowled. A ride on that hideous beast seemed more like torture than a rescue.

"Oh, no," he said. "Don't tell me you're one of those? A bike is a perfectly good method of transport. I promise I won't pop any wheelies, okay?"

"O-kay?" That word came often from his lips, she mused. An incantation, perhaps?

"Okay. Do you have a coat or something? It gets pretty cold on the road."

"My cloak is warm," she began, then stopped. She scowled and patted her sides, looked down at herself. Hadn't she been wearing her cloak? She didn't recall taking it off, so where—

"It must be upon the bridge."

"Wait here."

She watched as he retraced his steps, his long, dark figure searching on all sides as he went. He went to the walls on both sides of the bridge, searching the stream below.

When he returned, the quizzical expression in his eyes told her he held his own doubts about her.

"There's nothing there," he said. "You weren't wearing one when I passed you."

Elinor didn't care for the feeling that was creeping into her heart and mind. First, she had arrived on the bridge and she could not recall how she'd gotten there. In truth, she couldn't seem to recall much of anything before the glaring light and the arrival of the Drew creature. Now her cloak was missing. What next?

"That's okay. You can wear my jacket."

She started to protest, then gaped in silence as he gripped the collar of his leather surcote and simply ripped it open, straight down the front. No buttons, no laces, no clasps. Just a perfectly even tear in good, thick leather.

By Our Lady, he's strong.

He held the coat open so she could slip her arms into it. Wavering between curiosity and fear, she opted for fear as the more prudent guide for her behavior. She obediently donned the garment, and he walked away.

His steed stood waiting in such utter silence she couldn't even hear it breathing in the quiet night. It made not a murmur of greeting, nor did it look their way when they approached.

It was the ugliest horse she'd ever seen. *I doubt it is a horse at all. It has no real head and it goes on wheels, like a cart.* Yet he'd ridden it like a steed, and its leather saddle and saddlebags were somewhat like harnessing. Who could say what monsters devils might ride?

She looked at her companion in confusion. He'd said it was safe, but did that apply to mere mortals?

"Hop on like you'd ride a horse," he said. "Here, lean on me."

Elinor had little choice. She doubted that he would permit her to go free. And if he proved true in his offer of aid, she had never known a time when she needed it more. Touching his arm gingerly, she hiked her skirts, threw her leg over the slick black saddle and settled herself on the thing. She blushed as she caught the Drew creature staring at her legs.

Great lack, she thought, he could see all the way up to the points of her hose! She might be in hell, but she'd been raised a modest and genteel maiden and would act accordingly. Quickly, she tried to cover herself, but he held up a hand.

"Don't. Keep your skirt up. That way it won't get caught in anything." He picked up his extra head and handed it to her. "Put this on. I didn't bring my spare."

Elinor eyed the object with revulsion. The fellow chuckled, a not unpleasant sound.

"It may ruin your 'do, but it'll keep you from ruining a lot more in an accident."

He lifted the thing and settled it down over her head. To her surprise, Elinor could see out of the huge eye hole, though things about her were tinted in a pale, unearthly shade. The man fastened the piece of neck-skin beneath her chin, and then it came to her—it was a hat! A helmet, in fact, much like that of a knight. *Sir Drew?* She would have smiled at her new realization but a wave of sickness swamped her and she tilted in her seat.

The man caught her and steadied her, then stepped awkwardly before her to straddle the beast. He reached around behind him and pulled her arms about his waist.

"Hold on," he called out.

He made some quick motions, and then Elinor's ears were assaulted by the beast's spluttering roars. The animal jerked forward and took flight. She screamed, clamped her arms about the man's waist and hid her head, helmet and all, against his broad back. One quick glance up at the stars wheeling overhead cured her of looking up. Her curiosity had some limits. She hung onto the rider in charge of the beast and waited for the awful journey to end.

The emergency room buzzed like a hive of agitated bees. Friday night, a full moon, springtime—it brought out the best and the worst in people, Drew Ingraham knew from grim experience, even in a small community like Sebastopol.

There had been some trouble admitting the young woman, because she wasn't carrying a purse with her costume-party outfit and she had no identification or proof of medical insurance on her person. Also, as she was clearly a foreigner, the red tape started rolling out from behind the admitting desk until Drew signed a voucher to act as the responsible party and pay all her bills. He felt it was the least he could do for her. For all he knew, he had hit her with his bike and sent her tumbling to the hard stone of the old bridge, though he'd have sworn she'd been falling long before he'd neared her. Besides, he had no desire to get snarled in a fishnet of bureaucracy. From the look of the heavy silk dress she was wearing, he guessed she could probably afford to repay him.

He shook his head as she sat next to him on the waiting-room couch and gazed, rapt, at the jabbering TV hanging on the wall. He had no idea why he should do such a thing for a complete stranger. He needed—and wanted—responsibility for another person right now about as much as a submarine needed screen doors.

At least he had a name to put to her now. The Lady Elinor Elizabeth Justinia DeCourtenay, she'd told the admitting secretary with haughty pride. She hailed from England, she claimed, though he thought her accent sounded a bit off the mark from what he knew of British speech. She'd rattled off an address straight out of an Agatha Christie novel: East Somethingfield on the Whatsis, and she'd quietly insisted she knew of no telephone number where anyone who knew her could be reached. Finally, Drew had stepped in to say he thought she might have a head injury, and this seemed to expedite the admitting process.

Now, as he sat beside Elinor on the couch in the waiting area, he wondered where she'd been going in that odd costume and why she hadn't been carrying so much as a purse. Venners Creek Bridge spanned a pleasant little stream in the middle of nowhere, well away from most of the yuppie homes and wine-tasting resorts of Sonoma County. He doubted, too, that the peach and apple farmers of the area were in the habit of throwing elaborate costume balls in their leisure moments. Had she been going to meet someone on the old, moonlit bridge? If someone as lovely as Elinor DeCourtenay were waiting for him, he thought, he'd sure as hell be there on time, if not early.

The idea brought him up short. Had he slipped his cable? Not only did he have no intention of getting involved with anyone, but he'd narrowly missed running the woman down with his bike. Add to that her general aura of otherworldliness, and you had a recipe for deep trouble, he told himself.

Still, he couldn't see any harm in looking.

And he liked looking at Elinor DeCourtenay, even

now, as she sat, disheveled and shell-shocked. With her honey hair and fair skin, deep greenish-blue eyes and delicate features, she reminded him of an exquisite old miniature he'd seen once in a museum—especially in her Renaissance or whatever costume. That long skirt, he already knew, covered a pair of the most luscious, appealingly long legs he'd seen outside of a lingerie ad. What would it be like—

"Ms. Courtenay?" A nurse interrupted his reverie.

Drew touched Elinor's shoulder. "That's you."

He rose and watched as she followed in the nurse's wake, a slender figure in trailing skirts and his black leather jacket. They disappeared behind the swinging doors to the ER. In less than five minutes, however, the nurse popped her head out the doors and beckoned him.

"Does she speak English?" she asked when he got inside the doors.

"I think so. Second language is my guess. She said she was English, but she's got the weirdest accent I've ever heard. More like French or Dutch."

"Uh-huh. Then you don't know her?"

"No." He jammed his fingers into his back pockets. "I just missed hitting her with my Harley out at Venners Creek Bridge. Thought I'd better bring her in."

The nurse gave him the fish eye, as if to say he was on the suspect list as Elinor's assailant, then led the way to a curtained cubicle. Inside, Elinor was perched on an examining table, clutching Drew's leather jacket. Her chin held its proud tilt, but her eyes were wide with apprehension. Her posture seemed to soften when she saw him—or maybe he imagined it.

"Elinor," he said softly, coming to stand before her. "The nurse needs to look at the cut on your forehead. And at the rest of you, to know if you're hurt. Don't be afraid."

"Nurse?" Elinor asked doubtfully. She raised her chin another notch. "No. No witchcraft. The De-

Courtenays do not hold with witchcraft. Unless the witch is properly trained and an avowed Christian, of course."

The nurse snorted. "I'm a board-certified RN, ma'am, and I'm halfway to my master's in emergency care. As for my religious beliefs, like any good American citizen, they're my own business. I don't hold with witchcraft, either, but if you don't let me examine you soon, my superiors are going to swoop down on their broomsticks and start asking why."

She crossed her arms and gave Elinor a stare of equally royal dignity.

Elinor glanced at Drew. He nodded. She shrugged off the jacket.

"Very well. You may tend to my wounds."

"Thanks a bunch, your ladyship," the nurse muttered, picking up a blood-pressure cuff.

"You are welcome."

The nurse went through her routine with swift, practiced moves. When she finished, she stood back for a moment, tapping her cheek.

"Well, that's a clean cut over her eye. Shouldn't trouble her too much. Won't even need stitches. Keep that cold pack on it while I step out and get the doctor. I want him to take a look at her. There's a small chance she's got a concussion."

She started to exit through the curtain, then turned back to Drew.

"Oh, by the way. I think you're off the hook for assault with a deadly hog." She seemed about to say more, then vanished out the curtain.

He turned, startled to hear Elinor chuckle softly.

"Your woman is the very like of my dear old Margaretta, God rest her soul. She never knew her place, either, and her tongue could slice a meat pie six ways. Still, her gentle hands gave the lie to all her barbs."

Drew thought he caught the gist of her words. Listening to her reminded him of listening to Shakespeare, a vice he'd harbored in absolute secrecy during his hell-raiser days. Had Elinor DeCourtenay done the same in her youth? She could be an actress, caught up in a part.

The doctor came in, a fellow only a year or two older than Drew, with running shoes that squeaked as he moved about Elinor, doing his own quick exam. Elinor scowled at him every time he touched her, and when he reached out and asked her to tilt her head back so he could shine a light in her eyes, she gave him her own version of the fish eye.

"Is this how you would address a lady?" she asked, her tone low and cool enough to refrigerate ice cream.

The doctor, however, had not a clue. "One quick look, miss, and I'll be done."

"One may hope."

Drew choked back a laugh. For all her beauty and confusion, she never seemed to lose her grip on her pride. Who was she?

"That's a fantastic costume you've got there, Ms. DeCourtenay," the doctor was saying as he stepped back from the table. "You must be in town for the medievalists' fair out at Ragle Ranch Park. I really got into that stuff in college. Got to be a pretty good jouster, if I do say so myself."

"Medievalists?" Drew asked.

"Yeah. It's a national organization of people who like to dress up and drink mead and stage sword-fights on weekends. Some people come from Canada and other countries to be in on these things. My guess is she wandered away from the site, took a bump on the head and is a little bit disoriented. I don't think there's any concussion, but it won't hurt to take the usual precautions. The nurse will give you an instruction sheet on your way out on how to care for her for the next eight to twelve hours. Of course, if you do see anything strange about her, give us a call right away."

And off he went, squeaking his way out to the triage

27

area. Drew kept hearing his last words—*if you see anything strange about her*. He looked at Elinor, waiting so patiently and royally on the exam table. He couldn't think of anything about her that wasn't strange.

The nurse returned with the release form and instruction sheet. He listened with only half an ear. No doubt the doctor had made the correct diagnosis—a mixed-up medieval fan with a bump on her head. Drew could even imagine her having sworn to stay in character, quaint speech and all, for the duration of the weekend.

Eight to twelve hours. The rest of the doctor's words sank in. Did they expect him to care for this lost lady fair for the rest of the night—and more?

He scanned the instruction sheet. Eight to twelve hours, yes, it said, but it recommended a watch of several days, in case a slow bleed in the brain should develop. Days? He couldn't do it. No way. There had to be someone else she knew around here.

When the nurse left, Elinor slid down from the table and handed him his jacket.

"I am obliged to you, sir, for your safe escort to this house of healing. I must go. I am needed elsewhere."

Drew went after her and took hold of her elbow. "No, you don't," he said, surprised even as the words left his lips. "I'm taking you home. You may have a concussion."

She gave him a look of such freezing disdain that he let go of her elbow.

"As you say," she murmured. "I shall go home."

She glided through the curtain, headed for the big blue swinging doors. Drew followed. He caught up and held the door for her and she swept out into the waiting area. Outside, she stopped and looked about her.

"Which direction shall I take to find the Oakfield road?"

"Is that out by the meadow?" he asked.

She considered this for a moment, then nodded.

28

"The easiest way is to go out the main drag and then cut over to the interstate, but I think you'd better call home, instead."

"Drag? Call home?"

"Yeah. You do have a home, don't you?"

She nodded.

"I thought so." He led the way down the hall. "There's a pay phone around the corner. You can call someone to come and get you. I'll call for you, if you want."

She looked at him as if he'd just sprouted feathers. When she spoke, she used the soothing tones reserved for talking a crackpot down off a high ledge.

"Yes. Call to them for me, please."

He turned and went to the bank of phones that stood at the corner beyond the admitting desk. She followed, skepticism written in the set of her mouth.

He dug out a quarter and lifted the receiver. "What's the number?"

"Number?"

"Their phone number."

"I don't know any such number. Please, sir. I must go home. My brother and my sister . . ." She broke off.

"Yes? Your brother and sister? Where are they?"

"I cannot tell you. It is too dangerous. I know not where your loyalties lie."

"I see."

Damn. She sounded like a paranoid nut. Could she be an escaped mental patient? It wasn't out of the question.

Yet something in him didn't buy the image of Elinor DeCourtenay as a loony on the lam from the local bin. She just plain seemed lost.

"Okay," he said at last. "You're going home with me. I can't take you back out to the park in this condition."

She peered at him, as if measuring his words and the quality of his character, all at once. Finally, she nodded her assent in the aristocratic manner he was coming to see as her trademark. He handed her his jacket and helmet once more.

I'm going to regret this.

Taking a royal waif under his wing was hardly his style. Moreover, the longer she remained under his care, he sensed, the more involved he would become— he could feel it.

Elinor DeCourtenay with her gorgeous legs and her quaint old costume, her old-world manners and her bewildered yet proud demeanor, spelled nothing but trouble. Too many questions surrounded her. He'd help her out this one night and then send her on her way.

Fog was rolling in by the time they'd ridden all the way to his house out by the Russian River. He pulled up to the old detached garage behind his house and halted. Elinor dismounted and followed him inside, into the kitchen.

"You can put the jacket and helmet on the chair," he told her. "I'm going to make up the bed for you."

He looked at her for assent. Her upright, royal stance began to crumple into a good old-fashioned faint.

He stepped across the room and caught her arm. "Okay, what do you say we skip the formalities?"

Slipping an arm about her shoulders, he guided her to the little bedroom, where he helped her off with the jacket and helmet. Bending to slip off her shoes, he motioned for her to lie back on the pillows. When he'd covered her up with the well-worn quilt, he squatted beside the bed.

"You rest. I'm going to be waking you up to check on you every hour, so don't get any ideas about losing consciousness on me. If you need anything, just yell. I'll be right nearby."

She looked at him with those fathomless blue-green eyes and finally nodded.

"Yes, Sir Drew," she whispered.

Her lacy dark lashes fluttered downward. In a matter of moments, sleep overtook her.

Drew eased back onto his heels. He looked at his watch. Eleven-thirty. He'd better start a pot of coffee. He had a long night ahead of him.

Roger Aston's horse made it across the bridge before it went to its knees. He managed to roll out of the saddle in time to spare his legs from being mangled, but even after he came to rest, the world still spun around him. His body shook with a violence that seemed ready to dislodge his very bones. With great effort, he shifted to his side and retched out the full measure of his evening's meat and drink.

When he'd finished, he barely had strength to roll to his back. He closed his eyes against the whirling stars and treetops.

It had happened again.

He had mounted the winds and traveled away. Where, this time? And, more importantly, when?

"And where is the DeCourtenay bitch?" he growled.

Another spasm of nausea grabbed at his entrails. He curled into a ball, gasping.

The fit eased. The pangs had struck him worse than on his last venture. If he traveled this way much more, he thought, the journey might well kill him. Why had he used the magic this time?

Elinor DeCourtenay.

Ah, yes. That had been his reason, this time. He'd been spinning his web around her for months, years, drawing her closer and closer to him, binding her up in his plans.

Elinor. He'd had the mother, but the mother had still chosen that milksop Gerard DeCourtenay, defying him and his love for her, even defying her parents in her pursuit of Gerard's money and position. Only her belly, fat with DeCourtenay's child, with Elinor, had made them bend to that unwanted marriage.

31

Coral Smith Saxe

He'd seduced the mother.
He'd ruined the father.
He'd have the daughter.
And he'd make all of them pay. Time and again.

Chapter Three

Drew stooped down beside the bed and put his hand on Elinor's shoulder. He shook her gently, as he had three times before during the night. She groaned and turned away from him.

". . . isn't time for Matins . . ." she mumbled into the pillow.

"No, but it's time to sit up and tell me your name," Drew said, drawing her back toward him.

"Oh, Sister, leave off . . ." Elinor's eyes opened. "Oh, 'tis, you, Sir Drew." She seemed to sink into the pillows. "I thought I was . . . home."

"Sorry." He sank back on his heels. "Ready for a pop quiz?"

She gave him a blank stare.

"Never mind," he said. "Just answer a couple of questions." He raised his hand. "How many fingers am I holding up?"

"Three."

"Good. What's your name?"

33

"The Lady Elinor DeCourtenay."

"You're consistent at least. Do you know where you are?"

"In your home?"

"That's right. Do you know how you got here?"

"Yes. On your dreadful black beast."

He nodded. "Fair enough. So you're no biker chick."

"Biker chick?" she echoed, her eyelids beginning to drift shut.

"Never mind. Go on back to sleep."

She followed his order at once, sliding down among the pillows once more and curling into a ball under the threadbare quilt.

The nurse had said to watch out for any out-of-the-ordinary confusion or sleepiness. She was sleepy but she was as easily roused as the next person. Confused? She gave some bizarre answers but she never faltered over them. She might be confused but she wasn't in doubt, if that made any sense.

Drew watched her sleep, studying her serene face for some clue to her identity. There was nothing there— no clues and nothing to tell him why he had the strangest feelings about her. Nothing in the smooth skin, nothing in the tumbled fair hair, nothing in the set of her brow. Yet the feelings were there.

He twisted up and away from the bed and left the room. Going to the kitchen once more, he retrieved his mug of cooling coffee in the dim glow of the range-light over his stove. He moved to the window over the sink and stared out at the darkness, softened by fog enveloping his house.

He should probably turn her over to the police to handle as a lost or missing person, whatever the proper term was for people in her situation. But that seemed unfair. She deserved a chance to remember on her own before she was plunged into the system and handed around from agency to agency.

If she felt better in the morning, he'd take her out to

34

that medieval fair the doctor had mentioned and turn her over to her fellow lords and ladies. Her memory might return if she was back in a familiar setting.

Because she couldn't stay here. Not with him. He'd worked long and hard to get to the point that his own, solitary company pleased him, that he felt sufficient unto himself. He'd made a life for himself in this ramshackle house, in this new town, in his new trade. He knew one or two people in the area, but he didn't want any real ties. He didn't need any complications, especially one like the woman who was sleeping in his bed right now.

What was more, he didn't like the feeling he had when she talked as if she'd dropped in from another planet. The light in her eyes, the firm sincerity in her tone, made him—God forbid—believe her. And he didn't want to believe her.

Actually, he told himself, he believed that *she* believed. Which meant she was at least a couple bulbs shy of a chandelier. A clinical case, if anything. His old pal, Dr. Will Curran, psychiatrist and hog-riding fool, would have a field day with her.

Worst of all were the other feelings he had when he looked at her.

In spite of her odd behavior, her face, her form, her slightly musical voice, all went straight into him and connected up with something so startlingly primal and possessive it caused him to tense even now. In a matter of hours, she'd managed to penetrate several of the barriers he'd constructed with such care and dedication, barriers built to keep out the likes of Elinor. Okay, so he'd never met anyone the likes of her. The principle remained.

It wasn't mere desire, or lust. He'd felt those many times, looking at other women, thinking of them. But the intensity of this feeling, the sheer force of it, coupled with a powerful urge to surround her and fight off all intruders, struck him like a blow to his solar plexus.

35

He'd never felt such an impulse before. Never.

Not even with his wife.

He tossed the dregs of the coffee into the sink. He set the mug aside and paced the short length of the kitchen, running his hands through his hair.

Damn! He hadn't wanted to think about any of this. He hadn't wanted to think of LeeAnne.

She was gone. The end.

Her death had closed the book on many things in his life, and he liked it that way. Needed it that way.

He'd get over this, too, he told himself. This encounter with Elinor was just a small ripple in the straight-flowing stream of his life. Once she was returned to her fellow jousters and jesters, everything would go back to normal.

Elinor stood before the small crystal urn, gazing with wonder at the bubbling, dark liquid dripping within and inhaling the delicious aroma issuing forth from its steaming confines. Master Coffee, Sir Drew had called it, as he had poured in grains that looked for all the world like good, rich soil. Could this squat object truly be a man?

No, she told herself with a shake of the head. "Master Coffee" sounded more like a term of endearment, she decided, not unlike the way the men sometimes called good ale John Barleycorn. She smiled with pride at her deduction, wishing she had some means of making a drawing of the object. How Joanna and Thomas would enjoy seeing it.

Her nose caught a new scent. Following its lead, she turned to where Sir Drew was placing platters of hot food upon a small table.

"Such fair odors!" she said. "I am famished."

"Hope you like bacon and eggs. Lots of cholesterol, but I won't tell if you won't."

Elinor pondered his words for a moment. "I see. I gather this is a fast day for you, and you break it on my account." She frowned. "I would not have your soul on my conscience."

Sir Drew motioned for her to take a seat at the table. "Don't worry about my soul. It's my arteries I'm looking out for. But not this morning."

"Ar-ter-ies," Elinor murmured as she sat down.

When she'd woken that morning, she'd been bewildered at her surroundings, yet, to her surprise, she'd also felt a sense of safety and comfort in Sir Drew's home. It was beyond fathoming, like so much of what was happening to her, so she'd let it pass.

She looked down at her plate. Sir Drew might be the most peculiar being she'd ever met, but his food smelled delicious. Her stomach reminded her she hadn't eaten for many, many hours. She had decided to take a chance on Sir Drew's hospitality—she might as well eat his food.

She looked over the silver he set before her. The knife she recognized, and the spoon, but why in the name of St. George had he given her a tiny pitchfork? She watched Sir Drew use his. He seemed to wield it like a stabbing knife, then scooped the eggs with it like a spoon. It didn't look as if it would be too difficult to manage.

"If you're feeling better, we'll drive out to the medievalists' fair this morning," Drew said. "Someone's bound to know you out there."

Elinor winced as the sharp points of the pitchfork poked her lower lip. Sir Drew wasn't looking at her, she noted with relief. He must think her horribly ill-bred not to know how to use such obviously dear and elegant utensils.

"Mmm, yes, perhaps," she said, taking another stab at her eggs.

"I don't think there's any concussion. You were fine all through the night. And you seem okay this morning."

Elinor looked at his slightly bleary eyes and the faint,

fair stubble on his cheeks. "You kept vigil all night," she said softly. "God bless and thank you, Sir Drew."

He looked up at her, his eyes suddenly cautious. "It's nothing."

"I've been a most burdensome guest, I fear. Would that I had some way to pay my debt."

He stared at her for a moment, then suddenly bent his head over his plate. "Don't bother."

His curtness stung her. She'd meant to be polite. Knights were sworn to be courteous to gentlewomen, she thought, straightening in her chair. Did he take her for some peasant or strumpet?

Ah, but such excellent food, she thought, coming back to the reality of her physical needs. She'd mastered the little pitchfork, finished her eggs and bacon, and now began on the plate of toasted bread before her. She could find no fault with his table.

Sir Drew got up and poured dark brown liquid from the urn called Master Coffee. He carried small cups of the liquid to the table and set one down in front of Elinor, who sniffed it rapturously, then took a sip. Her eyes went wide with surprise at the bitter taste and the flame-hot temperature of the beverage.

"Sorry. It's not the gourmet stuff. Do you want milk or sugar?"

Elinor, at a loss, nodded. Anything would be better than this concoction.

Sir Drew went to a tall white chest and pulled out another container, brightly painted with pictures of cows, and brought it to the table. He held it over her cup and said, "Say when."

White milk streamed into her cup. "Halt! 'Twill overflow!"

"Okay. Here's the sugar." He pushed a small bowl to her. "I'll let you handle this."

Elinor tasted the so-called sugar, whiter than any snow she'd ever seen, let alone sugar. It was potently sweet. She smiled and tipped the bowl up to pour some into her cup.

"Don't you want to use a spoon?"

Her hand froze. "Spoon? Oh. If you say so." She scooped out a bit of the white stuff and let it fall into the now-creamy brown drink. She gave a cautious sip and smiled broadly. " 'Tis marvelous! What did you call it?"

"Don't you know?"

"I know it comes from the Master Coffee. Master of the Coffee . . ." She brightened. "He is the master of the coffee. Then this drink is called coffee?"

Drew looked at her for a moment. "Yes," he said at last. "Coffee."

"Delicious. Oh, if only the sisters could see me thus. Breaking my fast with a pitchfork and drinking coffee from the master of all coffees."

"The sisters?"

"Aye. At the Abbey of Wednesbury. 'Tis where I live, or did live. I came home to Oakfield House but two months ago."

"You're—you're a nun?" His voice sounded oddly choked.

She shook her head and took another sip. "No. My vows have not been made."

"A nun." Drew walked away from the table and stood before the window, his hand rubbing across his chin. "I think we'd better get you back to your friends as soon as we can."

"As you say, Sir Drew."

"It's not Sir. It's just Drew."

Elinor nodded. "Forgive me. I do not yet know your ways."

He didn't answer, only turned and left the room. Elinor stared down at her coffee, wondering again what had angered him. She scarcely seemed to set one foot aright.

He would take her back to her friends, he'd said.

39

That sounded wonderful. But which friends did he mean? And where were they?

She felt slightly dizzy as she recalled last night's adventure on the stone bridge. A fog seemed to surround all her memories. Try as she might, her memory still failed to supply any details of what had happened between the time she had arrived in the courtyard of Castle Clarisdoune and the arrival of Sir Drew on his smelly, noisy black beast.

She gave up and finished her meal, sensing it would be a long day and her body would need the sustenance. Perhaps there were no answers to be found by cudgeling her brain. What she needed most was to make her way home.

She went on a search for the garderobe and made use of it, in all its cool, white elegance. When she emerged, Drew stood waiting for her in the hall, helmet in hand.

"Do you have everything?" he asked.

"I had not much to begin with. Only my cloak, and I left it . . . back where I came from."

"Okay. Wear my jacket. Let's ride."

Though its roaring breath still stunned her, the ride on the dark beast no longer terrified her. She simply closed her eyes against the dizzying passage of the landscape.

She knew Drew possessed the Master of Coffee. Perhaps this was Master of the Beasts.

That idea frightened her. She still did not know if demonic forces were at work upon her. Drew had certainly shown her no malice. Yet he stood as master over both the Master of Coffee and the Master of Beasts. He must possess powers far beyond her knowledge of either men or magicians.

Before long, her curiosity nagging at her like a noisy child, she ventured a look around as they sped down the cool, winding road. The black pathway spun out beneath them as smoothly as a marble floor. Overhead, on either side of the road, the tallest trees she had ever seen shaded their way. These towering monoliths smelled sweetly of pine, a scent she knew, but their trunks glowed as red as Friar Leary's ginger beard.

The shadows of these giants dropped away, changing places with broad, rolling meadows, and here and there a sizable cottage or a strange, pastel castle or fortress. Shining metal monsters passed them on the road, at speeds unthinkable, and Elinor had to hide her eyes when one of these, as large as any house, stormed by with a blare of fearsome trumpets.

At last, the beast slowed and Drew steered it onto a road more similar to those she knew, of hard-packed dirt, rutted from the wheels of many vehicles. Elinor opened her eyes to see what could only be a market fair—a real market, with tents and stalls and banners floating on the wind, proclaiming the various wares for sale.

Relief and joy sang within her. The familiar scents of wood fires and animal dung, straw and dust and cooking foods were like ambrosia. Drew had brought her home!

She could hardly wait until the Master Beast came to a standstill before she jumped down and tore off her helmet. How sweet was the sight of people dressed in normal, everyday garb and the clamor of voices and musicians and sellers hawking their goods. She wasn't mad, after all! And she wasn't in hell. Whatever had happened to her to make her see all those strange and disturbing wonders—it was over. She was back where she belonged.

"Here you are," Drew said, lifting the visor on his helmet.

"Yes. And, oh, how grateful I am to you, sir!" She handed him the other helmet. "It's so good to be home! Which market fair is this?"

Drew's shoulders lifted. "It's the only one I know of."

" 'Tis no matter. Thank you a hundred, thousand times!"

"See anyone you know?"

"Nay, not yet. But there's bound to be someone who knows my family and how I may find my way home. I hope—oh, look! They're going to have a contest of arms!"

"You go on."

She looked at him, suddenly dismayed. "Pardon me, Sir Drew. It's not that I wish to be relieved of your company. Indeed, will you not join me? This looks like a most merry business." She smiled and gestured at the gathering crowd.

"I've got work to do."

She tilted her head to one side and regarded him. "You work too much, Sir Drew," she said. "You have the look about you of a man whose nature is out of sorts with his occupation."

Surprise registered in his blue eyes, then apprehension. He quickly covered both with a wry smile.

"Yeah, well, it keeps me off the streets. You go on and find your friends. Have a nice life, Elinor De-Courtenay."

She placed a hand on his arm. "I'll never forget your kindness to a stranger. May you have all the blessings of life piled tenfold upon your head, Sir Drew."

He smiled once more, briefly, and she thought she saw a wistful sadness behind it. Turning the beast around, he walked it a short way off before kicking it into roaring action. In a twinkling, he'd vanished, back toward the road, back to his life in the strange, wondrous world where he belonged.

Pondering the mystery of all she had seen and done in the past hours, Elinor walked toward the center of the marketplace. Drew had gone, with his amazing steed and his curious speech. Had she been caught up in a miracle? A fit of madness? A dream?

If it had been a dream, she thought, it was one she

might wish to have again. The blue eyes and strong chin of the Dark Knight of the Bridge, as she had dubbed him in her fancy, were images forever graven in her mind. The memory of his strong arms and gentle hands touching her refused to give way or fade in her mind. Of all men, he was one she would have liked to know, had he been a man of her position and country.

But such wishes were folly. He'd been plainly anxious to be rid of her. And she fit into his world as well as a fish on horseback. No, she'd wakened from her dream of Sir Drew of the Wonders. Time to shake the sleep from her eyes.

She had things to do. A brother and a sister who were depending on her to meet their father's debts and secure their home from Roger Aston.

It would be no easy feat. She had been ready to pay any price, even if it meant compromising her faith and the virtue of her body by joining him as mistress. Today, she felt a wave of sick, gripping fear at the very notion of giving her body to Roger. She fought it off and stepped briskly into the throngs of fair-going folk. DeCourtenays did not shrink from duty.

But first, she thought, she had to find someone who could set her on the right road to Oakfield.

Drew opened a drawer of his tall, red tool box and drew out a tray of shining wrenches. He carried the tray over to the large table where a stripped-down 1941 classic Harley Knucklehead stood, its front end anchored in a viselike wheel block. After sliding the tray onto the table beside the rear wheel, he shrugged out of his jacket and rolled up his sleeves.

Work. Routine. Solitude. Just what he needed.

He surveyed the motorcycle's engine, squinting in and around the many parts fitted with such efficiency under the flaking, teardrop-shaped tank. Selecting a tool at last, he went to work, his hands finding their way around the battered but not beaten machine with practiced ease.

He'd been working on bikes since he was twelve, though doing it for a living had never crossed his mind until a few years ago. When he'd set up this shop, he'd been amazed at the amount of money he could make in restorations alone. The money didn't interest him, but it did keep the wolf from the door. What interested him, most of all, was the freedom to be his own man, twenty-four hours a day, seven days a week.

The dim, cool garage, with its bank of good, bright lights over the work area, was the first place he had come when he'd returned from dropping Elinor at the medieval fair. It was easy to lose himself in his work. He had come today to shake the image of a tall, slender figure in a dusty blue gown, standing all alone in the midst of that bright, noisy circus.

Better to focus his attention on crankpins, cams and valves, he thought. Far safer. More relaxing.

But as he began to tap, twist and pull, taking the Harley's engine apart bit by worn bit, he couldn't seem to lose the sound of Elinor's light voice and musical accent. Even amid the odor of overcooked engines, solvents and ancient motor oil, he couldn't shake the scent of her hair as he'd lifted her up to wake her through the night.

It was irritating as hell.

What was it about her? he wondered, grimacing. She wasn't even his type.

His type. He gave a snort as he tossed a grime-caked nut and bolt into the waiting pan of solvent. He'd had only one lover in his life: LeeAnne of the chestnut hair and velvet-brown eyes. All other women had been such minor blips on the radar screen of his love-life, they'd hardly mattered at all. It was LeeAnne who'd commanded his every thought, from the first instant he saw her until the day she died. And long afterward. If he had a type at all, LeeAnne had been its embodiment.

He stretched out a leg and hooked the bottom rail of a battered stool with the toe of his boot. Sliding it toward him, he sat and chose another tool.

Elinor, however, had registered more than a blip in the few short hours he'd known her. Maybe it was her otherworldliness and her quaint speech that intrigued him.

It was a quirk, he told himself. A fluke. He'd had a weakness for Shakespeare and swashbuckling movies since he was a kid. *Robin Hood* and *The Black Swan, The Black Shield of Falworth*. That was probably all it was.

He rapped gently at the frozen bolt, then reached for his wire brush to clean it.

Thank God he had his work, he told himself, enough work to keep him just busy enough, just tired enough so he could sleep in peace. This old Knuckle might take weeks of steady effort to restore it to the sort of glory its owner had so eagerly sketched. That was all he needed to stay on track.

He continued to dismantle the old bike, taking his time, doing everything methodically, carefully, as he always did.

But images of a leggy blonde in his kitchen kept coming back to him. Elinor studying his refrigerator. Elinor tapping on the glass of his windows, blinking in amazement at his toaster. She had wandered about his modest, cramped kitchen like an awestruck tourist on the streets of New York. Her long braid had rippled down her back, and her dress had swayed and trailed about her as she stared at each appliance and fixture, large and small, giving soft exclamations of wonder and delight.

He'd watched her from the corners of his eyes as he fixed breakfast and had felt a not unpleasant mixture of amusement and desire mingling inside him. Maybe *he'd* been the awestruck tourist, watching this curious and beautiful image from another era pass before his eyes. He'd certainly never known anyone so completely enchanted by a can opener.

She'd also eaten a meal that would put a lumberjack out on the couch. He'd found himself looking her over as he got up to get more bread for toast. She was round in all the best places, but he couldn't see an extra bulge anywhere else on her tall frame.

He shook himself as he recalled his prolonged observation of her body. All right, so she was easy on the eyes. And inspiring to the libido. But that didn't make her any less weird. And just because she had legs that looked as if they went all the way up to her armpits didn't mean she wasn't a crackpot with delusions of royalty. There were plenty of women with big blue eyes and deliciously full breasts and . . .

Swearing under his breath, he placed his tools aside and wiped his hands. He headed into the house for lunch, hoping that satisfying one appetite would diminish the pangs he felt from that other, more mercurial hunger.

He was finishing off a cold sandwich when he caught the glint of metal on the floor by the fridge. He bent down and pulled out a chain of flat, gold links. Dangling from the end was an odd-shaped circle of gold.

He hefted it in his palm. It felt heavy enough to be solid gold, he thought, and it was obviously handcrafted. He turned it over. It seemed to have notches carved into its back and some squiggling shapes incised there. The marks meant nothing to him. All in all, it most resembled those round-faced, benign suns in old drawings.

It must be Elinor's. No one else could have dropped it. No one else had been inside his house for months.

The thing looked valuable. And Elinor had not had so much as a purse on her. Grimacing, he knew what he had to do.

What he didn't know, or didn't want to know, was

why he showered and shaved before hopping on his bike and riding back out to the park.

Things were not right. Elinor felt as odd in this place as she had with Sir Drew and his flying beast.

She'd passed several hours strolling about the fair, gazing about her, first in delight, then wonder, then confusion. Hunger and thirst also plagued her, but she had no coins with which to purchase food or drink.

And things were not right, she thought again. These people dressed as she did, used words familiar to her, carried objects she knew well, yet so many other elements rang false. For one thing, gentles associated with peasants and worse with shocking ease and tolerance. Many of them even touched one another and walked hand in hand! Now and again, great thundering eagles coursed through the gray-blue skies, huge and sleek with wings so bright the sun glinted off them like burnished silver. She craned her neck to follow their path, covering her ears against their fearsome roars, yet these fair-goers gave them ne'er so much as a glance. They were as unamazed as she would be at the sight of a chicken in the manor yard.

There were colors and textures to their clothing that were utterly foreign to Elinor, scents in the air that bore no equal in her memory. An abundance of folk went about with spectacles on their noses. Many chewed on whole legs of roasted fowl wrapped in precious paper. One woman, attired in a gown much like Elinor's, traveled beside her companion in a wheeled chair that rolled along as if drawn by invisible ponies.

Strongest of all, she could not cast off the sense that she was being watched, watched by something evil. This tingling sense added the greatest share to her uneasiness.

Was she in hell? Perhaps she'd landed on some distant star, or wandered into a camp for madmen. Or perhaps she was the crazy one, spinning about in the midst of a madwoman's fevered dream.

Questions spun, unanswered, in her head, until a blast of horns captured her attention. Easing her way toward the front of a cheering throng, she saw two men preparing to wage battle with swords and shields. Their blunted weapons showed this to be a contest for sport, not a blood-duel. Since her feet were aching and her stomach growling, she reckoned the contest might offer distraction and a chance to rest. She found a hard, square bundle of straw near the edge of the circle and sat down.

The opponents swaggered to their places in the center of the ring. Cheers and catcalls greeted them from all sides. A plump woman in a tight, revealing gown jiggled up to the contestants and raised her arms. With a shout, she signaled for the battle to begin. The clash of metal upon metal rang out over the crowd, which howled with delight at the spectacle.

Still, the creeping, uneasy sensation of watchful eyes penetrated Elinor's awareness. She scanned the crowd. No face looked familiar. No one appeared to be paying attention to anything save the battling swordsmen.

She hugged her arms close around her. A soft, creaking sound reminded her she still held the leather surcote Sir Drew had given her. She wondered if he would think she'd stolen it. He hadn't asked for it back before he'd ridden off, and she'd had no way to follow the track of the speeding beast.

Despite her doubts about Sir Drew, she clutched the surcote to her, enjoying the subtle tang of something spicy mingled with the unmistakable scent of a male. Numerous metal fittings and buttons were scattered here and there on its dark surface, but she didn't dare test them for fear some spell might be unleashed at her touch. She might think him handsome and chivalrous, but she still wasn't convinced he wasn't a sorcerer of some sort. She simply held the coat under her chin and took odd comfort in the feel of it against her.

The crowd suddenly bellowed its excitement, and she looked up at the combatants. As she tracked the flash of their broadswords, her eye caught a glimpse of a face in the throng.

Her heart skipped a beat, then regained strength, thumping hard.

A tall man stood across the ring, his head turned, scanning the crowd. Elinor could see his long, sleek, black hair, a telltale streak of white slicing through it, just above his temple.

"God preserve me," she whispered to herself, frozen where she sat.

Roger Aston.

Chapter Four

Elinor gripped Drew's jacket more tightly. Roger Aston—her tormentor, her pursuer, her creditor and judge—was here in this mad, confusing world. Had some malevolent spell brought them both to this place? Surely it must be so, but when she searched her mind for another scrap of intelligence, some memory that would tell her what evil trick had been played upon them both, all she could summon up was white-hot pain and fear.

Her mind raced. Why was she so fearful? True, she misliked and mistrusted Roger. But she'd given her word to go to him, had she not? That had been their bargain: Elinor would spend one night alone with Aston, and in return, he would withdraw his petition for repayment of their debt to him for one full year. She did not know if the bargain had been kept by either of them.

Once again, her whole being rebelled at the very notion of sharing Roger Aston's bed. She couldn't shake the horror of it, which seemed to have doubled in strength since that moment when she'd gone to offer herself to him.

But perhaps she could go to him in this public place, perhaps strike another, less objectionable bargain with him. She knew she had made an oath, not merely to Aston, but to Thomas and Joanna, as well. They had to be protected, at all costs.

Still, she couldn't move toward him. Something had changed between her and Roger, something she couldn't summon from her memory, try as she might. If he so much as touched her, even looked at her . . .

Panic rose quickly in her chest, threatening to choke her. She looked at the spot where he had appeared, only to find him gone. Had he seen her? Their eyes hadn't met. Sweet Jesu, she thought. What if he was coming after her even as she sat, goggling and gasping like a goose trying to swallow a wagon wheel?

She leaped up and plunged blindly into the crowd. Jostling and weaving, she ran, her mind bent only on the goal of escaping, of putting as much distance between her and her enemy as she could manage. She gained the outskirts of the crowd and made ready to sprint across to the market stalls set up under the shelter of the trees beyond. If she could reach the maze the shops formed among the tree-trunks, perhaps she might evade him.

A hand, iron-strong, reached out and seized her arm. Elinor screamed and struck out at her captor, throwing all her weight behind her clenched fist.

"Whoa, Elinor! Don't panic. It's me."

She looked up. It wasn't Roger who held her. It was Sir Drew.

Without another thought, she flung herself against him. His arms wrapped around her, and she trembled there in his embrace. Devil he might be, but she'd rather take her chances with Lucifer than with Roger Aston.

51

Before he could utter a word, she pushed away from him, yanking on his arm. "Quickly!" she cried. "We must be off! We are in great danger!"

She began to run, but he held her fast. She pulled frantically at his arm. "Please! If you will not aid me, then I beg you, do not hinder me!"

He reached up and put his hands on her shoulders, holding her gently but firmly in place. "What kind of danger?" he demanded.

She labored to catch her breath. In that instant, she realized she had spoken amiss. Drew was not in danger. Not yet. But if Roger were to see them together, might he not turn on Drew as well?

"Just let me go," she panted, twisting her arm in his grip. "I'll not trouble you again, I vow!"

"Somehow I don't feel real confident about that," he said. "Look, if you're in danger, I can get you out of here, fast."

She looked at him, torn between longing to accept his offer and her duty not to drag others into danger with her. How could she dissuade him?

"Besides," he continued, pulling her gently over to the shelter of a low-hanging oak. "I have something of yours and you have something of mine." He gave a pointed look at the coat she was still clutching under one arm.

"But I—you mustn't—"

"Tell me later. You're shaking like a paint-blender. Come on. Let's go." He took her arm, and they hurried toward the entrance to the fair.

Elinor felt waves of horror, fright and guilt rising within her. Rolling with those waves, however, was a bright, winged creature, hardly big enough to be noted, but real all the same.

Hope.

Elinor picked up her feet and raced toward it, her hand in Drew's.

Drew spurred his steed, and with Elinor mounted

behind, hurtled past the meadows and the tall, red trees. They flew faster than any horse could ride, even Roger's white champion. He urged the beast ahead, the great animal moving so fluidly, Elinor fancied it was eating up the smooth black road beneath them.

Before long, they turned onto a bumpy dirt road. Drew slowed the beast, then reined it into silence. He helped Elinor dismount, then dismounted himself and led the way up a lovely wooded path where dogwoods waved their creamy, cuplike blossoms overhead.

Removing his helmet, he laid it on a wooden bench. He sat down on the back of the bench, his boots resting on the seat.

He studied her for a long moment.

"Okay," he said at last. "Talk."

"Talk? Of what?"

Elinor pulled off her helmet and set it on the bench beside Drew's. She raised her eyes and gave him what she called her "Yes, Mother Agnes?" look of bland innocence.

He scowled. "When I found you at the fair, you looked like you'd just checked out of the Bates Motel. What—or who—scared you back there?"

She hesitated. Now that she was far from Roger's reach, at least for the moment, she wasn't sure how much she should tell. Drew already treated her as if she were a trifle crack-brained—would this merely confirm his suspicions?

There was also the humiliation of telling of her family's predicament and how it came to pass that the DeCourtenays, once one of the oldest and most respected names in all England, had fallen into such embarrassing need. She wasn't sure how someone of his world, as she was coming to think of it, would respond to such a tale. In hers, she knew, many folk would feel revulsion at the DeCourtenays' folly.

Moreover, Roger Aston was dangerous, perhaps deadly. If he thought Drew stood in his way, or that he could get to Elinor through him, he wouldn't fail to come after him.

She looked up to see Drew's light blue eyes fastened on hers, his expression skeptical and yet concerned. He'd cared enough to bear her away from danger, at a mere word from her. She owed him some explanation.

"I—I am sorry to have frighted you and dragged you from the fair. I was, perhaps, a bit overexcited by the combat and the crowd."

He cocked an eyebrow. "Overexcited?"

"I was mistaken. I thought I saw someone I knew, but upon reflection, I believe it was not he."

"Uh-huh." He held his gaze on her face. "And who did you think it was?"

Heat rose in her cheeks. She was abominably poor at lying and well she knew it.

"I thought perhaps it was an old enemy. Someone who couldn't possibly be here. Someone who knew my parents. 'Twas but a foolish fancy, doubtless brought on by the strangeness of these past hours. Perhaps even the blow to my head. Forgive me for—for startling you so . . ."

She trickled off. If she said much more, she would be in it even deeper. Some sense told her Drew wasn't the sort who'd abide a liar.

He reached into one of the slits in his cotehardie and drew out a handful of glimmering gold. He let the object dangle before her.

"What is that?" The thing looked familiar, and yet she could not place it.

"You tell me."

She shook her head. "It is a medallion, a necklace. It must be quite valuable." Did he mean to offer it to her?

He twitched his fingers, and the medallion swung like a pendulum. "I found it in my house."

"It is not yours?"

He shook his head. "And if it's not yours . . . ?"

54

She stiffened. "Be plain, sir."

"You said you were in trouble. That you had enemies. This thing looks old and valuable. Does this have anything to do with the trouble you're in? Is this why you think someone is following you?"

"Are you saying I stole it?" She managed to keep her voice cool and even, though the heat of outrage was rising in her.

"Are you saying it's yours?"

"It is not. Not that I know of . . ."

Her voice trailed off.

Save her, but she had seen the medallion before. It had hung around Roger Aston's neck. How had it made its way into Drew's house?

"Ah. Forgive me. As you know, I had a blow to the head. Not all things are clear to me every moment. It *is* my medallion."

She held out her hand to take it. He pulled it out of her reach. She glared at him. How dare he toy with her as if she were a naughty child to be teased?

"You changed your mind awfully quick, princess," he said. "Pretty convenient memory you have there."

"I told you. I did not recognize it at first. Now I have remembered and I wish to have my property returned." She extended her hand once more.

He seemed to consider this for a moment, then offered the medallion again. She reached for it, yet as she clasped it in her hand, he held fast. She met his cool, even gaze with all the icy poise she could summon.

"You want to tell me more?" he asked softly.

"There is no more to tell. It is mine. Pray you, release it, sir."

He stared at her for another long moment, his steady gaze causing her to wonder if he was about to erupt into outrage, which perhaps was her due, or if he was deciding to merely take the medallion, abandon her in the woodlands and ride off into the gathering evening.

She swallowed against the fear that settled in her chest when she thought she might lose her one friend in all this strange world.

"Please," she said, more softly. "If you be a man of honor."

He looked away, his gaze moving slowly, taking in the enormous trees and tall stands of bracken ferns. Elinor held her breath.

"All right." He loosed his hold on the chain. "Play it your way." He stood up. "Now what?"

Now what, indeed?

"I must find a way home," she said, slipping the medallion over her head. The touch of it made her shiver at first, then it quickly warmed and seemed to comfort her with its weight. "Which is the road I must use?"

"Back to England?"

She blinked at him. "*Back* to England?" Another shiver coursed through her. "Ah . . . what do you suggest?"

"Well, this is California," he said. "England's a long way off. I thought maybe you knew someone here in the U.S."

Icy fear began to spread along her arms, raising the hairs. A long way from England? She couldn't have traveled so far in such a short time! And what were Caliphorneeah and You-Ess?

"I know of no one here," she said slowly. "Only you." She hesitated, then asked, "The bridge where you found me—is it in Cal . . . Cafil—"

"California? Yes. It spans Venners Creek. Sonoma County, not far from the Bodega Highway." His expression was wary. "Are you having trouble remembering again? Even on the Concorde, it's a long haul from England to the States. Don't you remember flying here? Going through customs?"

The last bit of heat departed from her cheeks in a great hurry. She moved unsteadily to the bench and sat.

Indeed, she was having trouble remembering. But she hadn't forgotten the bridge. It spanned the stream that ran through Great Oak Field, that pleasant vale where the DeCourtenays had dwelt for centuries. It was the Oakfield Bridge. She knew it—its stones, its shapes, it color and texture. And she knew as sure as she drew breath that Oakfield Bridge and her home were in England.

"Elinor? You okay?"

She didn't know if she was Oh-Kay. Or who Oh-Kay might be, she thought giddily. But she did know one thing: she was very, very lost.

She could not tell Drew the thoughts racing around in her head. How could she tell this powerful, unshakable man that she was beginning to fear she'd lost her way and her wits? In the end, all she could say was that she was not sure what to do next. He shrugged and asked if she wanted him to take her to someplace called the Port of Air.

"But you don't have any money, do you?" he asked before she had a chance to reply. "No credit cards, no purse, no passport, not even a stick of gum."

She shook her head and held out her empty hands. He pressed his lips together, as if smothering a sigh, and then offered her his hand.

"Come on. It's getting late. There's not much we can do on a Saturday night. You can stay at my place till Monday. In the meantime, I'll make a few calls. Maybe you can hock your necklace."

"Hock?"

"Pawn it? Sell it?"

She clutched at the circle hung about her neck. "No. No, I cannot sell it. It—it is too precious to my family."

"More precious than getting back home to them? If you hock it, you can always get the money together at home and send for it."

"No."

"Okay. Like I said, we'll play it your way." He

plopped his helmet on her head and led the way to his beast. "Let's go."

They rode out of the woods and down the wide roadway. This time she felt brave enough to keep her eyes open for the entire trip.

Trees and berry briars lined their route. Splendid cottages peeked from behind groves of trees or stood out proudly, set back on green meads of perfectly groomed grasses. Such gardeners as must live in this country, she thought. It made for a fair landscape.

Her curiosity was particularly piqued by a passing glimpse of two women, dressed in leggings very like Drew's. What would it be like to go about with no skirts to catch on things or drag in the dirt? There had been no—

Ninny!

She interrupted her own thoughts. Here she was in the strangest world, with the strangest man, perhaps lost, perhaps ill, perhaps enchanted, and she was still overcome with wonder at gardening and clothes. Her father used to say she should have been named Catherine, for she was the most curious Cat he'd ever seen. Still, that curiosity needed to be focused on learning more of where she was and how to get back to her home and family.

Once they had arrived at Drew's, he guided her through the house, showing her the various rooms. With a few quick words and gestures, he showed her the Bath Room, as he called it, gave her towels and cloths, and told her to feel free to use anything she needed.

"And where shall I sleep, Sir Drew?" she asked as he was about to hurry away.

"In there, in my bed again." He pointed to a door in the opposite wall of his bath chamber.

"But I would not put you out of your bed."

"My couch makes into a bed. I'll sleep there." He retreated once more.

"God 'e good e'en, Sir Drew," she said to his departing back.

" 'Night."

He didn't look at her, only continued down the hall toward the kitchen. She heard a door close behind him.

Sighing, she closed the door to the bath chamber. With every passing moment, she was deeper in debt to the dour Sir Drew. The DeCourtenay pride was being put to the test.

However, now was not the time to ponder the mystery of Drew Ingraham, intriguing though he was. There was another, more urgent matter to decipher.

She fingered the medallion. It added a new dimension to this matter, along with the sight of Roger at the fair today. She needed time to sort through the possibilities. She looked around her and smiled.

A short time later, she sat soaking in Drew's magnificent white bathing tub. Despite her confusion and anxiety, she was delighted with this giant, white-clawed basin. It was by far the most elegant, useful construction she'd yet encountered in this new world. Hot water without buckets or fires. Cool water with just a turn of the hand. And so smooth against the backside! She settled back and allowed the steamy warmth to surround her. Slowly the sharp bite of her cares began to lessen as her weary muscles warmed in the heated water.

Feeling relaxed, she played with the metal knobs that controlled the water-spouting, examined the bottles and jars on the windowsill above the tub, and sniffed in rapture at the fragrant green cake that rested on the wee shelf near her hand. She gave the cake an experimental lick and discovered that its taste failed to equal the pleasure of its scent. Soap! she concluded, smiling at her small victory over confusion.

Never mind the luxury, she scolded herself, just concentrate on resolving this mystery.

She took inventory of what she already knew.

For one thing, she was terribly lost. According to Drew, she wasn't in England, but in some place called Caliphorneeah. He'd asked her if she'd flown here—saints, did he think she was a witch or a sorceress? Even the bridge, the Oakfield Bridge, he'd said, was in this new land and had a new name.

Secondly, Roger Aston was here. Though it was yet possible she had been mistaken at the fair today, she doubted it. Few other men looked like Roger. Few other faces were so firmly imprinted upon her mind's eye.

Thirdly, she was in the home of a fair, courteous knight, who held dominion over some of the oddest creatures and contrivances she'd ever witnessed, in dream or in waking.

Last of all, she had arrived in his world wearing a necklace of obvious value and importance, about which she could recall nothing. All she had was a vague feeling about it, a sense of familiarity but no more.

It was a paltry store of information. Worse yet, she had fewer explanations for her situation.

It could be that she had fallen under an enchantment, a spell that rendered her incapable of seeing the world in ordinary fashion. Perhaps that was why her memory was so feeble. It was a most unsatisfactory explanation.

There was another she liked even less. Had a power that belonged in the hands of the angels fallen into the talons of Roger of Clarisdoune? Her father had ofttimes said that Aston possessed the luck of the devil himself. Some spell of Roger's own making might have brought them both to this land of wonders.

It was a mad, fantastic notion.

And it rang with truth.

She ducked under the water, soaking her hair. Her thoughts were taking an eerie turn. While no one would deny that there were evil powers in the world, still, the idea that she might be caught up in something unearthly chilled her very bones.

Massaging some of Drew's sweet-smelling soap into her scalp, she considered her plight. Somehow, Sir Drew played a part in this fantastic tale. But was it for good or ill? She was reluctant to consider it—too many disturbing feelings were roused in her at the thought of the tall, comely knight who'd carried her off on his steed.

She dipped her head beneath the water again, shaking her head vigorously to release the multitudes of bubbles clinging to her hair. She sat up, smoothing her hair back from her face, letting the ends trail down her back into the water. If only Sir Drew had some wondrous concoction to clear her whirling brain as easily as this soap cleared her hair.

"Aiigh," she muttered to herself. This puzzle had more layers than an onion, more threads to unravel than a carpet in the king's great hall. Solving it might be beyond her reach. Still, she had to do something, and if she was to act in prudence, she needed at least some solid bits of truth to guide her.

She got out of the tub and wrapped herself in the small but fluffy-soft towel Drew had provided. As she combed out her hair, she wondered if she looked as odd as she felt.

The women at the fair had looked much as women did in her own land. Some of the menfolk had stared openly at her, and she'd felt their eyes on her even as she walked away. The latter was nothing extraordinary, she decided. Mother Agnes had always said men were goats, forever disposed to viewing the world through their codpieces. Men in this land were like those in her own.

Her eyes widened as she stared at herself in the mirror, comb upraised. Was Sir Drew one of those randy goats?

Lord knew she'd seen him stare at her. A rueful smile

curled her lips. Most of Drew's stares had been of amazement and skepticism, she observed, not of love or lust.

She grimaced as she yanked on a nest of tangles. Such thoughts were not only frivolous but useless as well. No wonder Mother Agnes named them sinful—they distracted one from more important matters.

Only one matter held real import in her life. She had to get home to England. Joanna and Thomas were in England and they were unprotected by family.

She frowned. A shiver of fear had traversed her spine at the thought of her sister's name. Just why, she couldn't say, but she felt a sudden, sharp fear for her little sister's safety.

Drew had said it was a long way back to England. So be it, she thought grimly as she dressed. She'd walk, run, crawl all the way if she must. She'd even fly, if she could find a wizard to teach her the skill.

She had to get home.

Maybe she'd drowned, Drew thought. The way she'd been turning the faucets on and off and flushing the toilet for no reason, anyone would have thought she was a gleeful and fascinated three-year-old who'd escaped her mom's watchful eye. Now, an hour later, he'd gone into the kitchen to get a cold beer from the fridge and heard her, still in the bath, splashing and humming to herself.

He took a long pull of his beer, hoping to banish his embarrassingly adolescent urge to have a peep through the bathroom window at his beautiful guest. The impulse passed, but its subject lingered in his mind. Elinor was taking up too damned much space in his life. If he was to be free again, he had to find a way to get her home or at least reconnected with her own people.

He'd been working in his shop, running over a list of possibilities in his head. He'd said he was going to make calls, but he'd been unable to think of just who to dial.

"Hello, Santa Rosa Police Department?" he muttered. "Uh, I just picked up a woman that I almost ran over and she says she's from Camelot or Sherwood Forest or something and I want to know how to send her back. No, she doesn't have any ID. She doesn't know what an ID is, let alone a car, a coffee maker, or a fork, or a faucet . . ."

Yeah, right, they were going to listen to that. They'd be coming after *him* with the nets and the Thorazine cocktails, not her.

Next on his list had been Missing Persons. She'd seemed so frightened on the bridge and at the fair. She'd gone white when he'd told her she was in the U.S. Maybe she was on the run.

That led him to Immigration and Naturalization. She could be an illegal, on the run from the INS. But that was a goofy notion when he considered it. How many medievalist/Shakespearean actresses tried to sneak into the country—in costume yet—to find work? It made about as much sense as for him to sneak into Italy to find work as the pope. And the Lady Elinor DeCourtenay did not strike him as someone planning to be a hotel maid or a migrant farm worker.

Next, the British Consulate came to mind. This was the most promising so far, yet he wasn't sure how they could help him beyond putting him in touch with Scotland Yard or Interpol. And that still didn't rule out the possibility that he'd come off looking more like a crackpot than she, just for getting involved—

He straightened up suddenly. Crackpots! That was it. He knew who he'd call first. And, in this case, he wouldn't have to go through any red tape, fill out any forms, sign his life away, or wait until offices were open once more. All he had to worry about was whether Dr. Wild Will Curran, Ph.D., M.D. in Psychiatric Medicine, was in love this weekend.

Chapter Five

Elinor wandered about Drew's small, spare bedchamber. Plain as a monk's cell, the only comfort it boasted was a bed, four pillows, and a closet full of good—though unusual—clothing.

She touched the surcotes, leggings and other items so cleverly hung in the wardrobe. The fabrics were sumptuous, a delight to the touch. Close-woven wools and linens that might have been spun from the downy silk of milkweed puffs made up the majority, while on the shelf above, a number of items of a soft, faded indigo were neatly folded and stacked.

She touched the shift she wore. Stains edged the hem. A sniff of the sleeve brought smells of dust, foods and the musty-bitter sweat of the Master of Beasts. She lifted the sleeve of a smooth, white cotehardie, comparing the two.

Moments later, she had stripped off all her garments and carried them into the bath chamber. She plopped them into the bathtub and ran water over them, then swished the luscious green soap in the water until there were bubbles all about. That done, she turned off the water, dried her hands and padded back to Drew's wardrobe.

She slipped into the elegantly simple cotehardie and buttoned its many buttons. The sleeves hung down beyond her fingertips, but she rolled them up to her wrists and smoothed her hands over the cool, fine-woven fabric. Bending, she saw that the hem of the cote ended just above her knees.

She shrugged. No one would see her, so no one could judge her immodest. It was clean and fresh-smelling and would serve her well for a night's rest. Already the sun was going down; with no candles, torches or lamps in sight, she would do what most folk did at nightfall: go to sleep.

She hurriedly scrubbed and rinsed her clothes and hung them here and there about the bath chamber to dry. The light from the windows was nearly extinguished by the time she returned to Drew's plain bed and knelt down to make her prayers. At last, she climbed under the bedclothes, sighing with gratitude at the soft support of the well-stuffed mattress.

Rest was what she required, for she could do nothing about her plight in the dark of night in a strange land. On the morrow, she'd set about finding the road back to England.

Luck was with him, Drew thought. Or Cupid, anyway. Wild Will was at home—alone, for a change.

It had taken him longer than he'd thought to get up the nerve to make the call. He'd chosen to use the shop extension, for the sake of privacy, but even then he'd picked up the receiver and set it down twice before he finally dialed.

It wasn't just the nature of the call that held him back. It was the fact that he was making this call at all.

He couldn't remember the last time he'd spoken to

Will, but he suspected it had been nearly a year ago. Truth to tell, the only calls coming in or going out on his phone, at least in recent memory, had all been related to his motorcycle restoration business. He wasn't sure what sort of response he'd receive.

"Yo, Will. It's Drew." He waited, unable to go on until he heard Will's reaction.

"Drew? Drew Carey, the very famous actor?"

"Drew Ingraham, Doc."

He felt relief. Will knew his voice. He was yanking him, a sign of Will's affection.

"Drew Ingraham? *The* Drew Ingraham? My late friend and cohort in crime?"

Exaggerated coughing and gasping erupted on the other end of the line. Drew started to smile.

"Beg pardon," Will said. "Just a mild myocardial infarction. I'm better now. I get this way every time an old friend comes back from the beyond."

"How are you, pal?"

"Not bad, actually. I sold the Big Twin, fell in love seventeen times, got arrested for smuggling underage houseplants across county lines, and was elected home room president. Didn't you get my Christmas card?"

"You mean the one that said 'You may already have won'?"

"That's the one. First class, all the way, that's me. How're things at the hermitage? Seen any miracles?"

"I'm witnessing one right this minute," Drew responded. "Will Curran at home on a Saturday night. What happened, Doc? Get in a car wreck and end up in a full body cast?"

"Maybe *I'm* trying the reclusive bit. I've been wondering how it suits my old pal Ingraham. God knows, we never see him, his mother and I never get any letters, comes a Friday night, he never calls—"

"The day you decide to go into seclusion is the day they find Big Bird drunk in an alley off Sesame Street, a hen in Spandex tucked under each arm."

"You saw the papers, then! Big scandal. Kermit's doing damage control, but I don't think this is going to help, come the next pledge drive."

Drew laughed and felt himself loosen up at last. Wild Will was the same, rain or shine—a nut who helped other nuts for a living. His friends and his clients could depend on him to take them and their problems seriously, but not solemnly.

Drew envisioned him as they spoke, a small, compact dynamo seated cross-legged in the middle of his vast living room, holding the cordless phone against one ear with his shoulder while his hands busied themselves with a book he was speed-reading, or perhaps the latest catalog of exotic plants or cutting-edge electronic toys. Twenty-four hours a day were never enough to occupy Curran's brilliant, searching mind.

"Look, Doc," Drew said, plunging in. "I've got a hypothetical for you."

"Just like that? I don't see you for seven centuries and you call me up out of the blue asking for free advice? I'm wounded, Ingraham. I really am."

"Take two aspirin and call Dr. Ruth in the morning," Drew retorted amiably. "You going to listen or not?"

"Same old Ingraham." Will made clucking noises over the phone. "You gotta get over these delusions of grandeur, Your Royal Heinie. But, since you've already interrupted my quiet evening of nude lacrosse and fish sticks, I guess I can give you a listen."

"Thanks. Here's the deal. I want to know what you head doctors do when you meet a patient and you're not sure if they're bona fide bananas or if they've just had too many coconuts land on their skulls."

"Tropical metaphors. Sounds exotic."

"No. Just wondering how you could tell."

"You left out one other possible diagnosis, young Dr. Kildare."

"What is that, Dr. Zorba?"

"The one that concludes that said patient is neither

67

bananas nor coconuts, but has all his oars dipped firmly into the blue lagoon."

"Meaning he's sane?"

"Maybe. Guess again."

"Meaning he's faking it?"

"Aye, captain."

Drew blew out a short breath. "I should have known this would be complicated."

"Welcome to my world. Wait till you have to factor in all their relatives, lost childhood pets and sexual predilections along with all the clinical and recreational drugs they may have ingested within the last few decades."

"Yeah, I know. I never said you didn't earn your megabucks, Doc. But can you at least give me some of the preliminaries? I mean, after you've eliminated concussion or something like that, how can you tell what's really up with them?"

Will gave a short bark of laughter. "If I could've figured that out in one phone conversation, I'd have saved myself a lot of time and money on piddling stuff like med school and residency. But if you can give me some details about this hypothetical client of yours, I might be able to give you some clues."

Drew caught the faint emphasis Will placed on the word hypothetical. Lying to Will was next to impossible. Not just because of his training but also because William Curran and Andrew Ingraham had attended the same schools for the first twelve years of their education. They'd ridden bikes together, then graduated to their shared passion for motorcycles. They'd fought together, played ball together, gotten drunk together, moaned over girls together. Will had been the best man at Drew's wedding to LeeAnne. He'd also been a pallbearer at her funeral. And though Drew had kept to himself almost exclusively for the past three years, Will would always be the one person on earth who knew him best.

"I don't have it all thought out," Drew said, hedging as best he could and hoping Will wouldn't press. "But I can tell you some of it."

He sketched an outline of what he knew about Elinor. He maintained the switch in gender and he left out the information that the hypothetical person in question was at this moment lounging not-so-hypothetically naked in his bathtub.

"Hmm," Will murmured when he'd finished. "I think you can pretty safely rule out the bang-on-the-head hypothesis. The guy's been checked by a doc and is up and functioning. People can get their wires crossed from a head injury, but it wouldn't manifest itself in the ways you've described."

"So we're talking bad brain chemicals? Personality disorder? Escapee from the funny farm?"

"Don't be crude, ya lousy philistine. But yes, that's the route I'd go with the information you've given me. At least to start out."

"How? What would you do next?"

"Ah. Assessments. Now that's where the fun starts."

Drew grabbed for a pen, yanked a page off his wall calendar and began to take notes. By the time Will had finished, he'd covered the entire sheet, even writing upward along the edges.

"So, when is this opus coming out?" Will asked.

"Hmm?" Drew was still scribbling.

"When does the book come out? You said this was all hypothetical. I assumed you'd decided that being out in the boonics all by yourself was the perfect place to write a novel."

"Oh." Drew straightened up from the shop table and dropped the pen. "No. No novel. Just thinking."

"The wood ticks are getting to you, aren't they?"

"Another diagnosis by phone, Doc?"

"Touché. Okay, no more snooping."

"Bull feathers."

"Have it your way." Will's voice softened. "You know

what I mean, man. Take care of yourself. Get out once in a while. Wear your galoshes. Brush after every meal."

"Always use zip codes?"

"Mail overseas packages early."

"I'll consider it. Back at you, Doc."

Drew hung up the phone. He grinned. It had felt good to talk to Will again in their old, bantering way. He hadn't thought it would go so well, especially after all the time he'd spent alone. He wasn't sure he knew how to talk to friends anymore. It was good to know that Will hadn't written him off.

He stared at the page of notes before him and recalled why he'd made the call to Wild Will. It was a long shot, but it was a start. At the very least, armed with the questions Will had provided, he could find out more about his mysterious, beautiful, uninvited guest. Then, maybe, he could get her out of his house and off of his mind.

As long as he didn't do anything foolish.

Like touch her.

Or kiss her.

Or take a good long look at . . .

He slammed the brakes on that train of thought. It was late. He needed some rest. Alone.

He slipped his notes into his shirt pocket, locked up the shop and crossed the yard to the house.

Elinor felt as if she were coming up from under very deep water. Murky shapes shimmered before her, closing around her like a gathering school of large fish. She didn't know if she was under water, yet she had the thought that if she didn't get out of this place soon and fill her lungs with wholesome, freeing air, she might die.

One of the shapes loomed larger, pressing against her sides and then her back, with serpent-like motions both seductive and sickening. She fought the languor she felt in her own limbs, lashing out at the thing. Her lungs were beginning to burn—she was under water and she needed air.

Get away! she screamed, though she knew she couldn't be heard. The serpent-shape moved off, then darted back, its body or tentacles wrapping about her, dragging her back from the freedom almost in sight above. She struggled, twisting and turning, clawing at the thing that wanted her life.

She gave a great heave and was hurled backwards, her body slamming into a rock or a wall. . . .

Everything was peaceful in the house. Drew felt relieved. She must have finally made it out of the tub and gone off to bed.

Just to make sure, Drew went to the bathroom door and listened. He heard nothing. He knocked softly and when there was no answer, went in.

A short yelp escaped him as he switched on the light. The room looked like a Friday night blowout at the Sudz 'n' Dudz. Wet clothes hung from every available hook, towel rack and fixture. Stockings, dresses, underwear and even ribbons dripped everywhere, the water puddling below each item and then gathering momentum to join with its fellows and form tiny rivers all along the age-slanted linoleum floor.

"Okay, this is too much," he growled. He leapt across the running streams and yanked open the door to the bedroom. He opened his mouth to bark out an order, suddenly filled with righteous fury.

But when the light from the bathroom fell across his bed, all words stopped short in his throat.

Elinor lay on the bed, the covers tangled and tossed aside as if she'd been wrestling with them. She was breathing uneasily, emitting small, whimpering sounds. Her long hair was everywhere, the heavy, damp strands spread across the pillows, the sheets, even tumbling over the side of the bed.

She was wearing one of his shirts, one of the white ones from his former life as a corporate player. It was modestly buttoned and covered her hips, but below the tapered hem, Drew got a good look at the long, long legs he'd glimpsed when she'd stepped over his bike-seat. They were every bit as shapely and firm as he'd thought, rising up to the softest, most intriguing . . .

Her scream nearly stopped his heart. She came bolt upright in bed, striking out at the air before her. She didn't scream again, but her frantic sounds spoke eloquently of fear and desperation.

He crossed to the bed and took her hands in his, holding them gently down and speaking to her in a soft, reassuring voice. It was some time before she actually seemed to see him. When she did, she gasped and scrambled back up onto the pillows, yanking her hands out of his grasp.

"Elinor," he repeated. "Elinor? It's Drew. Don't panic. You were just dreaming. You're awake now."

"Oh, God," she panted, her back pressed against the wall. "Sweet Lord, what's happened to me?"

It was Drew. Elinor shook her head, relieved to see that his familiar face didn't disappear or alter as . . .

"You were having a dream," Drew told her. "A bad one?"

She nodded, her heart beginning to slow its frantic hammering. "How did you—did I cry out?"

He smiled. "Yeah. But it's okay. I don't think they heard you in Nevada."

She took several deep, slow breaths as she gathered her wits. "I'm sorry. I hadn't meant to disturb your rest."

"I wasn't sleeping. I just came in from the shop." He motioned toward the bathing chamber with his head. "Nice setup you made in there. You planning to stock it with trout?"

She raised her hands in confusion. He pointed.

Leaning around him, she peered into the lighted room. Water was running everywhere over Drew's smooth, elegant floors. Damp air was already wafting into the bedchamber.

"Oh. Oh, no!"

She leapt off the bed and went wading into the mess. She apologized while snatching clothes off their hanging places and tossing them into the tub.

"Surely you must find me the most burdensome guest ever to visit this household! I crave your pardon. I only wished to clean my garments. I've never done it before and I didn't know so much water would—"

"It's okay." He joined her efforts to stem the tide, handing her towels and bringing a mop and bucket.

"But your lovely bathing chamber. If I've spoilt it, I shall repay you, I promise—"

"Hey. Don't worry about it. This is an old house and it's seen worse."

It wasn't much comfort.

"There," he said a short time later. "I think we caught it before it reached the high tide mark."

He gave her a hard look as he wrung out the mop. "How about you? Are you all right? That was some slug-fest you were into there on the bed, especially for someone who was sound asleep."

"I am much improved." She shivered at the memory of her dream, but concealed it. "Thank you for waking me. Dreams ofttimes have the air of reality, do they not?"

"Yes. Do want a drink or something?"

She shook her head. "In truth, I am ashamed of my silly outcries. I'm not a child to be wailing in the dark over a mere dream."

His eyes were still on her when he straightened up from the bucket. "No need to be ashamed."

"Still, you must think me as giddy as a leaf on the wind," she said as he went to put away the mop and pail.

She gathered up the soaking towels from the floor. The air in the bath chamber was no longer as warm as it had been. She plopped the towels into a basket on the floor and looked down at herself. Her whole front was soaking wet, the fine white fabric clinging to her like a second skin.

Something made her look up.

Drew leaned against the doorsill, taking a long, slow look at her, from the top of her head to her feet and back. She felt a blush creeping up over her breastbone and into her face. The shine in his eyes was both disconcerting and flattering. No one had ever looked at her in such a way—as if he could gaze at her all day and never grow weary of the sight. The thought sent a curling tendril of sensation throughout her middle.

Mesmerized by his attention and caught by her own response, she stood frozen. She knew she should do something—move or cover herself . . . or what?

"Oh," she said at last, jumping a little. "I beg your pardon, Sir Drew. I borrowed one of your cotehardies to wear while my clothes were drying. I hope I've not spoilt it utterly by getting it wet. I must apologize again for my lack of care. I've always had laundresses to clean my clothes."

He looked up at her face, bright lights still flickering in his eyes. "It's okay. I don't mind."

She swallowed over a tight lump of excitement rising in her throat. The longer she gazed at those lights in his eyes, the more she felt they were igniting tiny sparks within her.

"It's okay," he repeated. His tone was cool. "I'll toss it in the dryer."

"Ah."

He took a step toward her. "You'll have to take it off, first."

"Oh! Oh, of course, yes." Her fingers went to the top button, then stopped. "Oh. You—I—" She edged toward the bedroom door. "I'll just . . . If you don't mind . . . I need another garment . . ."

He nodded. "Take another shirt out of the closet."

"Thank you," she murmured. "I shan't be a moment."

Scuttling to the closet, she fumbled for another of the white cotehardies. She shivered as she stripped the wet shirt—as Drew had called it—from her bare skin. Her fingers felt like someone else's as she tried to hurry into the dry one.

She held the wet garment out before her as she returned to the bath chamber to hand it to him. With a muttered thanks, she turned and fled to the bedroom once more, clambering into the bed and pulling the covers up to her chin.

"Good night, Elinor."

"Good night, Sir Drew."

The light in the bath chamber was extinguished. She listened for his footsteps retreating down the hall, then hopped from the bed and softly closed the door to the bedroom.

Jumping back into bed, she buried her hot face in the cool pillow. Thanks to the wet, clinging fabric of that shirt, Drew had just seen details of her physical form that not even her mother had seen since she was a child.

It was embarrassing. It was a bit frightening.

Then why did she feel so pleased and excited?

Perhaps it was this place. This man. This spell she seemed to be under. Things were happening so quickly. A short time ago, her days and even her hours were in order, clear and unchanging in their routine. Even her emotions had been more neatly regulated.

But here, now, she went from sleep to nightmare, rest to terror, sleeping to waking, embarrassment to pleasure, suspicion to desire all in a matter of moments. Drew might be accustomed to it, but she wasn't. Her mind and senses flooded with new topics to savor and to consider, she lay on the bed and tried to bring order to her experiences.

She was beginning to turn the matter of the medallion over in her mind when the sun came streaming into the room, and she realized her weary body had given up on her querulous, ticking mind and sent her off to a dreamless sleep. Tomorrow had come. It was time to begin her search for a way home.

When Elinor rose, Drew was not to be found. She called his name, made a tentative search of the house, but he was gone. Her clothing, however, had been returned to the bath chamber, dry and fresh-smelling. She dressed quickly and went to the kitchen.

Drew must be in the outbuilding he called his shop, she guessed. As she went about, opening cupboards and pantries, she wondered what he did there.

Shops were for smithies, weavers, carpenters, she mused. Drew was fair spoken, despite his many odd words. He carried himself with pride and elegance and he owned the Master of Beasts and the Master of Coffees. He couldn't be a common laborer.

Then again, judging from the paltry stores in his cramped bit of a pantry, perhaps he was a common workman. She discovered a container of dried fruits, some wee wafers, and a packet of dried wheat sticks. Not much for keeping body and soul together, but she'd make do. If a man so healthful and strong as Sir Drew could survive on such fare, then so could she. She crunched and chewed, and washed the meal down with the good water from the well-spout in the kitchen basin. Not knowing what else to do, or where to start on her journey home, she went outside to the shop.

Standing on tiptoe, she peeked in at the window in the outbuilding's door. Drew stood by a brightly lit table, grooming another of his ugly horses. The beast—scarcely as big as a pony—perched atop the table, and while Drew took gleaming instruments to its hide and legs, it maintained a statue-like poise.

"The strangest animals," she murmured.

She knocked on the door and heard Drew call out, "Come."

76

He glanced at her over his shoulder as she entered. "You're up early."

"I'd say not. At the abbey, we are required to rise whilst it is still dark to recite our prayers. Then a brief rest, then prayers again at cock's crow."

"Sounds like the army."

Elinor chuckled. "I have heard it described that way. And not always in a complimentary tone."

She moved further into the large, high-ceilinged room, giving both Drew's black beast and the one on the table a wide berth. Still, her interest was roused by the sight of Drew's long, strong hands selecting tools and putting them to use with steady, silent competence. Oh, for a pen and parchment, she thought, to draw those skillful fingers. Such an image might never illuminate one of the texts she worked on at the abbey, but she didn't care. Her own fingers itched with the need to sketch.

"So, you're a nun," Drew said, breaking into her reverie. "What order? That's what you call it, isn't it? An order?"

"Aye. The sisters at Wednesbury are Benedictines."

"You don't dress like a nun."

"I am not a nun. I have yet to take the veil. We dress in habits while we are in the enclosure and we may dress so outside. But we are not so compelled."

She edged closer, her eyes still on his hands.

"Things are loosening up, I guess," he commented. "I see you found your clothes. Nothing shrank?"

She glanced up. Once again, he seemed to be taking inventory of her figure, from top to toe. Flustered, she stepped back, her skirts held out wide.

"I believe that everything is its proper size."

"Good. That's a pretty fancy costume, as far as I can tell."

"It is my last good gown. Please give my thanks to your servants for their care."

"My servants?"

"Aye, the ones who do your washing."

"Oh, them." The corners of his mouth lifted. "You must mean Mr. and Mrs. Kenmore. Sure, I'll tell them."

"Thank you."

While she puzzled over his mirth, he turned back to his work. Servants and laundry were soon forgotten as she watched in fascinated silence. He was actually removing pieces from the animal on the table-top . . .

She gave a gasp, causing him to nearly drop the tool he held.

"It is a clockwork!" she cried. "Not a beast, but a machine!"

He pointed to the creature. "This? Yeah. It's a machine. What did you think it was?"

She felt herself flush. "A steed. Perhaps an enchanted horse."

He gave a brief grin. "Not exactly. It's a Harley. A motorcycle. They have them in your country, too, you know. Norton bikes are good machines."

"From Chipping Norton?"

He shrugged. "I don't know. I've been a Harley rider since I saw my first street bike. But these old babies are the best."

"Old? But they look quite new."

"I do my best. Sometimes I get one in pristine condition and all it needs is a rubout and a polish. Others I have to send out to be re-chromed and painted. But the ones I work on are all at least fifty or sixty years old."

Half of what he was saying was comprehensible to her, but she decided she liked listening to him. The light of interest sparkled in his eyes, his face was animated, and there was pleasure in the deep tones of his voice. She smiled at these pleasant signs of life in her usually dour host, felt proud that she'd come upon a way to evoke them.

"But how do they move?" she asked, following the bent of her own curiosity. "They have wheels, yet no horse or oxen to draw them. And I see no ropes to pull them or waterworks to propel them."

She rounded the opposite side of the machine on the table, peering in and around the metal parts in its center. "It must then be a clockwork, yes? You must wind it?"

He chuckled, a warm, throaty sound. "No. Not exactly. Come look at my bike. This one's all torn apart."

He went to the Master Beast and ran a hand over its back. "Look," he said, pointing to the heavy cluster of metal underneath. "This is the engine. And this is where the fuel . . ."

Carefully, thoroughly, he went over the ingenious creation with her, stopping to answer her questions, never flagging in his patience.

"Are there many such motor-cycles?" she asked.

"Yes and no." He stood up beside the "bike" as he referred to it. "There are a lot of motorcycles, but these oldies, the Knucks and the Shovelheads, the originals, they're hard to come by. Some people spend years just hunting for parts before they have enough for a whole bike."

He smiled. "There are a lot of old legends about how somewhere, out in the desert, there's an old abandoned warehouse with hundreds of these bikes just sitting, in pristine condition, right off the factory line back in the 1930s and '40s. Somebody left them there, maybe when the war started, and all you have to do is go out and find them."

"And have you been there?"

He laughed outright this time. "No, not me. I'm no dreamer and I'm not looking to get rich quick. I make enough on the work I do and that's all I need."

"Then you must be a contented man."

The laughter left his eyes in the passing of a breath. His face grew cool and formal once again.

"I don't know," he said. "I suppose I am. As contented as the next guy." He stepped quickly to his work table.

Coral Smith Saxe

"Did you get any breakfast?" he asked, turning his eyes to his work.

"Aye. I did make free use of your pantry. I hope 'twas not too forward of me."

"No. Help yourself."

She hesitated. Something she had said had caused the lights of life to dim in his face. Perhaps one did not speak of money or contentment in this land. Surely she was ignorant of many of its customs.

Drew said nothing more, giving her the feeling she'd been dismissed. She felt foolish just standing by, yet she didn't know what to do.

Idleness was not her custom. At the abbey, there was a rigid schedule and a never-ending round of tasks. At home, there were obvious demands of the mistress of the house, as she had recently become upon her mother's death. Here, she had no idea what she should or should not do.

Drew's bare pantry came to mind. Perhaps she could help him there. Domestic work would never be numbered among her talents, yet she might expand his stores a bit. It would be some compensation for his charity toward her.

"I shall be outside on the grounds," she said.

"Fine," came the terse reply.

She went out, closing the door quietly behind her. She looked about, admiring once more the tall, red-barked trees, the lush ferns and shrubs ringing the clearing where his house stood. Surely there would be good game for the taking in those bushes and the forest beyond. There would be berries among the brambles, mayhap, and even a few wild onions. With luck, she might also come upon some clue to the truth of where she was and how she might return home. She pushed up the sleeves of her gown and set out to explore.

Chapter Six

Drew had managed to get lost in the intricacies of valve springs and oil lines for several hours. It was a skill he'd worked hard to perfect after LeeAnne's death and he was glad it hadn't deserted him.

Elinor's question about his contentment had rattled him. Not surprising, he thought as he set about cleaning his tools. Most everything about Elinor rattled him in one way or another. But her question, expressed as it was with a piercingly honest look from her remarkable eyes, had all but undone him.

It was a question he hadn't asked himself in years—if ever. When she had posed it to him, however, it seemed vitally important, in the way that the tiniest missing engine part makes all the difference in starting a bike.

She hadn't asked if he was rich. She hadn't asked if he was happy. She'd asked if he had found contentment.

Had he?

He'd survived the rocks and jolts of a reasonably normal childhood, despite the loss of his parents in his sophomore year at San Jose State. He'd finished college with a good degree, had married the woman of his dreams. He'd started a successful business, right out of school. Surely he'd been content.

Then LeeAnne had died. He'd set his own terms for handling that shock: pulling out of the firm, selling his home, moving here. It was what he'd wanted. He'd made a new life for himself, and yes, he did enjoy his work. No one bothered him. He'd been able to get past the grief and rage of LeeAnne's death, hadn't he? And now he was living in peaceful routine in one of the most beautiful areas of the country.

Contentment? Sure, why not?

Bull feathers

He was cleaning his hands when some odd thumpings and tweets began to pierce his consciousness. Tossing his rag aside, he went to the door and peered out.

"Holy—!"

He yanked open the door and tore across the yard.

"Elinor! What the hell are you doing?"

She only gave him a smile and a wave and turned back to her task. He skidded to a stop next to her and grabbed her arm.

"Are you nuts? You can't do that! Those are—"

"Sparrows," she finished cheerfully as she bagged another with her homemade net. "There's a lovely fat one!"

He grabbed the stick and net out of her hands. He pulled the netting loose, and the bird flew free with a desperate-looking flap. He held the trap up in front of him.

"You can't go around snagging birds! What were you doing?"

"Just as you say. I was catching birds." She looked at him with a mixture of irritation and wonder.

"What for?"

82

"What for? Why, for our supper, of course!"

"You eat sparrows?"

"Of course. They lack much meat, but two may make a meal out of a dozen or so."

He looked down at her feet. A saucepan was at the ready on a wooden crate. From inside the crate came cheepings and scratching. He could guess their source.

"How were you going to—you weren't going to eat them live, were you?" He couldn't help it, he had to ask.

"La, no! That would be unsavory. Nay, their necks must be wrung, then their feathers plucked, then they must be gutted, I believe, before—"

"That's okay," he said hastily. "I can fill in the rest of the details myself."

He lifted the pot and then the crate. Elinor cried out as her quarry escaped into the air with a rush of brown wings.

"Sir Drew! Did you not realize they'd fly free?"

"Yep." He set the box down. "Elinor, we don't go around strangling sparrows. For all I know, they're protected birds."

"Protected?"

"Okay, so I doubt sparrows are on the endangered species list, but all the same, we don't hunt them for food. We don't need them."

"Don't need them?" She placed her hands on her hips. "You must be more frugal and self-denying than the Franciscans! Your pantry is scarcely greater than this box, and I saw it is but half full. Summer may come soon, but such a larder won't last more than a week or two. I was but trying to add to your provisions."

He sighed. "Come with me."

He led the way inside and showed her the cabinets where he kept his packaged foods. "There's plenty to eat, especially for one person living alone."

Opening the refrigerator, he pointed inside. "And in

83

here, plenty more. What won't keep can be frozen." He opened the upper door and showed her the frosted packages inside.

"Frozen?" Elinor stuck one finger in and touched an ice-rimed can of juice. She drew the finger back quickly and sucked it as if it were burned. "It is colder than February!"

"Yep. And what's more, if I run out of all of this, I can just go to the market and buy more."

"You have no gardens. No orchards."

"I don't have time to do all that. And I'm the only one here."

"Except for me. I wanted to repay your hospitality."

He shut the fridge door and leaned against it. "I appreciate the thought. But please, don't go decapitating helpless birdies on my behalf. I have enough food for both of us."

"Very well, Sir Drew."

"It's just Drew."

"Aye."

He looked around the kitchen. It had been hours since he'd eaten and he guessed it had been the same for her. At least, he hoped she hadn't tasted anything too strange out in the woods while he'd been working. She seemed savvy enough about hunting the birds— were there more weird survival-in-the-woods skills she possessed?

"Tell you what. I have a couple of calls to make, then I'll order us something from Capriccio's. You like pizza?"

"I don't know."

"Well, you can give it a try."

He started for the door, then paused. "I know it must be kind of boring around here for you. If you want, you can read. I've got some books in the front room. Or watch TV. Or listen to some music. I may live out in the sticks but I do have most of the comforts of home." He paused again. "I guess I'd better show you.

84

After a quick introductory course in operating modern electronic equipment, she looked mystified but game to try. She was standing agape before the TV when he left.

He hoped he wouldn't find her frozen there hours later, hypnotized by the shopping channel.

He used the shop phone again, for the sake of privacy. Showing up on a bridge in the middle of the night, washing clothes in the bathtub, he thought as he looked up a phone number; hauling sparrows out of the sky for supper. Things were getting just too weird. He had to take action. He dialed quickly and waited for an answer. He didn't have to wait for a second ring.

"Santa Rosa Police Department. How may I help you?"

Pizza.

How had she reached the age of twenty-one and never heard the word, let alone tasted such a marvelous food? From the instant Drew brought the aromatic pie into the house, Elinor was enchanted. Surely it was the food of the angels.

"It is Italian, you say?" she asked, savoring the scent of her second piece before biting off the pointed tip, as Drew had done.

"So they say. I don't think they eat it in Italy, actually. Or else it's considered peasant food and only fit for Americans. But it's based on some Italian dish, I guess."

Elinor sipped at the rich red wine Drew had poured. It was a bottle from local vineyards, he'd said, and it was as fine, or finer, than any of the French or Spanish wines she'd tasted. He'd also brought out an icy cold salad of crisp greens from his winter cabinet. She couldn't recall ever having a finer meal. When she said as much to Drew, he chuckled.

"You're a poor man's dream come true," he said.

"Some guy's gonna be delighted to date you."

"Date?"

"Take you out to dinner."

"Ah."

She occupied herself with her pizza—she'd seen the word written out on the box, so she knew how it was spelled—and wine. She hadn't made much progress in finding her way home, but she'd accomplished a few things this day.

Though Drew had put an end to her efforts to catch some fowl, she had found several aromatic and medicinal herbs along the forest path. She'd wound the fresh-pulled plants with grasses and strung them up in the little room off the kitchen, where two more large white boxes, a bit like his winter cabinet, sat side by side. She'd peeked inside them, but they were empty and thumped hollowly when she closed their doors. Barrels for storage, she'd concluded.

She'd soon have them filled with as much good provender as she could find about the estate, she'd vowed. Drew's charity would not go unrewarded.

At last, Drew pushed away his plate and drank the last of his wine. He pulled a piece of paper from a pouch in his surcote and unfolded it carefully, clearing his throat.

"I have to ask you something," he said, his eyes meeting hers before veering off once more. "Do you think maybe you really did hit your head back there on the bridge the other night?"

She swallowed a bite of pizza and considered. "I did hit my head. Your nurse bandaged it for me. It is healing well."

"Do you think you might have hit it harder than she thought? What I mean is, I think maybe you got pretty mixed up out there on the bridge. Am I right that you've been a little confused?"

His eyes showed earnest concern, warming her and putting her at ease. Slowly, she nodded.

"My head feels well enough. Still, I find your ways and your world most unfamiliar. I understand I am not in England. But there is oft so much I cannot comprehend I begin to wonder if I am dreaming."

The set of his shoulders softened.

"Okay. I have a friend who's a specialist in this kind of thing. He helps people who are . . . confused. He gave me some questions to ask you that might help us to find out what's happened." He raised the piece of paper. "Here are the questions, if you're willing to try. This isn't a test. It's just another way to find out if there's anything wrong with the way your brain is working."

Elinor looked up from her pizza and raised an eyebrow. "My brain is wholly inside my head. You cannot see its workings lest you crack my head and lay it open." She eyed the knife he'd used to slice the bread.

"You may be right, but I'm not going to do that. Just humor me. Ready?"

She chewed the last bite of her pizza, swallowed and gave a beatific sigh. She used her napkin to wipe the delicious sauce from her fingertips, then folded her hands before her. "Very well. I am prepared."

"All right," he said, and cleared his throat once again. "Who are you?"

She looked at him with mild annoyance. She'd told him this several times already. Still, he'd said these questions might help to find out if she was dreaming or perhaps mad. It seemed best to go along with him. "The Lady Elinor Elizabeth Justinia DeCourtenay," she recited, just as she'd insisted Joanna and Thomas recite their identities on the Oakfield Road. "Daughter of the late Gerard, Baron Newborough."

"And where were you born?"

"At Oakfield House, my home."

"What day is this?"

She thought this over. "I came here of a Friday evening. That would make it—oh, dear, the Sabbath." She felt a terrible pang of guilt that she'd disregarded the holy day. She vowed to make a penance as soon as she was able.

"What month?" Drew asked.

"May."

"What year?"

"The year of our Lord fourteen hundred and twenty."

"And who is the president of the United States?"

"Sir Fred Rogers?" She'd seen such a person on the picture box Drew had called Teevee.

"Ah-ha. O—kay, let me rephrase that. Who's on the throne of England?"

"His Royal Highness by the Grace of God King Henry the Fifth."

"What time is it?"

She got up and walked to the window. She squinted up at the sky first, then down at the ground. "It is difficult to ascertain with certainty, for the sun seems to set earlier for you, yet I believe it to be nigh onto seven o'clock in the evening."

She saw Drew looking at the clock he wore strapped upon his wrist. He raised his brows. "Seven-ten. Very good."

She smiled and went back to her chair. He waited as she took another sip of her wine, then returned to his testing.

She was skeptical that all these queries would yield any great truth about her situation or her condition. What could be gained by asking her to draw the hands of a clock? It seemed downright silly to list the past kings of England or name the states bordering this mysterious land of Caliphorneeah. Still, she cooperated. Perhaps Drew's friend was a scholar well versed in divining such wisdom. And if he was, might he not help her to find a way out of this confusion?

At last, he'd exhausted all the items on his list and had filled several sheets of paper with her replies. He capped his pen and set the pad aside.

"Have I sustained a brain injury?" she asked.

"I don't know. I'll have to show this to my friend and ask him. I'm not trained in psychology."

"And what is that?"

"The study of the mind."

"I see. And the brain and the mind are thus the same?"

He frowned. "Good question. I believe that's what we assume."

"But what of the heart? And the soul?"

He shrugged expansively. "I can't really say."

"Do you believe one possesses a heart and a soul and a mind?"

"Yes. But I can't say I know where those things are located within us, beyond the physical presence of two organs called the heart and the brain."

He toyed with his wineglass and she lifted the bottle, offering to pour him more. He stretched out his arm and she filled his glass with the deep ruby liquid.

"You ask the darnedest questions."

"I?" she asked, smiling. "Hark at this fellow, who only moments ago asked me which is the larger, a mouse or an elephant."

He grinned in return. "Touché. But I didn't make those questions up. Is it because of the convent? Is that why *you* ask such unusual questions?"

She helped herself to another piece of pizza, which was cooling but still tasty.

"I don't know. Surely everyone should be concerned about the conditions of his or her own heart and soul and mind."

"True. Maybe that's the trouble these days. Not enough of us give those things a thought on a yearly basis, let alone daily."

"Have you lost your faith, Drew Ingraham?" she asked softly.

He looked startled, then angry, but he quickly hid those feelings behind a light smile.

"I don't know that I had any to begin with. I should probably check in the lost-and-found. Maybe someone else picked it up."

"I feel my own slipping away, ofttimes," she confessed, surprised at herself even as she said the words. "So many injustices. So much sickness and suffering. So many people who feel no shame for the pain they cause."

"Has that happened to you? Has someone caused you great pain?"

She felt the impulse to say yea to his question, to trust the honesty in those pale blue eyes. Yet she also felt the same reluctance she'd felt before when she'd been faced with telling him about Roger and her family's fate. For reasons that weren't clear to her, she didn't want to reveal too much. And she didn't want to appear a pathetic victim to this man, of all men. She employed his ruse of making light of the subject.

"Who has not in this life? Yet, here I am, hale, whole, and in possession of all my teeth."

He chuckled. "Yeah. I guess I don't have much room to complain, either. It's not like I've been shipped off to fight in the Middle East or had to give up a kidney or an eye or anything." He sat forward. "You haven't been in the service, have you?"

"In the service of whom?"

"Of your country. The army?"

She giggled. "I? A soldier? La, Sir Drew, your imagination carries you away."

He looked a bit sheepish. "I just wondered. A lot of women these days are in the military, so I just thought I'd ask. But I suppose not many nuns go into the army, unless they serve as nurses or chaplains."

"I am not one. I worked in the library at the abbey, most days."

"Then you must like to read."

"Aye, when I may. Though I have but little Latin and less of French. I looked at your books while you were out. How fortunate you are to possess so many! Our library at the abbey is but little larger than your collection."

"That's too bad," he said, rising and going to the bookcase. "I don't have anywhere near as many as I used to have. But you can't go around with the whole world packed on your back. That's why we have public libraries."

He reached out and pulled a large book off the shelf. A piece of paper fluttered out of the pages.

Hopping from her chair, Elinor bent to snatch it up. "Hey, wait. What was that?"

He reached for it as she hid it behind her back. She tried to dodge him. In an instant, she was pinned against him, her face but scant inches from his. She froze in his embrace.

Chapter Seven

Elinor stared up into Drew's face, her whole being suddenly alert with the sensations of being held snugly against his front. Heat flooded through her. Time seemed to hang in the air somewhere outside of them. In the intense awareness of that long, long moment, she saw that brightness spring up in his eyes, those blue sparks.

She wanted to move, to touch him. She wanted to see what changes her touch might work upon him, for his touch was surely working wonders on her.

His hold on her tightened, ever so slightly. She almost jumped with the realization that she might not be the one in charge, that he might decide to test her with touches of his own. The very notion tantalized and terrified her.

Flustered, she pulled the paper from behind her back and handed it to him. He retreated, and she breathed a ragged breath of relief. The heat in her face deep-

ened, though, as she watched him studying her handiwork.

"This is great," he said slowly. "I'm no art critic but
I know this isn't just some kid's scribbling."

"Forgive me. I saw the paper and the crayon there
on the shelf and I—I couldn't resist."

"I'm glad you didn't." He looked at her, his eyes in-
quisitive and admiring. "You're an artist."

She felt a thrill of pride at his words. No one had
ever said such a thing to her. Her skill at drawing was
appreciated only as a gift from God in the abbey, and
she was never allowed to take credit for any work she
did. And she had never dared say the word "artist"
aloud in reference to herself.

Yet Drew Ingraham had said it. He'd said it aloud
and with admiration, while looking at a mere sketch
she'd made while looking out the window of this room.
The light in the trees had intrigued her, and she'd done
her best to capture the scene before the sun went
down. It had satisfied her—she'd given no thought to
what others might think of it.

Delight mingled with the excitement she'd felt in his
embrace. Drew liked her work.

She watched as he strolled around the edges of the
room, the drawing in his hand.

"You're an artist," he murmured. "You're a nun—or
at least almost a nun. You're English. Somebody must
know who you are."

Elinor's joy dimmed. He was only interested in solving the puzzle of who she was and how he might be
rid of her. She should have known.

"Aye. Mayhap tomorrow some key may come to us."
She began to gather up the dishes and the remains of
their meal. "It shan't be long till I am away."

His hand was suddenly on her arm.

"I'm sorry," he said. "I didn't mean to sound like I
couldn't wait to get rid of you. You haven't been that
much trouble."

"Many thanks, my lord," she said coolly, moving away. "I shall return these plates to the kitchens. Have you a bottlery? There is yet a glass or more of this good wine to be drunk. I shall store it there if you will tell me where to find it."

He dropped his hand to his side. "Never mind. I'll take it with me." He tossed her drawing on the chair and took up the bottle. "I have to get back to work."

And with that, he was gone.

Elinor sat down in her chair, her eyes stinging with tears. She'd known she'd been a burden to him, but she hadn't realized how much he resented her. Even before he'd said the words, she'd known the truth: He couldn't wait to be rid of her.

"Nay," she whispered fiercely to herself. She pounded her fist on her thigh. She wouldn't cry. De-Courtenays were survivors. It would take more than a dour knight and a thoughtless word to bring her low or make her surrender to hopelessness.

And she would prove it—to herself, and to Drew Ingraham.

Drew had risen early again, eaten breakfast at a roadside cafe, and made his way across the vineyards and into the city of Santa Rosa. Feelings of guilt and stupidity had ridden with him.

He'd behaved like an idiot last night, a real chump, he thought as he parked the bike and went into Will Curran's office. He wouldn't blame Elinor if she took a swing at him. But what he had to do this morning was too important to delay.

"Well, at least she's consistent," Will said, tilting back in his chair.

"Consistent?"

Drew stopped pacing around the room. Will had read through the wine-and-pizza-stained notes. Now he gazed at his friend over half-glasses, steepling his fingers in what Drew always called his best The Doctor Is In attitude.

"What do you mean by consistent?" Drew asked.

"Look." Wild Will Curran flipped the wrinkled pages with one finger. "Lords, ladies, barons, kings, England in the fourteen-hundreds, Henry V, it all fits. She's got the fifteenth century pretty solidly and accurately placed in her mind. At least to the extent that I know anything about Hank Vee and his ilk."

"Okay, so she's consistent. I knew that already. But does that mean she's nuts?"

Will winced, broadly.

"Okay, okay, does that mean that her *mentis* is *non-compos*?"

"No. Not necessarily." Will grinned. "I know, it would be a lot easier if I'd just say she's a full-tilt loony, let's get her into the county psych ward on the double. Or if I said she's sound as a dollar. But from what you're telling me, and from what I can see in this simple assessment, it sounds as if she's functioning as well as anyone else out there and she's no danger to herself or others."

"All of which means I can't have her committed."

"Which you don't want to do, of course."

"What do you mean, of course?"

"Well, speaking as your old compadre and not as a shrink, I'd say this lady has gotten under your skin in a big way."

Drew scowled. "That doesn't solve my problem."

"No. No, it sure doesn't. In fact, it makes it a hell of lot more complicated, because if you're hung up on this Lady Elinor, then you aren't seeing anything about her very clearly. I wish you'd bring her in."

Drew shook his head. "I don't think she's ready for that."

"So you do believe her?"

Drew made a wry face. "Damn. Yeah. No. Hell, I guess I do. At least a part of me, my gut, tells me she's not a liar. The only alternative seemed to be that she's a crackpot. And I can't prove that either."

"What do your glands say?" Will's grin was cherubic.

"Leave my glands out of this. I'm not one of your patients, so don't start with me. I'm on to your tricks, Doc."

"A bit paranoid, are we?"

Drew made an obscene gesture. "I'll try to find out more from her, Doc. But I doubt she'll give me much to go on. She's totally fixed on this Henry V thing."

"There are worse delusions."

"This is true."

"You say she goes about dressed in medieval-style clothes?"

Drew nodded.

"Well, here's something you might try. Put her into contemporary clothes. Play current music. Show her around town. See if anything in the twentieth century clicks with her."

"Shock therapy?"

"Please, Ingraham, if you're going to play shrink, at least get the terminology straight."

"Never mind the lecture, Professor Peabody. I'll try it."

Will rose and waved hands over Drew's head, blessing him. "Good boy."

Drew gave him a sour look, then offered his hand, a bit shyly. "Thanks. I can pay you—"

"Don't insult me," Will said good-naturedly. "Besides, I have no idea how to write out a diagnosis code for this. Your insurance company would want to come live with you—and maybe me—for a long, long while if I told them you came to me for help in identifying a cross-century-dressing sparrow strangler."

Drew winced inwardly at Will's description. It didn't cover all he knew and felt about Elinor, but it was scarily accurate in its own way.

He shook hands with Will and left the office, headed

for the Santa Rosa Police Department. He introduced himself and, after filling out forms with all the information he'd given them over the phone the night before, he was ushered in to see the sergeant in charge of covering missing persons.

He left the SRPD with no more confidence than he'd had when he went in. It had been tricky to explain that he thought Elinor was lost, or maybe delusional, and then justify why he hadn't brought her in to the department.

Still, the sergeant had said she'd pursue the matter as far as she could—which was only a short way, given that she hadn't had a chance to interview the subject.

He rode home, dogged by unanswerable questions. What he needed, he decided, was what had always served him in the past. He needed action. He decided to act on Will's suggestion and surround Elinor with the ultimate test of the twentieth century.

"Mall?"

"The mall. You must have something like them in England. Shopping centers?"

Elinor stared at the sprawling acres of buildings surrounded by more acres of cars. She shook her head. "Is it a market town?"

"That's it. Yes. I hate the damn things myself, but you've got to have something other than your costume or one of my shirts to wear."

As they entered the glassy gates of Mall, she blinked. The outside was well fortressed and built of smooth, plain stone. Inside, it was a teeming mass of people of every kind, dressed in many different costumes, strolling about looking at goods displayed behind huge glass walls. Music was all around, and noise, and smells, and she felt, for once, somewhat at home. It might be different in its details, but this Mall was unmistakably a market faire, like many she had attended in the past.

Drew led her to several of the shops offering clothing

and shoes for sale. Everywhere she turned, there was a variety from which to choose. More wonderful yet, she wouldn't have to wait for the tailor or the cobbler to make them up for her. She could wear them right out of the shop.

"There are so many," she murmured to Drew as the saleswoman directed them to rack after rack of gowns hanging on narrow bars. "How can anyone choose?"

"Beats me. I just stick with the basics."

She stood back and surveyed him from head to toe. "Your attire is most appealing, but it is not for a woman to wear."

"Women wear these all the time." Drew motioned to the saleswoman. "Can you show us some jeans and T-shirts?"

The woman looked disappointed, but led them to the shelves at the back of the shop where blue jeans of every type and style were lined up with tops of every hue. Elinor went straight to the soft, pre-washed denims and ran her hands over the fabric. She looked at Drew. "These?"

"If you like them."

"They are wondrous fair."

They left the store with Elinor's gown in a shopping bag, along with two more pairs of jeans and three more tops. In her new clothes, she'd fairly skipped into the shoemaker's. Never before had she felt such freedom! No wonder men went about in breeches. When she got home, she vowed she'd introduce them to all the nuns at the abbey.

She looked up at Drew. He turned his head away.

"Is something amiss?" she asked. "Do I look improper?"

"No. Well, maybe." He stopped before a small building decorated with a map in many colors and a long list of words. She watched as he ran his finger over the list, stopped at a certain one, then took her hand and led her away.

They halted before yet another clothing shop.

"Vic-tor-ia's Secret?" She glanced at him. "What sort of secret?"

"Uh . . . yeah. This is where I think I'll leave you in the care of someone else."

Drawing her inside the door, he motioned to one of the shopkeepers.

"She needs a little of everything. New wardrobe. Whatever she likes."

He was gone from the shop before Elinor could ask what secrets she might purchase.

"That's all right, hon," the shopkeeper said. "Some men adore it in here, others would rather just have you model our stuff for them at home. Now, let's get your size and then let's shop!"

Drew paced outside the shop for a few moments, then, feeling like an idiot, turned and crossed the corridor to the music store across the way. He hadn't bought any new music in a long time and had tossed out virtually all his old tapes and CDs because they stirred up too many memories of LeeAnne.

The jazz section brought up better images. A cursory visit to the rock and pop racks, however, made him shake his head in wonder. He'd never imagined he'd be so out of touch with current music. Half the names were unfamiliar to him. It was as if he'd been on a remote island for the past three years.

What the hey. Maybe it was time to take a chance.

Counting Crows looked intriguing, so he picked up the CD and moved along the aisle toward the classical recordings. The thought occurred to him that Elinor, with her penchant for all things medieval, might enjoy hearing some music from her favorite time period. Trailing a hand along the little cards labeled with the names of artists, instruments, genres, he came to one marked "Early Music." He was examining something by a group called Anonymous Four when a man's voice drifted across from the other side of the stacks.

"Indeed, I am sore pressed for time this day, but mayhap, on the morrow I might return and you could show me more of this machine."

Drew frowned. He would have wagered there wasn't another soul in all of Sonoma County who spoke with that weird accent. But it was unmistakable. This had to be one of Elinor's countrymen.

He moved along the aisle and rounded the corner at the opposite end. Feigning deep interest in cassette tapes for learning Mandarin in one's car, he cast a side-long glance at the source of the voice he'd heard.

A tall man, lean and elegant, stood chatting with the salesgirl. His hair was dark, sleeked back into a pony-tail at the nape of his neck, and he was dressed in what Drew recognized as a high-priced, designer suit. Drew edged closer, now studying recordings of the Great Political Speeches of the '30s and '40s. The man's laughter was warm and beguiling, and when Drew cast another look at the pair, he saw the salesgirl nearly melt under the brilliance of the fellow's smile.

A charmer, Drew thought. Very smooth. Not unlike any number of wealthy types he'd known in his old incarnation. But while their accents had spoken of prep schools and board rooms and snowy ski slopes and sunny resorts, this guy sounded like Chaucer in the original.

Just like Elinor.

He pulled out a tape of the "Former Soviet Red Army Marching Band and Chorus On Parade," and turned with the intention of engaging the salesgirl with a question. The man turned his way at the same instant. Drew saw a startling streak of silver that slashed through his dark, sleek hair. His eyes, which rested upon Drew for the briefest moment, hardly seeing him, were as icy as glacier-fed streams.

Drew turned back to the rack of martial music and replaced the tape, taking his time and pretending to be

100

engrossed in comparing recordings of Scottish pipe and drum bands. The man in the costly suit followed the clerk to the counter at the front of the store, paid for his purchases and left. Drew moved swiftly to the counter, a tape of Hawaiian slack guitar music in one hand and the Counting Crows CD in the other.

"Interesting combination," the girl commented as he slid them across the glass countertop. "Will this be paper or plastic?"

"I'm sorry?"

"Paper money or plastic. You know, cash or charge?"

He grinned, knowing how out of it he must appear to this beringed and multi-pierced girl.

"Right. Uh, plastic."

Fortunately, she grinned back as he fished for his wallet.

"It's okay," she said, rings glinting as her fingers flew over the keys on the cash register. "You looked a little distracted."

"Yeah, I guess I was." He passed his card over to her and she inserted it in the credit-check console. "You like the Crows?"

"Yeah," he lied. "You?"

"They're all right. I'm more into the imports, though. There are some really tasty groups coming from the Netherlands these days."

"That guy who just left. Was he from the Netherlands?"

"Mr. Gucci with the platinum card?" She chewed on a fingertip. "I don't think so. Bought some super weird stuff, though. Real old classical stuff. Asked a lot of questions. It was like he didn't even know what a CD was!" She giggled and shook her head. "But I wouldn't mind him comin' around again. I mean, he's pretty old, but some of the rich old guys, they know how to treat a girl, you know what I mean?"

Drew shrugged. She pointed to him with a red-black fingernail. "Now, a guy like you," she began with a beguiling smile, "you're the—oops, there it goes."

She read the clearance code off the credit console and punched in the total of his purchases. The receipt cranked out and she handed it over to him with a pen. "Just sign by the X."

He was scrawling his name when she asked, "You save your carbons? We don't have the new kind of carbonless receipts yet, so I've gotta ask."

"No," he said, pushing the receipt and the pen back to her.

"Then I'll just toss 'em," she said, snapping out his copy and dropping it in the bag with his recordings. He watched as she slipped the carbon into a slot in the counter behind her.

"There you go," she said, handing him the bag. "Come back anytime."

"I'll do that," he said, turning on his warmest smile.

Her smile widened and she waved as he left the store. Outside, in the mall, he strolled back toward Victoria's Secret and made sure Elinor wasn't waiting for him. When he saw she wasn't, he waited a few moments, then returned to the music store.

"Back already?" the salesgirl trilled.

"Yeah." He stuck one hand in his back pocket, feigning shyness. "I—uh—I just remembered. My accountant told me to start saving the carbons. Makes it easier to file."

She pouted. "Oh, I wish I could, but I'm not supposed to mess with the carbons once they've been put in the bin. It's like a rule or a law or something."

He rubbed his hand across the back of his neck. "I know it's not a lot of money, but Marv will just about chew my butt off if I don't bring him back his paper. Last time, when the band was out on tour, I had to go under my bed and all through the bus afterward, just to collect all the stuff so he could file. Man, is this gonna tick him."

"Aww." She softened, looked around the store. "Well,

Don's on break. I guess what he doesn't know won't hurt him." She crooked one of her blood-red fingernails at him and he followed, wondering at the lengths to which he was willing to go to find out the truth about Elinor DeCourtenay.

Elinor soon learned why Drew had been reluctant to come in and help her pick out these items. Such undergarments were not to be believed! Scraps of satin and silk, filmy edgings called lace, tiny braies that stretched and smoothed over her derriere, small bodices called bras designed for the sole purpose of encasing the breasts—all these were called lingerie, the woman of the shop said, and most women had as many or more of these items as they had outer garments.

Elinor, clad only in a bra and panties of pale rose satin, stood and surveyed herself in the full-length mirror. Her first glimpse of herself in this vast expanse of glass, her body almost as naked as a newborn infant's, had caused her to emit a muffled shriek that had brought the saleswoman knocking at the door of the tiny dressing chamber. She'd apologized, yet even after the woman had gone, it had taken her several tries before she could bring herself to face the image in the glass.

In the end, her curiosity had won the day. She stood examining the reflection in awe and wonder.

Mother Agnes would have been shocked, of course, and many lectures on vanity, modesty and chastity, along with a suitable penance, would have followed, had the good abbess witnessed the sight of her wayward abbess-in-training openly staring at her own nearly nude body. But Elinor had never seen such mirrors as these, and she was curious to see who and what she was in the flesh.

She'd known she was a woman and that she was neither homely nor stunningly beauteous. But she hadn't been prepared for the surge of pride she felt as she looked at the way all the lines of her body seemed to satisfy the rules of proportion and how her womanly curves seemed to also show health and sleek strength.

She touched the skin above her breasts. Did other women of this place enjoy looking at themselves? Was it a sin to them?

Drew hadn't wanted to see her. He hadn't come in. Did he not find her body pleasing to the eye? Or was he acting as a gentleman ought with a chaste maid?

She made a face and shook her finger at her image. She was lusting again. She wanted Sir Drew to see her in these garments. She wanted him to look at her as he had the night she'd stood before him in that wet, translucent shirt. She wanted to show him she was indeed a woman and not merely a burdensome child.

Never in her life had she had such feelings, such impulses. Never in her life had she entertained such thoughts about any man. Every moment seemed to bring new revelations.

"How ya doing in there?" the shopkeeper called through the door of the dressing chamber. "Everything okay?"

Elinor jumped, blushing, then recovered her poise. "Yes. I am quite o-kay. I should like to wear these garments."

"Sure thing. Just take off the tags and hand them out to me."

Elinor pulled off all the bits of paper that were stitched to the clothing and pulled her new jeans and top on over them. She spent a few moments savoring the ease with which the device known as a zipper worked up and down, then slipped her shoes back on and went out to meet Drew.

It had taken a bit of finessing, but he'd pulled it off. With the convenient arrival of a customer desperate for a new release of Shaker hymns on CD, Drew had managed to fish out not only his carbon, but the one just below it on the pile, the one from the man with the silver-streaked hair.

Out in the mall once more, he sauntered over to one of the large tubs containing twining ficus trees and stood in its partial cover. He took the carbons out of the music store bag, crumpled his own and studied the other.

Roger Aston, the name read. The signature below was a crabbed scrawl that might denote Roger Aston or Barbara Walters, for all he could tell.

"Aston," he muttered. Aston-Martin was all that came to mind. Well, he thought, at least it was British. So it might be that Elinor was telling the truth when she said she was from England.

But had she come with a companion?

The thought roused a mixture of emotions. Not only was he more curious than ever, he felt called to meet the challenge of solving this mystery. There was something about Aston that had put his senses on alert, something oily and unpleasant, despite the man's obvious taste and charm. Conflicting urges fought within him; a desire to confront Elinor with the identity of this fellow clashed with an equally powerful urge to keep him the hell away from her. Added into the mix was a hot little spark of jealousy at the notion that Aston might be Elinor's lover. Or husband.

He shoved the carbons back in his pocket and headed for a bank of phones tucked under the escalators. It was time to call in an old favor.

As he waited for a teenage boy to finish his leisurely chat with his girlfriend, Drew realized that for the second time in three days, he was about to put in a call to someone from his old life. Back in the old days, when he'd been hustling for his communications consulting firm, he'd been on the phone day and night. Nowadays, his calls were few and virtually all to clients or Harley restoration contacts around the country.

The boy vacated the phone. Drew stepped up, fishing

coins from his jeans pocket. He wondered again at the lengths to which he was going for the sake of a lost lady.

"Sir Drew, Knight Errant," he muttered to himself as he dropped money into the pay phone. "Windmill-tilting a specialty."

The shopwoman followed Elinor out of the store, to where Drew was waiting. He handed over another of his shining cards to the woman. She returned shortly with a full shopping bag and the card.

"She's gonna be gorgeous," she told Drew. "Great taste and a bod to go with it. I could die."

"Bod?" Elinor asked as the woman left.

"Body," Drew said.

"Ah." She recalled her thoughts in the shop and felt warmth creeping into her cheeks. Everything about her seemed to conspire to bring lustful themes to the fore.

"Want some lunch?" he asked.

"Lunch. That's a meal, yes?"

"You got it. Come on. The food's not fancy, but it's fast."

The stalls with all the foods, despite their lights and noises, were much like the stalls she knew at markets all over the countryside at home. There were many, many exotic dishes to choose from, but Drew led her over to a stall decorated with a glowing red dragon.

"How about dim sum? It's not bad here."

Elinor resorted to the universal word of acceptance and approval. "O-kay."

She was delighted to see that dim sum was little pasties or tiny pies filled with meats and vegetables and spices. There were three different sauces to eat with them, and she could almost manage the fork by now.

"How do you do it?" Drew asked as she reached for her tenth little pie. "I've never seen anyone put it away

106

like you who wasn't a professional athlete or a full-time farm laborer."

"I eat too much?"

"No. Obviously not, from the way those jeans fit you. But most women I know are constantly moaning over the size of their thighs and the next diet they're going to go on."

"I don't know of such things. I have a body. I feed it, I clothe it, I keep it warm. I work hard at the abbey. A body needs food to keep the soul within it, does it not?"

"I guess that's true." He was silent for a moment, then asked, "How do you like the mall and your new clothes? Feel more at home?"

"Yes, I suppose. Mall is very like the market fairs near my home, and I do so like the clothes you purchased for me. You must allow me to pay you for them as soon as I am able."

"No, it's no problem. I'm just glad you're back in regular clothes."

She chuckled. "How regular they may be, I know not. But they are most comfortable and ingenious."

Somehow, he seemed disappointed with her answer. She couldn't imagine what he was expecting, unless it was a greater display of gratitude for his largesse. But he waved away her thanks.

They ate in silence. Elinor tried not to ask so many questions and reminded herself not to stare when someone or something exotic passed her, which seemed to be happening every other moment. Maybe Drew would be happier if she fit in with his world.

She studied him for a moment. He'd scarcely touched his food. When he glanced up at her at last, his eyes seemed clouded and dark. She wiped her hands on the paper napkin and folded it carefully beside her plate.

"What is it?"

"What's what?"

"I see questions in your eyes." She folded her hands

in her lap. "You may ask of me what you will."

"Thanks." There was a hint of a smile at his lips, then it vanished. "Did you come here alone?"

"Nay, I did not. I came with you, on Harley." She paused. "Is this another brain functioning question?"

"No, no. I don't mean here," he said, knocking on the tabletop. "I mean here." He waved his hands to include the immediate world. "When I found you on the bridge the other night, were you alone?"

She felt a warning tickle of apprehension at the nape of her neck. "I told you. I thought I was pursued."

"And who was pursuing you?"

She clutched her hands tightly in her lap. "Why do you ask this of me?"

"I'm interested. You drop into my life, you're all confused, you keep saying you're from England but you can't call anybody there—it's pretty mysterious. At the fair the other day you said you thought you'd seen someone you knew, and I don't think it was your dear old Auntie Gertrude. If someone is after you, don't you think it's important for me to know who it might be?"

Her apprehension grew. She didn't know where to look. "Why do you ask this?"

He leaned across the little table and dropped his voice. "Did you come here with someone else, Elinor? A man, maybe?"

She stared at him, still silent. She knew what he was about to say, yet she couldn't speak to stop him.

"A man named Roger Aston?"

Chapter Eight

She'd known it was coming. Still, she felt as if she had been thrust into icy water.

"Who?" she whispered, choking on the single syllable.

"Aston. Roger Aston."

She gazed at Drew, the knight she had trusted, the man about whom she had been entertaining such sensuous and, she saw now, foolish fancies. How had he come into possession of that hated name?

"I don't know what you—"

"Cut it, Elinor." His voice was cold. "I can see it on your face. You know this guy Aston. Did you come with him? Is he—a relative? A friend? Your lover?"

"Nay. He is none of that to me."

She made an effort to steady her voice. She was Elinor DeCourtenay, *the* Lady DeCourtenay, not some foolish household serving girl. And she had done no wrong. She need not tremble at the tone in Drew's voice nor feel shame at his questions. Still, something prompted her to be cautious.

She drew herself up and regarded him with a cooler mien. "I do know a man of that name. Of what matter can it be to you?"

He leaned back in his chair but the intensity in his eyes did not diminish. "Why don't *you* tell me?"

She matched his gaze. "He is a man of my country. A neighbor."

"A neighbor?" He shrugged slightly. "Pretty nice neighborhood."

"It has been home to my family for generations past. From the time of the Conqueror. Indeed, William of Normandy gave the land to my—"

"Yeah, I've heard the pedigree. Is Roger Aston's lineage as long as the DeCourtenays'?"

She shook her head. "He is but a lord by decree alone, and that as recently as his sire's lifetime. His background is most common, truly."

She lifted her drink with chilled hands and took a bracing sip. She waved a hand, hoping to dismiss the subject.

"I must thank you again for all the lovely clothes you have bought for me this day. Such finery is not easily found in my land."

A long pause followed her words. Then: "So, you're not going to tell me."

She sighed and studied him. His face held no evil intent she could see. But his expression was guarded and more than a bit suspicious. There was something else, something she could only glimpse at the back of those clear blue eyes. Was it pain? Jealousy?

She was being a fanciful ninny, she told herself. The fellow had just spent good coin on her, had taken her into his home, had seen that she had had the services of a physician. He'd fed her, clothed her, nursed her. He was a kind man, for all his gruff and solitary ways. He deserved some explanation.

"Roger Aston is Lord Lewes, master of Clarisdoune, which borders my family's land. He and my mother's father had some business together, as had his father before him. There is no love lost between the Astons and the DeCourtenays. We associate with him only . . . as needs must."

"Hmm. So you didn't come here with him?"

She spread her hands. "Did you see aught of another living soul with me upon the bridge the night you found me?"

"No, but—"

"That was truly my first night in your land, Sir Drew. I have since seen no one else of my acquaintance."

"I see. Even at the fair?"

"Where . . . where did you learn of Roger Aston?"

"Ah. So that's how you want to play it," he said, shrugging. "Okay. Then I'll just say you must have muttered the name in your sleep."

"A person may say many things in her sleep, to be sure."

She waited for him to speak again, to object or even to rail against her. His distrust of her was plain.

He said nothing more about it, leaving her at a loss for words, as well.

At last, he rose.

"We'd better get back. I have some work to finish in the shop."

She rose to join him, gathering the shopping bags together. She was grateful for the change of subject.

"A man must needs work. Even a knight. Whilst you labor, I shall prepare a meal. It is the least I can do to repay your many kindnesses to me."

He shot her a stern look. "No sparrows, right?"

"No sparrows." She smiled in spite of herself, but the humor did not penetrate her spirits.

He knew about Roger, she thought as they rode home. How, she knew not, but it was plain he hadn't

111

merely heard her mutter the name in her sleep. And he wanted to know more.

Yet how could she bring herself to tell him?

Roger had reduced her family almost to beggary, had hounded her mother even as she mourned the death of her husband. He'd cast nets around them all, brought them low, and she knew that his black deeds were rumored to extend to more than her family alone.

Tell Drew that she'd made a bargain with Roger—a night in his bed in exchange for lenience on the note they owed him? She'd prefer to walk to Scotland and back, barefoot.

Another thought made her catch her breath. Roger was no respecter of persons when it came to getting what he wanted or when it came to doing harm.

Sir Drew's act of kindness to a strange young woman might have brought him into dire peril.

She trembled as she clung to her rescuer's waist. God in heaven. Her foolish bargain might cost Drew more than just clothing and a few nights out of his own bed.

Roger sat on the balcony of his hotel room and sipped his wine. The spirits available in this place were excellent, the equal, at least, of wines he'd had in Italy and France. As he sipped, he pondered what his next move should be. He had gone traveling through time before, but never in this fashion. In the times before, his amulet had been whole and he had managed to return to his home-time, as he called it, with relative ease.

But the trips were getting harder. He had been ill for days this time. He'd lain in that foul meadow for what seemed an eternity until he had staggered up and managed to mount his horse. He recalled stumbling into some kind of market fair, but he'd been too dazed to notice much. The farmer he'd sold the beast to had been rather goggle-eyed, but when the man asked if he was from someplace called Hollywood, Roger had simply nodded and the man treated him like an amiable maniac from then on.

The horse had brought him good money—cash, he had insisted. The man drove him to his bank, and when they parted, Roger found a nice inn in the town. A notice at the innkeeper's table offered something called American Express. Roger inquired about it, took it with him, filled out the application, and gave it to the innkeeper to post. He retired to his room, ill again with the effects of time-travel and had ventured out only twice since then: once to the market fair to purchase some clothing and then to a pawnbroker's shop, where he got a rather nice sum of money for some of his jewelry.

The American Express card had arrived yesterday morning, and he had returned to the market to buy more items for his personal comfort. He didn't intend to stay long, but he didn't intend to do without, either.

But here was a quandary: He wasn't at all sure he could return to his own time. Or to any other. The little DeCourtenay bitch had taken half of the amulet with her. She had run from him, then, and he had lost her in the mists before he reached the bridge and went hurtling into the void between centuries. Where had she gone? Had she traveled with him? Or had she been left behind when his incantation had been uttered?

He'd seen no sign of her at the bridge. And the nearest farmer, the one who'd bought the horse, hadn't seen anyone meeting her description.

He set down his goblet. The bridge. It had been the same. The same bridge from his time. He'd stake his life upon it.

That had never happened before. In the past, he had arrived in England, his home country. This time, it seemed he was in some strange place called America. They'd heard of England, so the people told him, but this was not the same place.

Yet Oakfield bridge was here. Was the bridge the key to solving his quandary?

He pushed back his chair and bounded into his room. In a matter of moments, the innkeeper was summoning him a cab.

Some things in Drew's land—or time, or whatever this was—had not changed from her own, Elinor noted. Vegetables were still vegetables, though they came from the tall white cupboard where winter was ever-present. Drew's pantry boasted breads of finest ground flour, wines decanted in rich colored glass, and exotic items with their images painted with exquisite accuracy on their containers. Perhaps he wasn't so ill-prepared to face the lean months, after all.

Her duties at the abbey had included only the routine turn at scullery work in the kitchens and helping out with baking days. At home, as a girl, the family had had a multitude of servants, cooks, hunters and others to prepare and serve meals. Still, she reasoned, how difficult could it be to put together a dish of meat or a stew? After all, her mother had seen to it that Elinor had learned to keep kitchen and household accounts, a daily task Elinor had hated, for it seemed every dried pea and chicken bone must be listed and inventoried and tallied in maddening detail. But the lessons had yielded at least a nodding acquaintance with the ingredients of a good meal. She went to work with a will.

Cooking, mixing, wiping up spills and passing back and forth from the kitchen pantry and table to the hearth, where the fire needed such careful tending, soon had her in a more-than-rosy glow and a less-than-rosy temper. She decided she should speak to Drew about modernizing his kitchen, for it was really quite a bother to carry foods from the kitchen to the fire in the next room.

At last, she pronounced the main dish done. Laying aside several pieces of bread to be toasted and laid out

114

as trenchers, she rose, stiff in the legs, and went to the bedroom to change into clean attire. As she washed in the cool white privy basin, she began to regain her spirits. She hummed a little tune as she thought of Sir Drew entering the small dining hall to find a solid feast prepared, as was only fit for a good knight of his caliber.

A dark thought intruded. Drew might be a knight, but were his clockwork steeds and gentle ways any match for Roger's evil power?

She frowned as she went to change into some of her new clothes. Drew knew about Roger. That meant that wherever she was, Roger was here as well. She wasn't utterly mad. Her scant memories were accurate, though scattered. That was some encouragement.

Perhaps there was a way to meet with Roger here, on more neutral ground, and settle their bargain in a way less shameful than the one she'd been driven to before. She might salvage her dignity and honor, as well as her family's fortunes.

She prayed that Roger was as yet unaware of Drew. Time was not on her side, she thought with a rueful laugh. She had to find Roger Aston and treat with him once more—in secret.

Smoke was the first thing Drew smelled as he approached the house. He tossed aside the oily rag he was using to clean his hands and raced indoors.

"Elinor!" he shouted, bounding into the living room where great gray puffs were billowing from the hearth. "Elinor!"

He barreled into the narrow hallway and yanked open the bedroom door. She turned to him with a smile, a hairbrush in her hand.

"God 'ee good e'en, Sir Drew," she said sweetly.

He stood frozen for an instant at the sight of her. She appeared to be clad solely in yards of glossy, honey-gold hair. She stirred, ever so slightly, and he caught a glimpse of lace, a shimmer of satin, and realized she was, at least, wearing undergarments. Undergarments in no way consonant with his idea of a nun's habit.

"Fire," he managed to blurt.

She gasped. "In the house? Oh, saints, we must to the well!"

She vaulted toward him, tresses flying. He caught her by the shoulders. "Wait," he commanded, gathering his scattered wits. "Stay where you are. Keep the door closed until you hear me call. If I tell you to get out of the house, go out through the window, understand?"

She nodded and he spun away, slamming the door on an image that, in any other circumstances, would have rendered such a feat impossible, or at any rate, unthinkable. But the smell of smoke and the heat in the small house reminded him of the danger and he sped back to the living room.

There, on the hearth, lay what appeared to be every pot and pan he owned, along with a multitude of dishes, bowls, spoons, forks and knives, along with, inexplicably, a hammer and tongs. In the fireplace itself, an old stainless steel mixing bowl glowed in the light of the flames. What looked like a cookie sheet covered with charcoal was lying among the embers. The smell, he thought, was a disturbing blend of pork rinds, stale beer and burnt toast. And maybe cheese. "What the—"

"Is the house afire?" Elinor's voice floated up the hall. "Please, Sir Drew, let me aid you! I've dealt with fires before!"

"I believe it," he muttered.

"Pardon?"

"Yeah, come on out," he called. As he said it, he realized she might well emerge clothed just as she had been a moment ago. He felt a quick struggle within himself, between panic and potent desire. The latter won the contest; TKO in the first round.

He heard her padding footsteps behind him. "Oh, heavens preserve me!" she wailed. She dropped to her knees before the hearth and reached for the smoking cookie sheet.

"No!" He grabbed her arm and pulled her back. "Are you nuts?" he demanded. "You almost set fire to the house with this junk, you want to burn yourself, too?"

She looked at him, and to his surprise, her usual cool and composed features crumpled and tears began to fill her eyes.

Unthinking, he pulled her into his arms. "No, don't," he murmured. "It's all right."

"It isn't." She shook her head where it nestled against his chest. "I've been naught but a vexatious burden to you from the moment you first encountered me. 'Twould be better had you left me there upon the bridge."

He felt her long, lithe shape enfolded in his arms and felt the little sob she tried to suppress. He felt his heart contract even as his mind told him to be wary. Elinor, the Lady Elinor, who had stared down ER nurses and commanded doctors to mind their manners, who brought new meaning to the word haughty, was trembling in his arms, a vulnerable, human woman.

Brought low by soup and toast. Or, at least, that's what he could deduce from the culinary evidence before him.

A wave of tenderness washed over him. Even if he wasn't fully convinced, she seemed convinced enough that she was lost and alone in this world—hell, in this time. So far, she'd been managing with admirable aplomb. Now, of all things, cooking dinner had reduced her to tears. Brought low and into his arms, her skin against him like—

For a moment, he froze. *Her skin*. Saints preserve him, as Elinor would say. He was holding a beautiful young woman wearing the most minimal and seductive garments imaginable. And they were alone, in his home, far from anyone or anything but the silence of the redwoods and the gentle mists rolling over the hill from the sea.

He was in real danger.

And he didn't care.

The fire might be fading but he was warming rapidly. His body, held so long in check, had decided that the silken presence of Elinor was just what it wanted most in all the world and that it would brook no denials. He ventured a caress, his hand connecting with the smooth coolness of her shoulder blade.

Just a touch, he told himself. Just a touch and he'd be satisfied. After all, she hadn't fought his embrace. And it didn't seem as if she was in any great hurry to pull away.

A slide of satin, a whispered sigh.

Just a touch, where the soft angle of her back began to bell out, ever so gently, into the sweet, delicate curve of her hip.

Just a touch. Of his lips against her hair.

And perhaps just one touch more, to take a handful of that thick, waving mass of gold, feel it slide through his fingers, as fine as—

"The trenchers!" Elinor pulled away and whirled to where the bread continued to char. " 'Twill be spoilt!"

Drew stood in confusion at the sudden interruption of his idyll. Had he misjudged her signals? He'd felt her softening in his arms, warming. It had seemed she wanted him to touch her, or had at least not been repelled by the idea.

He watched as she wrapped her hand in a towel and pulled the cookie sheet from the flames. The pathetic lumps of blackened bread smoldered on the tiles of the hearth.

"Oh, 'tis ruined, after all," she moaned. She reached for the bowl of smoking liquid. "But the charlette, I

118

believe, has been preserved." She set the bowl on the tiles and looked up at him with a shy, proud smile. "I've never cooked before."

"Ah."

It was all he could think to say, in the face of her guileless cheer, at the sight of the weird milky broth with the strange lumps bobbling about on its surface, in view of Elinor, kneeling at his feet, clad in a lace and satin camisole set—a view that could easily raise the enthusiasm of a corpse.

Elinor rose, carrying the bowl of stew. "Let us sit at table, then, before this chills."

She walked ahead of him, her long hair swinging about her hips. Drew followed, mesmerized. She set the bowl on the table in the kitchen and stood back, admiring her handiwork. A few moments passed before she seemed to realize how she was attired.

"Oh!" she gasped as her hands brushed down her front. "Oh. Sir Drew, you must excuse me!" She scurried from the room, calling out behind her, "I must needs dress for dinner!"

Drew went about like a somnambulist, opening windows and doors to let the smoke escape and the cool, moist evening air blow through the house. He banked the fire and placed the screen in front of it, stepping around the debris of Elinor's initiation into cooking.

He had been too concerned with the fire and then too entranced by her nearness to give much thought to what she had been doing while he was in the shop. His house wasn't exactly an English country manor but it was fitted out with the basics, including a perfectly good gas range and oven. What had possessed her to try to cook over an open fire? Maybe she was one of those people who thought all Californians did was drink margaritas and barbecue mahi-mahi steaks.

But then again, who would try to barbecue a loaf of bread and some soup?

Coral Smith Saxe

He grinned. Lady Elinor DeCourtenay, Baroness. The one and only.

A warning bell sounded in his mind. Careful, Ingraham. Don't go getting all emotional. It never pays.

He turned as Elinor reentered the room. She was dressed in plain blue jeans once more, and a long, tailored white shirt that featured a high, buttoned-up collar. He was relieved. He was disappointed. He was annoyed with himself.

"Is there aught amiss?" she asked.

"No," he answered. "Let's eat."

To say the meal was abysmal was like saying Vladimir Horowitz could really tickle those ivories. The charred toast, which Elinor insisted on scraping and salvaging, was laid on plates, and the charlette, as she called it, was ladled over each chunk. The result was a mixture that looked like nothing so much as Campbell's Cream of Elephant soup, Drew thought. As it was meant, in Elinor's words, to be eaten "in solitary"—images of confinement with bread and water came to Drew—there was nothing else on the menu to turn to when the palette wearied of the main dish. As it soon did, for both of them.

"Is this . . . a traditional dish where you come from?" he asked, toying with his spoon.

"I suppose. I fear it didn't quite turn out the way I hoped."

"You cook a lot?"

"Oh, no. I seldom did more than scullery work at the abbey, and at home we of course have servants for such work."

"Must be nice."

"I suppose. But it is, of course, an easier job at home. You really might gain advantage, Sir Drew, were you to move your stores and pots and ice cupboard into the next chamber. 'Twould make cooking less taxing if a body did not have to bring the food so far to the hearth."

"Isn't the stove working?"

"Stove?"

He pointed into the kitchen area. "The thing with the burners."

She slumped. "Aye, me. Have I gone amiss again?"

He chuckled. "No. Well, yeah. You just forgot about the invention of the cook-stove."

She bounced up from the table and went to examine his range. He dashed after her. God only knew what she might do with a gas burner.

"You heat pots on these rings of flame?" she asked, watching his demonstration.

"Right, remember?"

"I shall now."

He sighed inwardly. Will's notion that Elinor's memory would be triggered by the trappings of the twentieth century was falling apart under test conditions. She seemed as staunch as ever in clinging to her fifteenth-century pose.

"It seems a good invention," she said, crossing her arms and standing back to give the range a once-over. "Still, I don't know. One may control a good wood-burning fire. Your range-stove might take it into its head to break or misbehave, and then where would you be?"

"You're right. But all the same, I'll take my chances."

They returned to the dinner table, where their meal sat congealing. Drew grabbed their plates and began to clear the table before any excuses needed to be made.

"Tomorrow would be a good day to head down into the City," he said, hardly realizing he'd come up with a plan. "We can visit the British consulate and see if they can help you."

"I shall be ready to travel at cock-crow."

He laughed. "Have you heard any roosters around this place?"

She smiled. "No, I have not. No wonder I sleep so

late—no cocks to crow, no bells to ring, no little sisters or brothers bouncing into my chamber—"

He took the glasses she was carrying to the sink. "You have sisters and brothers?"

A long moment hung silently between them. The look on her face told him that she was debating what to tell him.

"I have a younger brother and a younger sister," she said softly. "Thomas and Joanna."

"And they're at home, in England?"

"Aye."

He hesitated himself. This had to be done with care, he sensed. "Tomorrow, when we go to the consulate, maybe you can contact them."

"They are with friends. In the country."

"I'm sure they can find the number. You'll just have to tell them where."

She brought the silverware from the table. "If you say so. Surely I've seen many wonders already."

The note of despair beneath her words pierced him. He took the silverware from her and set it in the sink. The impulse to gather her in his arms and comfort her returned, but the memory of her secretiveness made him resist. He wasn't sure she wanted his comfort.

"If they're out there, we'll find them. Even from overseas there's a lot that they can do. And if they can arrange for you to get back home, so much the better."

"Aye. That is what I need most of all. To go home."

"So . . . you go on and go to bed. I'll clean up."

"Oh, no. It isn't meet for a man of your station—"

"Yes, it's plenty meet. Go ahead."

She gnawed at her lip as he watched her debate between her duty to serve in the kitchen and her duty to obey. Or was it something else that made her think twice about staying with him?

He lifted his chin toward the hall. "Go ahead." To get his eyes off those sweet lips, he turned back to the sink and began to run the water.

"Very well. God 'ee good e'en, Sir Drew."

"Good night," he said over his shoulder. "And . . . thank you for dinner."

There was a pause. Then, "You are most welcome, good sir knight."

The softness of her voice made him grip the dish-cloth in his fist. He held tight until he heard her door close down the hall.

When she'd gone, he scrubbed the charred remains of the meal from the pots and restored his living room while nursing an Alka Seltzer nightcap.

Tomorrow would turn the trick, he told himself. With a little luck and persistence, she could be on her way back to England. He'd be free and alone once again.

The soft opening strains of John Gorka's "Love Is Our Cross to Bear" wafted from the radio, plaintive and melancholy. It caught him off guard, in that way music sometimes could, slipping past his defenses and into his heart, where so many memories and longings slept. He stood frozen in the dark, listening as guitar and voice blended, creating a solid, physical ache in his chest.

At last he moved, reaching to punch the Power button on the stereo tuner and shut off the song.

"What is this," he muttered, "a conspiracy?"

A dreadful din woke Elinor. Short, shrill rings hammered at her ears, rousing her from sleep with a start. Those weren't the abbey's bells, she knew. And they weren't the alarm bells from her childhood at Oakfield.

She located the source of the sound. It was a shining white box on the table next to the bed. The rings went on and on. At last, she lifted its lid.

"Yo, Drew. It's about time."

She dropped the thing on the floor and scrambled back in the bed. The box-lid had spoken!

"Ingraham? What's the deal?" The box spoke again,

123

though it sounded more distant and muffled from the floor. "Look," it went on. "Don't you think you're going too far with this hermit stuff? Hell-ohh! Earth to Drew!"

Elinor leaned closer to the box. "Who are you?" she asked. She was annoyed at the weak sound of her voice. "I insist you make yourself visible to me, spirit," she commanded, her voice gaining strength.

"Whoops!" the voice said. "Wrong number. Sorry, lady."

There was a click, then a great swarm of bees buzzed through the box. Elinor picked up the box-lid with two fingers and gingerly set it onto the table. A moment later, it began a low howling.

"What a dreadful device!" she murmured. She picked up a pillow and plopped it down over the infernal thing. "Whyever should Sir Drew have such a box? It is a nuisance and a traitor to restful sleep."

She swung her legs out of bed, yawning and stretching. She hadn't heard the cock crow, but judging from the light behind the draperies at the window, she guessed it was full morning. She recalled that Drew had said they'd go to a city to find a British counselor or some such. She'd best hurry.

She washed, got dressed and went out into the hall. "Sir Drew?"

There was no answer. She headed for the kitchen. It looked untouched and cold, though clean.

She heard a familiar roaring in the yard and saw Drew bring his machine to a halt near the back door. He came in looking red-faced from the wind.

"I brought you some breakfast," he said without preamble. "It's not much but we can get more in the City when we get there." He handed her a bottle. "Have some of this. I've already eaten."

"Thank you." She was drinking the delicious orange nectar from its quaint container when she recalled how she'd wakened earlier. She set the drink aside. "Sir

Drew, I fear me I've broken your talking box."

He gave her a puzzled frown.

"The one at your bedside? It was shrieking at me and so I lifted its top. It spoke to me in a saucy, impertinent manner and then began to wail when I put it down. I placed a pillow over it to make it quiet and I hope I did not smother it in doing so."

"You smothered a box by my bed? Oh, the phone! The phone rang?"

"Aye, it did. Most cruelly."

"Did the, uh, voice, say who it was?"

"Whoops. He said he was Whoops."

"Whoops?"

"Aye. And he also said your name. Are you truly a hermit, Sir Drew?"

He shrugged. "Well, whoever it was, he'll call back if it's important." He rose and offered her a helmet. "Ready to ride?"

The wench in the music shop was too young and freakish, Roger decided. Too gauche.

The one in the tanner's shop, however, was of a very different stripe. She had made a point to place her card in his hand as he'd left with his purchases.

"Call me," she'd said. "Let's have a drink."

It had been long enough. It was clear that he wasn't going to be able to depart from this place—or time—until he understood what had gone wrong on that damned bridge the other night. If he was stuck here, he wasn't about to do without, in any sense of the word.

He knew how to "call" someone, as they put it. He had an elegant, if small, suite of rooms in a fine inn. He had money and even one of those cards that people used in place of money.

What he lacked was a vehicle. He couldn't escort this or any other woman about the town without an automobile. In this place, everyone rode about in them.

Alas, the innkeeper where he was staying had informed him, while money might go a long way toward securing a vehicle, one needed a license for driving one. One also needed such a license merely to rent a car, as they called them here.

Here, in the darkness of this tavern, however, there were many fine citizens in possession of just such licenses. They carried them about in their purses, even inside their clothing.

In a moment or two, he'd have selected his "helper." Then he could have his car, his women and his fun.

And all the while, he'd be on the watch for a certain lady by the wretched name of DeCourtenay.

Chapter Nine

The City, Drew told her, was also known as San Francisco. Elinor found it noisy, frightening, astonishingly beautiful and exhilarating. Just the first glimpse of it from afar, its turrets and towers piercing the sky, took her breath away and made her long for paints and paper. When they'd crossed the vast orange bridge that guarded it, she'd felt as if they'd flown off into one of her wildest fancies. By the time Drew had guided Harley through its many hilly streets and vast thoroughfares to the building where the British consulate was housed, she was speechless.

Inside the consulate, Drew approached a woman behind a table in the entry hall of the building. Above her hung several bright flags flanking the portrait of a handsome woman in a glittering crown. Some duchess or countess, Elinor surmised.

"May I help you, sir?"

Drew took Elinor's elbow and gently urged her forward. She made a small curtsy.

127

"Well, it's a little hard to explain—"

"Would this be a matter for Immigration Services, sir?"

"No. At least, I don't think so." Drew let go of Elinor's elbow and rested his folded hands on the high tabletop. "Is there someone I can talk to about this lady here? She's a British citizen, I think, but she doesn't seem to know or remember—"

The woman cut him off with a cough. "I see. Perhaps you would like to speak with our community liaison, Miss Sloane? She frequently helps visitors who've become lost or . . . ill?"

"Lost, yes. Ms. DeCourtenay is lost and we need help getting her back home."

"Very good. Let me just ring Miss Sloane and see if she's available."

Drew took Elinor's elbow again and led her a little ways from the table.

"It is 'the Lady DeCourtenay.' You must give her my title or—"

"It's okay. She's sending us to someone who can help. You can tell her all your names when we meet her. Have you remembered anything new? Anything that might help her find you a way back home?"

She shook her head. "That is why you must tell her my full name, Sir Drew." She wanted to tell him that she thought they might never find her home if she was, as she suspected, out of time as well as out of place. But the woman at the table was beckoning them.

"I'm so sorry. Miss Sloane is in a meeting across town. She won't be back until late this afternoon."

"Is there someone else we can speak to?" Drew asked.

The woman shook her head. "The consul proper doesn't generally handle such matters and he's not in today, either. You may come back this afternoon and I will make sure that Miss Sloane is informed of your needs. If I might have your name and some particulars?"

Elinor listened as Drew dictated a brief message. She wondered if any other folk came to this place looking for help. . . .

Her heart cartwheeled in her chest. Roger! She was about to ask if the lady in waiting to the consul had seen him, then halted. After denying Roger to Drew, she couldn't very well bring him up now.

"Do you give aid to many lost travelers?" she asked the woman. "It seems a service most welcome and necessary."

"Yes, ma'am, though we don't as much as other consulates, as our countries do share a common language. I must say I can't quite place your accent, however. I used to pride myself on my ability, rather like Henry Higgins." She sighed and smiled. "I suppose I've been over Stateside too long. Are you Cornish, by any chance?"

Elinor drew herself up stiffly. "I daresay I am not. I am an English lady, born and bred in Staffordshire."

"Forgive me, ma'am. I meant no offense." The receptionist shot a glance at Drew. "Is there anything else I can do for you this morning?"

"No, thanks. We'll check in later."

"Very well. Good day to you, sir. Madam."

Elinor nodded and allowed Drew to lead her back out into the street.

"Cornish! Sir Drew, I believe you have been duped."

"How's that?"

"That woman was no Briton, I vow. I, from Cornwall?" She sniffed. "It is to laugh. No, I believe we shall find no aid in her establishment."

"All the same, I'll take my chances," he drawled. He placed his hands on his hips and stared around them. "Well, we've got some time to kill. What would you say to some breakfast?"

She brightened. "I should say, welcome, Sir Break-

Coral Smith Saxe

the-Fast, and pardon me for keeping thee waiting so long."

"I second that emotion," he said with a chuckle. "And I know just where to go."

A short time later, they were purchasing flaky buns and fragrant coffee from a food shop nearby. Elinor also petitioned for more of the orange nectar, cheese, fruit, thin slices of roasted meats, and mushrooms soaked in a seasoned oil. Drew grinned and paid for them all, save the smoked fish she requested.

"Sorry," he told her. "It's a rule with me. No anchovies on the bike or in my house."

With their picnic packed into Harley's saddlebags, they went flying over hills and along busy roadways. Before long, they arrived at a vast park, with meadows stretching to cliffs overlooking the ocean. Drew steered straight for a castle in the midst of the green.

"Have you leave to be on this lord's land?" Elinor asked as he secured the motorcycle and started off with their foodstuffs.

He grinned and held out a bottle and cups for her to carry. "No problem. This is a public park."

They picnicked on a bench near the castle. Though she tried not to stare, Elinor had never seen so many odd specimens of humanity as those that strolled, rode, hopped, rolled and ran past them: brown people and tan people, jugglers and singers, people in clothes that fit like the skin on a snake, people with hair colors rivaling a stormy sunset.

"Welcome to San Francisco," Drew said with a grin.

She started. "Pardon," she said. "I did not mean to gape like a country mouse in London-town." She leaned closer to him. "Surely there are many minstrels and circus-folk about in this park?"

"Princess, you don't know the half of it."

"I have been sheltered, indeed," she murmured, watching a pair of well-armored youths race past, wheeled shoes propelling them at literally breakneck

130

speeds. "Mother Agnes would have much to say about going about among such folk."

"Is she your Mother Superior?"

"She is." A gusty sigh escaped her. "And while she is a good and a saintly and a most capable lady, she tries my soul to its limits some days."

"Tough, huh?"

"As capable of bending as a brick."

He laughed and refilled her cup with the orange drink. "How long have you been at the convent?"

"I entered when I was twelve."

"Twelve? Wow. I'm surprised your parents let you go so young."

She shrugged. " 'Twas a matter of expedience. In the beginning, my mother and father sent me for my education, along with the hope that I should learn less headstrong ways."

"Something tells me they had to give up on that one."

"You have hit squarely upon it."

"And later? Why did you decide to stay? Or maybe you didn't."

"I did choose to stay." She looked off toward the sea. "It was not long before I came of age to be married. I begged to remain rather than be wed to someone not of my choosing."

"Your parents had someone particular in mind?"

She gave a short laugh. "Three someones, in truth. Two for insurance lest their first choice decided a wife with ideas of her own and a taste for drawing at all times of the day was not to his liking."

"I didn't know they still did arranged marriages in England. What about your sister and brother? Are they married?"

"No. They are not of age."

Pulling her legs up beneath her on the bench, she perched cross-legged and tossed bits of bread to the birds waddling about on the grass. It was good to speak of her home and family, yet she was uncomfortable speaking of marriage to Sir Drew. She wasn't sure how he'd respond to stories of a young woman who refused to marry, even when her parents chose model men as her suitors.

"So you just stayed in the convent so you wouldn't have to get married?"

"And so that I might do the one thing I loved and cared for most—my drawing."

"You're certainly good at it, if that sketch I saw is any indication of your talent."

"I don't know if I possess talent, but the nuns are generally pleased with my work and they have trained me well. It is an orderly life and peaceful."

"But you still weren't happy."

She looked at him, surprised. "No, I was not," she said slowly. "How did you guess?"

"The way the light in your eyes went out when you switched from talking about your art to talking about training and orderliness."

She turned away, self-conscious before his knowledge of a reality she hadn't fully admitted to herself.

"I have not the meekness to be fully content as a sister. Perhaps one day I shall."

"You're going back?"

"It is my home." She managed a smile. "My artwork is there."

"Art! That reminds me. The whole reason we came here. Come on. You ain't seen nothin' yet."

Drew tossed the remains of their picnic into a nearby barrel. Pulling her by the hand, he led the way over the meticulous lawns and paths and right up to the castle door.

He paid some money to an attendant as they entered the building. Taking her hand again, he led her into the center gallery.

Elinor stopped still, her mouth open, unable to keep from gaping like a carp in a pond.

132

"Dear, beloved Sir Drew," she breathed. "You've brought me into heaven."

"Not heaven, princess. The Legion of Honor. It's a museum."

"Museum?" Elinor looked at him, dazed delight illuminating her whole face. "Nay, this is a paradise."

Drew felt her radiance creep in and settle around his heart. He had guessed she'd be interested in visiting an art museum but he hadn't been prepared for her to be completely blown away at the first glimpse of the foyer. She was entranced, enchanted. If they didn't take things slowly, she'd blow a fuse before they even made it to the Renaissance collection. But he felt a rush of pride that he'd thought to bring her here.

"Whatever you say," he replied. "Let's take a look at the map and you can pick out what you want to see first."

She shook her head over the paper he held out. "I can't say. Can there truly be so many rooms as this? And are they all filled with paintings?"

"Not just paintings. There's sculpture, crafts, prints, textiles, historical objects, furniture—"

"Hold, hold. I cannot bear it. Lead me, Sir Drew."

"If you say so. Just remember I'm a mechanic, not an art historian."

He took her on a tour of what he recalled of his favorite works. She trailed beside him in stunned silence, her eyes as huge as a child's, as if she wanted to absorb the works right into her body through her vision.

When they reached the special exhibition of Rembrandt sketches and paintings, she stared for a long moment, then covered her face with her hands.

"Elinor?" Drew reached out a tentative finger, brushing aside a lock of her hair. "Princess, what is it?"

She lowered her hands. Tears edged her eyes. Her lips trembled.

"I can never do it."

"Do what?"

"Be a painter. By our lady, this fellow has undone me."

"Rembrandt?"

"Aye." She gestured toward his *Self-Portrait*. "How can I ever paint again after I've seen that? Such vanity! Such arrogance ever to dream of it."

Tears spilled over and onto her cheeks.

He didn't know what to say. He was no artist. He could appreciate art but he'd never been reduced to tears the way Elinor was at the sight of this old master's work.

Having no words, he followed his instincts, pulling her into his arms and holding her close. She buried her face in his shoulder and trembled there. The silk of her hair flowed beneath his hand as he swayed with her, murmuring inarticulate sounds of comfort until he felt her body relaxing.

And when she raised her face to his, he placed a kiss at the corner of her mouth, tasting salt and honey together.

He was almost undone by the hunger that surged up within him, a hunger not just of desire, but a soul-deep yearning for contact with another. With Elinor.

God, how he wanted her.

Someone coughed nearby. He recalled where they were and eased away from her.

"Come on," he whispered. "Let's go sit."

He led her to a bench and eased her down, turning her away from the painting that had brought her to tears.

"You must find me an ut—utter ninny," she hiccupped, wiping at her cheeks with the backs of her hands.

"No. Lot to take in, eh?"

She gave a little gasping laugh.

"Aye. That's scarcely the half of it." She brushed her

hair back and stared up at the ceiling. "Oh, my Lord, I know I've been proud. But did you have to bring me this low?"

"Hey."

He took her chin in his hand and turned her face to his. "Don't do that to yourself. Do you think you're the only one who's ever felt inadequate in comparison to one of the greats? Rembrandt himself probably whined all over his studio when he looked at stuff that other painters did."

"Think you so?"

"Absolutely."

"Does he live in this city?"

"Who? Rembrandt?"

"Aye. Perhaps I could speak with him, if he would see me."

"Princess, Rembrandt's been dust for hundreds of years. Didn't you see the date on the plaque? It was painted in 1640."

She made a little gulping sound, then straightened. "Ah. No. I missed that."

"You want to go on? Or have you had enough for one day?"

"No, I wish to go on. Is there more?"

"Much more, but I'm trying to be selective. If we tried to see everything, we'd be here all week." He stood. "I tell you what. Let's leave the high arts and go see some plain old furniture."

They made their way to another wing, where model rooms from various periods were set up for viewing.

"And you say no one lives in these rooms?" Elinor stood behind the velvet ropes and peered into the Baroque sitting room.

"They're just for show. If people used all this stuff, it would get worn out and broken and dirty and be lost forever."

A tour group shuffled in, surrounding them. Drew maneuvered himself out of the crush, but when he

135

turned to speak, Elinor had vanished. He spun about in the hallway.

"Oh boy."

Breaking into a trot, he managed to reach her just as she stepped nimbly over a rope and into another room. No guards were in sight, but he knew it was only a matter of time before someone passed by.

"Elinor, you can't go in there," he hissed from outside the rope. "It's not even finished yet—didn't you read the sign?"

"This is an outrage," she exclaimed. She motioned for him to come in. "Thieves and vandals!"

"I'm gonna regret this," he hissed, stepping over the rope. "What are you talking about?"

"These are Lady Carrowe's things! They belong in Alderbrydge House."

"Who's Lady Carrowe? No, wait, don't answer that. Let's just get out of here before *we're* arrested for theft and vandalism."

"I shall not be removed from here until I see justice done. The Carrowes are true friends and I cannot stand idly by and—"

He took her arm.

"Princess. Listen to me. This is a museum. The sign outside this room said that this is an exhibition in progress, with stuff from Germany, England and Belgium, thirteenth through sixteenth centuries. It doesn't say anything about anyone named Carrowe. It does say to stay the hell out or get busted, big time."

"Very well. Conduct me to someone in authority."

"Whatever. Just come with me now."

Elinor deigned to let him help her back over the ropes.

"Hmph. Clever thieves to take a lady's house right out from under her roof."

A security guard rounded the corner. "Is there something I can help with?"

"No, thanks," Drew said, drawing Elinor down the hall. "We were just leaving."

"Why did you not tell him that Lady Carrowe was robbed?" Elinor demanded.

"Because if I did, we'd be escorted off the premises by some guys with great big butterfly nets."

She pulled free and confronted him. "And prithee, what does that mean?"

"It means, princess, that while I'm getting used to all your delusions about the fifteenth century and Henry V, the rest of the world isn't ready to hear it. You'd be locked up if you charged into the curator's office and started claiming that you want their medieval room back."

She scowled. "It is not right."

"Yeah, well, life's not fair." He looked at his watch. "We still have a couple of hours left before we have to get back to the consulate. Let's go get some fresh air."

The wind off the water was refreshing, Elinor admitted.

They were standing at the end of a long pier that jutted out into the great inlet Drew called San Francisco Bay. Elinor spooned another bite of the thick, creamy stew from her paper cup, appreciating both its flavor and warmth as the breezes slapped at her cheeks and hands. After the hushed and rarefied atmosphere of the museum, she enjoyed the racket and bustle of the harbor, with its great clanking machines and shrieking gulls. The shock of seeing Ariane Carrowe's furnishings in this time and place was beginning to fade.

Drew was still giving her sidelong glances. She knew she needed to tell him her suspicions about where and when she was from, but it was difficult to form the words, especially when he was regarding her as if she were about to begin cackling like a hen.

137

And then there had been his kiss.

She pushed that memory aside, hard. She couldn't afford to be drifting off into lust. This was too important.

"Is your chowder okay?"

She started, then gave him a smile and lifted her cup. "Delicious."

"Best there is." He shifted so that he was facing her, one elbow resting on the rail. "So? How do you like the City?"

"Need you ask?" She spread her arms wide, the breeze whipping at her hair and clothing. "I do think it the most astonishing place I've ever been. Oceans and mountains and palaces and paintings and noise and clam chowder—wondrous!"

He caught her about the waist and pulled her to him. Whirling her about, he began to dance her down the pier.

She laughed in delight and shrieked for fear they would collide with passersby and end up in a tumble of arms, legs and hot chowder. He laughed with her, gazing down into her face with an expression she'd not seen there before: sheer delight.

He halted and pulled her closer. She put a hand on his shoulder to steady herself. Her head was whirling.

"Elinor," he said softly.

"What, my lord?"

"Just this."

His lips descended to hers. She closed her eyes and surrendered to their magic.

It might well be folly. It was most likely sin. She no longer cared.

Even if she had cared, could care, she was helpless to prevent it. At this moment, she wanted his kiss more than life itself.

She raised a hand and slipped it beneath the hair at the nape of his neck. With a sharp, in-drawn breath, he pulled her still more tightly against him, deepening the kiss.

And she'd thought the Legion of Honor museum was paradise.

Chapter Ten

All too soon, he was lifting her arm away from his shoulder and easing her back, out of his embrace. She looked at him in dazed wonder.

"I think . . . I think we'd better take it easy," he said.

Nothing in her memory had ever been as easy as kissing Drew. Still, she nodded and stood back, straightening her jacket. He turned and leaned on the railing.

"So, who is Lady Carrowe?" he asked, spooning up more of his chowder. "The one you said owned the stuff in the museum."

"She is . . . a friend. She and her husband have been most kind to my family. I should not like to think I had a chance to do her a kindness and failed."

"You didn't fail. You obeyed the law."

"I?"

"And you kept me and you both out of the nut-hatch."

"Nut-hatch?"

"Lunatic asylum."

"Truly? Is it deemed madness in your land to thwart thieves, even such bold ones as put their ill-gained goods on display?"

He tossed his empty cup into a nearby barrel, then met her eyes squarely. "Elinor. You've got to stop this fifteenth-century business. It's starting to give me the willies. And it's going to get you into trouble."

So they were back to their old problem. Yet the time they'd shared—and the kisses—had they not wrought a change between them? Could she trust him with the idea she'd been pondering over the past days?

She scraped out the last of her stew and tossed the paper cup after his. The wind caught hers and it overshot its mark. He ran after it and put it into the barrel. By the time he'd returned to her side, she'd composed some of what she wanted to say.

"I thank you for your concern and for your patience, Sir Drew. I know that I am a bother and that my ways are foreign to you."

"That isn't what I said—"

"Pray, let me continue." She put her hand on his arm. "This is a difficult matter."

"All right. Shoot."

She ignored his command, having no weapon to fire. "You ofttimes have brought it to my attention that I do not comprehend time as you do. You say that this is a year far in the future of my time. Rembrandt, the divine artist—you say he lived some while after I should be in my grave. Yet here I am, alive and seeing his paintings. You tell me that when I speak of my time I may get into trouble. Sir Drew, I believe I am in trouble already."

"Go on."

"I believe that I have traveled through time."

She watched his face. His expression didn't change. "Sir Drew? Did you hear my words?"

"Go on."

"Very well. Though I cannot say much more, for I know so little. All I know is what I sense and what sense I can make of the world about me. There can only be one explanation. By some means, magical and unseen, I have been transported from my own world of the year 1420 into your world of the 1990s."

"And from England to America?"

"As you say."

He jammed his hands into the front slots of his jacket and strolled away. Trailing a step behind, she wondered if she had been too hasty in telling him her ideas. They were fantastical, after all. But surely he could be made to see—if he kept an open mind . . .

He halted at the end of the pier. She waited, unwilling to see his face.

"Princess, that is just about the biggest crock anyone's ever dished out to me."

Her heart sank. She had her answer. Not all his words made sense, but she apprehended his tone all too well. The time they'd spent, the kisses—they hadn't been enough, after all.

She turned and began walking back up the pier.

"Elinor!"

She kept walking, though the boards beneath her feet reverberated with the impact of his running steps behind her.

"Elinor. Wait."

She stopped and turned. "I don't wish to continue giving you the Williams."

"It's willies, not Williams."

She headed off again.

"Wait, wait." He caught her elbow. "I shouldn't have corrected you. I'm sorry, Elinor. Really."

"Don't be. It merely adds to what I have been trying to tell you. You must forever correct me because I do not know your ways or your words. I am not of your time."

"I know that's what you said. But, believe me when

I tell you that's impossible. Time travel isn't possible. And even if you did come forward in time, how did you manage to get to the United States? You must have traveled through space, too, and yet you don't have any memory of how you got to California, do you?"

"No. However—"

"Princess. Elinor. It simply isn't possible. There has to be some other explanation." He let go of her elbow and looked off into the distance. "Isn't there something else that happened to you?" he asked softly. He met her eyes. "Isn't there something else you want to tell me?"

"You are implying, sir, that I am a liar."

"Elinor, you've got to admit—"

"I admit nothing save that you are no true knight nor a gentleman, sirrah. I shall make my own way."

Anger bubbled up within her, anger mingled with pain. She stalked away from him before hurt took the fore and caused humiliating tears to fall.

"You don't have anywhere to go," he said, dogging her. "And you don't have any money."

"I shall go back to the consulate. They at least may believe a fellow Briton and render aid without impugning my honesty."

"Okay. Then let me drive you there. After that, I'll leave you alone if you want."

She halted, considering. It was true that she had no idea how to get to the consulate. The city was vast, she knew that, too, and it would be easy to get hopelessly lost among its steep hills and narrow dales.

"Oh-Kay."

"What do you mean, she isn't coming back?"

"I'm sorry, Mr. Ingraham. Her meeting ran quite late and she had to catch a plane to New York. She went straight to the airport with Consul Sherwood."

Drew ran his hand over the back of his neck. "Isn't

there anyone available who can help her contact someone in England?"

"I can certainly do that, sir, if the lady will tell me
the party she wishes to reach."

He looked at Elinor, who held herself stiffly away
from him, more regal than the woman in the portrait
overhead. She stepped closer to the counter.

"If you please, I should like to contact the Abbess of
Wednesbury."

"One moment."

Drew watched as Elinor stood, hands folded before
her, waiting with the patience of a pilgrim. Smooth,
Ingraham. Very smooth. Tell her she's full of it. That's
the way to handle a loon like her.

He grimaced. There were no loons like her. Artist
nuns with delusions of fifteenth-century origins. Beautiful waifs who looked like the sweetest sin a man could
conjure up. Exquisite liars with secret lovers in Armani
suits.

Whoa, pal, he told himself. You're crossing into Will
Curran's territory, and it's not Elinor necessarily who's
the patient.

"Sir? Miss?"

He joined Elinor at the counter. The consul's secretary had a puzzled look on her face.

"I beg your pardon, miss, but the Abbey at Wednesbury is undergoing restoration at this time. The only
line in is via the National Trust, and they say there's
no . . . abbess there these days."

"What about your friend?" Drew turned to Elinor.
"Lady Ariane Carrowe, didn't you say?"

"You might send a message, aye. Lady Ariane or
Lord Tristan Carrowe, Alderbrydge House, in Shrop-
shire."

"Very good."

This took longer. When the secretary returned, she
was shaking her head. "I am sorry, but this one is
rather a dead end, as well. This also led me to the Na-

tional Trust. Most of Alderbrydge House was destroyed in the war. No one lives there now."

"In the war?" Elinor covered her mouth with her hand. "Mercy, I had no idea."

"No idea?" The woman shrugged. "I suppose it does seem a long time ago to you younger ones." She raised her brows. "Is there anything more I can do for you?"

Drew looked at Elinor. She shrugged, forlorn.

"No, thanks," he said. "When will Miss Sloane be back?"

"Monday, sir."

They left the building and stood by the bike. "Now what?" he asked.

"I . . ." Elinor sagged. "In truth, Sir Drew, I know not."

"I know I'm gonna regret this, but let's go home."

"To your home?"

"Yes."

"But you said—I told you—"

"We both said a lot of things. Let's go back to my place, get some rest and tackle this thing again tomorrow with fresh heads."

She put her hand on his shoulder. "Thank you, Sir Drew. You are indeed a courteous knight."

"Yep. That's me."

They rode straight home with the chill wind of the bay changing to the warmth of the tawny hillsides near Santa Rosa. The shadows of the trees were long as they drove the River Road and wound up the long drive to Drew's home.

It seemed to Elinor that days had passed since they'd left home that morning. Time was indeed problematic, she thought ruefully as she climbed the steps to the back door.

"I'm going to put the bike in the garage," Drew called. "I'll be in soon."

All she wanted was a change of clothing and a bite of supper, she thought as she retreated to the bedchamber. Her eyelids were already drooping.

She bent to unlace her shoes. Something behind the night table caught her eye. She tugged the table out from the wall and lifted the object.

It was a small rectangle of paper with a glossy finish on one side, as if it had been glazed. The back was plain white, and dull, except for the words "LeeAnne at Half Moon Bay" scrawled across the top, followed by a broad, curling script that she deciphered with some effort:

For Drew—Body and Soul—LeeAnne.

Elinor turned the paper to the glossy side and saw the likeness of a woman, so perfectly rendered it almost seemed she was alive. Painters and artists in Drew's world must be creatures of near-angelic skill, she thought. Even the great Rembrandt could not have captured an image with such accuracy.

She pondered the face. It was exquisite: small and fine-featured, with laughing brown eyes and a cloud of brown hair. LeeAnne. Who was she? Relative? Friend? Lover?

She felt a sudden pang. She hadn't imagined Drew with any other woman. He was so solitary, indeed, a veritable hermit. She should have known. Drew wasn't a boy. Of course he must have had lovers. Here was yet more proof of her inadequate understanding of this world.

The idea of Drew with a lover did not please her. Especially when the woman in question was so beautiful and had written such passionate words to him.

Body and soul. She could imagine some of what it would be like to share such a complete, intimate bond, particularly with Drew. His kisses alone had nearly undone her. With his powerful, lean body and his gentle talented hands, he would be sheer delight to explore and touch. And though she ofttimes puzzled over the

146

content of his thoughts and the meaning of his words, she saw in the light of his clear blue eyes a sound soul, one that she'd like to reach.

She sighed and tucked the picture back behind the table. No matter how sweet and fair her fancies, she could never belong here. Not in this land or time. Not to Sir Drew Ingraham. He had his life and his world, and she had hers. That had been made all too clear to her today.

She pulled her shirt off over her head and felt a tug around her throat. The medallion and its heavy chain twisted in the fabric for a moment, then fell free. She lifted it and felt its weight.

Another puzzle.

It was time to begin her search in earnest, on her own. Drew had tried all he could, but he didn't believe her. She must find her way out of this world, back into hers, without the aid of her gallant, solitary knight.

"Yo, buddy, what's the deal? Your phone has been truly screwed up. You used to be a consultant on business communications, remember? Did you forget about that old-fashioned thingie, the telephone?"

"Rich." Drew tucked the phone under his chin as he wiped his hands clean. "Sorry about that. I've been out of town. What have you got for me?"

"Wait a minute, wait a minute, where the hell have you been? People down here in San Jose have been saying you went to Nepal, others say you went on the road with Aerosmith. Nobody's talked to you or seen you since . . . since . . ."

"I know, Rich. Since the funeral."

"You okay?"

"Yeah. I'm fine. Just needed to get away."

"Yeah, well, it's good to know you're still in the land of the living. So, who is this guy Aston?"

"That's why I left a message for you the other day. Did you find anything on his credit file?"

"It's pretty interesting. You might want to come down and look this over."

"I've got to have something now."

"Okay."

There was a pause and the sound of shuffling papers. Rich would be in front of his computer, of course, fiddling with some program or other, while he tilted back in his ancient desk chair, speaker phone freeing his hands to use the keyboard while he talked. To say Rich Woessner was a hacker extraordinaire was an understatement. To say his methods bordered on the criminal was to put not too fine a point on it. He was the one person from the old consulting firm who Drew felt was an actual friend. He again felt a pang of guilt for neglecting his old relationships. He marveled that his friends would even speak to him.

"Here we go," Rich said over the ever-present bleeps and clicks of his system. "For one thing, the guy's from Cleveland."

"Cleveland?"

"Yeah. For another, he's an insurance adjuster. Fifty-five years old."

"Anything say the card's hot?"

"Not that we can find so far. But here's the deal. It's a new application."

"How new?"

"Less than a week."

"What about other credit?"

"That's the weird thing. He doesn't have any other credit cards. Never has had, not that anybody can figure. He got this one on one of those deals with the bank. You know, you get a card if you can show a big enough balance? Well, his was a whopper, so I guess they were falling all over themselves trying to keep him happy. Rushed the whole thing through."

Drew blew out a harsh breath. He tossed the rag onto the workbench.

"You there, man?" Rich asked.

"Yeah, I'm here."

"So what gives? You're not back into consulting or I would've caught word on the 'Net. What's a reformed hell-raiser turned entrepreneur turned monk doing with a middle-aged insurance guy from Ohio? A rich one, at that?"

"That's what I've got to find out. Name of the bank?"

"First Maritime. Small potatoes but with big ambition."

"Santa Rosa branch, right?"

"You got it. Want to know where they sent the card?"

"Wait, let me grab a pencil."

"You won't need one. What's the best hotel in your area? Or at least the snootiest one?"

"Mm, the Forest Springs Inn, if we're talking Santa Rosa."

"That's the joint."

"Not too surprising, the way this guy lives."

"Watch your back, man. Insurance men are like secret Ninjas."

"Yeah, in your world, maybe." He paused. "Sorry I've been out of touch. I owe you, pal."

"Naw, you don't. I still owe you for what you did for my sister and her old man. Let me know what you find."

"I'll do that."

"And don't be such a stranger. You got my e-mail address, right?"

"I don't have a computer, Rich."

"Are you sure you didn't go to Nepal? It's like you're livin' in another century, Ingraham. I'll bet you don't even have a microwave."

"Yep. I just snag me a squirrel, clean it, toss it into the smokehouse out behind the cowbarn."

"Whoa."

"I was kidding."

"Oh. Okay, whatever. Catch you later."

"Thanks again."

149

Drew hung up the phone and pondered this latest information. *An insurance man from Cleveland, my ass.* Since when did insurance get so lucrative that mere employees could afford imported suits? And when did Midwesterners sound like they just stepped off the set of Masterpiece Theater?

He knew it was no coincidence that this Aston and Elinor had shown up in the same place at the same time. But their connection still eluded him.

He went into the house. Elinor was nowhere to be found. He'd urged her to take a walk while he finished some work in the garage, so that must be where she'd gone.

He scrawled a note to her, left it on the kitchen table and went to change. A short time later, he was on his bike, heading for Santa Rosa and the very exclusive Forest Springs Inn.

"Now, where might I locate a wizard?"

Elinor stood on a corner of the high street in the nearby village of Riverton. She'd decided she must do one of two things: find Roger himself or learn the magical means to transport herself back to her own world.

To her surprise, there were one or two shops in High Street which seemed to offer just the services she required. At any rate, there were talismans and cards of foretelling in the window-cases, signs of suns and moons and stars over the doors, and the scents of burning herbs wafting out onto the stone path that ran in front of the shops.

She stood before one shop that seemed especially promising, but she hesitated, suffering pangs of guilt. Consorting openly with witches and magis was tantamount to consorting with the Devil himself. Mother Agnes would have fainted away at the very notion, but Elinor had no choice. Magic was what she required.

"Is there something I can show you?"

She looked up to see a young woman with long red

fingernails standing in the doorway to the shop. Elinor gathered her courage and entered.

The place smelled pleasantly like a chapel, with incense heavy on the air and candles lit all round. Elinor relaxed and began to explore.

There were many books, but they only added to her confusion. She had not guessed that magic was so openly practiced and embraced in Drew's world. There were books on how to cast spells and foretell the future, illustrated tomes showing people twisting their bodies like knotted ropes in the name of health and vigor. Some books claimed to be about Heaven, and others about Earth. Others told about gods and goddesses, as pagan as any heathen clan. There were many books with titles featuring the words energy, healing, visions, spirit, nature, angels, herbs and mysteries. None of them mentioned time-travel or magic trips across the ages.

Elinor tried another store. An eager young man in ragged clothing followed her about the shop, chattering about cabalistic gatherings and aromas and leering at her in a cheerful state of lechery. Everything he showed her seemed to be a tool for invoking lust, fertility or sexual attraction. She stared at him blankly, as if she'd never heard such terms before, then, smiling demurely, trod heavily on his foot as she passed out the door.

The last shop yielded no better results. However, the friendly shopkeeper, who cradled a kitten on her shoulder, did impart some news that chilled Elinor like an icicle dripping over her spine.

"Time travel, huh? You know, that is *soo* strange. Somebody else was in here just yesterday asking about that, and, like, nobody has asked about that stuff in a long, long time. And all of a sudden, two of you in the same week. It was totally amazing because he kind of talked like you, too. Are you from England or something?"

Elinor could barely speak. "Yes," she murmured. "England. Was this, this person, was he—"

"Yeah, real good-looking for an old guy. You know, like maybe John Travolta's age. He didn't look like Travolta, but you know, his age."

"I see," Elinor said blankly. "What did he look like?"

"Tall, nice bod, what I could see of it under his suit. One of those 'do's with the ponytail down the back—you know, kind of out of style but still okay for older guys. And he had a streak in his hair, a really cool one. Didn't look bleached at all. Hey, are you okay?"

Elinor felt the color leaving her cheeks, and the icy feeling sinking toward her toes. She gripped the edge of the counter with both hands.

"Whoa, you better sit down," the woman exclaimed. She hurried out from behind the counter and guided Elinor to a chair near the books. "Have you been fasting or something? You look like major hypoglycemia. Let me get you some tea with a little honey. Sit there. Be right back."

The woman scurried through a beaded curtain into a back room where Elinor could hear her clinking dishes and metalware. She crossed her arms about herself, trying to get warm. She'd known Roger was here, in this world, if not in this town. And it was no surprise that he'd be looking into magical shops. What chilled her was the knowledge that he was seeking information about traveling through time.

She'd been right. There had been a small part of her that hadn't wished to believe it, that had hoped her confusions were nothing so exotic. Now it was confirmed, and the truth was shattering.

"Here," the woman said, carrying in a steaming mug. "It's just blessed thistle tea with sage honey but it should give a boost to the ol' blood sugar and get your circulation going again. You went whiter than skim milk."

Elinor sniffed the tea and then took a cautious sip. It was mild and sweet and had a familiar flavor. She

knew thistle teas were wholesome, in general, so she
relaxed and allowed the soothing drink to warm her
suddenly chilled hands and heart.

"Better?" the woman asked.

She was seated on the floor, cross-legged. The kitten
hopped into her lap and settled down. Elinor nodded
and tried a shaky smile.

"Old boyfriend?"

Elinor almost choked on her swallow of tea. "Pardon?"

"Well, like I said, you both have the same accent,
you're both looking for the same stuff, and you just
about keeled over when I described that guy to you.
Oh, no. I haven't—he isn't—you're not, like, on the run
from him, are you? Like domestic violence?"

Elinor summoned her composure. She was utterly
unaccustomed to sharing her personal problems with
anyone, let alone a shopgirl. It was not only unnerving,
it was unseemly. She managed to shape her smile into
something more dignified.

"Oh, la. Nothing of the sort, I assure you. You
guessed aright at first. It has been a fast day for me and
I am not so hearty as I supposed. Thank you for your
kindness." Elinor set the cup on a nearby shelf. "Many
thanks. I must be away." She rose, grateful for the return of her strength.

"You sure? I think maybe you ought to stay. I can
burn a little sage, put on some music. Get your head
clear before you take on the world again. Or that guy."

"He is naught to me," Elinor said, feeling the lie almost scorch her tongue on its way past her lips. "All I
required was a bit of sustenance. Thank you again."

"Okay." The woman set the kitten aside and rose to
follow. "Want me to let you know if he comes back?"

What Elinor wanted was to scream. The woman was
most doggedly persistent!

"Here's my number. Just call and I'll let you know."

"Very well. You're too kind," she said, taking the card

the woman practically thrust into her hand.

"My name's Reya. You take care, 'kay?" She was pursuing Elinor out of the shop. "And get some carbohydrates—pronto!"

Elinor scuttled down the street, stuffing the card into the knapsack she'd borrowed from Drew. Great lack, had the woman nothing better to do?

She glanced back over her shoulder and saw that the woman was still watching her. In her flustered state, she entered the next shop she came to. Once inside the door, she peeked through the glass to see if Reya would actually follow her.

"May I help you?"

She jumped at the sound of a man's voice behind her. She beheld a thin, wizened man wearing a pristine white surcoat decorated with a narrow scarf of striped silk running down the front. A few wisps of white hair crossed his bald pate and he sported a neat white beard.

He was standing behind a long, beautifully lit glass counter. Inside the glass case and on the top of the counter, all around, were ornaments of gold, silver and precious stones. They lay on yards of rich black velvet, each piece a glittering sun, star or flower of delicate craftsmanship.

"May I help you, miss?"

"Carbo-hydrates?"

Chapter Eleven

The phone in Roger Aston's suite at the Forest Springs Inn went unanswered. Fortunately, Drew had a contingency plan. Using a gift-wrapped bottle of Glenfiddich and a note from, ostensibly, a lady who'd glimpsed Aston in the lobby last night, he'd lured the Englishman into the hotel bar, where he now sat, awaiting the "lady's" arrival.

Drew waited and watched as Aston had one drink and ordered another. He was about to go over and strike up a conversation when a stylish woman beckoned the Englishman to her table.

He had to hand it to the guy, Aston seemed to be a magnet for females. Aston joined her, and the pair were soon chatting and smiling like old chums. Old chums with something more than friendship on their minds, of course.

It wasn't too long, either, before Aston and his pretty companion left the bar together. On his way past, Aston ordered the bartender to send champagne to his suite at once.

"Sure thing, buddy," the bartender muttered as Aston departed. "As soon as hell freezes over."

Drew chuckled. "One of those, eh?"

The bartender flushed. "Sorry. I shouldn't have said that."

"It's okay by me. I used to captain the bar at the Claremont while I was in college. Some of the guys who'd come in there acted like they were God and Elvis rolled into one."

"Tell me about it. You'd think with all that money they could afford a personality transplant." He grinned. "What can I get you, sir?"

"Another lemon-lime. Too early in the day for anything with hair on it."

"Coming up."

"So, who is that dude?" Drew asked. "He looks kind of like that Brit—you know, the guy in *Silence of the Lambs*. Except for the hair, of course."

The other man shrugged as he set a fresh drink before Drew.

"I don't know who he is. Never saw him before Saturday night. All I know is he's got a lot of spending cash—which he uses for everything except tips—and he thinks the whole world should bend over and kiss his . . . foot."

He took up a clean cloth and began polishing shot glasses. "The lady who serves bar in here on nights says he's a big hit with the women—well, you saw him just now. Must have one hell of a line."

"There's no justice," said Drew. "I always figure there's just that scent of money coming off these guys. Gets 'em every time."

"Yeah, and I guess it doesn't hurt to drive a Jag luxury model and wear a chunk of gold the size of Rhode Island around your neck."

"Like I said, there's no justice." Drew drained off his

soda and laid down money for payment and a tip. "Well, take it easy, man. Don't let the bastards get you down."

"Back at you."

A stroll through the parking lot revealed only one Jaguar—a luxury edition in silver with a discreet sticker on the back license plate frame: "Lion Imports: Sales, Leasing, Rental."

"Bingo."

Returning to the hotel lobby, Drew phoned the Department of Motor Vehicles. All that netted him was the information that the car was rented, not leased or sold. The license plate number only led back to Lion Imports.

He decided that going on the offensive was the best bet for his next call. Lion Imports was only too happy to tell the irate homeowner who'd found their silver Jaguar in his personal parking space for the third day in a row that the matter was not in their hands.

"You'll have to take up the matter with Mr. Hardesty, the gentleman who rented the automobile," the customer relations manager told him. "I'm not permitted to give out his address but I can give you his phone number."

Drew jotted it down, thanked the man, and pressed the cut-off lever on the phone. A second later, he released it and punched in the number he'd been given.

"Tropical Pets, this is Dave Hardesty speaking."

Drew's mind zipped over the possibilities. Tropical Pets? What was going on?

"Hello?"

"Yes, sorry about that, I was just running some numbers through my computer. Mr. Hardesty, this is Ronald Wentworth at the Santa Rosa Police Department, office of Traffic Safety."

"Yes? Is there a problem?"

"Mr. Hardesty, there's been a complaint that your car's been abandoned in a parking space in downtown

Santa Rosa and we are notifying you that it's being towed as of one P.M. this afternoon."

"My car? Is this a joke? My car's parked right outside of my store. I can see it out the window right now."

"Do you drive a silver-gray Jaguar, license plate number AJ572K?"

"No, I sure don't. You people have made a big mistake."

"Mr. Hardesty, we are a government agency. Our records show that that car was rented to you by Lion Imports, using your California State driver's license. Are you saying that you know nothing of this vehicle?"

"Yes. Whoa, wait a second! Let me check something."

Drew heard the phone clunk, then some rattling of papers.

"Sir, I'd like to report that my driver's license is lost. It's not in my wallet, where I always keep it. I haven't looked at it for days. It could have been stolen."

"All right, Mr. Hardesty. You need to report the loss to the DMV immediately. We will be forced to impound the car in the meantime."

"Fine with me," said the hapless Hardesty. "I had nothing to do with it."

"Very well. Have a good day."

Drew hung up. It was likely that he'd just violated a dozen different laws and statutes, but somehow he felt it balanced out in light of what he was beginning to learn about Roger Aston.

"This is one tricky bastard," he said under his breath.

Elinor knew more than she was telling; he'd already decided that.

But did she know less than she should?

The shopowner chuckled, a pleasant, slightly wheezy sound. "That I can't help you with, miss," he said. "You need a café, maybe?"

"A café. Oh, yes. I crave your pardon, sir." Elinor began to back out of the shop.

"Better you should crave a bagel," he said. "But before you go, miss, could I see that piece you're wearing?"

She looked at where his gnarled finger was pointing. She lifted the gold necklace. "This?"

"*Ja.* May I see it closer?"

"I suppose." She moved closer, keeping the counter between them. He seemed like a kindly soul, but who knew in this strange world?

He took the ornament in his hardened palm and hefted it gently. Then, tilting his head, birdlike, he studied the sun-face hanging about her neck.

"This is very old," he murmured. "Very old indeed. From your grandmama, *ja*?"

"Aye, sir," she said. "At least, I believe it so. I am not certain."

"Such a nice way you talk," he said, giving her a grin. "Most kids today, *feh*! But you're from England, *ja*? A different language they speak there." He chuckled, then went back to examining her medallion.

"This necklace," he said, handing it back to her so it wouldn't thump against her chest. "Where iss the other piece?"

"I know of no other. Why do you ask?"

"I have seen only one other like this in all my days. In Austria, many, many years ago, I saw such a one. It was a rose, one piece the bud, but when you added the other behind it, it became a full-blown flower. Most pretty. Most unusual. And very old."

"I've not seen other pieces. Just this one."

"Here, I show you."

He held out his hand and she placed the heavy medallion in his palm once more. He turned it over and with his little finger pointed to a spot in the gold.

"See this notch here? And this one? They're meant to hold something else behind this section. Another

159

piece that completes the picture. Makes something more of the piece than this."

Elinor squinted and could just barely make out the notches he indicated. "I believe you are correct, sir," she said, wonderingly. "I've never taken the time to observe it in such detail. You have the eyes of the master craftsman."

The man shrugged eloquently. "Eyes, yes, those I've got. And time, too. But you, *meydele*, you don't have so much time, eh?"

She couldn't help herself. There was just something about those soft old gray-green eyes that spoke of wisdom and compassion.

"Nay, sir. I don't believe I have. In truth, I know not what time means, of late."

"You're young! You're immortal!" he said, smiling. Then his smile softened. "But not so young as a fellow might think, eh? You got what *my* grandmama would call 'an old soul.'"

Elinor felt that the man was too close to the truth. She sensed she could trust him, as she trusted Drew. But Drew thought she was mad or perhaps ill or even a liar. She had no reason to believe that this man would react to her story any differently than Drew.

"Mayhap," she said, smiling back. "But I must be going. Thank you."

"It was nothing. Come in again and chat. As you can see"—he gestured around the empty shop—"people aren't exactly beating down my doors these days."

"Blessings on you," Elinor murmured. "I shall try."

She left the shop feeling lighter. She stole a glance down the street. The woman Reya was nowhere in sight. She breathed more easily. But now where should she go?

Near the end of High Street, she saw a sign that gave her a new hope: Library. If the owner of the library could be persuaded to let her look at his books, she might find the answers she sought.

She saw a woman and a child entering the place. She followed in their wake.

According to Drew's best guess, Elinor had been gone for over six hours. When they'd had breakfast together early that morning, he'd told her to go for a walk and she'd said that was probably what she'd do. How far could she have gone on foot?

He'd been riding around Santa Rosa most of the afternoon, trying to scare up more information on Roger Aston, but he'd run into nothing but dead ends. Riding home, he'd decided he had to sit down with Elinor and get her to talk about Aston, whether she liked it or not.

The house had been empty when he returned. All signs told him Elinor hadn't been there all day.

He'd hopped back on the bike and headed out, checking the nearby Armstrong Woods park first, then cruising around the back roads.

This is nuts, he told himself after an hour of driving. Why was he hunting for her? So what if she'd disappeared from his life?

She was a grown woman, he argued, still searching. He hardly knew her, when it came right down to it. She'd been secretive and evasive with him from the first moment he'd picked her up on the bridge. She'd flooded his bathroom, nearly set fire to his house. She strangled sparrows to cook into casseroles. She was also, he felt sure, mixed up with a wiseguy of some sort who falsified credit information, swiped people's driver's licenses and used them to set himself up in luxury. Why should he care about her?

Okay, okay, besides the obvious physical stuff.

It's simple, his sensible, reasonable self told him. She's a lost nut-case and you're a chump.

True enough, he supposed, turning onto yet another country road. He'd certainly been enough of a chump in the past. LeeAnne had shown him that when he got involved, he was involved down to the last atom in his being.

Damn! He thought he'd given all that up. He'd put as much distance between himself and the world of waifs, hucksters and just plain liars as he could.

He'd just forgotten to make sure none of them dropped out of the sky right in the path of his front wheel.

Lost waif, he thought as he turned into the familiar driveway of a modest suburban ranch house. That was why he was doing this. For all her oddball ways and aristocratic airs, he sensed Elinor was a lost soul, wandering about in a strange world. Why he'd been picked by the fates to be her guardian he couldn't say, but so far, he was all she had. If she was lost in the varied and sometimes weird environs of Sonoma County, he was the one who had to find her, Roger Aston or no Roger Aston.

Two small comets burst out the front door of the house as he cut his motor and dismounted.

"Drew! Drew! Drew!" they screamed, barreling into him with the full force of their meteoric joy.

"Whoa, whoa," Drew cried, scooping up the bouncing four-year-olds, one under each arm. "How the heck did you two get off your leashes?" he demanded with mock sternness. "Don't tell me you gnawed your way out of your cages again?"

"Drew! You gotta see it! We got a hamster—"

"—when it's Mommy's night off—"

"—you never came over when we—"

"—we use the pot all the time now, ya know—"

"—and then we're going to the beach and you can—"

"Yo! Tuck! Cubbie! Get off the man!"

A man's voice rumbled through the yard like a dozen bowlers making twelve simultaneous strikes. Drew looked up from the chattering, wriggling twins to greet his old friend Bear Olson.

Bear's nickname was apt, as he walked with the

heavy, stolid gait of a Yosemite black bear and was
built along the lines of a robust grizzly in summer. In
his boots and jeans, Drew thought, his beard and hair
haloing his face with a nimbus of white-blond curls,
he looked as if he could hold his own against an oncoming Buick. Yet the gentleness with which he ex-
tracted his twin sons from under Drew's arms gave just
a hint of old Saint Nick, as well.

"Ingraham," he rumbled, grinning.

He set the twins down and they shot toward the
house, scrambling to be the first inside. Drew watched
with wincing amusement as the pair narrowly missed
losing fingers and ears on their way through the screen
door.

"Bear," Drew said with sudden awkwardness. As
with Will Curran, it had been a year or more since he'd
last been to this house or seen Bear.

"Uh, it's been a long time, I know. The twinks are
getting pretty sizable."

He stuck out his hand. Bear clasped it in a bone-
crunching welcome.

"We've missed you, man. Yeah, the boys are really
sproutin' up. Hey, wait'll you see Jennie. First grade
and I'm already thinkin' about girls' school." He jerked
his woolly head toward the house. "Comin' in? Rita's
got sun tea."

"Yeah. But just for a quick one. I need to ask a favor."

"Say the word, man."

Drew followed Bear to the house. His feeling of awkwardness was compounded by another sensation, one
he wasn't sure he could name. It was a mingling of
pain, relief and warmth at Bear's easy acceptance of
his sudden return. For all his bulk and brusqueness,
the big man had a grace Drew wasn't sure he himself
could equal.

Rita Olson floated into the room, a willowy redhead
with an air of serenity that would have been simply
pleasant if one didn't know she was the mother of two

163

gale-force four-year-olds and a six-going-on-forty-year-old. Her lightly freckled face broke into a sunny smile at the sight of Drew.

"Hey, you," she said softly, coming to give him a hug. "How the heck are you, anyway?"

"Better," Drew replied, the word surprising himself even as it left his lips.

"Good," she said firmly, giving him a pat on the cheek. "Time and space, that's what I told Bear you needed. Come on in, have a sit."

"I can't stay long," he told her as they went into the small but cozy kitchen. "I came to borrow your old man."

"I suppose I could let you have him for a bit," Rita said as she pulled out glasses and poured iced tea all around.

"What you need?" Bear asked, chugging the fragrant tea.

"I need help finding someone. You know the area, and it'd be pretty easy to cruise it on your bike. Can you spare the time and the gas?"

"Like I told you, just say the word."

"Who are you looking for?" Rita asked, her gentle eyes looking worriedly at him over her glass. "A kid?"

"No. A woman. Her name's Elinor. She's English. I think she might have gone for a walk near my place and gotten lost."

Rita's eyebrows went up, but before she could ask the question that was so clear on her face, Bear interrupted. "Can do. You okay with the sprats, babe?"

"Sure, but—"

Drew cut her off gently. "I'm not sure how far she's gotten or if she's okay. She's not too familiar with the area and she's a foreigner. I think we'd better get out there soon."

Bear rose to his feet, draining the last of his tea. "Just let me grab a jacket."

Rita raised her brows again at Drew, her eyes widening. "Well?" she prodded.

Drew's awkwardness renewed itself. "She's an acquaintance. I've just been helping her out for a few days until she can get back to England."

"Ah. Will we get to meet her?"

Drew shook his head and smiled, staring down at his hands. "All right, Mama Bear, don't get all stirred up. There's nothing going on."

Rita unfolded herself from the chair where she'd been perched, cross-legged. "Did I say anything?" she said, all innocence. "All I asked was if we'd get to meet this woman who needs a search party in greater downtown Riverton."

"Hey, babe," Bear said, returning to the kitchen. "The boys are building a cart so they can bring the critters out to meet Drew. Tell 'em we'll be back. There's duct tape in the hall closet if they get too rowdy."

"Duct tape?" Drew asked, laughing.

"Heck, yeah. The parenting tool for the nineties," Rita said, walking them to the door. "We haven't had to use it yet, but it's comforting to know it's there."

Bear and Rita kissed good-bye and Rita gave Drew another hug. "Glad to have you back," she whispered. "Don't be such a stranger, 'kay?"

As he and Bear drove away on their bikes, Drew considered their welcome. No "where the hell have you been," no "long time no see," no "jeez, you could have at least called." No questions about what he'd been doing all this time. Just a warm greeting and acceptance.

He'd forgotten what it was like to have friends.

But this wasn't the time to be mulling over the nature of relationships or his past. He'd enlisted Bear's help to find Elinor and he didn't want to waste time.

They pulled over at a turn-out near River Road. Bear offered to search along the old county road to the west.

Drew would go east, into town. In an hour they'd meet back at this spot.

As he described Elinor, Drew stuck to the concrete facts as much as he could. He left out the business about Henry V, time travel, and Elinor's general air of otherworldliness. He just warned Bear that she might seem a bit disoriented and that she was a bit of a British snob.

"Kind of like royalty, huh?" Bear asked.

"A lot like royalty," Drew said. "If she gives you attitude, just tell her Sir Drew sent you to look for her."

"Sir Drew?" Bear chuckled. "This is one lady I have got to meet."

They rode off in their separate directions, Drew feeling like an idiot for telling Bear what Elinor called him. But he couldn't have let Bear encounter her completely unprepared for either her uppity manners or her weird way of speaking.

If he were a beautiful lost loony with a medieval fixation, where would he go first? Or, alternatively, if he were a woman who'd run afoul of the law in a foreign country, where would he go to find a new hiding place?

He tried the resort hotels and motels, the supermarket and the bus depot in the back of the John Deere dealership. No one had seen her. He even went to the little watercolor gallery on Jennings Street and the art supply store tucked within Mattison's Hardware. No luck.

An unpleasant thought struck him: She might have gone to find Roger Aston. He was about to turn around and head back to Santa Rosa when a sign over a little shop caught his eye. "Magicke, Mirrors, and Memories," the hand-carved words read.

"This might be the place."

He fought the urge to sneeze as his nostrils were treated to an atmosphere made up of equal parts burnt sage and sandalwood perfume. A girl stood behind the counter, popping her gum and bouncing up and down

166

to the music pouring into her ears from her head-phones. She waggled her long red nails at him and then went right back to her copy of *Vogue*. Drew went up and waved a hand in her face to let her know he wanted to actually speak to her.

The kid was no help. Too addled by whatever was coming from the incense burner to know who was coming or going in the shop, Drew figured.

Still, he decided he was onto something with the magic angle. He tried the two other stores on Main that dealt in New Age items. In one, a nervous young guy with an undernourished beard eyed him warily and said someone answering Elinor's description had been in but she hadn't bought anything and besides so many beautiful chicks came into his shop every day he couldn't keep them all straight.

"Wow. Yeah, I can relate." Drew kept his sarcasm well hidden in his bland tones.

In the last shop, the young woman seemed normal and friendly enough, but when he began asking about her customers and if she'd seen a woman of Elinor's type, she began to freeze up. By the time he left, he felt as if his face had been frost-bitten. But he also knew something else. The woman was lying. She knew something. Maybe it was about Elinor, maybe it wasn't, but she was protecting someone.

He stood on the sidewalk outside of her shop and looked up and down Main. He was striking out. If he didn't find Elinor soon, he'd come back into this shop. And he wouldn't take no for an answer.

His frustration mounted. Where the hell had she gone?

He decided to walk the length of Main, peering into all the store fronts as he went. She must be hungry, he thought, as his own stomach registered a complaint. Had she gone into the deli? God knew the woman could eat.

Coral Smith Saxe

He passed a jeweler's, a café, and a real estate office, the public library. Where the hell was she?

Nothing. All those books and not one had contained so much as a hint on how one might leave one's own time and be blown away to a far-flung era and place in the twinkling of an eye.

Elinor's stomach growled once more. "We're fasting," she told it. "Remember?"

Her stomach didn't care to recall, she thought. No more did she, not while the scent of heaven-created pizza wafted on the breeze from some nearby establishment.

Her hunger was compounded by the memory of Drew's cozy little house. And of Drew himself.

She could go back. She knew that he would take her in. But she didn't want his pity or his charity. She must find her own way.

Something caught her eye. She smiled. It was a cross, mounted atop a high, narrow spire.

Hitching up her knapsack, she headed for sanctuary.

At least he had a lead.

Drew stood on the walkway in front of the library, feeling a mixture of elation and frustration. She had been in the library; the librarian had described her to a perfect T. And it had not been long since she'd left it—alone. Thus far, she hadn't met up with anyone else, and it was likely she'd been in town this whole time. He didn't want to think about the possibilities of what might happen, even in a few seconds, to someone as unwary as Elinor, even in this sleepy little town.

His brow wrinkled as he recalled the stacks of books on the carrel where the librarian said Elinor had sat. Books with titles such as *Magick and the Black Arts; Spelles, Charmes, and True Wisdom*, and *Are You a Good Witch or a Bad Witch: Wicca for Beginners*. What

was she up to, planning to sacrifice some more sparrows?

He glanced back up the street, at the way he had
come. He needed to think like Elinor, he told himself.

Oh, yeah, Ingraham, he thought. Like you're going
to get inside the head of a beautiful crackpot who
thinks Mr. Rogers sits behind the big desk in the Oval
Office.

He turned away from the stores he'd already inves-
tigated. She was alone, she was searching for something, answers of some kind. Witchcraft. Magic.
Metaphysics. Religion.

He closed his eyes for a moment as it came to him.
Religion, yes. She was a nun.

He rounded the corner at a fast pace, his bootheels
ringing hard on the pavement. The church was less
than a block away. He gained the front steps of the old
stone building and yanked open the doors.

He almost yelled with relief at the sight of the blond
head in one of the front pews. The old wood floors
creaked beneath his feet, and Elinor turned in her seat.

"Sir Drew, I—"

"Where the hell have you been?" he exclaimed, his
relief changing quickly to anger. "You've been gone
over six hours!"

"I came to see if I could find—"

"Are you nuts? Wandering around these country
roads alone? Don't you know what can happen to a
woman alone these days?"

She rose and placed her hands on her hips. "Nay, I
fear I know no such thing. As I've told you before, I
know little about your world. You said I should go for
a walk. Here is where I walked!"

He glared at her. "Why didn't you ask me to take
you?"

"You have made it clear my presence is a burden to
you. I am capable of looking out for myself."

"Oh, right. The lost nun from Nowhere-on-the-Thames, who doesn't know the difference between a coffee maker and a crankcase!"

"If you are so lacking in respect for me, why have you bothered to follow me?" she demanded, her eyes glinting.

"Because I thought you might be in danger! I see I was mistaken."

"More than you know, sirrah!"

"Right. I'm out of here. Find your own damned way back to wherever the hell you came from." He swung around and headed up the aisle.

She gasped. "Your tongue shall send you there first," she hissed.

"My wha—?" he spluttered, turning once more to stare at her. "I—you—"

"Even a nun from Nowhere can show proper conduct in church."

"You want to see proper conduct?" He covered the distance back to her in one long stride. "You want proper conduct?" he said, pointing a finger at her. "I ought to toss you over my shoulder and haul you to the bus station right now!"

"You may try. But your motorbeast shall have to be bolstered with pillows for a month ere your rump rides easy once more!"

"My rump!" he bellowed. "You think you—"

He couldn't help it. The grin had to come. The treason of his face urged the rest of him on, and before he knew whether he was fighting or floating, he had pulled her into his arms. Her own burst of laughter was lost as he set himself to the task of kissing her smiling lips, long and thoroughly.

His laughter faded as she warmed to him, going soft and willing, her lips no longer mocking or challenging but communicating sweet messages of pleasure. He felt a moan rising from deep within himself, felt it humming in his throat, pouring itself into her.

He had no plans for the next year or so, he thought to himself. *Maybe I'll be ready to stop then. . . .*

Chapter Twelve

"I gave her cakes and I gave her ale / and I gave her sack and sherry / I kissed her once and I kissed her twice / and we were wondrous merry!"

Drew and Elinor jumped apart. Elinor stared at the man who was singing and nearly jigging down the aisle toward them. She had been so lost in Drew's kiss, in the delight of his embrace, that this small man, with his merry song and almost elfin face, seemed to be something out of an old tale.

Drew groaned. "I should have known. Bear called you, right?"

"Correct, amigo mine. Rita had an emergency at the clinic and had to go in to work. I took over the search so Bear could go home and take care of the young terrorists in training. And I see you have found what—or who—you were looking for?"

Drew jerked his thumb at the fellow. "This is Dr. William Curran. Wild Will, this is Lady Elinor De-Courtenay."

The man bowed with a flourish. "At your service, ma'am."

"Lord Curran."

"Lord Curran. Hmm." Curran stroked his beard. "I like the sound of that. What do you think, Ingraham? Shall I buy a duchy or something and tack on another title?"

"Shrink is bad enough," Drew drawled.

"Shrink?" Elinor couldn't follow this, but she was growing accustomed to the feeling.

"A derogatory appellation which my so-called friend here insists upon using in regard to my esteemed occupation." Curran looked injured.

Elinor turned to Drew for help.

"Psychiatrist," he said. "It's an old joke."

"Indeed." The man rubbed his hands together. "I've been waiting to meet you, Lady DeCourtenay. Drew hasn't told me nearly enough about you. Therefore, let us make our exit from this place and tear a joint or two at my humble abode."

"I thought you gave up dope," Drew muttered.

"Very amusing. Don't try the wiseguy act on me, old friend. It won't wash."

"Right. But we've got to—"

"—get right out there and head for my place. I just got a hunk of venison and I'm ready to grill out, as we say here in the land of mesquite and the free-range margarita."

"Venison?" Drew gave a sardonic smile. "Using the barter system these days, Doc?"

"As a matter of fact, it did come from a grateful patient. He wanted to give me his hunting dog, but I settled for the catch instead."

Curran was already leading the way out of the church. Drew nodded to Elinor and they followed.

Lord Curran's motorbeast was far more complicated and decorative than Sir Drew's, she noted, colored a brilliant red and sporting many more levers and circles upon its top. It was most eye-catching, but she decided she liked the simplicity of Drew's black and silver Harley.

Will Curran's home was like his motorcycle, though on a grander scale. Its lower story nestled into the hillside, as if it had been carved into it. The upper levels, she saw as they dismounted, soared up into square towers which seemed to be made entirely of glass. Boxes full of brilliant flowers stood suspended below the windows, dripping a rainbow of blossoms down the walls to the stonework below.

"Such a beauteous manor," she murmured as she and Drew followed Lord Curran toward the wide front doors.

"Head-shrinking pays."

She reached up to touch her temples, puzzling over this bit of news. What value could there possibly be in a smaller head? Sir Drew's and Lord Curran's looked the size of any ordinary man of this land or hers.

The inside of Lord Curran's house was as interesting as the outside. It lacked the coziness of Drew's, but then it was built in more lordly proportions. Her well-trained eye for beauty and line could appreciate much of the design of the house, though she also saw objects and structures beyond her ken. She was drawn at once to the paintings on the walls, a mixture of images both startling and delightful.

"Welcome to Casa Loco," Lord Curran said, spreading his arms wide. "Can I get you something to drink, Elinor?"

She started at the familiar use of her first name, then remembered that Drew had done the same. It seemed to be the custom, however unsuitable.

"Aye. I should welcome a drink."

"You name it, I've probably got it. Unless you want vintage Red Chief strawberry soda—that I don't have."

"Ah. Wine, if you please, Lord Curran."

Drew groaned. "Don't do it, Will—don't read out your wine list."

Curran looked mildly offended. "I'm sure Elinor can make up her own mind about what she wants to drink."

"Red or white wine?" Drew said quickly.

"A claret?" she asked, shrugging.

"Coming right up." Curran grinned at Drew. "Your usual, Ingraham?"

"If I can't have Red Chief."

"Make yourself at home, Elinor," said Curran. "I'll be back in a flash."

She gazed after him in wonder. Lord Curran was an unusual fellow, it seemed. If he could come and go in a flash, he might be the wizard she sought.

"So many books," she murmured, crossing to the wall of shelves in the great hall. "Lord Curran is a scholar, aye?"

"Definitely. Though he isn't Lord Curran. Call him Doc, if you want to call him anything."

"And paintings. And sculpture," Elinor murmured, strolling about. "He has many interests."

"Yeah. He knows a little about everything, and what he doesn't know, he'll find out if it kills him."

"You are fond of him."

He grinned. "We go back a long way."

"A childhood friend?"

"Don't look so surprised. I did have a childhood, you know."

It was her turn to grin. "Aye, I fancy you did. And the pair of you were the bane of your mothers' lives."

"Like you?"

"I?" Her face was all innocence.

He stepped closer. She shivered, a small pleasant sensation, at the way his eyes looked her up and down.

"Try to deny it," he drawled.

He reached out and ran his finger down the length of the braid that hung over her shoulder. A ripple of

175

sensation followed his touch and settled in the center of her.

"I can just see you, a kid in blond pigtails," he murmured, "driving your mom nuts by falling into mudholes and cooking up weird stuff in the fireplace."

She shook her head, smiling. "Not I, sir."

"Yes, you, princess. I bet you colored on her wallpaper."

"I was a model child."

"You were a brat."

His fingertips came to rest on her hip, did a little swirling dance there. Her heart danced along.

"I was a paragon of virtue and sweetness."

"You swung on the chandeliers."

"I sat sweetly and sewed."

"You lie."

"I lie."

His eyes were smiling, his lips smiling, and so close. She didn't care if it was impossible, foolish. She willed him closer, closer—

"And here we are. Claret for the lady and me, Fat Weasel ale for the barbarian—" Will stopped short. "Orrr . . . I could go out and come back in again."

Drew moved away easily. Elinor felt her cheeks heating.

"Lord Curran. You said that you should return with a flash," she said, striving for a light tone. "I saw no lightning."

"I'll remember the pyrotechnics next time. However, I'm as hungry as a curly wolf. Come join me in the kitchen, you two, while I start the food."

He grinned at Elinor. "Ingraham says I'm an insufferable braggart when it comes to my cooking, but I'm sure you'll keep me humble by giving me the honest praise and honor that I so richly deserve."

She returned his smile. "I shan't lead you to sin, Lord Curran. Though I've a feeling you need no conduct in that direction."

"What does she mean by that?" Curran demanded of Drew. "Have you been filling her head with your callow lies, Ingraham?"

"She's got eyes, Curran," Drew said. "And ears."

"And lovely ones they are, too."

"Watch it, Doc. You're on the thin edge."

"Don't listen to him, Elinor. He's turned bitter in his old age."

"Has he, indeed?"

Drew ignored them both and headed for the kitchen. "Come on. Let's rustle up some grub."

Curran made a rude noise at his retreating back, then offered his arm to Elinor. "Shall we, my lady?"

"I should be delighted, Lord Doc."

Will Curran had not been exaggerating about his culinary skills. He kept Elinor and Drew entertained with both his antics and his expertise in the kitchen, after which they set a table outside on a large wooden dais. Will lit soft lamps hidden among the trailing vines and flowers, and they ate outdoors, with the sounds of the insects and the calls of night birds. Elinor savored the breeze that ruffled her hair and seemed to carry off her tensions and cares.

"What is Casa Low-koh?" she asked as they sat lingering over dessert and more delicious coffee. "Is it in the Cali-for-nian tongue?"

"Spanish. Means the Crazy House," said Drew.

"Crazy. A madhouse?" Elinor turned to Will with wondering eyes.

"No, although there have been occasions—never mind." Will smiled. "No, it's just a psychiatrist's joke. I guess working with crazy people all the time gives you kind of a warped sense of humor. But what do you think of my abode?" he asked.

"It is a marvel. So many windows and plants! And such comfort. It is as if you live half in the earth and half in the clouds."

"That's Doc, all right," Drew commented.

Coral Smith Saxe

Elinor ignored his sarcasm. "It is a most commendable state, Lord Curran, don't you agree? One's mind should be on heaven, yet one's feet should be firmly planted on the ground."

"I don't know. There are a lot of times when I wish I could fly in those clouds. And sometimes I wish I could just burrow underground and hibernate." He lifted his cup. "What about you, Ingraham?"

Drew rose from his chair. "I'm a wheel man, myself. Give me a road to ride over. If you two will excuse me?"

When he'd gone, Will looked at Elinor and shrugged. "That's the trouble with kids today. Machines, machines, machines."

She rose and began gathering up the empty plates and cups. "I believe Sir Drew speaks lightly when he's most serious," she said. "Indeed, I believe it could be a trait he shares with his good friend Lord Will?"

"Whew." Will whistled through his teeth. "You got us there. Does it bother you?"

She shrugged. "From time to time. But it amuses me, too."

She and Will cleared the table while Drew was gone. In the kitchen, he introduced her to another cupboard called the dishwasher, where, he claimed, dirty plates and pans would be transformed into clean ones with but the twist of a knob. She took his word for it. His house was too full of wonders to be limited by anything so mundane as a greasy platter.

"You have many books," she said as they worked side by side. "And you are a physician. You must be quite learned."

"Pshaw, ma'am. I'm just your ordinary garden-variety dilettante."

"Is that like a sorcerer?"

His laughter rang out. "No, though some people look on my profession as something akin to the black arts."

"You heal mad men and women?"

178

His glance at her was shrewd. "Are you worried about your mental health?"

"Nay—"

"Drew's?"

She looked at him in surprise. "Nay. Should I be?"

Will waited a bit before answering. "He's been alone out there for nearly three years. I've seen him maybe twice in all that time. As a friend, I worry. As a doctor, no. I've known Drew since we were tadpoles. There's not a sounder nut, even if we couldn't be more different." He gave her a reassuring smile. "I'd trust Ingraham with my life. And believe me, sweet lady, I love my life."

"I can tell," she said softly. "You may not have contentment, Sir Doc, but you have the life force in you fair to bursting."

"And you, Elinor? I'd say you're one of those full-of-life folk, too, but your lovely eyes say you're far from contented, yourself."

She felt suddenly shy, wary. "Is anyone content at our age, my lord?"

"Yep. I've met 'em. Some were locked up for their own protection, it's true, but I've known a soul or two who I'd say were bona fide happy and at peace with their lot in life. But you're avoiding the question. What would it take to make Elinor DeCourtenay content?"

She smiled at him. "Thou art persistent, sir." She sobered. "I cannot say, in truth. I do not know what Sir Drew has told you of me, but I am a stranger here. More strange than any ordinary traveler. I suppose contentment would be to find my way home again."

"And where is that?"

She wiped her hands on the towel he handed her. "England."

"That much I guessed. Whereabouts?"

"You would not know of it. Truly." She set the towel aside. "And only a wizard could find it, I think."

"There's that word again. What if I said I was a wizard. What would you do?"

"I should ask you how I might go home again."

"I recommend flying."

"And would you give me the spell to make me fly?"

"I'd buy you a ticket if you wanted. Though I don't believe Ingraham would be happy about that."

She looked away. "I believe he would know great relief were I simply to vanish. I think he would scarcely notice."

"Beep! Wrong. I've known him longer than you, begging your pardon. You have his full attention, trust me. Why else would he have mustered the troops to find you today?"

"That is why I am so irritating to him. He wishes not to be bothered."

"Beep! Wrong again. That's zero for two, Ms. De-Courtenay. That surly act of his is mostly show. He's been hurt in the past, and he might be scared but he's also fascinated." He leaned back against the counter, arms crossed over his chest. "Fascinated by you. And I can't say I blame him."

She began sliding silverware into an open drawer. "You are a flatterer, my lord."

"Yep. But I also have impeccable taste in women, as Drew himself will tell you. If you'd stumbled in front of my bike—"

"Yo, Doc," Drew called from the great hall. "Come here and show me how you've got your CDs organized. It looks like you arranged them all by last names of the audio engineers."

Lord Curran excused himself. Elinor was relieved he was gone. She liked him very much and his flattery was sweet, but she was uncomfortable with the piercing quality of his brown eyes. For all his joking and whimsy, Will Curran was a shrewd judge of people. If he'd stayed longer in conversation with her, he'd have had her confessing herself to him, telling him about

180

Roger and her thoughts on how she'd come to be here. She didn't need another person to call her a liar or a fool.

She explored the kitchen as she finished wrapping the leftover food in thin sheets of metal that folded as easily as paper. How different this house was from Drew's, she thought. It was as if Curran poured his life into his house, while Drew held a more practical view, believing that a house is but a shelter from the elements. Neither was fully satisfactory, she felt, but she couldn't tell just why.

She shrugged and went on working. It didn't matter. The only house she needed to concern herself with was Oakfield.

"She's incredible," Will told Drew as they moved out of earshot of the kitchen.

"Yeah," said Drew. "But I know nothing about her, and you were the one who said she could be leaning either way on the sanity question."

"That was before I met her. You didn't say she was gorgeous or an artist or that she was interested in just about everything under the sun."

"I didn't want to bias you ahead of time. But now that you've seen her, what do you think? Am I gonna end up in the middle of the night with her deciding to reenact the Wars of the Roses, starting with me?"

"Planning on living with her?" Will's eyebrows waggled.

"No. In fact, as soon as I can get her down to the passport office or wherever, I intend to put her on a plane back to England." Drew ran his hand over the back of his neck. "It's just . . ."

"Just?"

"It's just that there's something nagging at me. Like she's not telling me everything. I think she's mixed up in something dangerous. Whether she's in it by choice or by force, I don't know."

Drew told Will about his encounters with Roger Aston so far. "There can't be two people in Sonoma County with that same weird accent."

"Why not?" Will raised his hands. "Coincidences happen all the time."

"This one's just too big. They've got to be connected."

"So, no one can seem to locate anyone she knows, she might be connected with a shady character, she's gorgeous, sexy, and intelligent, and she's hooked on the fifteenth century. What's the problem?"

"She thinks she got here by traveling through time."

"Oooh-kayy."

"Weirdsville, huh?"

"Yep. That one's on the edge, all right. Still, she doesn't seem to be a threat to herself or anyone else. She's actually a pretty savvy lady."

Drew twisted the glass he'd been holding in his hands. "Now I'm back to square one."

"Yeah? That kiss in the church didn't look like square one to me. I'd say more like you'd rolled a six and were well on your way to collecting the orange chip for Sports and Recreation."

Drew groaned. "I don't want to play Trivial Pursuit, Doc. Not with her or anyone else."

"And the kiss?"

"Things just got out of hand for a moment. Damn. Everything about her winds up in a dead end or weirdness! It's like she really did fall out of the sky."

"Hmm. Angels are still pretty big these days."

Drew shot him a black look, then softened. "Sorry, Doc. This whole thing's got me chasing my tail. I wasn't looking for this."

"Yeah," Will said.

"You don't believe me?"

Will shrugged. "It's not up to me."

"Don't give me that smug psychiatrist bull. Talk to me straight, because there's no way I'm paying you for your time."

Will took a moment, studying his boots. Then he looked at Drew, and the laughter usually present in his eyes and tone was gone.

"I'm not saying this as a shrink, Ingraham. I'm saying this as a friend who's known you a hell of a long time. I know your history with LeeAnne, man. I know what you lost when she went down that night. I know it snapped something off inside you like a light switch. And I watched you pull away from everyone and everything. It was like you left the country. All you took with you was your bike and body."

Drew leaned his long form against the bookcase. "Go on."

"That's all. You've been away. Do you know this is the first time you've been in my house in over a year and a half? Bear said Cubbie and Tuck weren't sure who you were at first, then they recognized your bike.

"Maybe she did drop out of the sky. Maybe she's a spy for some bike repair shop in Cotati. Maybe she's one of the casualties who were sent roaming when they closed down the state mental hospitals. Maybe she's just a beautiful dreamer. But whoever she is, she got you out of your cave, pal. And I don't think there's many of us out there who could have done that."

Drew rolled his shoulders and pushed away from the bookcase, scowling.

"You're the dreamer, Doc. It's not her. It's just the circumstances around her. And like I said, this whole search today only convinced me more that she needs to be on a British Airways jet, pronto."

"Clear enough. But I'll butt in just one last time."

"Can I stop you?"

"Nope."

"Okay, shoot."

"If you don't want her, can I have her?"

Drew's fist had flown before he'd thought. Will's reflexes were as fine as ever, thanks to years of martial arts training. He ducked easily and came up with a cocky smile.

"Damn you," Drew growled. "That was low."

"Just testing. Never lie to a shrink, pal. It's my stock in trade."

"I thought that was lawyers."

"Don't try to change the subject. You need to decide what you're going to do about that beautiful lady in the kitchen." He gestured in that direction. "Speaking of which, it's pretty tacky leaving her in there all alone. We can't let her think we're old creeps who think women belong in the kitchen. Not that there's anything wrong with being a homemaker, of course."

"Oh, yeah. Elinor's a real homebody," Drew said. "You should see what she can do when she gets cooking."

"Really? May I?"

"Watch it."

Lord Curran offered them lodging for the night but Drew declined. Elinor started to protest that they couldn't ride by night, but then she recalled that the Beast had a brilliant lantern on its front which illuminated the road at night like a bonfire on a hilltop. Sir Doc gave her a light, warm suit to wear over her clothing to keep out the wind and night air. They made their farewells, with Sir Doc and Drew exchanging fond insults until the Beast's roars drowned out all words and they were swallowed up in the darkness around them.

She felt as if they were all alone in the world, the two of them, flying through the night. She was growing to appreciate, if not actually enjoy, racing about on this unusual mechanical steed.

She leaned against Drew's back and sighed. She was weary from her daylong search, and the good food and wine had made her sleepy. It was good to be braced against Drew's broad back, even with her helmet as a barrier against any real feeling of his warmth against her cheek.

She'd enjoyed his warmth when he'd kissed her in the church that afternoon. He'd seemed willing and ready to kiss her again in Lord Curran's hall. And she had wanted so much to be kissed, to kiss him back.

It was puzzling. He embraced her with such heat and tenderness, yet he was so contemptuous of her, so distrusting.

What was it Sir Doc had said? Drew had been hurt, but she had his full attention. She didn't know what to make of that.

Ah, well. She yawned and nestled against him once more. As she did so, Drew's hand grasped hers where they were clasped about his waist and gave them a hard squeeze.

"Don't go to sleep," he shouted back to her.

She nodded and lifted her head. The chain of the medallion shifted beneath her clothing.

She straightened even more, allowing the chill of the night to nip at her here and there.

She knew what her next step would be. Louis Feldon the jeweler could be her best hope.

Chapter Thirteen

Rita Olson called early the next morning, inviting Drew and Elinor for a barbecue that afternoon. Drew wanted to refuse but knew he couldn't. Bear had done him a favor, no questions asked. Drew owed him. And now that contact had been reestablished and Rita's romance antennae had been raised by Elinor's name, he knew she wouldn't accept any refusals.

Elinor had looked wary when he'd told her.

"You don't have to go if you don't want to. It's not a command performance. I can tell them you're sick or something."

"You would lie for me?"

He winced. "No. Not if I can help it."

"I had hoped to go into your village again this afternoon. But I do not want you to lie to them. And they are your friends. You should be with them."

"Then I guess we'll go."

* * *

The Shore Unknown

Introductions went smoothly. To Drew's great relief, Elinor didn't mention anything about time travel or Henry V to Rita and Bear—he wanted to explain all that himself, in private.

As far as Bear was concerned, any friend of Drew's was a friend of his. Rita, however, was another matter. Drew caught the cordial but measuring look she gave Elinor when they met. The Mama Bear was on guard.

Tuck and Cubbie took to Elinor right away, but it was Jennie, Bear and Rita's daughter, who took her in hand and led her on a tour of the modest suburban property with all the dignity and aplomb of a museum docent. Before Rita could intervene, Jennie had whipped out a brush, comb, pins and ribbons and was soon seated atop the picnic table, "doing" Elinor's hair, chattering away as if they'd been lifelong friends.

"She's really beautiful, Drew. And incredibly patient," Rita confided to Drew as they watched from across the yard. "Jennie's going to talk her leg off."

"If Elinor doesn't go bald first," Bear added.

"Oh, God, that's right." Rita looked at the men with wide eyes. "The only hair Jennie's ever worked on is Barbie's, and you don't want to know how that turned out. It's a thing with girls—I think Mattel is starting up a hair club for dolls."

Drew laughed. Despite Rita and Bear's fears, Elinor seemed to be having a fine time. He was glad that she appeared to have passed muster with Rita. He observed that she listened to Jennie with respect and interest and talked to her like a normal human being—something he noticed many people couldn't manage when they got around kids.

"Elinor will be all right," Drew said. "She's not Barbie and she's got hair enough to occupy a squadron of little girls. Man, Jennie's growing up, though."

"I know. Too fast. When I was twelve I wasn't half as wise as she is at six. It's scary."

187

"You and Bear are doing a great job with her. The twinks, too."

"Thanks. We try, though with Tuck and Cubbie, some days it seems more like crowd control."

"That's why I told you their nicknames should be Duck and Cover, not Tuck and Cubbie."

"Tell me about it."

Rita popped the lid of the ice chest and handed out a beer to Drew. She dragged up two patio chairs and motioned for Drew to sit while Bear went to tend the grill.

"Okay," she said. "Tell."

Drew twisted the cap off his bottle and reached for Rita's. As he uncapped hers, he said, "What do you want to hear?"

"The whole megillah."

"All right." He handed over her beer and settled back into his chair. "I was born to poor but honest sheet-rock miners in the south of France—"

Rita slugged him on the arm. "Cut it out. That's what I'd expect from Curran, not you. First of all, how did you meet her?"

He sighed. "She fell out of the sky—ow! Damn, woman! I'm telling you the truth." He rubbed his arm where she'd slugged him again. "I mean it. I was riding my bike out on Venners Creek Bridge. One minute there was nobody, then, all of a sudden, she falls smack in the road, there on the bridge. I almost hit her. She's got some kind of amnesia or a block or something. She says she time-traveled here from England and that she really belongs in the late 1400s. She loves to draw and she can snag a sparrow on the wing with just a net."

Rita stood up. "Give me that beer."

"Why?"

"You don't need alcohol. You're loaded on something already."

He stared at her. "You're serious."

"Hell, yes, I'm serious. I may not have known you as

188

long as Will and Bear but I know you well enough to know you're not a liar. So you've got to be sniffing, smoking, drinking or popping something to tell me a load of horse hockey like that."

"Holy—" he muttered. He handed her the bottle. "Here. You're right. I don't need this. I'm losing my marbles, fast."

"Ohh—kayy." She took the bottle and set it aside. Squatting down before him, she put her hands on his knees. "You in some kind of trouble, friend?"

He shook his head. "No. Not the kind you're thinking, Mama Bear." He patted her hands. "But you just woke me up to something."

"I gotta go see that the twinks don't use the cat for target practice," she said, glancing over at her sons. "You just sit here and un-lax. You're with friends, remember?"

As she walked off, he ran a hand over his face. He'd just been on the receiving end of some of his own medicine. He owed Elinor a big apology.

He looked over to where Jennie was winding Elinor's hair into Princess Leia-style cinnamon-bun braids. Beams of afternoon sunlight caught fire in the strands, warming the blond strands to a glimmering gold. She was so oblivious to her own beauty, he thought. So different from LeeAnne, who knew her every asset down to the last eyelash and how to best magnify and use each one.

Scowling, he shook off the memory. This was just what he'd been afraid would happen if he got back with his old friends. It was inevitable that he'd begin thinking of LeeAnne.

Elinor was what mattered right now. Rita's reaction to what he considered to be the facts about Elinor had shown him what it must have felt like for Elinor to have shared her weird but earnestly felt suspicions down on that San Francisco pier. He needed to tell her, to apologize.

That is, if he ever got a moment alone with her.

Rita gathered up the plates and led the way into the kitchen. Elinor followed, carrying cups and silverware.

"I'll wash and you dry?" Rita asked. "Our dishwasher's on the fritz again." She grinned. "You'd think with these mechanical wizards all around, every appliance and doorknob in this house should work like new."

Elinor smiled. "Drew's possessions work well, though I suspect it is because he scarcely uses them. He keeps bachelor's hall."

"That's probably true," Rita said, running steaming water into the basin. "But I don't think the same thing applies to my old man. We're just so busy with the kids and making ends meet these days that we never think about mending the linoleum in the kitchen till the middle of the night when it's too late and we're too tired."

She began to slide the dishes into the water, which was foaming like a beaten egg white. Elinor took up a dry cloth hanging near the basin and stood ready to dry the dishes, glad she knew at least this much of housekeeping.

"But your lord is a good man, I can tell," Elinor said. "And you have such merry and healthy babes."

"Yep, we're really blessed on that score." Rita handed her a plate to dry. "But those babes need new shoes almost every week it seems, and there's not a big bunch of cash left over at the end of even a good month. We're all right, of course," she said hastily. "We're making it. But when a working dishwasher gets to be a big-time luxury, it gets a little depressing."

"I've never had one," Elinor murmured.

"Oh, I'm sorry." Rita raised a soapy hand. "I didn't mean to sound like a weenie. I grew up without a lot of this stuff, too. And I guess I still think of Drew as having bucks to burn, the way he did back in the old days."

"He burned bucks?" Visions of smoked game came to mind.

"Yeah. Practically printed his own money, he was so successful in his consulting business. And he always spent tons on his friends. I think that might be one of the reasons why he stopped coming around. When he quit his business, he didn't have all that spending cash anymore, and, well, I've always wondered if he felt we wouldn't feel the same way about him if he wasn't such a big spender."

Elinor rubbed away at the goblet Rita handed her. From what she could grasp of Rita's words, she gathered Drew had once been wealthy working at a business, not a trade as he did now. Here was a chance to satisfy some of the curiosity she'd been storing up since she'd met Drew.

"Why did Drew quit his business?" she asked. "He is a stubborn man, but I believe he's not a fool. Why should he abandon his security?"

Rita shook her head. "Oh, honey, he had his security blown out from under him the day his wife died. When he lost LeeAnne, he didn't seem to care if he lived or died."

Elinor managed to snatch up the bowl she was holding before it could crash to the floor. She set it on the counter and stood, gazing out the doorway to the yard, where the twins were riding horseback on their father. Drew grinned at the three of them from his seat under the willow, his long legs propped up on a crate.

In all the time she'd spent with Drew, she hadn't even guessed. Grief for his loss wrestled with jealousy inside her.

"Elinor? You okay?"

She turned to Rita, who was looking at her with friendly concern.

"I—I—I don't know. I mean I didn't know that . . . LeeAnne . . . had died."

"Oh, God. Me and my big mouth!" Rita reached out to her, her hand dripping suds on the rug. "*I* didn't know *you* didn't know. I just assumed Drew had told you. Or that Will or somebody would have, by now, anyway. I'm so sorry, Elinor."

"It is oh-kay." Elinor held out her hand for another plate to dry. "There was no reason he should confide in me."

"No?" Rita's green eyes studied her. "You really didn't know anything about it?"

Elinor shook her head, embarrassed. She'd known there had been a LeeAnne in Drew's life, but it had only fleetingly occurred to her that she could have been his wife or that she could have died. Except for that single portrait, Drew's home showed naught that spoke of a woman's presence in any way.

Rita took the plate and the towel from Elinor's hands.

"Come on. These can wait," she said, putting them on the counter. "I think maybe I'd better fill you in, 'cause now that I think about it, Drew may not ever get around to it."

She wiped her own hands on the sides of her flowery skirt and beckoned for Elinor to follow her into the quiet front chamber that was called Rita's Office. She closed the door behind them and waved Elinor over to a padded bench.

Elinor sat, heart aching. She wasn't sure what was coming, but she knew it had to do with Drew's pain, the hurt that Sir Doc had spoken of last night.

Rita came to sit on the floor in front of Elinor, a box in her lap. Setting the lid aside, she began to sort through many scraps of heavy paper.

"Here," she said, pulling one out. "This is one Will took of LeeAnne when he was in his photography phase." She handed it to Elinor and pulled out another.

"And this is them at their wedding. Will was best man, but he insisted on being their photographer, too. Typical of Wild Will—all of his photos turned out to be the best ones, even better than the ones by the professional photographer LeeAnne hired." She gave Elinor a sharp glance. "I'm sorry. I should have asked you if you wanted to see these. Is it too much?"

"No, it is well." Elinor shook her head.

"I mean, you and Drew both keep saying that you're just friends and that you're going back to England soon, so I thought you might like to . . ." She put her crossed hands over her heart. "I hope it's okay."

"It is well," Elinor repeated.

She wasn't sure how convincing that sounded, but she wasn't about to let go of these pictures. She studied the picture of LeeAnne Ingraham first. This one portrayed her whole body, not just her head. She was every bit as lovely and delicate and exotic as she'd looked in the picture Elinor had found in Drew's home.

"She was very beautiful," she murmured.

"Oh, yeah. She was always getting offers to model. But she said she just wanted to be Mrs. Drew Ingraham. That was enough for her. From anybody else, that statement would have had us all gagging. But when LeeAnne said it, we believed her."

"If this picture speaks aright, they were already in love when they married," Elinor remarked, turning to the wedding picture.

She could see the adoration in the faces of the two people standing together, hands clasped. LeeAnne was gazing up into Drew's face with a glowing smile. Drew was returning that adoring look, doubled.

"Tell me about it. I think a wrecking ball hit him the first time he saw her. We were kind of surprised at first, because you know how cautious he is and he was already talking about marriage within a week of meeting her. But when we saw them together, we knew this was it, the real thing for both of them."

"How . . ." Elinor cleared her throat. "How did she die?"

"She was crazy about sailing. Drew bought her a boat as a wedding present and they were out on it almost every weekend. I don't think Drew cared for it as much as she did, but hey, that's love for you. He'd have taken up bungee jumping if LeeAnne wanted to do it."

Rita brushed her hair back from her face and handed Elinor a yellowed piece of thin parchment.

"There's the death announcement from the newspaper. LeeAnne's family was pretty important, so it was a huge deal down in San Jose."

Elinor read the words on the parchment:

LeeAnne Searles Ingraham, drowning victim. Entrepreneur-husband Andrew Ingraham declined comment. Funeral arrangements pending.

"She drowned?"

"Yeah. Ironic, isn't it? She was so crazy about sailing and had raced boats and been on sailing trips down to Mexico and back, but she ran onto the rocks just off Half Moon Bay."

Rita wiped a tear from the corner of her eye. "Drew was a basket case. Hardly made it through the funeral. The next week, we got a call from some of his business partners asking us where he was. We hadn't seen him. Finally, three weeks later, he showed up on our doorstep, looking like he belonged in a casket, too. He said he was okay, but he'd sold his share of the business, bought a house in the redwoods, and wanted to know if Bear knew anybody around here who wanted a bike restored."

"And that was when he went into seclusion?"

"That was it. Bear sent a couple of folks to him with classic bikes to restore. Drew called and thanked him, then we hardly saw him again until yesterday, when he came and asked Bear to help him find you."

Elinor could hardly take all this in. Her feelings were like a tangled rope. She felt terribly sad for Drew who had lost the love of his life when they were so young. She was touched by the story of their love. She was gladdened to hear that he was visiting his friends once more.

Those feelings were all well and good. But she also felt a tiny chill feeling of relief that LeeAnne was dead. Jealousy had been roused in her by the picture she'd found in the house, but she'd been able to contain it as long as no one spoke of such a person as LeeAnne, who'd offered "body and soul" to Drew.

Jealousy flickered up within her once more. She didn't want to know that anyone else had been Drew's lover. She didn't want to know that their love had been known to all as the epitome of passion and devotion. And she didn't want to know that Drew was still grieving the loss of his lovely, adoring, perfect mate.

No wonder he doesn't want me, she thought, hot tears stinging at the back of her eyes. No wonder he's so anxious to have me gone.

"Hey." Rita touched her knee. "Hey, it's okay. It was an awful thing. But it's great that he's back with us, now. And that he's got new friends, like you. I'm sorry if I upset you."

"It is oh-kay," Elinor replied. With a mighty effort, she cut her tears before they could begin to flow. "It is a most sorrowful tale. Poor Sir Drew."

"Yeah." Rita put all the pictures and papers back in the box and replaced the lid. "But it looks like he's starting to put it behind him, and that's what's important."

She rose gracefully from her seat on the floor.

"Come on," she said. "Let's get those dishes done so we can get back out there before those two head for the garage. It's one thing to listen to them talk about motorcycles. Once they get near an actual bike, they can't keep their hands off of it. We won't see them again for a week."

A clap of thunder rolled overhead.

Rita shrugged. "Good old Sonoma County spring weather. But you're probably used to rain where you come from, huh?"

"Indeed."

Drew and Bear met them at the back door, each with a twin in tow. Jennie followed, her arms full of the frightful-looking poppets she called Bar-bees.

"It just opened up and started pouring," Bear reported, shaking rain droplets from his hair. "Didn't even see it coming."

"You going to be okay riding to work?" Rita asked. "You want to take the car?"

"Naw, I'll be fine. But I'd better hit the shower and get ready. It's after five."

"We'd better be going, too," Drew said.

"No way!" Cubbie and Tuck howled in chorus.

"Actually, you can't go, Elinor," Jennie said crisply. "You promised you'd play dress-up, and in this household we keep our promises. Right, Mom?"

"We try, hon, but we don't lecture our guests on their moral obligations, either." Rita grinned at Drew. "At least, we try not to."

"You gotta stay, Drew," Tuck said, wrapping his arm around one of Drew's legs. "You haven't even seen the snakes yet."

"Or the banana slugs!" piped Cubbie.

"How can you resist?" Bear clapped Drew on the shoulder. "Play it your way, man. But you're welcome to stay. Beats you and your lady gettin' soaked on your bike." He offered his hand to Elinor. "Nice to meet you. Now you know where we are, come on back anytime."

"Thank you."

"Well," Rita said an hour later. "I thought this was just a spring shower and it was gonna let up by now."

The rain drummed on the roof as they sat in the comfortable front hall of the Olsons' home. The wind had picked up, and Elinor thought she heard a high note in it that didn't sound like a storm that was losing force.

"Is your husband safely inside?" she asked.

"Oh, yeah. The plant's only about ten minutes from here. He's cozy."

Rita turned from the window and shooed the children from the room, sending them off to bathe before bedtime.

"Bear said he was working security again," said Drew as Rita curled up on the couch once more. "I thought he was out of that, working for Hal in the bike shop."

"Hal's struggling. And he's getting too old to really do the volume he needs to pay Bear full-time what he's worth." Rita grimaced. "Bear hates pulling night guard, but it's the only thing he can get right now. And you know how dependable he is. Eagle Operations called him to come work and he couldn't say no."

Elinor saw a flicker of pain in Drew's eyes. He hid it quickly.

"You guys are okay, though, right? You know, all you have to do is say the word—"

Rita smiled and put up her hands. "No, no. We don't need your cash. We just need you. We're fine, really."

Bells rang in the kitchen. Elinor jumped a bit but was pleased that she knew the bells belonged to the machine called a telephone, which allowed people to speak to one another over long distances. Rita went to answer its summons.

"It's raining pretty hard out there," Drew said. "But we can make it home if you don't mind getting wet."

"I'm used to rain. I shan't melt."

"Okay, we'll—"

He broke off as Rita returned.

"Guys, I've got a really big favor to ask."

Getting Jennie to bed was easy, Drew thought to himself grimly. All Elinor had to do was talk dolls, tell

197

her a story and tuck her in. The twins were another matter altogether.

He'd never realized how much they looked alike when they were buck-naked, dripping wet and on the run. He'd never known kids were so slippery. He now knew why Bear and Rita sometimes just resorted to shouting *Hey you* at them, rather than try to sort out which twin was climbing the shower curtain and which was finger-painting with the toothpaste.

And how the hell had they gotten hold of the vacuum cleaner, let alone hauled it all the way up to the top bunk?

He emerged from their bedroom damp, weary and frazzled. Elinor was sitting in the front room, demurely sipping a glass of wine. He glowered at her as he sank onto the couch.

"It's late. They've been playing all day. Why aren't they tired?"

She started to grin. He raised a brow at her. She ducked her head and poured him a glass of wine.

"They are excited that you are with them," she said in soothing tones. "You're someone new. Children will test a new guardian."

"Yeah, well, they tested me and I flunked. I have a whole new appreciation of Bear and Rita."

Outside, the wind was now at a frenzy, lashing the bushes and trees, while the rain drove across the yard in sheets. Drew found wood under a tarp on the back deck and laid a fire in the fireplace. No sooner had it built to a nice flame than the lights went out. He heard the loud clack from the answering machine in the kitchen. A quick check of the fuse box and a peek out at the surrounding neighborhood soon proved that the whole area was without power.

He located an extra flashlight for Elinor, but she'd already lit candles and was gathering extra blankets to lay over the sleeping children. He joined her in Tuck and Cubbie's room. Both boys were sleeping half out of their bunks.

"Saints," Elinor murmured as they slid them back into place and covered them up. "These children sleep like lobsters."

"How's Jennie?" he whispered.

"She's well, I think. She's restless in her bed and was sleeping with no bedclothes. Perhaps she sleeps like her brothers, ever in motion."

They returned to the front room and sat once more in the glow of the fire. The house was growing chilly, Drew noted, now that the power outage had halted the electric baseboards that heated the house.

"You should see if Rita has another sweater or something you could put on," he told her.

"I am well," she said, sliding down to be nearer the fire. "I'm accustomed to rooms much colder."

He slid off the couch and joined her, bringing their wine with him. "Might as well finish this off. It looks like we're in for a long night."

"What is a pile-up?"

He poked at the fire. "It's a bad accident. Several cars—in this case, ten—all run into each other at the same time. Lots of people get hurt. That's why Rita got called to the hospital on her night off."

"God save us," she murmured. "Such a terrible thing."

"Yes. Accidents often occur on nights like this, and a power loss makes it worse."

"I should never have thought it so until tonight, but despite all your wonders, you can still be rendered helpless."

"True. We're kind of spoiled." He set down his wine. "Elinor, I owe you an apology."

"I, Sir Drew?"

"On the pier the other day. In San Francisco. I had no right to call you a liar. I'm sorry."

She gazed at him for a long moment, her face shad-

199

owed in the dim light. "I forgive you. I have burdened you overmuch with my presence and my problems."

"That's not it—"

"Daddy?"

Jennie stood in the doorway, rubbing her eyes with her fists. Elinor was on her feet in a flash.

"Your father is at work, sweeting," she said softly. "Your mama as well. It's Drew and Elinor with you."

"Daddy, there's porkchops in the hall closet."

"Is she sleep-walking?" Drew whispered, getting up.

Elinor placed a hand on the little girl's forehead, then kissed her there.

"She's feverish." She took Jennie by the hand and led her toward the kitchen. "Come, wee one, let's have a drink of cool water."

Jennie went with her, sniffling. "I'm really hot, Daddy. Can't we have the air conditioning on?"

"Sure, hon," Drew said, following. "You're sick. It'll be cooler after you have a nice drink and get some aspirin."

"Tylenol, Daddy. Mommy says kids gotta have that."

"Do you know what that is?" Elinor asked from the sink.

"Yeah. Acetaminophen. It'll take her fever down. I'll go look for it."

By the time he returned with the bottle and an extra candle, Jennie was seated on the floor with Elinor's arms around her. The water glass was spilled on the floor.

"She can't breathe," Elinor said, her voice soft but edged with alarm.

"She's had asthma, I think. A couple of years ago. If she's got a chest cold, that could be setting it off."

Jennie was wheezing where she sat.

He spun around and raced for the bathroom again, this time almost colliding with Tuck. He grabbed up the little boy.

"Jennie's having trouble breathing, pal. Do you know

where your mom keeps her breathing medicine?"

"Nebs," he said, pointing to the hall closet. "You gotta use the neb machine."

"Show me."

It was useless, he saw as soon as he found it. Even if he knew what medication went into it, it ran on electricity and there was still no power. Tuck couldn't think of anything else Jennie could use, and Jennie, between gasps, could add nothing, either.

"Call Mommy," Cubbie said, joining them. "She's a nurse."

"Can't. Phone's out." Tuck looked at Drew. "Right?"

"Right." Drew squatted down by Elinor. "I'm going to have to go out. I'll find someone with a cell phone or get the paramedics myself. Can you handle things here? I won't be long."

"I shall be fine. But for Jennie's sake, do hurry."

"I'm on my way."

"Godspeed."

It was taking too long.

Elinor had sent the twins back to their beds, bathed Jennie with cool cloths and made her comfortable before the fire, but the little girl's breathing was growing more labored. She seemed to rally now and then, only to cough and lapse once more into the hoarse struggle for air. There had to be a way to help her breathe more freely.

There was still no power. The talking-phone did not work. And Drew hadn't returned.

She tucked blankets in around Jennie and added another log to the fire. As she was gazing at the flames, she tried not to think of pile-ups. Drew would come back. He had to—

She knew what to do.

She shot up off the hearth and raced for the kitchen. Moments later, she was lugging the largest pot she could find. Water sloshed over its sides onto the carpet, but she managed to get it to the hearth. With the fire-irons, she made a space on the grate that held the logs and carefully lifted the pot into the flames.

That done, she whirled up and out the front door. It took a maddeningly long time, it seemed, to locate the plants she was looking for in the dark, with only the flickering stick-lantern to guide her. Yet she knew she had seen them earlier that day, near the front of the house. She set the lantern down and began grabbing handfuls of wet greenery.

Chapter Fourteen

"I never imagined I'd be so glad we're lazy weeders," Rita said, rocking Jennie in her lap. "Or that this man here drives like a fool on fire."

"You drove like a madman?" Elinor glared at Drew. "You could have been piled up! Then where would we be?"

He shrugged and grinned, his arm draped over Bear's broad shoulders. Both men were bleary-eyed and unkempt. Drew's trousers were drying into a solid mud-cake and a growth of blond beard stippled his cheeks.

Elinor couldn't be angry with him. When he'd returned at last, in the still-driving storm, he'd brought with him cars with many lights, white-coated physicians with medicine to aid Jennie, and, blessedly, the little girl's frantic parents. Jennie had been so cheered by the sight of her father and mother that Elinor's eyes had gone starry with tears.

"We owe you both," Bear said. "Especially you, Elinor. The paramedics said if you hadn't gotten her to breathe that herbal mist, she might have . . ." He broke off and looked away.

"Nay," Elinor said. "Nay, Sir Bear. Not your fair Jennie. The real help came with you."

"And our man Ingraham," said Rita warmly, nodding at Drew.

"Aye."

"Mom, I'm hungry," came a voice from under the makeshift tent by the hearth.

"I hear ya, Cub," said Bear. "Come on, Ingraham. Let's go do some damage in the kitchen."

"I think we'd best be moving on, pal."

"Hey, what's the matter? Afraid we'll ask you to babysit for us again tonight?"

"I don't think I'll answer that. But Elinor looks done in. This is not good for Anglo-U.S. relations."

Elinor smiled. "I am weary. Forgive me."

"Just in case you're wondering," Drew said to Bear as they mounted up on his bike. "Jennie told us last night there were porkchops in your hall closet. You might want to check it out."

"I'll do that. Elinor, anytime you want to come and pull up my front lawn, you head right on over."

Elinor chuckled and patted the big hand that clasped hers. "I'll remember that, Sir Bear."

Back at Drew's, Elinor went straight in and started a hot bath in the bathing chamber. She laid out towels and soaps, brushes and combs, along with clean clothes from Drew's wardrobe.

"Go," she said, shooing him along the hall. "You have been out in the cold and the rain. I don't want to have to go out and pull up herbs to care for you."

"You're pretty pushy for a Brit."

"Leave my country out of it. Go you and scrub the land off your own person."

He turned and gave her a long, lazy look. "You're not

exactly a dewdrop yourself, princess. Why aren't you taking a bath?"

She raised an eyebrow. "Sirrah, you do forget yourself."

His departing laugh was wicked. She went to change her clothes, smiling. When he emerged, she had breakfast prepared and he'd refilled the tub for her.

By the time she'd finished her bath, he was sound asleep in the front room. She pulled a blanket from the bed and covered him, almost staggering with her own weariness.

He reached up and pulled her down to him. Her soft shriek of surprise was cut off by his lips meeting hers, warm and searching and perfectly inviting. She struggled against his arm for an instant, but his hold on her was of iron, pinning her against his chest. The warmth of his body seeped into her skin through the shirt she wore. She surrendered and accepted the pleasure of his kiss.

"Mmm," he murmured at long last. "So sweet. 'Night, princess."

She hardly breathed, sure that this was some trick. She shook him gently. He was asleep.

Crawling out from under his arm, she went to her own rest, smiling, bearing the heat of his lips and his body with her into her dreams.

"You must be into some serious stuff," the youth said as he wrapped Roger's parcel. "We don't get many people in asking for mandrake root. I keep trying to tell my ladies who come in that it's a wicked aphrodisiac, but, well, you know chicks."

Roger took the package.

"I do indeed," he drawled. He tapped his chin with one long finger. "Tell me, have you seen aught of a lass with a necklace like this one? A comely wench, flaxen-haired?" He held up the medallion that hung over the front of his cashmere sweater.

The young man squinted, then shook his head, one greasy lock of hair falling over his spotty forehead.

"No, I'd remember a chick wearing that big a chunk of gold. But wait a minute—I did have one in here who talked like you. A real babe. Wanted stuff on time-travel." He grimaced. "Kind of frigid, though. Totally ignored me."

"Did she really?" Roger clucked softly. "Unimaginable. Yet she could be the female I seek. Is there more you can tell me? Whence she came? Was she alone?"

"You talk so cool. She did, too, like I said. She was definitely alone, 'cause I never would've tried to hit on her if she was with a guy. But that's all I know. She just came in, didn't buy anything, went back out again. Stepped on my foot like I'd offended her or something. Chicks, man."

"Chicks indeed," said Roger, resisting the urge to step on the fool's foot himself. He wasn't surprised that Elinor had done so—such egregious young hounds were intolerable. No wonder the women of this time were so bewildered about their femininity and so grateful when a true gentleman came along.

His quarry was near, he could feel it. Visiting the bridge hadn't gained him the other half of the medallion, but it had convinced him that the bridge itself was of the same era as he and Elinor, however difficult that was to fathom. Elinor had been on the bridge, the medallion about her neck, when he'd crossed over. The spell he'd invoked must have carried them both to this time and place, by simple virtue of their proximity.

One thing nagged at him, aside from the fact that he hadn't yet laid hands on Elinor, and that was, ironically, the matter of time. He'd never before remained so long in any other time than his own. Moreover, on those other occasions, he'd always had the full medallion with him and no traveling companions; Elinor's journey with him had been an accident. Like many

other spells and charms, this one could well dissolve
or terminate itself after a certain length of time.

He could be running out of time. But then, so was
Elinor. They both would be trapped in this far century,
on this strange shore.

He nodded and bowed to an elderly woman in lime-
green trousers. She beamed upon him as she passed.
It was good to know that his charms worked in any age
or clime he chose.

At least, on most. Elinor DeCourtenay had not been
so enamored of his ways, despite the fact that she'd
pledged to bed him for a night. Even after being plied
with wine liberally laced with potent herbs, she'd
balked.

He shrugged and pulled a shining key from his
pocket. He was acquiring greater skill in operating the
roaring machines that carried people everywhere in
this land. Two days of instruction was all it had taken,
though he still preferred the sensation of a live horse
beneath him. He got into the Jaguar, as the clerk in the
rental shop had called it, and set out onto the road,
taking care to follow the lines painted on the roadway.

Elinor was here. She'd been the one at that odd fair,
sitting on a hay bale, clutching a leather surcote. She
was here and she had his medallion.

All that remained was to find her. And while that had
proved to be more difficult than he had first imagined,
he knew he was closing the net about her even now.
She'd been in this village, in these shops. While he'd
gone east from the bridge, it seemed she'd gone west.

Guerneville, Rio Nido, Forestville. He zipped past
the little towns with their quaint names, headed back
to Santa Rosa. Perhaps he'd take up residence in one
of the rustic inns along the river. Wherever he chose,
on the morrow he'd begin his search in earnest.

Tonight, he had other matters to attend. Time limits
or no, he wasn't about to give up his pleasures.

He returned to his hotel, where a shower and a

change of clothes refreshed him and a glass of wine took the edge off his irritation at the delays he'd met in finding Elinor. Then the Jaguar bore him away again, into the town.

"You're right on time," the brunette purred at him as he stepped from the car and took her arm.

"I should never dream of keeping a woman like you waiting. Shall we go in?"

"Mmm, yes. I hope you're hungry. This is the best restaurant north of San Francisco. You must know somebody big to get a reservation for tonight."

"Just took a bit of magic. And, my dear lady . . ." His eyes swept over the tight little red gown she wore, a gown that he hoped would come off more easily than it appeared to have gone on. "My appetite is growing by the moment."

Her eyes glinted with amusement at his suggestion. "Is it? Well, we'll have to see what we can do to . . . satisfy you."

The restaurant, as she'd called it, was pleasantly dim and their corner table conducive to intimacy. Roger smiled at his companion over the rim of his wineglass. Women of this time were so amiable, he thought. What wouldn't they do for a bite of supper and a bottle of wine?

They'd do far more than Elinor DeCourtenay, he recalled with bitterness. Indeed, he thought, feeling the brunette's hand slide across his thigh beneath the table, this one with him tonight probably wouldn't even need the aid of his helpful herbs. And if she balked at some of his more . . . interesting requests, well, it was no difficult matter to convince her of the wisdom of indulging his little pleasures.

He ripped the loaf of fresh, crusty bread in half.

No, it would be no problem convincing her. One way or another.

*　　*　　*

The phone roused Drew. He stumbled off the couch and caught it on the fourth ring.

"Yeah?"

"Mr. Ingraham?"

"You got him." He scrubbed at his face, squinting at the clock. Four-thirty? How the—

"This is Sergent Coombs of the Santa Rosa Police Department. Missing Persons. We spoke the other day?"

"Oh. Oh, yeah. I'm sorry, I was just—never mind. Did you find anything on Elinor DeCourtenay?"

"I'm afraid not. I checked national and international, and that name doesn't come up anywhere."

"Anyone fitting the description I gave you?"

"Now, that was a yes. One in Oklahoma, one in Alaska. The FBI are looking into both."

"FBI?"

"Yes, sir." There was a pause. "Whenever there's an MP report that goes unsolved for a certain length of time, it's automatically handed over to them."

Drew had to say it. "Because of the suspicion of foul play?"

"That. And the possibility of fraudulence."

"I see." He pulled up a chair and sat down. "And have you handed this matter over to them yet?"

"Do you want us to?"

Drew sighed. "Yes. No. No," he said more decisively. "That is, if we can avoid it?"

"Time is running out, Mr. Ingraham."

"Look, I don't think this is a case of fraud. This lady is genuinely lost. If we can find her family or some friends and do it discreetly, we'll save her a lot of embarrassment." He straightened in the chair. "Tell you what. There is one name she remembers. Roger Aston. Can you run a check on him?"

"Sir, you might be better served by a private party."

"You know any PIs in this area who have international connections? This is just going to come back to your desk, I'm afraid, Sergeant. And, as you said, time is running out."

There was a heavy sigh on the other end. "All right. I can look into the name. Spelling?"

After Drew hung up, he sat by the phone, staring out the kitchen window. He'd said it. He'd said he believed she was just lost. But was that really what he felt?

Elinor came in. "I heard the phone bell ring. What time is it?" She squinted out the window. "Nearly sunset?"

"We slept the day away."

"Such sloth," she said with a yawn. "Mother Agnes would be most displeased." She glanced up at him, then looked quickly away. "I beg your pardon. I know that you do not like me to speak of my . . . past."

"No, it's all right. Maybe talking about it will help you . . . remember something. Something that we can use to help you get home."

She shook her head. "Nay. I have thought and thought till my brain is a-weary. Have you eaten?"

"No." She was changing the subject. "Is Mother Agnes the one you wanted the consulate's secretary to call?"

"Aye. But that gained us nothing." She rose and went to the pantry. "May I have some of this bread, Sir Drew?"

"It's just Drew, remember?" he said, his irritation rising. "And you don't have to ask. Just help yourself."

He watched her pad about the kitchen in her stocking feet, her long golden braid swaying and brushing over her hips as she moved. He'd been impressed with her calmness and her skill in the storm last night. She'd proven she wasn't just a somewhat goofy misfit, utterly out of touch with reality. She had acted coolly in a bad situation and she had, very possibly, saved little Jennie's life.

But did she have to be so damnably lovely? And lovable? She was exotic, yet as cozy as a homemade quilt.

Odd, yet as desirable as any Playmate of the Month.

And as maddening as a . . . as a . . .

Woman.

He glowered, feeling his body warming to his thoughts. He wanted her with an aching need that surpassed anything he'd felt in a long, long time. It wasn't just deprivation, though that was a factor he freely acknowledged. He wanted Elinor herself, for herself, not just any body, willing or unwilling. He wanted to have that golden braid in his hands, wanted to wrap it about his wrist and pull her gently to him, binding her in his arms. He wanted those hips against his, wanted those long—

"Eggs, Sir Drew?"

He jumped. "No. Yes. Yes, and don't call me Sir. It's Drew. That's all."

She looked puzzled at the annoyance in his tone. "Very well. Drew. I shall cook eggs for us both."

"Thanks." He rose. "I've got to . . . got to see if the garage is okay."

"Oh-kay."

He went outside, wincing as pine needles and small rocks dug into his bare feet. It took some of the fire out of his libido, he noted grimly, though it didn't extinguish it by a long shot.

He clamped down hard on his desires. He still didn't know enough about her. Even if she was lost, he didn't know if he could trust her. Trust was all-important, he reminded himself.

He'd trusted LeeAnne. Given himself to her heart, body and soul. He'd rushed her into marrying him and never bothered to learn more about her than the fact that she was beautiful, adoring and utterly desirable. She'd had a hold on him so strong that by the time he learned the truth about her, it was too late to do more than hang his head in humiliation.

No, he wasn't going to be a fool twice. His body could scream at him all it wanted. He wasn't going to bed

Elinor DeCourtenay. At least, not until he knew who she was and why she was here.

He recalled kissing her last night, just before he fell asleep. He'd wanted to wake up and gather her in, hold her through the day and night. And much, much more.

He prayed fervently for solid information. Soon.

To his surprise, it came sooner than he could have hoped.

Elinor was in the front room, drawing, when the phone rang later that evening. Drew picked up the kitchen phone.

"Ingraham? It's Will."

"Doc, good to hear from you—"

"Sorry, but I don't have much time. I'm on my cellular and the battery's running low. I think I spotted your man here in Santa Rosa. The guy you think is involved with Elinor."

"Where are you?"

"I'm at La Belle Vie. He's here, having dinner with a woman. I'm about two tables over. They seem to be very good friends, if you know what I mean. I walked past his table a couple of times, trying to catch the accent, and you were right, it's the same as Elinor's."

Small comfort, Drew thought.

"Thing is," Will continued, "they're on dessert now and from the looks of things, they're not going to linger over cognac afterward. I can follow him, but I'm here with a date myself."

"It's okay, pal. I know where he lives."

"I know this is going to net me big scoffs, but I've got a gut feeling about this guy, now that I've seen him."

"I won't tell the shrinks' union. What's your hunch?"

"Be afraid, Ingraham. My shrink radar is detecting crazy coming off this guy in waves. Don't trifle with him."

Drew's fist tightened on the phone. He didn't know whether to be relieved or outraged. One thing he didn't feel: surprised.

"Ingraham? My signal's starting to go."

"Thanks, Doc. Don't do anything with Aston. I've got it covered."

"Okay. Just remember what I said. I know from crazy."

"I hear you."

After he hung up, Drew leaned against the kitchen wall. His first impulse was to hop on his bike and collect Aston from La Belle Vie himself. His second urge was to storm into the front room and shake Elinor until she told him everything.

Good sense intervened at the last second. Aston had probably left the restaurant already—Drew had no hope of catching up with him tonight. As for shaking Elinor, he knew it would only earn him her fear and anger.

It was his fear for her that was gnawing at him now. However, for the first time, he had an ally. Will had seen, and he believed.

Elinor had clammed up on him often enough. It was time to take a new tack.

Crazy or not, it was time for Roger Aston to do some talking.

On the second day after the storm, Drew summoned Elinor to speak on the talking phone. She was pleased to hear Rita's warm voice issuing forth from the box, and not the worrisome Whoops person. Rita invited her to come shopping with her.

"Thank you, it is a most generous invitation," Elinor replied. "But I have not the money to buy things."

"Well, I need some way to show my gratitude for what you did the other night, and I won't take no for an answer. Is there something special you need or something I can do for you?"

"I—I should like to visit the library in the village."

"That I can do. Jennie's been doing just fine and she has soccer practice tomorrow right after school. What do you say I pick you up and take you to the library, then when soccer's over, I'll swing by the library again. You can even use my card."

"I would be most obliged. At what hour shall I be ready?"

"I'll be there at a quarter to three, okay?"

"I shall be ready."

Elinor handed the speaking device to Drew, who placed it back on its box.

"I shall be going into the village with Rita on the morrow," she told him. "Will that be oh-kay with you?"

"Sure. I have some stuff to do in Santa Rosa, so I'll be out most of the day anyway. I'm glad you'll have something to do."

Over the past two days, Elinor had gone back and forth in her mind, arguing over the significance of Drew's kisses. Her heart, her body, urged her to hold on to the dreams that were building within her. But her reasoning was more persuasive. She could be a friend to Drew, but to hope for anything more was folly. He had won the love of his life, a love without equal, according to his close friends. He was not looking for another.

She must accept this and go on with her search for a way home. If she lingered—well, she didn't want to think of the pain that could ensue.

The following afternoon, Rita drove up to the house and Elinor had her first car ride. At least, that was what Tuck and Cubbie called the trip in the little red vehicle.

Jennie joined them, and they proceeded into town. In front of the library, Rita showed Elinor how to lift the smooth metal latch on the car door and how to release the lock on the harness across her lap and chest. Feeling younger than Cubbie and Tuck, who sat grinning and waving, Elinor managed to step out of the car and shut the door, swinging her hair well back out of the way.

Rita leaned over and spoke out of the window. "Pick

you up right here in two hours, 'kay? If I'm a little late, don't freak—Jennie's practices sometimes run over."

"Oh-kay."

Elinor watched the car as it chugged away, leaving a small puff of gray smoke in its wake. Drew had such good friends, she thought. It was difficult to believe that he would have chosen to shun them for so long. Doubtless, their faces brought up too many memories of all he'd lost when his LeeAnne had died.

She turned and looked up the street to Louis Feldon's shop. Now wasn't the time to stop and ponder. She had a vow to fulfill.

"Ah, the lovely *meydele* with the sun medallion," Louis said with a broad, welcoming smile. "So, did you get something to eat, miss?"

She returned his smile. "Aye. I did, thank you, sir."

"And you wish to know more about your necklace, *ja*?"

"Aye. How did you know this?"

He placed his hands upon his display table.

"It's not every day a pretty girl comes into my shop alone. Even more unusual she should have around her neck a rare piece of jewelry and know so little about it." He lifted a finger to his forehead. "So, I'm thinking. This pretty *meydele*, she had such a look of wonder on her face when I told her about it. And she's not the type that lets a matter drop"—he plunked his hand on the tabletop—"like that. She's curious, I'm thinking. She'll be back." He raised his hands, stretching them toward her. "And here you are."

Elinor shook her head in amazement. "Astonishing," she said. "And can you also foretell the future, sir?"

"You mean like those *meshuga* psychic-hot-line people?" His mouth turned down as if he tasted something sour. "Not me. But I can tell you this: When you've lived as long as I have and you've seen as much, then, well, it's not so difficult to see things coming." He clapped his hands together and rubbed them, eyes bright. "Now, let me tell you something about the past."

Elinor felt a shiver pass over her arms and neck. "The past?"

"Listen. Look."

He bent down and pulled a large, slender book from under the display table. Beckoning Elinor closer, he opened it up on the tabletop and paged through it. He paused at a page where a small sketch had been drawn alongside the close, neat lettering. He donned a pair of spectacles to study the entry.

"*Ja,*" he said, trailing a fingertip over the letters. "*Ja.* This is what I found. Here." He slid the book around until it faced Elinor. "There."

She bent to read:

Similar to the half-crown betrothal pieces of the Eighteenth and early Nineteenth centuries, sectional medallions such as the item shown in Figure 23a led to the design and crafting of many intricate and unique pieces in the early Twentieth century. The main body of the piece would represent perhaps a hand with a heart held in the palm. The heart would be so constructed as to detach from the hand leaving both parts to be worn separately. Though medieval in origin, such medallions did not gain great popularity prior to the Renaissance but in the early 1900s, brooches of this type were especially favored by such artisans as Tiffany, Cartier, and Grushkov. Sectional medallions figure prominently in a few major collections throughout the world, though valued more for their rarity and their interesting, sometimes whimsical nature than for either craftsmanship or use of precious materials. See also: Brooches, Coins, Talismans.

She studied the small drawing. It was indeed a hand, with a perfect heart cradled in the palm. An arrow had been drawn to the edge of the heart, indicating where the smaller section lifted away from the palm to become a separate piece. It wasn't much like her medallion in form, but the idea was the same.

She looked at the jeweler. "You believe that my necklace is such a one as this?"

"Could there be much doubt?"

She shook her head. "I suppose not. Would such a piece be made in England?"

"In my opinion, *ja*. The one I saw as a boy was in Austria. It might have been made anywhere in Europe. And the design was not Indian or Asian, of that I'm sure. What I would wonder is not where, but when your necklace was made."

"When?" Elinor wanted to laugh, though not from mirth. "When" was the most important question on her mind these days.

"*Ja*. If this was made in the 1800s or the twentieth century, it might be of some value. However"—he reached over and closed the book with a flourish—"if this is when it was made, then you got yourself something very different."

Elinor followed the heavy gold lettering on the front of the book: *European Gems and Jewelry of the High Middle Ages: A Collector's Introduction*. She looked up at the man, puzzled.

"The Middle Ages," he said, gesturing at the book, then at her medallion. "If your piece was made in, say, 1300 to 1500, it's not only rare, it's very old. Not many pieces with that much gold in them survived over the centuries, at least not in their original form. Most of them were lost or buried or stolen by looting soldiers. Or tax collectors. Pieces got melted down, too, you know, and made into other things that were more fashionable for the times."

Elinor took a step back. The year 1300, she thought.

217

Or 1400, perhaps? If what the jeweler thought was
true, then she wasn't quite as mad as she'd feared. She
was holding a piece of jewelry from her own time.
Something that might firmly establish, at least in her
own mind—perhaps in Drew's—that she had come
ahead, across centuries, to this time called the twentieth century.

But how?

She looked up at the man who stood before her, so
bright-eyed and interested. Kindness showed in the
lines that edged his eyes, she felt, and there was an air
of wisdom about him that said he'd been through
many struggles and joys in his life. Did she dare share
with him the wild ideas that were the only logical explanation for her confusing presence in this place?

"So? You want to know more?"

She started, wondering if she'd spoken aloud. He
was looking at her, nodding and pointing to the book.

"You want to know more?" he repeated.

"Aye."

He turned the book back around toward himself and
began flipping through the pages once again. He
stopped, ran a finger down a page, then flipped it over
and ran it down the following page.

"*Ja, ja,*" he muttered to himself. "*Ja*—aha! Here you
are, miss."

Elinor took the book again and read. By the time she
had finished deciphering the odd spellings and the curious, rigidly uniform letters, she knew she had been
right in coming back here today.

"Magic?" she asked softly. "This might be magic?"

She touched the rounded center of her necklace. It
was the very question she hadn't dared ask.

He raised his hands, palms out. "I know, I know.
You're thinking, the old fellow's a touch senile. A little
light in the head." He knocked on his balding pate. "I'm
not saying you should believe this, what is written
there. I just thought—"

218

"Nay," she said softly. "I do not think you are in your dotage." She cleared her throat, which had suddenly filled with incipient tears. "I—I cannot thank you enough. I was afraid to say it myself."

"Here, here," he said, leaning over and peering up into her down-turned face. "You don't owe me a thing, Miss—Miss—?"

"DeCourtenay," she said automatically. "I am the La—." She stopped herself. Drew had told her that inherited titles were not used here. "Elinor DeCourtenay."

"Louis Feldon," he said, extending his hand across the counter. "Pleased to make your acquaintance, Ms. DeCourtenay."

Elinor shook his hand, unable to resist the charming smile he bestowed upon her. "And I yours," she said, then wiped at her eyes.

"Elinor DeCourtenay, would you do me the honor of stepping out with me for a cup of coffee, maybe a Danish?" He grinned. "My treat."

"I—I should be delighted, sir."

"No, no. None of that sir anymore. I appreciate anyone under the age of fifty who still knows how to speak to a person decently, but from such a nice *meydele* as Elinor DeCourtenay, I'd much rather she'd call me Louis."

"Louis."

"Much better!"

She waited as he put away several items on the countertop and went through the process of securing his shop. On the way out, he caught hold of a mirror and held it up. He made a great show of separating and smoothing each of the two or three strands of hair left on top of his head. He turned to her with a grin.

"There," he announced. "Now I look fit to be seen with a lovely young woman."

She laughed softly as he gathered up some books

and led the way outside. He offered her his free arm with a courtly bow, and she took it.

He walked her forward about five paces, then stopped and bowed toward the shop next door to his own.

"Here we are, Elinor DeCourtenay. Max's Deli, where the coffee is reheated fresh every morning."

She wasn't sure she caught the meaning in this, but she surmised, from the twinkle in his eyes and the half-merry, half-insulting manner in which he greeted Max himself, that it was meant to be a joke.

He shooed her onto a bench by a small table while he fetched two steaming cups for them. On his way to their table, he scooped up two pastries from the tray on the display shelf and waved them at Max, who grunted and lifted his chin in acknowledgment. He pushed a cup and a pastry toward her and began ladling sugar into his own cup.

"A sweet tooth I have," he said pointing at the sugar dish. "My Molly used to say I wasn't going to have a tooth left but the sweet one, but, eh, life's too short to worry over a bit of coffee and pastry. Certainly it's too short to do without."

He slid the books toward her on the table.

"Here, look at this one on top. I got it from one of those *narishe* shops down the street where they sell weeds and rocks to the tourists. Still, it was written by a rabbi, so maybe it's not too crazy. Just the facts, ma'am, that's what I like to read."

She sipped her coffee—which seemed delicious to her unsophisticated palate—and turned the book around to read its title: *The Symbolism of the Kabbalah*. There was other lettering beneath it, a script she recognized but could not read. She half rose from her seat, her eyes wide.

"This isn't, it cannot be . . ." she stammered. "Oh. You said rabbi."

"*Ja, ja,*" Louis said, waving his pastry. "Like I said, it

220

may all be hooey. But I think if you'll look at—"

Elinor almost knocked over the coffee in her haste to rise. "You,—" she squeaked. "You're a Jew!"

She saw Louis's bright eyes suddenly flare. Fury crossed his seamed face for but an instant, then was replaced with a dignity that was as cold as it was polite.

"I am a Jew, *ja*," he said quietly. "Is this a problem for you, Elinor?"

She was lost again in this strange world. A Jew! With his own shop in the high street like ordinary people! And here she was—she gasped as she heard the warning words of Mother Agnes in her head—breaking bread with one.

She backed away from the table, still horrified and bewildered.

"But you wear no sign," she whispered. "No badge."

The flare lit Louis's eyes once more.

"No," he replied, setting down his coffee cup. His voice was soft. "No yellow circle. No yellow star. No pointy Jew's hat."

Elinor backed up another step. "I—I—"

She turned and bolted from the shop.

Chapter Fifteen

The sidewalk café was crowded with business people on their lunch breaks. Drew nodded to the maitre d' and pointed in the direction of a corner table underneath a bright Cinzano umbrella. As he wove his way through the maze of tables and scurrying waiters, he noted that his luncheon companion sat alone, dark glasses protecting his face from the midday glare.

The restaurant on Railroad Square in downtown Santa Rosa had been Drew's choice. Few meeting places could be more public, which was a safety feature he felt was necessary.

He ducked beneath the umbrella's rim and slid into his seat. Lifting off his own sunglasses, he gave his companion a cool stare.

"Lord Lewes," Drew began.

"Aye. And you would be . . . ?"

"My name isn't important."

"Very well. I doubt that it matters." Roger Aston sat back in his chair, tapping the edge of the menu against

222

his cheek. "Your message at my inn said you might have something of interest to me."

"That's right."

"Something or someone?"

"You were right the first time."

"Ah. And what might this something be?"

Lifting his own menu, Drew scanned its contents. "I think you know. You don't strike me as a man who's careless with his possessions."

"You are correct. And if you know that, you must also know that I don't suffer fools gladly."

"If you thought I was a fool, you wouldn't be here."

"Perhaps. But be warned. It would be foolish indeed to cross me."

Drew set his menu down. "Let's cut the posturing, shall we, Aston? Why don't you tell me what it is you think I have of yours?"

"It is a bauble. Of little consequence above sentiment. It would gain you little, even for the weight of its gold."

"I see. Something your old granny gave you."

"Something of that sort." Roger motioned to the waiter. "And now that you know what it is, I wish to have it back."

The waiter made his way through the crush to their table and took their orders for drinks. Drew waited until the young man had gone before he spoke.

"Since we're both agreed that neither one of us is a fool, let's cut to the chase." He slouched more comfortably into his chair. "How much would you give to get your granny's necklace back?"

"How do I know you have it?"

The guy didn't miss a trick, Drew thought. Reaching into his breast pocket, he pulled out a rough sketch he'd made of the medallion.

Aston studied the drawing with casual interest. He let it fall lightly to the tabletop.

"It looks very like the one I seek."

"I thought so. And I don't think there's a whole lot of duplicates out there." Drew refolded the paper. "So? What's your offer?"

Aston leaned forward. "Let us have it appraised, shall we? We can go now, to a place of your choosing. I shall abide by whatever price your goldsmith may name."

"My goldsmith advised me not to sell."

"A hard man and shrewd." Aston sat back as the waiter set down their drinks.

Drew contemplated his next gambit. He needed more information. Clearly, Aston was eager to have the medallion back in his possession and he was not in any way the sentimental type. The necklace had real value, but Drew was certain its worth didn't lie in the market price of gold. If it had, Aston wouldn't have offered to take it in to be appraised. There was something more.

"If we did go to a jeweler for an appraisal or even to a pawnbroker, they'd check to see if the piece was hot."

"Hot?" Aston raised an eyebrow over the rim of his drink.

"Stolen. And they'd check both the domestic and foreign sources."

Aston spread his hands. "I have nothing to hide. Indeed, sir, if anyone may be accused of being in possession of someone else's goods, it would be you."

"So this is a legitimate piece?"

Aston set down his drink. His eyes, already chilly, became positively frigid.

"Why don't you tell me what it is you really want?" he asked, his voice low but sharp-edged. "I've been more than patient with you. If you do not wish to sell this thing back to me, its rightful owner, then perhaps I would do well to summon a constable or a magistrate and demand it back."

"You could do that, but I think you'd have a hard time convincing them of who you are and what you're doing in this country." Drew sipped his drink. "You might start with explaining whose driver's license you're using."

Color shot up into Aston's face while the knuckles around his drink went white. Still, his expression and tone didn't change.

"So. We understand one another quite well."

Drew met his gaze. Inside, his heart was beginning to thud. Aston was dangerous. That was plain. If Drew had any sense at all, he'd turn him in right now. But where would that leave Elinor? He still didn't know how she was tangled up with this joker, and until he knew, he didn't want to risk letting her get hung out to dry.

"I'm an amiable kind of a guy," Drew said, tilting back in his chair. "What do you say we cut ourselves a new deal?"

"Why don't you tell me how you came into possession of my necklace?"

Drew waved a hand. "Found it. Out on a country road. You must have dropped it."

"I see. I'm seldom careless."

Shrugging, Drew said, "Hey, there's a first time for everything. You want to make a deal or not?"

"Show me the piece."

"I wouldn't carry a chunk of gold that big around with me. Thieves and bad guys are everywhere, you know."

"You shan't have a ha'penny till I've seen it."

"Okay. I tell you what. I'll call you in a couple of days. We'll set up another meeting. Then I'll bring it and we'll talk deal."

Aston hesitated. Drew saw the wheels turning in the Englishman's head but he wasn't sure what direction they were headed in—deal or dirty deal.

"I am not accustomed to waiting upon the whims of others."

"Well, that's a shame, because I'm not, either. If you

want what I have, you're going to have to wait until I'm ready."

"Then you do not actually have possession of it."

"I didn't say that." Drew rose and laid some cash on the table for his drink. "Like I said, I'll call you. And don't worry," he said with a smile. "I'll give the waiter my tip on the way out."

He wound his way back through the chattering diners, slipping a bill onto their server's tray as he passed. A low, wrought-iron fence enclosed the restaurant patio. Roger leaned an elbow over it, toying with a flower from the vase on the table.

"Isn't it intriguing," he said as Drew strolled by, "how, out of all this world of people, you knew the medallion was mine?"

Drew shrugged. "No more intriguing than why a grown man would be so hot to get his hands on an old lady's necklace."

He gave a brief salute and walked on.

Elinor looked up and down the street, hoping to see Rita's car. There was no sign of it. She groaned softly and cast a brief backward glance at the food shop. She knew that Louis Feldon was sitting by the window but she didn't look there. She couldn't meet his eyes.

Her mind was whirling, heart beating fast. A Jew! She'd never met one before, though she'd heard about them. There had been none in the villages or towns near her home, and she'd always been told they were expected to keep to their special, walled-in quarters in the bigger towns. They were not tolerated among even the lowest company of Christian folk.

If she'd had any doubts that she was lost in a strange land, they were erased by this encounter. What manner of society would tolerate Jews among them, doing business, eating with them? She'd always heard that Jews were so arrogant that they wouldn't even eat the same foods as Christians.

Yet here was Louis Feldon. And she had never for one moment guessed his true identity.

She sighed and leaned back against the wall of the shop. He seemed so—so ordinary, she thought. No, not exactly ordinary. He'd been funny and kind. He'd been interested in her necklace and its history.

What was it Mother Agnes had said? Jews were always interested in money and gain, unlike Christians, who were, according to Mother Agnes, self-sacrificing in all things. The Jews had once been expelled from England, for the crimes of their usury. No wonder he'd been interested in her necklace!

Miserable and confused, she went into the library and wandered among the shelves. Richly illustrated tomes called out to her from all sides, but her delight in their wonders was spoiled by her confusion and sadness.

Rita and the children arrived and carried her away in the red car. Despite Rita's protests, Elinor asked to be let out at the entrance to Drew's drive, choosing to walk the short distance to the house through the soft, misting rain that had begun to fall.

She blew out a deep sigh as she made her way slowly beneath the overhanging dogwoods. She was coming to appreciate and enjoy this land of wonders and uni-magined comforts. Yet, what could one make of a world where one could not wring the neck of a sparrow for one's meat but that tolerated Jews in the midst of ordinary folk?

She was lost and she needed to go home. She'd been saying this to herself for days. The necklace might provide a clue as to how she could accomplish this, yet such knowledge was in the hands of Roger Aston, whom she could not find or abide, and Louis Feldman, a Jew, someone she'd been told she should not seek out or abide.

And for her efforts, should she succeed in solving the riddle of her travel through time and over land, should she arrive home at last, she would gain a life without Drew Ingraham, forever.

A sudden thought brought her up short. In a land where Jews wore no sign of their status, anyone might be a Jew. Anyone.

She was staring at the wall and stirring a pot of soup on the stovetop when Drew returned. He came through the door with a smile that wrapped her in honey-warmth. The thought came to her that she could simply stand about watching him all the long day.

"Good news," he said, doffing his jacket. "I got a breather valve for the lubrication system on the Knucklehead while I was in Santa Rosa. Almost mint condition, too." He slung the jacket over the back of a chair. "That's going to cut my time by a third, at least."

"That is good news," she said. "But didn't you say that you charged a certain price per hour for your labors? Why should you wish to reduce the time spent when it takes money from your own coffers?"

He shrugged. "I'm not in it for the money," he said, coming to sniff the soup. "Besides, that'd be gouging. I ask a fair price, I work as fast as I can to do a first-class job. The customer's happy, I'm happy. That's all I care about." He turned and headed out of the kitchen. "I'm going to go wash up. Then I'll come back and help. We need to talk."

Elinor considered his words carefully as the soup scorched. She caught the smell in time to lift the pot off the flame before it was actually burnt. Except for a bit on the bottom.

Drew wasn't interested in making money. That meant he was a good Christian, she concluded. Yet his friend Will was quite wealthy, and, from what she had gleaned from Drew, Lord Curran's prices were higher than a giant's topknot. Did that mean that Lord Curran was a gouger? Was he not a Christian as well?

Together they set the table. Drew poured wine while

Elinor sliced bread and cheese to go with the soup. He waved a slim package before her.

"And for dessert, Ghirardelli's chocolate," he said, grinning. "Finest kind, and I've never met a woman yet who could resist it."

"Indeed?" She raised an eyebrow.

"Don't get all ruffled up. Just because you're a nun, it doesn't mean you aren't a woman."

"I am not a nun. Yet."

"My point still stands. Wait till you try it, you'll see it's the best chocolate you've ever had."

She didn't tell him she had no notion what chock-let might be. More important matters demanded her attention. Still, it was gratifying that he'd noticed her womanhood. Some small imp did a jig of delight up and down her spine.

She struggled to contain her feelings. If she continued to respond to Drew's slightest remarks with such—such surges, leaving him would be a hideous trial. What was the phrase Jennie had taught her?

Get a grip.

They made small talk as they ate. The meal was delicious, they decided, and Drew gallantly declared that the smoked flavor of the soup actually improved the taste. It was all so pleasant—the wine, the meal, the peaceful hour spent at Drew's small, cozy table.

And then there was the chocolate.

When Drew tore the wrapping away, she was disappointed. All that lay inside was a flat slab of what looked like hard, shiny mud. The only outstanding features it could boast were regular lines dividing it into pieces and small bits of rock dotting its surface.

"I believe any woman might resist this," she murmured.

"O, ye of little faith. This is no ordinary chocolate."

He broke off a piece and held it under her nose. She took a sniff.

"It is sweet."

"Now taste."

She opened her mouth to accept the morsel on her tongue. For an instant, her lips closed around his fingertip. He drew it slowly away, leaving a tingling path over her lower lip.

Then the taste of the brown, rocky morsel flooded her mouth. She closed her eyes and softly moaned.

"See?" There was triumph and amusement in his voice. "I told you it was the finest kind."

She opened her eyes and her mouth. "It is nearly as wondrous as pizza."

"You got that right. So," he said, holding out another bit of chocolate for her to taste, "do you still say you can resist?"

She chewed, enjoying the added flavor of roasted hazelnuts amid the sweet. "Alas, sir, the men of your world have indeed discovered a formidable weapon against my sex."

"If only it were that simple."

"Thank heaven it is not."

"Yeah? Why?"

She was on the spot. "Well, if love were as simple as feeding another person a certain food, then I fear we all should take advantage of such a love potion."

"And you wouldn't like that?"

"Not all lovers are true."

He looked away. "Amen."

She rustled around in the package for another bite.

"Moreover," she added, chewing blissfully, "while the gift of chocolate may win a lover to your side once, were I a man I should fear that she loved my chocolate more than me."

He laughed, and she was relieved to see the haunted look fading from his eyes.

"You're probably right. It isn't any secret that while a guy might take a hike, a chocolate bar is always just around the corner."

"Or a pizza."

He placed his elbows on the table and leaned toward her. "Hey, pizza and chocolate. I must be making big points with you, eh?"

She lifted her napkin, dabbing primly at her lips. "If food be your champion, sir, beware lest indigestion be your prize."

"You sure talk swell, ma'am."

"You have got that right."

His laughter was like friendly thunder, shaking the dishes and cups. When it subsided, he gazed across the table at her. That light was there once more, the light that had come into his eyes when he'd looked at her in the water-soaked shirt. The light that had been there when he'd danced with her and kissed her on the pier. Its blue fire caught flame somewhere in her middle, warming her throughout.

"Ah, Elinor."

Her ears savored the sound of her name on his lips. "What?" she whispered.

"What am I going to do with you?"

She gazed down at her plate. "What do you wish to do?" The words were like smoke, sliding off her tongue, impossible to capture or retract.

She felt his gaze on her, hot and questioning. She couldn't look up.

"I just want . . ."

The pause stretched out, filled with unspoken wishes and wants.

"I guess I just want to help you."

She met his eyes. "You are a kind friend."

He cleared his throat, helped himself to some chocolate. "So, how was your trip to the library today?"

She accepted his change of subject, relieved that she hadn't been called upon to answer her own question.

"It went well. Rita explained to me about public libraries. What a marvelous notion, especially when so many of your citizens can read."

"Not as many as we'd like, but we're working on it.

231

We're not as literate as you over in England, but then there's a whole lot more of us. And a lot of the people around here come from other countries, so it's harder to reach everybody."

Elinor thought of Louis Feldon. He was from another country, wasn't he? Heat rose to her cheeks at the memory of their encounter this afternoon, though she wasn't sure why.

"Elinor, I need to talk—"

"I met a Jew today," she blurted out.

Drew looked at her, pausing over his wineglass for a moment.

"You did?" he asked, his voice bland. "Any particular Jew?"

"It was a man. In truth, I had met him before. But I did not know that he was a Jew until today."

"And?"

"Why do not your Jews wear an ensign of their race?"

Drew set his wine down slowly. His light blue eyes registered a multitude of emotions: shock, anger, disbelief, sorrow.

Elinor felt her stomach drop. What had she said now?

"Please tell me you're joking."

She shook her head, then raised her eyes to his, pleading for answers.

"God almighty," he muttered. He rose and paced to the other end of the kitchen.

"What is it? Pray, tell me what is wrong."

He gave a short, mirthless laugh. "Princess, there are so many things wrong with what you just asked me, I can't even begin to count them."

She couldn't help herself. "Are you a . . . are you . . . ?"

"The word is Jewish, princess. And what if I were?"

She stared down at her hands. "I don't know."

"Well, I guess that leaves room for hope." He paced back toward her. "First of all, they're not *my* Jews.

232

They're not anybody's Jews. They're people, just like you and me. Second, they don't wear any kind of ensign, as you put it, because they're people, just like you and me. I don't wear a badge, you don't wear a badge, they don't wear badges. And nobody can make them wear them. Third, they're not just a race, they're people, just . . . like . . . you . . . and . . . me."

He ran his hand over the back of his neck. "Damn, Elinor, you didn't say anything about ensigns or badges to this guy you met, did you?"

She felt the heat in her cheeks begin to flame. This matter was growing worse by the moment.

"I—I didn't know what to do," she said, speaking to her clenched hands. "I've never met a Jew before. And when I realized he'd touched me, given me food from his own hand, I—I had to . . ."

She wrung her hands together, then looked up at Drew, trying hard to make him understand. "I ran away. I didn't know what else to do," she repeated. "In my world it is not meet to associate with infidels."

"Infidels!" The word boomed into the air, causing the wineglasses and plates to rattle. This time, the sound was neither gentle nor friendly. "Are you for real?"

"It is the custom in my world. If I have—"

"Your world!" The sound exploded out of Drew once again. "Damn it, Elinor, I've been pretty tolerant of this bilge about Henry V and Mother Agnes and castles and cabbages and kings! But this is too much. Stop it now, do you hear me?"

He slammed his hands down on the table before her. "You can pretend to be a lady fair from Camelot all you want, but not in my house, do you get it? Because I don't care if you're from 1400 or 42 A.D. or the Paleozoic era. A bigot is still a bigot, anytime, anywhere!"

"But, Drew—"

He was at the back door in an instant, snatching up his jacket on the way. She leapt up to run after him but he raised his hand, palm out.

"Stay away," he said roughly. "Just stay away from me right now."

He slammed out the door and was gone, swallowed up by the darkness. She heard Harley start up and race away, its brilliant front lamp slicing a path through the night. The red lamp at its rump showed briefly, then winked out as the trees hid man and steed from her view.

She turned blindly to the kitchen, not seeing the plates and cups with the remains of their dinner, their lovely, friendly dinner. It had all gone wrong.

Drew had been irritated with her before. He'd been impatient occasionally. He'd been reclusive and withdrawn. But he'd never shouted at her. She'd never seen such complete disgust with her on that handsome face.

The memory of that look brought hot, bitter tears to her eyes. That look had felt like a blade, severing the connection she'd felt to Drew. She had outraged him with her odd ways, trespassed against his morals. He thought she was a liar. He'd called her a bigot, and though she had no notion of what that word meant, she gathered from his tone that it was not a term of endearment.

She sank into the nearest chair, pushing the dishes away. She laid her head on her arms and wept.

Drew anchored his pool cue and lined up his shot along the rail sights. He slid his arm back and sent the ball across the table with a force that almost bounced it over the cushion on the opposite side.

"Nice shot," Bear commented as several balls scattered around the table, none of them finding a pocket. "If you were playing on the next table."

Drew glared at him. He'd come to the pool hall almost without thinking. All he could think of as he'd driven off from the house was how much he wanted to hit something. He'd seen the glow of neon ahead of him on the road and had swerved into the parking lot, cutting the engine of his bike abruptly and striding into the place.

Bear had been at his favorite table, a beer in hand. He'd waved to Drew through the dense fog of cigarette smoke, and Drew had joined him. Few words had passed between them, but then, Bear wasn't big on conversation, as a rule.

Drew stood back and watched as Bear took the bridge from its place under the table and made careful adjustments to the placing of his cue for a center shot. Bear might measure in at Kodiak proportions, but when it came to pool, he was as meticulous as a surgeon. It took a patient player and a good-natured loser to play with him. Tonight, Drew was both by virtue of the fact that he just didn't give a damn.

Bear made his shot and went on to set up for the next. Drew waved to the server and ordered a longneck for himself. He crossed his ankles and leaned back against one of the nearby posts.

"So, how's Elinor?"

Drew groaned. She was the last thing he wanted to talk about. But she seemed to be the only subject on his mind these days.

"She's okay, I guess," he said.

"Rita told me what you said about her. About her losing her memory or something?"

Great. Now, even the Bear-man wanted to chat about her.

"Yeah. She's got some problems that way."

"Shame. She's a nice lady."

"Nice, yeah. But a little weird."

Bear missed his third shot. Drew went to the table like a sleepwalker and surveyed the field. He wasn't ready to let Bear beat him in a shutout, so he concentrated on his most likely shot and pocketed the ball. He missed the next one and went back to his position by the pillar.

Damn, he thought again. Tonight had been so good.

He'd been happy to see her in the kitchen when he came through the door that evening, even if she had been threatening to cook. They'd laughed and talked like real people, almost. They'd enjoyed their meal together in the dimness of sunset, the light from the windows setting off the sheen of Elinor's hair and skin.

He'd fed her chocolate by hand, and he'd just about lost it when she'd closed her lips around his fingertip, just for a second, and taken the chocolate into her mouth. He'd sipped wine with her. They'd shared a peaceful silence, that most delicate of all events in the process of getting to know another person. And then she'd gone and dropped that bomb on him: "*I met a Jew today.*"

Who the heck had raised this girl? he thought, taking a hard pull on his beer. One minute she was the soul of sweetness and courtesy, the next minute a babbling dreamer or a righteous, spitting cat. And tonight, she was the most complacent, wrong-headed little hypocrite that ever—

"Yours," Bear said, slapping him on the shoulder.

Drew stood where he was, staring off into the distance.

Bear waved a paw in front of his face. "Yo, Ingraham. It's to you."

"Sorry."

"Your head's at home."

"What?" He glanced up in surprise. "What do you mean?"

Bear chuckled. "Make your shot, man."

"You're getting awfully chatty in your old age," Drew grumbled.

"Yeah. Rita's been workin' on me. I guess it's a good thing."

Another laughable shot and Drew was back at the pillar, nursing his beer.

"Tied you up in knots, huh?"

"What?"

"Elinor. She's got you in knots."

There was no use denying it. "Yeah."

Bear concentrated on his next two shots, then paused, leaning his big frame against the table. "Is she real mixed up? Like crazy?"

"I don't know. Maybe. She says the weirdest stuff. Like tonight, she asked why Jews around here don't wear badges."

Bear grimaced. "She's not a skinhead chick, is she?"

"Not that I can tell. And she's not stupid. But she acted like it was a perfectly normal question."

"Hmm."

Drew stood away from the pillar as Bear returned to his shot on the table. "What do you mean, 'hmm'?"

Bear took his maddeningly slow time and made the shot. After a long swig of his beer, he got around to his reply.

"Well, she's confused and she's from out of town."

"That's it?"

"What else would it be?"

"Prejudice, bigotry." Drew paced around the table. "Insanity. Lies."

"Lies?"

"Yeah. She could be a liar. A fake."

Bear ruminated over this as he eyed his next shot. As he lined up the cue, he nodded. "Yep. A fake. Trying to bilk you out of your millions."

He took his shot, made it. Drew felt the hit inside himself.

"Okay, so maybe she's not a fake. At least not like that."

They played in silence for a while. Drew concentrated, though he sensed Bear was cutting him slack to prolong the game. If he'd wanted, his big friend could have finished him off in a matter of minutes.

"What are you going to tell her?"

Fifteen or twenty minutes had elapsed, but Drew knew what Bear was asking.

"Hell, I don't know. It doesn't matter anyway. She'll be gone soon."

"Yeah?"

"Back to England, yeah."

Bear ordered two more beers. Then he asked, "You okay with that?"

"With her going?" Drew shrugged. "Sure."

His friend took a long look at him. "You know, when I say stuff like that, Rita always says I'm dancing around the real subject. You're doing that 'I don't have no feelings about nuthin' ' shuffle, she says."

Drew scowled and leaned over his cue. "I'm being honest about my feelings," he growled. "I'm mad as hell. How's that for a sensitive, New Age response?"

"Pretty good."

"It's the lies," he went on, stalking around the table for his next line-up. "It isn't just her prejudice that bugs me. It's the whole deal. No matter what she says or does, no matter how ridiculous, dangerous or downright rotten her behavior, she gives me the same excuse—she's a foreigner and she doesn't know how things are done here. Bull!

"How long is she going to stick to that lame story? Being a foreigner doesn't mean she's exempt from the laws of common decency or common sense. And nobody but nobody in this day and age, least of all someone so obviously articulate and intelligent as Elinor, could be so confused by telephones, sheet-rock or canned bloody peaches!"

He rammed the cue forward. Balls flew. The cue ball waltzed its way into a corner pocket.

"Damn, damn, damn. I'm sick of her lies!"

He clamped his hands on the rails, head hanging, breathing ragged. Bear placed a hand on his shoulder.

"I'm sorry, man," Drew muttered. "I've got to get out of here."

"Be safe."

He tossed some bills on the table and stumbled for

the door. A few moments later, he was roaring west along the River Road, away from Bear, Elinor and everything else.

But he wasn't alone. With him on the bike she'd always despised was the best liar of all time.

LeeAnne Searles Ingraham.

He picked up the scent of the ocean on the air. He was headed toward the Pacific, that great oblivion that had swallowed up the biggest mistake of his life and then spat her back out, ready once again to make him mourn his lost love and faith, to mock him in memory, and to keep him forever twisting in the wind of his own guilt.

All the world had seen him and LeeAnne as the perfect couple. That world had included Drew himself, until the day he finally faced the truth. His beautiful, adored LeeAnne was as incapable of faithfulness and honesty as a cat is of resisting fresh salmon. And, he'd learned in his slow, painful way, she was as sleek and graceful as any feline in her efforts to conceal her infidelities, as purring and affectionate in persuading him to overlook her indiscretions.

He crested the last rise and saw the moonlight silvering the waves of Jenner-by-the-Sea. After LeeAnne, he never could trust its beauty, though he knew the ocean wasn't really to blame.

Lies. Lies were bad enough by themselves. Yet, he had learned, wherever a liar is found, a fool is nearby—the fool who believes the liar. It was humiliation that had driven in the final nail. He had lost a love, lost a dream, lost an innocence he hadn't known was so vital. But in the end, it was the loss of his pride that had devastated him.

Lies. That was what galled him.

He wasn't about to play the fool again.

Not even with Elinor.

Chapter Sixteen

Roger looked down at the woman sprawled face down across the bed. Her skirt was rucked up about her hips, her hair a tangled briar-patch. He tugged the dress down over her derriere, making a moue of distaste as he did so.

They were so unappealing when he was finished with them, he thought. They made such a fuss while preparing to trap a man, and then, when it was over, when they got what they wanted—what they deserved—they were a mess. He seldom returned for a second time.

Except with Susannah. His precious.

Of course, that had been different, he recalled as he dressed. Susannah had been his first, and he'd been hers. Two innocents together. There'd been no need of seduction, bribery, coercion, persuasion, magic or herbs. She'd come to him, appeared to him in the forest grove, weeping and brokenhearted over some new mistreatment at her father's hands. And he'd been there to comfort her.

He shivered even now at the memory. He'd never forgotten that time, not the smallest sigh, the slightest brush of lip or hand. And when they'd finished and lay on their moss-cushioned bed, she had looked as angelic and as perfect as the moment he'd first taken her in his arms.

He scowled at the bed and its occupant. Not like this one, her face-paint a-smear on the bedclothes.

He leaned closer, listening. She wasn't snoring, that was a blessing. He'd smothered one once for snoring.

Idly he wondered if she was dead. He'd been a bit inebriated. He might have mismeasured the love-draught he'd slipped into her drink.

"Ah well," he said, smoothing his jacket. " 'Tis no matter. I shan't want this one again."

He wouldn't want any of them again for a good, long time. By this time tomorrow he'd have his medallion back. He'd be home.

He slipped from the room and down the stairs. No one saw him go.

His car waited outside, gleaming in the light of the moon that had finally moved out from behind the clouds. Cars were excellent, he decided as he started it up and pulled smoothly from the drive. He liked the speed and the ease of them.

They didn't go as fast as the wheeled horses called motorcycles, however. He'd found that out today, after his midday meal with the mysterious man who claimed to have his medallion.

He'd thought himself such a clever fellow, Roger mused. He'd walked hither and thither, trying to throw any who followed off the scent. But the man was no fox and no fox-hunter, for Roger had tracked him after all, and had seen him mount his shining machine and speed away.

It had been a grave mistake for the fellow, whoever he might be. Roger would know him soon enough.

And then Roger could go home.

241

Coral Smith Saxe

He wanted to go back. In his own castle, he was master in every sense. He could beat his servants if they were surly or displeased him—here they had to be cosseted and treated almost as equals. In his own time, he was titled, landed and moneyed, three great boons that set him above almost every law.

Oakfield was there, the Oakfield of his time. He'd made a vow to bring every last DeCourtenay to his— or her—knees, and that vow went unfulfilled as long as he languished here. He had looked upon Susannah's eldest daughter and he'd seen in her comely face not only traces of the girl he'd loved but the image of Gerard, her bastard father, as well. And in her firm chin and cool eyes he'd seen much of the disdain that had supplanted the love in his Susannah's eyes. That disdain wouldn't remain after he'd finished with her.

Still, there was more at stake back in his own time than Oakfield and the destruction of the DeCourtenays.

As he returned to his room at the inn, he recalled Gerard's funeral and smirked. He'd played the grieving and supportive neighbor, but of course, he'd been the one whose subtle slanders and financial trickery had eventually driven the weak, scholarly DeCourtenay to his grave. He'd been especially pleased at the way the seeds of doubt he'd sown had caused the local priest to balk and call for an investigation before he'd allow DeCourtenay's burial in consecrated ground. They hadn't managed to prove suicide, more's the pity, but it hadn't been for lack of trying on Roger's part. He'd had to be content with knowing his rival was dead at last.

And then, into the church Susannah had come. Robed in black, veiled, her lovely red hair hidden beneath her widow's weeds, she had cast upon him a look of such pure hatred and contempt that he wondered the angels above the altarpiece didn't gasp in outrage and fall off their perches. In her train came the boy, blond, gray-faced and teary-eyed. Roger dismissed

DeCourtenay's heir as a mere inconvenience. But after the boy had come Susannah's daughters, and it was there that Roger had had his first glimpse of his future.

The girl Elinor was tall and comely, and he'd made a note to bed her at the first opportunity. What a joke upon old DeCourtenay to have his eldest daughter seen about the shire with her belly bursting with Roger's seed and no husband in sight. It was almost delicious enough to make him regret the fellow's death, that he should miss his daughter—the daughter he'd sent to a nunnery to keep her pure—coming home in shame from Castle Clarisdoune, her tail between her long legs. Almost, but not quite.

It was the second girl, the youngest of the lot, that had given him pause. He'd almost cried aloud at the sight of that fair, fair face, wreathed as it was in clouds of deep red curls. She was the very image of her mother, his own Susannah, from her slanting blue eyes to her sweet, delicate chin and rosebud mouth.

His legs had trembled so much that it was the first time he'd ever been glad of the chance to kneel in prayer. He'd sunk to his knees, and there, in the chapel where Mass was being said for his rival and victim, the child's own father, he made a promise to himself that he would move heaven and earth to gain this child.

He would cherish her, raise her. She would have the finest of everything. He would grant her every whim, her slightest wish. Princesses would weep with envy. And she would love him with a love unquestioning and immovable.

She would never learn to despise him, as Susannah had. She would be pure and fresh and innocent. Just as Susannah had been on that day when she'd given him her maidenhood. She would be his greatest treasure and triumph.

Passion had become obsession in St. Michael's Church that morning.

He showered and got into bed, smiling at the vision

playing in his mind. Dallying in this world was pleasant enough, but his power and lodestar were both waiting for him in centuries gone by. He had to get back to the past.

His future depended upon it.

The heavy book with the yellow pages was a great source of information, he'd learned. A quick perusal of the one by his bedside provided him with the addresses of shops that carried herbs and occult items. He might need a few more of these before he was returned to his own time.

But most of all, the sunny-hued pages yielded a tidy list of establishments that specialized in motorcycles.

Drew came in late and left early the next day. Elinor tried to engage him in conversation, with only the smallest success. His answers were a word or a gesture and then he was off again, riding Harley, with no word of where or when he might return.

A short time after he'd ridden away, she set out on foot for the village. The sunshine of the day, the moist spring breeze, made little impression on her mood as she swung along the road, fear and determination battling inside her.

Louis Feldon's shop sign said "Open." She drew a deep breath, muttered a short prayer and stepped inside.

He was showing wedding rings to a young couple and only glanced her way as she entered. She trembled, yet held her ground, watching from a corner near the door.

The young couple radiated happiness and love. Watching their intimate little touches and smiles raised a longing in her heart. She wondered if she would ever share that kind of tender loving with someone. It seemed the pair created a world of their own, populated by two alone, where no others could enter or disturb.

The lovers concluded their business and passed Elinor on their way out. She was alone with Louis, who was putting away his trays of rings.

"So, miss," he said, his tone formal and cool. "May I help you?" He motioned to the glass cases before him.

"I wish you could, sir." She stepped closer. "Though I do not see what I seek in your jewel cases."

"Then you want to go somewhere else, maybe?"

"Nay, sir, for you are the only one who may serve my need. I've come seeking your forgiveness. I acted as a fool and as an ignorant foreigner who offends at every turn."

"And what makes you say this now, Elinor?"

"Even as I spoke yesterday, I saw that I had caused you hurt and offense. Though I confess I meant no deliberate harm, I know the result was harmful. If you can find it in your heart, I beg your pardon, most humbly."

He reached over the counter and touched her hands where they rested, folded tightly, on the glass top.

"I was hurt, Elinor. Not simply for what you said—I've heard far worse, believe me. But I was hurt that this lovely girl, this Elinor, should harbor ugliness in her soul. And sad that I should not have seen it."

She shook her head, not daring to meet his eyes. "I am so sorry, Louis. I did not know. Where I come from, your people are not . . . are . . ."

He pulled one of her hands loose and held it.

"Where do you come from, Elinor DeCourtenay? Don't say England, that's just geography. You're from someplace else altogether, aren't you?"

She looked up into the kindly old face and the tears began to well. "I am from England," she whispered. "But not the England that you know."

"Eh, eh, *meydele*, you're all mixed up." He patted her hand. "Take your time. Come. Sit."

He pulled her around the counter and steered her to a chair.

"Take my time." Elinor gave a tearful laugh. "That, my good sir, is just what I cannot do."

He scooted a stool near her. "Are you saying you're in the wrong place, Elinor? Or in the wrong time?"

She felt her heart leap at his words. "What if I say both?"

He peered at her, head cocked to one side. "With anyone else, I'd say see a doctor. But with Elinor DeCourtenay, I believe I'd give it a thought or two before I made up my mind."

She burst into tears. "Thank you, oh, thank you," she gasped.

He chuckled and handed her a kerchief. "Never mind that. Let's go have that Danish and coffee, shall we? Then you can tell me where and, more importantly, when."

In Max's Deli, in a quiet corner booth, Elinor related what she had pieced together thus far. Louis listened, nodding and urging her on with the story.

"And yesterday," she said, "I came to you and you were ready to aid me. To my shame, I repaid that great kindness with rudeness. I am most truly sorry, Louis, for any pain I have caused."

"Enough apologies," he said, waving his coffee spoon. "Now that I've heard your story, your behavior at least makes some sense. You're not a bad person, Elinor. You're just a creature of your own time." He stirred his coffee. "The Middle Ages were a very bad time for the Jews. Superstition and intolerance were everywhere."

"If ever I get back, I shall endeavor to improve the lot of your people, I swear it."

"I believe you will."

She smiled. "You believe me. I can hardly take it in. At last, I have someone I can talk to who doesn't think I'm a madwoman or a liar."

"The thought crossed my mind."

She chuckled at the funny face he made. "I doubt it

not. I'm sure I should have the same response had someone from this time dropped down before me on the Oakfield Road." She leaned forward. "Yet why do you believe me?"

"I don't know. I'm old enough, I can say those words now without shame. But you must remember that I have more proof than just your word. I've seen your necklace, and I'd stake my word upon it that it's as old as you say." He shrugged. "Not exactly what they'd want to hear on *Sixty Minutes,* but it's good enough for me."

He stirred his coffee with greater vigor, excitement in his eyes. "But the question now, I take it, is how do you get back?"

"Aye. If I but knew how I arrived, perhaps that would reveal the path back. But, as I told you, I can recall very little of the night I came here."

"Would you agree that your medallion may have something to do with it?"

"I would. And I've guessed, as much as you, that there is a missing half somewhere."

"That's your next step. Find the other half. Do you have any idea where it could be?" He looked at her with sharp eyes. "Would it be here in this time? Or in your other time?"

Her hands shook around her cup. She set it down before she answered.

"I believe it is here. Now. Roger Aston, my family's tormentor, is here, though I do not know if he has the piece with him."

"You fear to find him?"

"Aye. And nay. I must return to my family, my time, and I believe that Roger is a key to that. Yet I fear to see him, for he is of an evil nature. He means to do wrong to all who bear the DeCourtenay name, as well as any who give them aid and succor . . . oh, my saints!"

"What?"

"You have helped me. You have become my friend. If I've brought you into danger—"

He waved her words away. "Don't give it another thought. I'm old, I'm tough. I've been through nightmares no one should have to endure. I can handle myself."

"But he is a wizard, and cruelly cunning—"

He shook his head. "No, *meydele*. I learned years ago that no one can take anything away from me ever again. I own my soul, my own spirit." He shrugged and munched the last of his Danish. "Besides, I'm old. No one would see me as a threat, anyway."

"I pray it may be so."

"Me, too."

Elinor laughed with him, though she felt a twinge of guilt for involving this dear man in her troubles. Yet it was a balm to her spirit to have a friend, a friend who knew and believed her. That was sustenance enough, she thought.

Louis had to return to his shop, but before they parted, they listed together several ways in which Elinor might search for Roger and the missing medallion piece. Knowing that she would be going home either to an empty and lonely house or to Drew's cold contempt, she elected to visit the library. When she emerged some hours later, she was deep in thought over all she had read of Louis Feldon's people.

"Say hey, it's the lost lady."

She started. It was the pimply youth whose foot she'd stepped on when she'd last visited his store. He stood in the doorway of that establishment, leaning on the sill and drinking something from a bottle.

"Good day, sirrah," she murmured as she passed.

"Hey, did that dude ever find you? He seemed pretty hot to get back with you. Can't say as I blame him."

She turned and saw the impudent, leering grin on his face. A tremor of fear shook her but she stiffened against it.

"What dude do you mean?"

"The English dude." He ran a finger from his left temple to the back of his head. "The one with the streak? He was looking for you, just a couple days after you were in here. Bought some mandrake root—he must have had some serious sessions planned for you, babe."

Her stomach did a slow, sickening roll. "Ah," she said, struggling for composure. "Yes, I do recall."

"You must be the hottest ticket in town. Two guys chasing after you, the English guy and the dude on the bad bike. How can I get in on this action?"

Elinor swallowed the bile that was rising in her as the creature swaggered closer. She looked him up and down, giving herself time to restrain the impulse to kick him where it counted.

"I don't know," she purred. "Mayhap you can tell me."

"Whaddaya mean?"

"Did this English fellow say where he was staying?"

"Nope. But we don't need him to have fun, do we? I mean, he's old and needs that mandrake stuff. I'm at my peak, babe. I can do it till Elvis comes back."

"I'm sure you can. But one more question. This fellow, was he wearing a necklace like mine?"

She held the medallion out. He scooped it up, deliberately grazing her breasts with his knuckles.

"Yeah, sort of. He asked about it. About yours, I mean." He pulled on the chain, gently tugging her closer. "What is this? Some kind of club key? I could be so into you, sweet thing. Where do I sign up?"

She slid one foot forward, nudging his feet apart. "It's quite simple," she cooed. "You just sit yourself down . . ."

She hooked her foot up behind his knee and jerked his leg out from under him. He landed on the sidewalk in a sprawl, his drink spilling all over his shirtfront.

". . . and wait until hell freezes over." She shouldered

her knapsack and backed away. "Good day to you, sir-rah."

A brick wall smacked into her back. She gave a small shriek and looked up to see Drew scowling at the scene before him.

"Sir Drew—I—I was just—"

He brushed past her.

"Say, duuude," he said, hauling the youth up by the collar. "Hey, she didn't hurt you, did she, man?"

"N-n-no." His feet scrabbled to find purchase, but Drew held him up just high enough for his toes to scrape the paving.

"Oh, that's good. I wouldn't like to see a guy like you take a beating from a girl. I'd much rather see some-body like me beat the crap out of you."

Grinning broadly, Drew hauled the banner out of its bracket by the door of the shop, still holding the youth in one hand. With a flourish, he lifted the shopclerk higher and hooked his collar over the bracket. He dangled there, kicking and gulping, unable to free himself.

Drew gave him a not-so-gentle pat on the cheek.

"Okay, Sparky. I guess that's all for today. But let's mind our manners from now on, shall we? Because if you don't, Sparks old boy, I'm gonna have to come back here. And if I have to come back, you're going to have to learn how to pee sideways, do I make myself clear?"

The dangler nodded vehemently.

"Good boy. Later on, duuude."

Drew took Elinor's elbow and walked her away from the shop. She looked up into his face, seeing both his wrath and a bit of triumph there.

"I can defend myself, you know."

He grinned down at her. "Yeah, I know. I saw. But I just couldn't resist adding my two cents. I think he learned something from us today, don't you?"

She grinned. "Aye. Let us hope. I'd rather be wooed by one of Tuck and Cubbie's banana slugs."

She paused when they were out of earshot of the lad on the bracket. "I need to tell you something."

"About him?"

"No. About me. About what I said last night."

Drew started to walk on. "I think we both said enough, don't you?"

"I want you to come with me to meet someone."

He stopped. "Who?"

"Just come with me, please. It's back this way. Past our—pupil's shop."

He regarded her speculatively. "All right."

She led the way back up the street. The gangly youth waved and wriggled at them.

"Sir? Ah, sir? If you don't mind. . . . Ma'am? I mean I'm sorry . . ."

They passed the shopclerk without so much as a glance. No one else on the street seemed inclined to get him down either, Elinor noticed. She wasn't *so* out of touch with the times, she thought.

She ushered Drew into Louis's shop with a trembling but hopeful heart.

"Sir Drew," she said, extending her hand toward the old jeweler. "This is Louis Feldon. He's a Jew!"

Drew's face reddened, but Louis's laughter rang out.

"Pleased to make your acquaintance," Louis said, offering his hand. "Our Elinor, here, she's one of a kind, *ja*?"

"You can say that again. Drew Ingraham, sir."

Elinor felt relief and pride rush through her as the two men shook hands. This didn't solve all her problems, but she hoped it went a long way toward mending the rift between her and Drew. And it was warming to her heart to see two men she cared for meeting and shaking hands.

"I apologized to Louis for the way I behaved yesterday. He understands I'm rather a stranger in a strange land."

"He does?"

"Oh, *ja*. This one here, she's no bigot, at least not in her heart. She just didn't know."

"You're very understanding, sir."

"Well, Elinor, she's a special case, isn't she? Ones like her don't drop in every day."

"Not in my life."

"Nor mine." Louis beamed on them both. "So? How did you two kids meet?"

Drew looked at Elinor. She nodded for him to speak.

"She, ah, well, she was kind of lost—"

"Kind of lost—ho! That's a good one." Louis waved at Drew. "But go on. Never mind an old man and his jokes."

"That's pretty much it. She was out on the bridge at Venners Creek, I was riding by on my bike, and I thought I had hit her. She didn't seem to have anywhere else to go and she was having trouble remembering, so I took her to my place. That's about it."

"And your wife, she doesn't mind an extra mouth to feed?"

Drew colored again. "I'm not married."

"I see. Well, it's a good thing for our Elinor you were the fellow to come to her rescue. Not many would have been so understanding of her predicament."

"Well, we're doing what we can to get her back home to England. It's been difficult to find anyone—"

"Ho! I should say so. Not so easy raising folks who've been dead a few hundred years."

Drew stared at the ground, then at Elinor. She shrugged.

"Louis believes me."

Drew looked at Louis, who continued to beam.

"*Ja*, it's a pretty fantastic tale, eh? But there can be no other explanation. And once she finds the other half of the medallion, I predict she'll be on her way home in no time."

"Sir, I don't think you understand. This story . . . Elinor's been pretty confused . . . Well, there was the bump on the head she took . . ."

"Ah, I see." Louis looked at her. "He doesn't believe? Or he doesn't know?"

"He does not believe."

"Oh, my. Now, that does present a problem, doesn't it? Still, if I found a pretty girl like you, Elinor, I'm not so sure I'd want to believe, either."

"What do you mean?" Drew asked.

"Well, who would ever want this one to leave? To disappear into the past never to be seen again?"

"That's not what I meant," Drew said.

"That is all right," said Elinor. "You've been honest about your doubts, Sir Drew. And I know that you are not looking for someone to stay with you."

"Elinor, you're—"

"I just wished for you two to meet and for you to know that your words to me last night were not in vain. I know now that Jews are people and that my friend Louis is a gentleman of the first quality."

"Ah, how she talks, eh, Drew?"

"Yep," he said tersely, jamming his hands in his back pockets. "How she talks."

"Are you angry with me yet?" Elinor asked when they were out on the street once more.

"No."

"Louis is a good friend. I owe that to you. If you had not instructed me in how to behave and think in the company of his kind, I should not have gained such a friend."

"Instructed you. That's a nice way of putting it. What I did was yell and rave at you, Elinor. I'm sorry."

"I forgive you. And still, it worked out for the best, did it not?"

"Yeah. Well, maybe not for that shopclerk you took down this afternoon."

She chuckled. "You put such an elegant finishing touch upon his comeuppance."

"I was proud to be a part of it, ma'am. You're a real artiste."

He smiled down at her even as he recalled his vow of last night. He wasn't going to be a fool for her, he told himself, but he didn't need to treat her like dirt. After all, she had just proven the extent of her faith in his word by going to Louis Feldon and apologizing for her behavior. Feldon sure seemed satisfied with her explanations.

"Louis believes you, you said. About time-traveling and all of that?"

"Aye. And I know you do not," she quickly added. "But I accept that."

He decided to let it pass. "Are you hungry?"

"Aye." She grinned. "When have you known me to be otherwise?"

"Let's go find some eats, then."

"The Experience Fish?" she asked as they pulled up to the rustic little building tucked back behind the redwoods on the river.

"Yeah. Dumb name, but great food."

The Fish, as it was known to the locals, was one of the best-kept secrets of the Russian River area. Not snooty enough to be listed in the wine country tour books, a shade too expensive for the college crowd, and too down-home to attract the cyber-slaves working in high-tech industry around the area, it was perfect for a certain, special crowd of river rats. Drew hadn't been in for a long, long while. He was glad to see it hadn't changed.

He asked for a seat on the back deck. Elinor clapped her hands with pleasure at the sight of the river, still in spring flood, running just a few feet beyond their table.

"Want to share some carnitas?" he asked her as they read over the menu.

"How?"

"Never mind. I'm getting used to this."

He ordered for them both. The vast wooden deck was quiet as they waited for their food and drank ice-cold bottles of Carte Blanca.

"You call this beer?" Elinor asked. "Rather weak, is it not?"

"Don't start with me," he said, waving his bottle at her. "I know you Brits like your beer warm and strong enough to use as disinfectant, but you're in northern California. Home of Italian food, German cars, and Mexican beer."

"Carnitas are Italian? Like pizza?" Her mood brightened even more.

He looked her up and down and shook his head. "Remind me to have you checked for a tapeworm, princess. It does not seem real, the amount of food you can eat."

The waitress sailed over to them, sizzling platters held aloft. The sun began to set as Drew showed Elinor how to wrap the hot roasted pork and the condiments in the soft tortillas. Tables all around them were filling up.

"What did you mean today at Louis Feldon's place," he asked at last, striving to sound casual, "when you said you knew I didn't want you to stay?"

She wiped a bit of sour cream off her chin before she replied. "I know I've been a burden to you. And your friends have told me that before I fell into your life, as it were, you were most solitary. I've disrupted that. And . . ."

"And?"

"And I know that Louis was wrong in his hints that you might harbor . . . feelings for me."

"You do?"

"Aye. So, you needn't worry. Louis and I will find a way home for me. As soon as may be."

"Is that what you want?"

255

She looked surprised. "Of course. I cannot stay here, in this place or this time. I do not belong."

"You look like you belong here."

She did. From her soft blue jeans to the easy way she swayed to the music from the jukebox inside, she looked like a woman who was utterly at home.

He returned to his meal, struggling to shut out the images of Elinor at home—on his sofa, in his kitchen, at his table, wearing his shirts, sleeping in his bed. It was all going to end in frustration. He knew it.

And he'd made up his mind about her, hadn't he? That she was a liar, after all, and that he couldn't stand playing the fool again? He had to stick to that thought. It was time to have that talk with her.

He opened his mouth to speak but was thwarted again.

"And what to my wondering eyes should appear but the lovely Elinor and her faithful friend—"

"Don't say it, Doc."

Will lifted Elinor's hand and kissed it. "My dear, welcome to the Fish. Never has such beauty graced these termite-ridden environs." He turned to the tall brunette on his arm. "Never since you walked in, Christianna, dear."

The young woman rolled her eyes at Elinor. "He's cute but he's so full of it."

"Which is why you love me with a passion second only to that of Heloise for Abelard."

"Yeah, well, just remember what happened to old Abelard, sweetie," Christianna replied. "Meanwhile, I'm starved, Will."

"Please join us," Elinor offered.

Drew sat back and watched in amusement as Will regaled them all with stories of his various trips around the world. The band was setting up on the little corner stage when Bear and Rita came in, grinning like kids skipping school.

"Date night," Bear said to Drew as they ordered. "We

have a standing contract with a baby-sitter."

"Smart."

By the time everyone had eaten, the band was in full swing and couples were moving out onto the dance floor. Drew watched Elinor watching Bear and Rita two-stepping, her amazed interest plain on her face.

Will and Rita pulled her onto the floor with them for some line-dancing. It was Drew's turn to be amazed when she picked up the steps with ease, her loose hair whirling about her as she turned and slid and clapped in time with the others.

She returned to the table, laughing and breathless.

"That, at least, was like to some of the steps I know from home," she told him as she gulped some ice water. "But the others are quite foreign. Is it the custom for men and women to hug one another as they dance?"

"Yeah. Sometimes. See—not everybody dances that way."

The band, who were known for their eclectic repertoire, started in on a rocking old Chuck Berry tune. Couples began to dance apart.

"Come," she said, popping up from her seat. "Let's join them."

She was already on her way out to the dance floor. He sighed, prayed for strength and followed her.

Okay, he admitted after a couple of fast numbers. It was fun. Watching Elinor copy new moves was to be witness to the embodiment of sheer delight. Will and Bear jostled to partner her, spinning her off from one to the other and back to Drew.

Even the band seemed to get a kick out of her. Their lead singer screamed his way into a superior version of "Twist and Shout," while the lead guitarist postured and strutted whenever she came near, breaking into out-of-the-blue riffs from Eric Johnson and Jimi Hendrix.

The stars had come out over the hills, the river sparkled with reflections from the deck lights. Drew looked around in surprise.

He was surrounded by people—friends, music, joy. How had it happened?

"We're gonna take it down a notch here," the singer rasped. "You know this one. Little number called 'Fields of Gold.' Play it sweet, guys."

Drew stood staring as the opening chords sounded.

"Yo, Ingraham. You want to dance with your lady, you better act fast."

Startled, Drew looked where Bear pointed. Three different men were converging on Elinor as she stood near the bandstand, swaying in time to the music.

Will grabbed her by the elbow, whirled her behind him and cut in front of the oncoming trio. She spun into the middle of the floor, where Bear managed to hook her arm and circle her around, delivering her right square in front of Drew's astonished face.

She glanced about at the other couples dancing close and sinuous. He saw her look away, start to turn.

"Dance with me, Elinor."

Chapter Seventeen

Elinor was melting, floating.

She was dancing with Drew.

The music seemed to be a tune she'd heard all her life. Perhaps it was one she'd been waiting all her life to hear. Or perhaps it had been inside of her, waiting all her life to be played at this moment.

It didn't really matter, she decided as his arms pulled her still closer. All was music. The sound of his breath so close to her ear. The beating of her heart. The lights dancing on the river, tossing their sparkles across its ink-black width.

It might be sin to be held so close to a man. But a glance about her told her it was at least the custom.

She was not about to flaunt custom.

"Dance with me, Elinor," he'd said.

It hadn't been a request, exactly. Nor had it been a command.

It had been more like a statement, an agreement already made between them both. A statement of the truth of their desire for one another.

For all her confusion in this time, this place, for all her bumbling and errors, this was a truth she could not deny.

She was well and truly in love with Sir Drew Ingraham.

Dancing with him had given her, at long last, a way to express it. No more ponderings and arguments. No sensible, rational words. Just this simple act of holding him, being held by him. This was the truth she'd been trying to tell and the truth from which she'd been hiding.

She had fallen into the depths of his blue eyes long ago. Now she had arms and legs and hands and body to share with him. She could speak what she felt and not be tripped up by her own clumsy words.

They circled slowly, dipped and swayed, inventing the dance as they went along. She saw Rita with her cheek placed close to Bear's. She pressed her cheek to Drew's.

Oh, he was warm. And the scent of him was sweeter than new grass, headier than spiced wine.

He pressed a kiss to her hair. She melted still more.

She placed a hand over his heart. His hand covered hers, holding her there as she felt the steady beat within.

Cheek to cheek, hands and hearts.

They were dancing . . . they were floating . . .

"Elinor," he murmured against her ear.

The instruments slid to a stop. The cymbal shuddered into silence as the crowd applauded. With a crash and a wild shout, the musicians were off again, playing fast and furious.

Drew let her go. She stood, not knowing what to do. "Thank you, Sir Drew."

"It's just Drew," they said together.

Laughter eased the awkward moment. "Come," she said. "Your friends are seated."

"Your friends, too."

She smiled. "Thank you for sharing them with me. They love you so."

She turned and led the way around the dancing throng before she could say more. She wanted to hold the moments just past in her heart, unsullied by spoken words.

They danced several more dances, but Drew didn't ask her to dance close with him again. Before long, he said it was time for them to go, and they made their farewells to the merry group around the wooden table.

"I had a lovely time this evening," she told him as they entered the house. "Thank you."

He smiled. "It was my pleasure."

He took her jacket and helmet and hung them with his on the pegs by the back door. She got them each a cold drink from the ice cupboard.

"Dancing is thirsty work," she observed, sipping the orange nectar. "Do you dance there often?"

"I haven't been dancing in years."

"Whyever not?" She slipped into a seat at the table. "Rita, Lady Bear, told me that she and her man go there several times a month. I would go among my friends, had I such good ones."

He crossed to the doorway. "Yeah, well, I just haven't gotten around to it lately."

"Did you dance there oft with your lady?"

His face went as still as the wall near her. "Why do you ask?"

"Rita told me about your LeeAnne." Elinor reached out a hand to him. "I am sorry for your loss, Drew. I know that you loved her with the truest heart."

"Thank you for your sympathy."

"Is that why you do not go among your friends? Fair memories can be the hardest, I know."

"I guess that's true." He turned away. "I'd better turn in. Good night, Elinor."

She sat gazing at the empty doorway long after he'd left and gone to the bathing chamber. It hadn't been easy to speak of LeeAnne. Her jealousy was still strong. But she had vowed to be a friend to Drew, and friends shared such talk, didn't they?

"Aye me," she sighed.

She went off to her own bed and fell asleep at once. When she wakened she judged, from the silence and the depth of the darkness around her, that it was still the heart of the night.

She tried to turn over and go back to sleep. She knew it would be a futile effort, for her first thoughts were of Drew and LeeAnne.

She swung her legs out of bed and padded silently down the hall to the kitchen. She took the milk from the ice cupboard and poured herself a cupful. The kitchen was lit by the pale glow of the lantern that Drew kept burning across the yard by his shop. She carried the glass to the table by the window and sat, sipping the chilly milk.

Drew had had a wife. A wife he cherished above life itself, Rita had implied. How must that have felt, she wondered, to have someone so deeply committed to you in mind, body and soul?

And to lose that love to a terrible death. Tears filled her throat. Drew could be a difficult man, but she sensed that some of his taciturn nature hid a tender, albeit complex, soul. To know that he'd been so hurt filled her heart with pain and sadness, despite the flickerings of envy that darted in and out among those feelings.

She hadn't expected to come to care so much for any man that she would actually grieve for a woman who would forever be her rival. But she had indeed fallen in love with Sir Drew Ingraham—all of him.

She set the glass aside and pulled her legs up to her

chest. She wrapped her arms around them and rested her chin on her knees.

This was folly. Madness. Loving Drew was impossible. How could love abide or even grow when his heart was buried with his lady in the depths of the sea? Moreover, she herself was not a woman of his time or of his country. There was a gulf of ages between them, as well as of miles. Customs and speech and a myriad other differences set them at odds. For all she knew, at any instant she might find herself whisked back—or even forward—in time or transported to a land as distant as a star.

Love was a delicate plant in the best of circumstances, her mother had told her. It required time spent in nurturing, training, and in sheltering it from the wayward elements. Love across time and distance, between two people born ages apart, had but the slightest chance of surviving, let alone blossoming into flower.

She reached up one hand, pulled the ribbon from her hair and let it fall around her shoulders. Returning her chin to her knees, she sighed. Yes, she knew all the arguments against her feelings. She knew why she mustn't love Drew. And she knew why he didn't, couldn't, love her.

The nagging ache in her heart, however, cared naught for her arguments. Her willful body insisted upon reviewing each occasion when they had touched, kissed or embraced—in vivid detail. And her spirit, so long suppressed and trained to duty, order and denial, rose up like a meadowlark whenever she was around this man who, oddly enough, had narrowed his own life to a small patch of trees and a solitary workshop.

She was so lost.

Lost in time. Lost in a foreign land, away from the loved ones she'd sought to aid. Lost in understanding what had happened to her or what she might do to change her fate. Lost in loving a man who had no love to give her and who might disappear behind the veils of time and distance at any moment.

One hot tear slid down her cheek. She let it go. She was weary of holding her emotions in like a stern master with a lively horse. Who was there to care if she wept? If she was lost, then she might as well give rein to her feelings, for it mattered little whether she was brave and bold or faint and melancholy.

She let go a little sobbing sigh, hardly more than a whisper. But it was enough. Her eyes filled. She pressed her forehead to her knees, and the tears came.

A hand touched her shoulder. She jerked her head up, wiping at her face with the back of her hand.

It was Drew. He stood beside her, a look of questioning concern upon his face.

"I'm sorry," she whispered. "I was homesick."

He squatted down next to her. He was wearing blue jeans and a white shirt, unbuttoned and loose at the waist. The blue of his eyes had gone gray in the dim light, but his hair shone like palest gold around his head. He lifted a finger and wiped a tear from the tip of her nose.

"I'm sorry, too," he said, his voice soft and husky. "I wish there were a way that I could take you home, princess."

She shook her head and looked down, away from the tenderness in his eyes. Perhaps he only pitied her; still, she wasn't sure she could face him just now, when it seemed he cared so deeply.

"I shall find the key," she said, clearing her throat.

"I know what it is to miss someone you love."

She looked up at him in surprise. This was the most personal remark he had ever made to her. She reached out and touched his shoulder briefly. "I know you do."

He went on, almost as if speaking to himself.

"You think you've got it all under control and nothing can get to you. And then some little thing, like a song or even a color, brings it all back. You're there, with them, in your head, but when you turn to speak to them, there's nothing."

She looked away, out the window, suddenly shy at this intimate speech. He was speaking of LeeAnne, of course, yet she couldn't help wishing they were thoughts of her.

Saints, how wild these feelings were within her! She had never before understood all the fuss about human desire and the passions that surrounded the relations between men and women. Prior to this, her information had all been gleaned from high-sounding admonitions from the Church or the bawdy songs and smirking jokes between men in the stables. She knew enough to know what coupling was and how it might be accomplished.

The night she had gone to Roger and offered herself in payment, she knew that that was what he expected of her. It had been wrong, and now she knew more than ever just how evil the act could be, were it done without these powerful feelings of tenderness and true yearning to be joined one with the other.

She had those feelings now. As she looked into Drew's eyes and felt the warmth of his body just inches from her own, she almost felt as if she could melt into him, be absorbed by him, overtaken, and in that moment feel not the least bit conquered. It would be the most perfectly right feeling she could imagine.

Her breath was beginning to come faster now. She felt a shiver that set her trembling, even as a flush crept upward into her face. He was looking at her in such an odd, exciting way, as if he were half in pain, half in wonder.

He reached out and took up a handful of her hair. He wound his hand in it, giving it the gentlest tug, then slowly unwound the long strand. Still holding it, he lifted it to his cheek. His eyes closed as he drew it across his lips and inhaled its scent.

Elinor gave a brief, whispered cry. Her whole body

was suddenly tingling everywhere, as if she were sitting in a fine, stinging-cold rain. She had been longing for his touch, and now that he had obliged her, she wasn't sure she could endure it.

He let go of the lock of hair and leaned away from her. "Elinor," he said, his voice husky and soft. "I . . ."

She looked at him, waiting for him to speak again.

He raised a hand, gesturing vaguely. "I'm sorry," he said. "I can't."

He rose. Elinor felt his distance like a wrenching within herself.

"Why?" she asked. "Why can you not?"

He didn't answer, but he didn't move away. Her body was still alive with the effects of his one simple touch, and she craved more.

"Is it—have I done something ill?" she asked.

He groaned. "No, princess. You've haven't done anything wrong."

She couldn't help herself. "You wish that I was another lady."

He looked startled. "Why do you say that?"

She shook her head. "It is none of my affair. Pardon, Sir Drew. I did not mean to trespass."

"Is that what *you* wish?" he asked, his voice suddenly cold. "That you were alone with someone else?"

She gaped at him. How could he not know? She was ready to fling herself upon him, beg him to hold her, do whatever he would with her, just to be with him. How could he ask if she could possibly long for anyone but him?

"In truth," she said slowly, "you know that I know little of your customs. If I do not know the proper way of showing . . . my desire . . . or the meet words to . . . express depth of feeling, I beg your pardon for my clumsiness. So, as it is so with me, where perhaps you would be more . . . circumspect . . . I must be blunt."

She swallowed against her fear and forged on.

"I would be alone with you. I would have you touch

me, Drew, you and no other. And if it may not be soon,
or if it may never be, please tell me at once so that I
may—"

She got no further. With a hoarse cry, Drew fell to
his knees before her chair and pulled her face to his
with both hands. In the instant his lips took hers, Elinor knew she had not been mistaken in her boldness.
She knew little of kissing, but there was a hunger in
Drew's gentle, trembling hold upon her, a fierceness in
his posture that told her that whether he loved her or
no, at the least he shared the intensity of her desire
and was as desperate as she to give it full expression.

She raised her hands and laid them on his shoulders,
felt the muscles straining beneath the smooth fabric of
his shirt. He was being so gentle, and yet she sensed
he was struggling to keep from crushing her in his embrace. She slipped forward in the chair and parted her
knees, allowing him to gather her against his chest. For
a passing instant, she wondered about the forwardness
of such an accommodation, but in the next instant he
was kissing her throat, the light stubble of his beard
rasping at her skin and setting her a-tremble once
more. If she was a wanton, so be it. She could no more
willingly halt this tender struggle than she could sprout
wings and fly. She raised her legs, wrapped them about
his hips and pulled him still closer, into her heart, into
her body, into her soul.

Elinor's words played about in Drew's mind, even as
he surrendered to the wildfire that was licking all
around the place where he knelt, holding her in his
arms.

". . . perhaps you would be more circumspect . . ."

There was an irony, if ever there was one. His cir-
cumspection was all show. Inside, all the fevered
dreams and heated longings he'd been fighting against
for the last weeks were clamoring for release, threat-

ening an explosion that seemed likely to burn his world
to ashes.

Her plain words, her simple grace, had undone him.
He couldn't have resisted after that. And he hadn't
wanted to resist. He wanted to do just what he was
doing now, holding beautiful Elinor, kissing her, hearing her soft gasps that poured oil on the encroaching
flames.

He fought for control. It had been so long. But this
was Elinor, a waif out of step with the world, so wise
and yet so innocent. So unusual and yet as familiar as
his own face. He wanted to give her every courtesy—a
word she would use—and every pleasure.

He reached up and began to unbutton the buttons
of the shirt she wore. His shirt. It engulfed her slender
form but it also looked delicious on her, her long,
strong legs bare below the tails, her hands half hidden
by the cuffs. He resisted the mad impulse to bite the
buttons off, but his fingers picked up the pace, match-
ing his impatience to see and feel what lay beneath.

When each pearl button was set free, he slipped his
hands inside the shirt and circled her waist. The silken
feel of her skin, the pleasure of following the deep
curve of her long waist, made his head swim. He slid
his hands downward, to the soft flare of her hips, then
up over her sides again until they just brushed the soft
undersides of her breasts. He leaned forward and
rested his forehead against hers.

"You are so soft," he whispered. "So beautiful. How
can you be real?"

"I am as real as you," she replied. "But perhaps we
are in a dream together." She kissed his neck. "Let us
not wake."

That was fine with Drew. He was already deeply
committed to this hot, sweet endeavor. All sense of
time was blown away on firestorm winds. It might have
been moments later when he gathered more of her
molten-gold hair into his hands and rubbed it over his

chest and abdomen. Elinor's response was to sweep aside the front of his shirt and pull him to her, inch by slow inch, arching up to press herself against him, then sliding downward, using her own glorious skin to follow the path he'd made with the heavy strands of her hair.

Was it long after that that he had set her sideways in the chair and bent her back over his supporting arm, so that he could caress her fully, teasing and polishing and suckling until she was clasping his head and arching to him in an eloquent petition for more? It couldn't have been much later that he'd kissed his way down her long, slender legs, pausing to tickle the sensitive soles of her feet and lightly caress the delicate bones of her ankles.

But then again, it could have been hours.

She'd let free a soft, shivering gasp when he'd trailed his hand upward, up the satiny insides of her thighs to that point where she was warm and moist and so unbelievably soft. He'd raised his head to kiss her, holding her steady as she jumped a little with surprise at his gentle probing of her flowering flesh. She'd moaned when he'd pressed his hand there, and her thighs had closed convulsively around him, trapping him so that she could move against him in an urgent rhythm of desire.

It couldn't have been too long after that when he'd swept her into his arms and carried her to his bedroom. He'd managed to light a candle on the nightstand and he'd watched her shadow on the wall as she stood beside the bed to remove her shirt. When she had let it fall, she shook back her hair, and in doing so, the tips of her breasts were cast there in silhouette, rising in sharp detail from the lush fullness beneath. He could see the soft, slight curve of her belly and even the fine tendrils of the golden hair below, ruffled and dew-damp, he knew, from his own caresses.

This innocent shadow play was somehow more

erotic than any kiss or embrace he could have experienced. With fingers flying, he shook away his own clothes and quickly reached for the woman who had so recently turned his life upside down and inside out. He tumbled with her onto the bed and lost himself in the glory of her sweet body, her gasps and murmured praises. And if, in the passing of those brief hours, or those many long moments—he had no idea which it had been—he lost all recollection of his own past or his apprehension of the future, it was perfectly understandable. For making love to the Lady Elinor Elizabeth Justinia DeCourtenay, entering her, rocking her, pleasuring her till she cried out his name and clung to him, shuddering and heaving with the fierce joy of her release, was a more potent magic than Drew Ingraham had ever dreamed, even in his wildest imaginings.

And when his own climax overtook him, he was not surprised to feel his heart begin to break.

Chapter Eighteen

Elinor lay curled against Drew, who slept with one arm slung possessively across her middle. The light from the windows was soft and gray, telling her it was another cloudy day in the redwoods.

Kindly sun, she thought, smiling, to look upon sleeping lovers and not wake them with a cruel burst of harsh beams.

She had never felt so utterly spent and yet so completely contented and at ease. No wonder the old songs claimed that love made fools of us all. The night just past had made her feel as if nothing in the world could be wrong—and if it was, she simply did not care. Foolish. And delicious.

What wondrous revelations, she thought. In an instant, she had learned that her constant yearning had not all been one-sided. Drew had taken her into his arms and showered her with loving. This was not like the childhood kisses she recalled, nor was it anything akin to the rough pawings she had endured from Roger—

She stiffened. Dear Lady, she thought. *I remember!*

The night of her visit to Castle Clarisdoune, the night she had gone to Roger Aston and announced that she had come to pay his price—she remembered. Glimpses had come to her mind just now, images of Drew's magical, loving caresses and his sweet words in her ear, contrasting with Roger's ugly squeezings, pinches and crude, insulting descriptions of all he planned to do with her that long, long night.

She clapped her hands over her mouth to keep from shrieking at the remembered horror. Had she—had Roger—? Her mind scrambled through the bits that were flying across her memory, trying to ascertain whether Roger had completed his plans. It still wasn't clear. She knew he had touched her, had torn at her gown. One vision showed his hands running roughly over her breasts. Another revealed his sardonic, triumphant smile as he had descended the stairs to greet her there in his hall. Yet another picture tumbled into place, of Roger reaching out to hand her a goblet, with the candles, so many candles, glinting sparks off its jewel-encrusted surface.

Her stomach rolled. She wrinkled her nose. She could smell the noisome wine as if it were here in the room with her now. She closed her eyes and strained for the image that would tell her what she dreaded most to know. Had Roger risen above her as Drew had? Had he . . . ?

She couldn't think the words even in the privacy of her own mind. The only images that came now were of swirling candlelight and a sickening drop into the darkest hole imaginable.

She gently lifted Drew's arm and slipped away from his strong, comforting warmth. The delicious peace and contentment had vanished. Now she felt only disgust, horror and fear.

She tiptoed to the bathing chamber, closed the door and locked it. She crept to the mirror and looked at her face. Despite its being pale with fear, she could see soft, rosy areas on her cheeks, areas where, she knew, Drew's beard had nuzzled her in the act of loving. Her hair was in soft tangles, and as she swept it back over her shoulders, she saw fainter versions of the same rosy marks on her breasts.

She squeezed her eyes shut again, her throat tightening, threatening tears. It had been so lovely, so completely right. Coupling with Drew had been a honeyed, tormenting madness that they both had felt and both had ministered to one another, fanning that madness to a frenzy that had burned it away, returning them both to sweet sanity.

She had believed it had been her first time. She had never wanted any man to the degree that she wanted Drew, and she had never wanted to give herself to anyone so much. Her maidenhood was a precious gift, whether as a dower-right or an act of complete love. It could only be given once.

She opened her eyes and faced herself in the mirror. She knew she could never regret the previous night, but it was shadowed now by the fear that she had come to Drew in ignorance of her true state.

Would it have mattered, a voice inside her asked? She thought no, then yes. It would have mattered, as it did now. But she also knew that regardless of her state, she would have felt the same desire for Drew, the same joy with him.

Once again, she was left to wonder what the custom of Drew's world demanded. Should she tell him she had been with another before him? She couldn't exactly tell him that she had been forced against her will, for she had gone to Roger knowing full well his expectations of her.

She let water run into the basin and washed her face vigorously. She took up a hairbrush and went to work, raking out the tangles and smoothing it, then plaiting it quickly over her shoulder. One of Drew's shirts hung on a hook; she donned it quickly, buttoning it up to the highest button, suddenly uncertain of propriety.

There, she thought. She looked a bit more like herself. She might be able to face Drew now. She summoned up her composure, raised her chin and made her entrance.

"Drew—"

"Elinor—"

They both spoke at once. Drew was sitting up in bed, his face a study in puzzled concern.

"You first," he said slowly.

"As you wish," she replied. "I—there is something I must tell you. I should have informed you last night before we—before I—"

"I already know."

She looked at him in surprise and then felt the hot sting of shame spreading over her face.

"I am sorry," she said, her composure wilting on the vine. "I should have told you, but I wasn't sure and I—"

"You weren't sure?" His tone was incredulous.

"I know it sounds as though I am the wickedest and most ignorant of all females, yet I swear, Drew, I had no memory of that night. I still can recall only bits of it, and they are so flighty in my mind that I fear me they are but phantoms."

"That night?" He scowled, his light brows drawn low over eyes that had darkened to the color of the sea.

"The night you found me. I wasn't sure what had happened, I couldn't recall anything more than that I was being pursued. I never meant to deceive you. I only—"

"Whoa," he said, raising a hand. "Back up here. What are you trying to tell me?"

She hung her head, miserable at the prospect of speaking the words so plainly. Yet she owed him that much.

"I am trying to tell you that on the night you found me at the bridge, I had been with another man. I am not a maiden."

Elinor crossed her arms, wrapping them around herself as she felt the shame turn her hot and then suddenly cold.

"Uh-huh."

He didn't sound too angry, just confused. She looked up at him. He was looking at her with that mixture of baffled tenderness she'd come to know rather well by now. She lowered her head and waited. She wished he would say something, anything.

"Is it your time of month?"

Her head shot up so fast her braid slapped at her shoulder. She couldn't have been more surprised if he had asked her if she could whinny like a horse. She blinked at him, unable to think of any reasonable reply. She settled for the truth.

"Nay. I had my time but a few days after I came here." She felt herself flush again and thought she must be as red as a cardinal's cloak. "I borrowed some clean cloths but I did wash them and return them."

"Uh-huh." He patted the bed. "Come and sit down, princess."

She came forward, bracing herself for his anger. Gingerly she took a seat on the very edge of the bed.

Drew cupped a hand under her chin and turned her face to his. His eyes were still more quizzical than outraged.

"Do you know what it means to be a . . . maiden?" he asked gently. "Physically, I mean."

She nodded against his hand. "Aye. A maiden is a female who has never lain with a man and coupled with him fully. Her maidenhead is yet intact within her womb."

He took his hand away and pulled back the sheet. "Then, if you're not a virgin and you're not menstruating, how would you explain this?"

His voice was still so gentle. Was there a storm to come after this calm? She swallowed against her fear and looked where he pointed.

She gaped. Several smears of dark crimson showed against the pale fabric of the bed linens. It was a moment or two before she recovered her tongue.

"You—you d-did not cut yourself, Sir Drew?" she stammered.

"Nope."

She slid off the bed and onto her knees, hands clasped at her throat.

"Thank you, thank you, thank you, our dear Lady, St. Genevieve, St. Margaret, and all the rest of the saints who watch out for foolish girls!" she babbled joyfully. "Thank you for protecting me! Thank you for letting this be . . ." She hesitated, looking over her shoulder at Drew. "For letting Drew be the man who won my maidenhead."

She started to get up, sank back down, genuflected and cried, "Amen!"

She clambered up on the bed and gazed at Drew with tear-misted eyes. "I was wrong!" she said, knowing it sounded inane but she was just so happy!

He nodded, smiling back at her. But she noted that his smile was not so joyous as her own. She reached out to touch his knee.

"What is it?" she asked. "Have I again trespassed against your customs?"

He shook his head. "No. It's just . . ." He blew out a short breath. "You were a virgin, Elinor," he said in a soft, pleading voice. "I didn't know that. I . . ." He shrugged, helplessly. "I had no idea this was your first time."

She stared at him, then nodded. "I know. I am not as most women even in my world. A woman of one and twenty years could scarcely be thought to be any maid, save an old one."

Drew shook his head again. "But I knew you were a

nun," he said. "I should have guessed that you'd taken vows of chastity."

"One may be chaste and yet not a virgin."

"Yes, but . . ." He broke off and reached for her hands. "It just took me by surprise, is all. I should have known, after these past weeks together. Thank God I at least had the sense to use protection for us."

He reached out and pulled her around so that she was sitting in the circle of his arms, her back against his warm, firm chest.

"I didn't hurt you, did I?" he whispered. "At least, not too much?"

"Nay," she said, pleasure tingling through her at the touch of his breath against her ear. "I had been braced for it, but you breached me so gently, so courteously, I felt only impatience, waiting for us to be joined at last."

"God, I love the way you talk," he muttered, nibbling on her shoulder.

She giggled and twisted about in his arms. "I do not talk too much?" she asked, laying her arms over his shoulders. "At the abbey, we were expected to go in silence most times and use only dumb-show to impart our needs to others."

"Of course you talk too much," he said, chuckling. "But then, you're asking a man who's been talking to himself, if he talked at all, for the past three years."

Elinor touched his cheek. "We are more alike than I thought," she said. "How strange it is that fortune brought us together, and yet how agreeable."

"You got that right, princess," he said with a grin.

He kissed her then, and the sun had risen high and burned away the morning mists before they left their small paradise.

Drew couldn't keep from humming. Even a late breakfast of Elinor's lead-shot biscuits and varnish-removing coffee couldn't make a dent in his good mood.

He knew he was a walking cliché. He didn't care. The previous night and morning had been bliss, satisfaction, thorough delight. The long days and nights of imagining making love with Elinor were over, and the experience had been far more wonderful than he had ever imagined.

For the first time in a very, very long time, he felt at peace.

He was still humming when Rich Woessner called late that afternoon.

"Ingraham. This is me, is that you?"

"Woessner. It's me. What's up?"

"I put some spin on that Aston character you were looking for. Did you find him?"

"Yeah." Drew was glad he was out in the garage, out of Elinor's earshot. "Go ahead. Tell me what you found."

"It's not much, but I thought you might be able to use it. I got a line into the insurance offices where this guy claims he works."

"And he never worked there."

"Wrong. He not only worked there, he was a star in their claims-adjusting heavens. His jacket was full of commendations, promotions, perfect attendance records."

"You're joking."

"Nope. But here's where the going gets weird. Roger Aston's dead."

"Huh?"

"As in doornail. Died a couple of weeks ago on a trip to northern California."

Drew scrubbed at his face. "I don't get this. I've met the guy, face to face. He's alive. I thought the credit card was a major phony."

"I don't know. I would have bet the farm on it, too. All I know is that I got this info from Cincinnati, right

278

from the horse's mouth. He died in a spa up in St. Helena."

"This is so twisted. There's no way this guy could be legit. How could he have worked a scam like this?"

"Hey, pal, remember the business you used to run? We used to warn our clients about computer scams. Anything can appear in cyber-space and people will take it for real."

"But you wouldn't fall for that."

"Nope. But I can't imagine why an Ohio insurance company would have fake files in their data banks. Unless it's a decoy. And even then, unless it's some kind of sting against insurance fraud, I can't imagine why they'd bother with dummy documents."

Drew sank onto a nearby stool. "I can't figure it, either, Rich. Maybe the guy went into Witness Protection."

"Then why is your guy still using that name?"

"If I knew that, pal, I'd be a lot happier."

"Wish I knew more about this. Do you have anything new for me?"

Though it seemed a futile exercise, he gave Rich Elinor's name and some of the names she'd mentioned at the consulate.

"I haven't been able to come up with anything on her, though," he said. "Santa Rosa PD's even gone through their Missing Persons resources looking for her. We're turning up nothing."

"I'll do my best, Ingraham. Catch you later."

"Right."

Drew sat by the phone and stared off into space. His mood was considerably less light. Rich's news added so much confusion to the mix of conflicting information he already had that he felt like he'd wandered into one of those mirrored labyrinths at the circus. Every time he thought he had a grip on the truth about Elinor, Roger, and their strange relationship, another re-

279

flection sent him scurrying away in the opposite direction.

Before he could move again, Rita showed up in the driveway and whisked Elinor away for lunch and some window-shopping. Drew worked in the shop until sunset, when Elinor returned, smiling and carrying a pan of lasagna—more of Rita's gratitude for her help the night Jennie was ill.

They started to make dinner, adding bread, salad and wine, three foods that Elinor could serve without health-threatening results. The simple pleasure of preparing a meal together was almost enough to make Drew forget the puzzle he'd been struggling with all day. Every touch was magnified by the memory of what they'd shared the night before; every excuse to kiss was taken.

"Mmm," he murmured against her hair. "If you keep this up, we'll never get this meal on the table."

"Are you sure you're hungry?"

"Yep. I missed lunch. And if I'm going to have the strength to . . . continue . . . I'm going to need food."

She twisted in his arms and tucked a piece of bread into his mouth.

"Let it not be said that I withheld bread from a starving man," she purred.

He pulled her tighter against him as he chewed. She took base advantage of his situation, nibbling at his ear.

"Hungry, Elinor?" he said when he could speak.

She giggled. "When have you known me to be otherwise?"

"That does it."

He reached out and switched off the oven, where the lasagna was reheating. She gave a small shriek as he scooped her into his arms and carried her off to the bedroom.

*　　*　　*

Two hours later, they returned to the kitchen. Their meal was none the worse for the wait, Elinor noted. Indeed, she felt as though she could feast on the glow in Drew's eyes alone.

"You've got to stop looking at me like that," he said, slicing bread for them both.

"What way is that?" she murmured.

"That way that makes my mind turn to mush. Even your nose makes me want to take you back to bed. How am I supposed to get anything done?"

She crossed her eyes and stuck out her tongue. "Is this better?"

He laughed. "Not much, princess. Remind me to get you a burlap sack and a fright wig tomorrow." He handed her a glass of wine. "And maybe something to black out a couple of teeth. Oh, and could you rub some skunk weed behind your ears? That might help."

"That might work for you," she said, smiling in the candlelight. "But how shall you manage to make yourself unattractive to me?"

He grinned. "Shoot. It's hopeless, I guess."

"Vanity!"

"Just stating the facts, ma'am."

They ate the meal in comfortable silence. Elinor savored the food, the wine, the company. She'd gone about in a cloud all day. Even Rita had noticed it, but Elinor had brushed off her comments with a smile and some remark about the day and the lingering delights of dancing at the Fish the night before.

"Elinor, we have to talk."

She glanced up from her reverie and smiled. "If you wish, Sir—I mean Drew."

He led the way into the front hall and lit the lamps. Kicking off her shoes, she curled into a corner of the padded bench he called a couch. He took a chair opposite her.

"You look worried," she said, watching his hands as they twisted together.

281

"Yeah. I guess I am. Elinor, I went into Santa Rosa yesterday while you were in the village. I had lunch with someone you know."

"Lord Doc? Lady Bear?"

"Roger Aston."

She felt as if he'd tossed ice water over her. "Who?"

"No. Don't start with the denials."

"I wasn't—I—you caught me very much by surprise. Why should you dine with Roger Aston?"

"I asked him to meet me. I told him I knew how to find the medallion he's been looking for."

Horror and pain bloomed suddenly in her heart. "You couldn't," she whispered. "You didn't—"

He reached out and caught her arm as she tried to leap off the couch. "Stay. We've got to talk about this."

"What have we to say to one another? You have betrayed me, sold me without so much as a fare-thee-well to my worst enemy!"

"That's what we've got to talk about. What do you mean by your worst enemy? And other than the fact that I didn't tell you beforehand, how have I betrayed you?"

She yanked her arm out of his grasp. "It is not your task to dispose of my medallion or my life. I said that I should find my own way home and no longer burden you with my presence. Why could you not show me some patience?"

"Because you refused to tell me anything about this Aston. It was plain that he scared the hell out of you, but you kept brushing me off when I asked you anything about him or about your connection to him."

"So you chose to speak to him, instead?"

"That's right. Because even if he's one of the bad guys, Elinor, I figured he could tell me something about you." He ran his hands over his hair. "I'm afraid for you. I'm afraid you've gotten mixed up with something illegal."

"Such as?"

"I don't know. Smuggling, maybe. Or theft. Aston wants that medallion and he wants it bad. Now, you tell me. Is it stolen?"

"Not to my knowledge."

"Is it supposed to be used to pay somebody off?"

"Not to my knowledge."

"Elinor, you're making this harder than it needs to be. I'm serious, princess. Aston is trouble and you're mixed up with him. Whatever he's up to could land you in prison or worse. Even Doc thinks he's bad news."

"Your words are meaningless. If you truly believed Roger is dangerous, you would not have allowed your good friend Lord Doc to meet him."

"I didn't allow him—Will saw him in Santa Rosa the other night. Dammit, Elinor, why are you stonewalling me? I'm trying to help you, to get at the truth."

"I have been telling you the truth! And you refuse to accept any word of it, is that not right?"

"You're right," he said, his voice low. "I haven't believed you. I've got no right to expect you to trust me now. But can't you see? It's the weirdest damned story in the world—it's the stuff of fairy tales."

"I know it, aye. I am not a fool. Yet all other explanations fall short of the mark. Only one tale, the one I told you on the pier in San Francisco, answers all the questions. I am not of your time. And neither is Roger Aston. Through his sorcery or some work of magic around us in the night, or perhaps by the power of the medallion pieces alone, he and I have traveled across the reaches of land and of centuries, and have arrived in this time, your time, and in your land."

She buried her face in her hands. Tears of anger and frustration rose to her eyes but she resisted them.

"I no longer know what to tell you. Your scoffing, as well as the danger to which I know I have exposed you, have compelled me to hold my tongue. What would you have of me?"

Silence reigned. She couldn't meet his eyes.

"I guess . . . I'd have you tell me your story."

At long last, she lifted her eyes to his.

"Truly? You are not placating me because I am so distraught?"

"Placating's never been my long suit. As you probably know by now. Please, Elinor. I'm ready to listen."

A heavy sigh escaped her.

"I suppose I can no longer keep the whole story from you. As you have brought us all into danger at Roger's hand, I shall tell you what you wish to hear."

He remained where he was. Those eyes she loved held no lights in them as they regarded her, but neither did they hold any malice.

"As I have told you, Roger is of my own time. He is wealthy, powerful and, I believe now, altogether evil."

She scooted back into the depths of the couch, wrapping her arms about herself as she related the story of Roger Aston's influence over her family's fates.

"He loved my mother once, I believe. That, or he did seduce her in their youth. My mother would seldom speak of him. When she chose my father over him, he seemed reconciled and went away for several years.

"When he returned, I was still a child at home. 'Twas then our troubles began to mount. And while he was subtle, his hand ever concealed, the gossip flew unabated that Roger Aston was intent on conquering the DeCourtenays."

"Couldn't your father stop him?"

She studied her hands. "My father was a good man but never a strong one. His gentle nature, his slight frame and his scholarly interests not only kept him from seeing evil in others, but from combating it as well. My mother stood alone against Roger, and she was but a woman."

"What kind of troubles did Roger cause?"

"He was most crafty. He undermined Father's investments abroad, knowing full well that Father's attentions were on his books and not his moneys. Later, he set forth to ruin my mother, letting it be noised about that my brother, Thomas, was a bastard by one of my father's oldest advisers. We could never trace such gossip to Roger directly, but I overheard my mother one day, confronting him with the vile stories. He only laughed and said that she could prove nothing. And she could not. Not long after that, I was sent to the abbey."

"So he went after your finances, then your mother's reputation."

"And, in turn, my parents' marriage."

"What came next?"

"When our foreign income collapsed, my father had to find moneys at home. He traveled around to all our friends, trying to raise a bit of capital to invest. It nearly broke him."

"Wait, let me guess. Roger got there before him?"

"As far as we know, though none would ever confess it. My poor father came home sick from travel and worry. When he arrived, a new problem had arisen. My mother was again with child."

"Ah."

"Aye. And, as my father had been seldom at home, nor in the best of health when he was at home, her fruitfulness seemed suspect. Roger chose this time to step in and offer a loan against some of our estates. My father refused, of course, but to his great humiliation, found that our circumstances offered no other choice."

"I suppose cutting down on expenses was out of the question?"

"Don't be foolish. Our belts were already wrapping double about our waists. And my father had his pride. He had a son, whom he loved dearly. He couldn't bear the thought of leaving no inheritance for Thomas, who was but an innocent in all of these matters."

"Sorry, princess. You're right. Go on."

She sighed. "Now come the sorrows. My father accepted Roger's loan, but it stole the heart from him. In

285

due time, he could scarcely raise himself from his bed. Roger was like a carrion-crow, circling about us, always playing the concerned neighbor and friend. When he learned that the last of his London investments had been bankrupted, my father lost all hope of life. He died in his solar, a flask of poison, untasted, at his side."

"Untasted?"

"It was ruled that no drop had been drained from it. Yet we had to suffer an inquest by the priest when rumors claimed that my father had taken his own life. We were forced to wait several days before we were allowed to bury him in hallowed ground."

"Rumors from Roger?"

"Aye. And, I suspect, the flask was from him, as well."

"This guy is like the Energizer Bunny of evil, he just keeps going—never mind me, then what?"

"Then, for a time, all was at peace. My mother was terribly aggrieved by my father's death but she managed to keep up my fees to the abbey and was planning to foster my brother and sister with Lord and Lady Carrowe, our last good friends in the world. Roger was away, in Ireland, we heard."

"Talk about the luck of the Irish."

"Indeed. Perhaps the Isle of Erin spat him back, for back he came, trouble flying before him. First, it was the old trouble of money. He offered again to make us a loan, which my mother was forced to accept. Then he seemed to believe he was a part of our household, for ever when I visited, he was ensconced there, hovering about my mother, lover-like though no love was shared between them in any sense, my mother assured me.

"She seemed unable to refuse him anything, save her bed, however. Her wondrous strength was ebbing under his dark wing. I protested his presence, and soon he was bringing suitors for me, saying that I should be married rather than troubling my mother in her ill health."

Elinor folded her hands beneath her chin. This was a part that was hard to tell, especially to Drew. She felt the sting of shame in her cheeks.

"I could not bear to be wed. And I could not bear to be wed to any man of Roger's choosing. So, to my great shame, I fled to the abbey and stayed away, lest I lose my life to a loveless, possibly evil marriage." She hung her head. "I left my mother to Roger's black touch. It was not six months later that she joined my father in the churchyard."

Drew clasped his hands over hers. "I'm so sorry, princess. That bastard's had all of you in chains for years."

She shook back her hair, blinking back tears in the same motion. "I fear I have more to confess."

"You don't have to confess anything. You did whatever you had to do to survive. Your mother wouldn't have wanted you to marry something that Roger dragged in, would she?"

"No, I'm sure she would not. Yet, after her death, I became mistress of the household. Thomas is scarcely of age and he needs time to grow, to be a boy. So I took on the estate and I blundered, badly.

"I was in a world of sorrows, losing my parents. I was terrified when I saw the state of our coffers. Roger, I realized, was our chief aid and our chief creditor. I went to him to plead for clemency, for I could not make the necessary payment. He offered me what I asked, but at a price. I must come to him and share one night with him. If I but did that simple, that least of things, he claimed, then he would call that debt paid."

"He what?"

She lifted pleading hands. "I did not know what else to do. He can be most persuasive, and I did not grasp the full import of his bargain."

"Elinor, what he asked you to do is illegal about six

different ways—here and in England, too, I'll bet. It's extortion, it's—"

"It's wrong, I know that now." She slipped off the couch and paced the room, twisting her hands. "On the night you found me, I went to meet him. I know that I arrived at his castle courtyard, but after that, all is dark. I came to myself on the bridge, where you found me."

She turned and faced him, arms outspread. "Now you know the whole tale. That is the truth, about me and about Roger. If you choose still to disbelieve me, there is nothing more I can do."

She spun and left the room.

"Elinor!"

She didn't stop. Down the hall, into the bedchamber she ran, and when she was inside, she flicked the latch on the door. She could hear his footsteps, following her. She flung herself on the bed and packed the pillows around her head and ears, shutting out all but the faintest sound of his voice, calling her name.

Coward, she scolded herself. She should have stayed to hear his response.

But there had been something in his expression, some small hint of mistrust or disapproval. That was all that had been needed to set her in flight. Her confession had been enough to bear for one night.

Chapter Nineteen

Morning hadn't come any too soon for Drew. He didn't know about Elinor, but he'd spent what was left of the previous night using the bedsheets for origami. After a night of tossing, turning and fretting over time and truth, he was grateful for the first rays of sun through the windows.

He'd listened for sounds in her bedroom, even tested the latch, but found it still locked against him. He couldn't blame her for wanting to lock him out. Not just because she might be afraid he'd call her a liar again, but also because she was no doubt as over-whelmed as he by all that had been happening and all that had been said.

He toasted bread and made coffee, carried both out to the garage. In the quiet of his workplace, he felt less disoriented by the stories and notions and feelings he'd been sorting through all night. His mind began to clear and he began to tick things off in his typical style.

One, he believed her story. Yes, it was preposterous

in some parts, ridiculous in its overall impact, but he'd watched Elinor as she'd told her life story and he'd seen her relive it in the telling. He'd wager his life that no one was that good an actress.

Two, Roger Aston was even more dangerous than he'd guessed. If half of what Elinor had told him was fact, the man was a master at manipulation, at finances, at the seduction of minds as well as bodies. According to Rich, he might even be a clever computer hacker. It was also safe to say he was seriously obsessed with Elinor's family.

Three, the medallion was a key player in all of this. Elinor said Roger had half of it, like a broken locket. He'd made it clear he wanted it back and didn't care about the cost.

Four, he, Drew, was falling in love with Elinor.

When that item came up on the list, he had to set down his coffee mug. He hadn't even known it was on the list. But it was a part of the picture, to be sure.

It wasn't just that sex with her was sensational, beyond anything he'd ever experienced, bar none. That was a terrific plus, but the love he felt for her went way beyond the physical. He knew now that he'd started falling for her on that first night she'd stayed in his bed, when he'd stayed up all night keeping watch over her. There was something about her that had connected to his soul, right from the start. She'd planted a seed in his heart and it had taken root.

He sipped his coffee again. It was time to accept it. He was involved.

"Okay, Ingraham," he muttered to himself. "Item five?"

His coffee sloshed to the floor of the garage as he shot out of his chair.

It was so obvious that they'd overlooked it a dozen times already.

Item five was the bridge.

* * *

Roger's nose wrinkled at the smell of the shop. He was accustomed to the scents of his own time, which were earthy to say the least, but this was altogether different. These were the scents of oil and leather, yes, but also of metals and other alloys and compounds made by these modern men. They were not pleasing.

"Afternoon, sir. What can I do you for?" A man approached, wiping his grimy hands on a rag already blackened with oil.

Roger wanted to step back from the fellow so as not to dirty his new trousers and surcote. Instead, he held his ground and relaxed his spine, allowing his posture to become less regal. With a hearty grin pasted on his face, he stuck out his hand in greeting.

"Lookin' for help with my bike," he said, broadening his accent so that it sounded more like the people on his TV screen. "Guy down at Wiley's Wheels said you might be the man to talk to."

"What kinda bike?" the man asked as they shook hands.

Roger tried not to wince at the man's filthy touch.

"A Knucklehead," he replied, recalling the information he'd picked up at the last few shops he'd visited.

"Yeah? Vintage?"

"I beg your pardon?"

"What year?"

"Oh. Oh, I believe it's rather . . . I mean, I dunno but I think it's purty old."

"Like forties?"

"Yah."

"Can't do much for you with one that old. I'm strictly eighties on up. But I can tell you who can."

"And that would be . . . ?"

"Name's Ingraham. Drew Ingraham. Never met the man myself but I hear tell he's like a wizard with the old Knucks and Big Twins."

"Ingraham. A wizard, you say? And his shop is in town here?"

"Nope."

The shopowner walked to the long table near the front of the shop and began ruffling through mounds of paper. "Doesn't have a regular business. Works out of his garage, as I hear. Now, where the hey did I put that receipt with his number on it?"

Roger watched with well-concealed eagerness and impatience as the man shuffled through pile after pile, pulling out crumpled scraps and folded sheets and pages brittle with age or edged with grease.

"This Ingraham, he rides a Knuck himself, does he?"

"Oh, yeah. Absolutely cherry. Every piece on it original stock except for the saddle. Nobody wants to give up the ol' kidneys these days, eh?"

"Ah—no, I s'pose not."

"Not from around here, are ya?"

"What makes ya say that?"

"Well," the shopowner said, hefting up yet another pile from a lower shelf, "your accent is pretty much a dead giveaway. You're a Southerner, huh? Texas?"

"Texas. Yah."

"Yep, I can always tell—whoops—we-ell, there she is. Always in the last place ya look."

Roger was reaching for the paper before the man was finished jabbering. It was almost in his grasp, then snatched back.

"Well, now, wait a minute, it says something here at the bottom."

Roger ground his teeth. "What?"

" 'No BS' it says. 'Serious players only.' "

"BS? British subjects?"

The man gave him a startled glance. "Bull shovel-ings, pal. *Comprende*? You sure you're from Texas?"

"Ah. Yep, that's where I'm from." Roger recomposed himself, reached out for the paper once more. "And I'm a dead serious player. My pal."

"Well, okey-doke. Ain't nothin' to me, I guess."

Roger took the paper between thumb and forefinger. "Many thanks."

"Oh, hey. When you see Ingraham, tell him it was me that sent you, okay? He doesn't know me but he'll know the name. Hal Green."

"Count on it."

Elinor rubbed her eyes as she stepped to the door of her bedchamber. Drew had been pounding on it, shouting for her to get up and get dressed.

"What is the matter?" she croaked. "Is the house afire again?"

"Nope." He took her by the shoulders and spun her back through the door. "Just get your clothes on. We're taking your memory out jogging."

"And he says *I* am mad," she grumbled.

Nonetheless, his excitement had infected her. She pulled on clothing, washed and went to the kitchen, where Drew waited with a cup of coffee and toasted bread for her.

"What is it you wish to do with my memory?"

He was packing fruit and cheese and other bits of food into her knapsack.

"We're going to jog it. We've been overlooking an important piece of your story. Today we're going to remedy that."

Her brain was beginning to waken. "What piece?"

His grin was triumphant. "The bridge."

"You—you believe me?"

His grin lost some of its brilliance, but it didn't disappear. "I believe as much as I can. Can you accept that for now?"

She gathered in a deep breath. "I shall try."

"Let's ride."

It seemed an age since she'd fallen, sickly and terrified, on this very spot, she thought as they parked Harley off the road and walked to the bridge. It had been

293

night then, and all had looked different by moonlight.

Yet this was Oakfield Bridge, no matter what they called it nowadays.

"Do you have the medallion?"

"I have." She pulled it out from under her jacket.

"Okay." His voice sounded tight. "Why don't you take a walk?"

"What? Oh. Of course."

She handed him her helmet, jacket and knapsack. Together they walked to the very edge of the bridge.

"Drew, I—"

"Mmm?"

" 'Tis no matter."

Hands clenched around the heavy gold circle, she murmured a brief prayer. She closed her eyes and stepped onto the first stone.

Peering out, she saw the same scene. She looked over her shoulder. Drew was still there. Nothing had changed.

He was scowling in his concentration, she noted. He motioned with a nod for her to go on. She let go and moved ahead.

Step by step, her arms out to her sides like a child balancing along a wall, she made her way up the gentle rise of old, worn stones. All her senses were alive, alert, testing each step she took to see if anything felt different, or unusual.

She topped the rise and turned to look back. Drew stood at the foot of the bridge. He raised his hands and shoulders in a questioning gesture. She shook her head. He waved her on.

Slowly she descended the other side. The water under the stones gurgled and rushed along with the recent rains swelling the stream. Overhead, the apple trees were blossoming, shaking some of their first flowers onto the moist stones beneath her feet.

No apple trees grew near the Oakfield Bridge.

When she reached the bottom, she looked back.

Drew was still standing on the other side, watching, frowning.

She paused, waiting for him to speak or give some sign.

He turned away and went to lean over the low wall of the bridge. She crossed back and stood near him.

"You believed, didn't you?" she asked softly.

He shook his head.

"Aye. Perhaps for only the passing of an instant, yet you did believe that what I have said is true. That I do indeed belong in a time far distant from yours."

"I just thought it might jog your memory," he said. "I thought if I brought you back out here, you'd remember what the heck happened to you." He tossed a pebble into the rushing stream. "But it was just a hunch."

"Do you not think that I share your wish? I would fain recall what brought me to you, to this world and time. And I need, above all, to return to my brother and sister, who are alone and unprotected in my time."

"Then we should do what I said, back when you first came home with me. We should go to England. I'll finagle you a passport somehow. We'll go wherever you say, and you can see that you're just lost in geography, not in time. You'll be home."

She felt stung by his fervent need to be rid of her. He seemed so disappointed that nothing had happened on the bridge.

"Very well, then. Let us go. I don't know the way from here, but I am willing to trust that a knight of your experience would have traveled many places. Lead the way."

He shifted to his side, so that he rested his elbow on the top of the wall. "And what about—"

"Hello-oh!"

They both started. A woman was coming across the bridge toward them.

As she approached, Elinor saw that the woman was

Coral Smith Saxe

about double her own age, or more—it was difficult to tell in this world. She wore a gown splotched with brilliant red, which, upon closer inspection, turned out to be cherries—as broad as her hand—painted on the bright yellow fabric and a short blue surcote. A broad green hat was tied under her chin, and she carried a staff that made a rhythmic thumping on the stones of the bridge.

"Hello," the woman called again as she topped the low rise and bore down upon them. "Peach of a day, eh?"

Elinor smiled at the woman's cheerful grin. It would be impossible to fear anyone who wore such merry garb, she thought.

"It is indeed a fine day," she said.

The woman drew up to them, breathing deeply but not winded from her brisk pace. She looked at them both expectantly.

"You live around here?" Drew asked at last.

Elinor wondered if he thought this was another lost woman come to plague his life.

"I do. In fact, you're on my property right now."

"The bridge is yours?" asked Elinor.

"Yes indeed. But not to worry. Public access is always permitted."

"Thank you." Elinor couldn't contain her curiosity. "How came you by this bridge?"

"Heavens, been in the family for years! And still as sound as the day my great-great-grandfather brought it across country."

"He brought a bridge here?" Drew came to attention. "This bridge?" He shot a glance at Elinor.

"That he did. Eccentric collector, I guess you'd call him. One of the minor railroad barons who lived in San Francisco. He bought this land for a summer home." She went to lean on the bridge wall herself. "Lovely spot, eh?"

"Quite," said Elinor.

"That your bike?" the woman asked.

Elinor gestured toward Drew. "His."

"Nice," the woman said, waving her cane at Harley. "Had a Shovelhead, myself. Sold it a couple of years ago. Couldn't do the upkeep."

"Too bad," Drew said, a smile playing at the corners of his mouth. "I do restorations and maintenance."

"Don't say? Well, well, the world is growing smaller." She raised her cane in salute. "I'll be running along. You're welcome to use the bridge, just don't get into mischief."

She started off at a brisk place. Drew dashed to her side. "Wait, please, Ms. . . . ?"

"Talcott," she said, halting. "Delphinium Talcott."

"Ms. Talcott, we're very interested in this bridge. Can you tell us anything more about it?"

She laid a sharp gaze upon him. "Not from L.A., are you?" she asked. "I'm not interested in selling it, and you can't have it for any movie location, either."

Drew raised his hands. "I'm not from Hollyweird, trust me. If you—could we sit down somewhere and talk?"

Her glance went to Elinor. Elinor felt herself compelled to support Drew's plea.

"I recommend us both to you, lady," she said, stepping forward. "We are neither footpads nor cutpurses. And it would be a fair favor if you would but sit and talk with us." She hesitated. "Oh-kay?"

The woman looked as if she wanted to laugh, then she waved her cane once again, pointing ahead. "There's an old stump over there," she said. "I can spare a minute, I guess."

They trotted along after her—like a pair of lambs, Elinor thought. Delphinium Talcott might walk with a staff, but she was as hale as any good dame of her age and then some. She set a good pace down the road, and they soon came to a small meadow that showed evidence of having once been an orchard, like the surrounding land.

Lady Delphinium seated herself on the broad stump of a felled fruit tree. Drew and Elinor took seats in the cool, slightly moist grass at her feet.

"So, what is it that you want to know?" their hostess asked briskly.

"You said that your great-grandfather brought the bridge across the country. Where was it originally?" Drew asked.

"Oh, it was in England originally. Great-grandfather Talcott went over there on his honeymoon. He'd made his fortune in the railroading out here and he was filthy rich, I can tell you. He and his lovely bride went to Europe for their honeymoon, of course, which is what all the swells did back then. They were on a walking tour in England when they came across a bridge by a couple of old ruined houses. Well, Great-grandmama was just wild about the bridge. Thought it was the most romantic thing she'd ever seen."

"Let me guess," Drew said. "He bought it for her."

"Right you are. Great-grandpapa was just wild about Great-grandmama, so anything she was wild for, he had to get it for her. He bought every piece of it, lock, stock and barrel, had it taken apart and shipped Stateside. Took a whole year to get it here and another year to put it back together in just the exact way it was when Great-grandmama saw it over there in England."

"He loved her greatly," Elinor murmured.

"He did indeed. When she died, he came out here with dynamite and fuses, all set to blow it to kingdom come. But their littlest boy, a sprat named Wesley, he took on so the old man couldn't bring himself to fire away."

"So it's been here ever since?" Drew asked.

"On that very spot. We were worried that the Interstate might come through here and that'd be the end of it, but they headed off in a whole different direction and we were left here in peace."

Delphinium looked at them, her eyebrows raised. "And now, you two had better do some talking. Why're you so interested in my old bridge?"

Roger prowled about the cottage, rifling through drawers and boxes, cupboards and chests. He'd been annoyed when he'd found the house deserted. Now his ire was growing as he realized the medallion was nowhere on the premises.

"Come, little DeCourtenay," he cooed. "Come back and show yourself."

He knew it was folly to expect her to return at his bidding. Who knew where she and her modern lover had gone?

He stood at the foot of the bed, frowning. He could see them now, the blond man and the DeCourtenay girl, writhing and squirming together on this very bed. This Ingraham had taken his *prima noctes*, the upstart bastard. Roger didn't like virgins as a rule, but Elinor's maidenhead had been promised to him. It was his right and payment as her lord.

She'd fought him when he'd tried to claim his due that night. That was how all this mess had begun—the stupid git had balked at his advances and run out into the night. He'd been fool enough to want to dress her in the half of the medallion he'd once intended for her mother, but she'd been the cause of all this traipsing about, this cat-and-mouse game that had wasted so much of his time.

And now she'd had the nerve to bed with this Ingraham. He'd wager she hadn't fought her woodsman lover, the little bitch. No, she'd been lolling about in a luxurious bed, while he, Roger, was prevented from returning to tend to his own home and claim his little Joanna. Then, to make it worse, she'd dispatched her tomcat to parley with him over the necklace. It was too much.

Elinor DeCourtenay was worse than her mother. Hell, she was worse than his own mother, and that was saying a great deal. She had been a thorn in his side too long, and by God, he'd make her pay.

He bent over and ripped the bedclothes from the bed, flinging them aside. With a roar, he sent the pillows flying after.

"Where's the necklace?" he shrieked. "Did you give it to him? Did you give it to him because he made you scream like a cat in heat?"

He tore through the house, kicking over tables and upending shelves. Books, clothing, papers flew through the air. Lamps shattered. Glassware exploded.

When he came to himself, he was in the middle of the kitchen, foodstuffs all around him on the floor. He looked down at the mess.

"Such slovenly housekeepers," he murmured.

Chuckling, he stepped gingerly over the puddle of eggs, taking care not to ruin his shoes. Once outside, he glanced at the outbuilding nearby.

"No. No, the cat has it on her. I shall simply have to bide my time."

Elinor and Drew were quiet as they left Delphinium Talcott's house. The old lady had invited them home with her, where they shared their picnic with her and took a tour around Delphinium's quaint wooden house. By the time they left, she had regaled them with stories, shared family portraits, and showed them a map of England handed down from her ancestors. The brittle paper showed precisely where the bridge had resided in England—in a lovely old Staffordshire meadow named the Oaken Field. Elinor had almost wept at the sight of the brownish smudge where her home would have stood.

As she walked toward the bridge and Drew's bike, it

seemed to Elinor that a great peace had settled on her heart. Virtually all the pieces of the puzzle had come together. The problem of the bridge was solved, in her mind.

She glanced at Drew and wondered what he thought of Del's story. Did he believe Del was in league with her somehow? Or did he believe she was a cracked pot, too?

Drew started to mount the bike, then stopped. He turned to her.

"It can't be possible."

She shook her head. "No, it cannot."

"But it's true, isn't it?"

She felt her eyes fill with tears. All she could do was nod.

He gathered her into his arms.

"Elinor," he whispered. "Elinor, this flies in the face of everything I know and understand."

She raised her eyes to his. "And you think it is different for me? I am not a fool, Drew. Nor a liar. And I know a doorlatch from a donkey."

"I know you do," he said. "I'm sorry. It's all so strange . . ."

"But you believe fully now, don't you?"

"I'm starting to. God help me."

"God help us both."

He hugged her close. "I'm so sorry. So sorry I put you through all that crap."

" 'Tis done. You had to satisfy your own reason and conscience."

"Now what?"

"Louis says the medallion is the key."

"But how does it work? You tried it today. Nothing."

She pulled away from him. "I don't know. That is what we must find out. My sister and brother are waiting for me, Drew. I must get back to my own time and aid them."

"What about Roger?"

Coral Smith Saxe

She hesitated. She didn't like what she had to say.

"Roger is of my time, as well. I believe he and I are yet bound together in this matter. I must go to him."

Drew's look was black. "The man is a bottom-feeder, princess. Pond scum. I don't want you anywhere near him."

"He has the other half of the medallion. You yourself said he wants mine back at any price. He must know something."

"Yeah, well, let's see if we can get around that. Let's go home. I'm not ready to play by his rules yet."

Elinor doubted that anything else would be revealed. Not without Roger. Still, she concurred with Drew's assessment of him. He was the scum of the pond, indeed.

She hugged Drew tightly as they sped along the River Road. The vineyards were greening on the gentle hillsides and the recent rains had turned the earth to a rich red-brown. The late afternoon sunlight slanted through the tall redwoods, casting beams that looked strong enough to walk upon.

She was going to miss this place, she thought. It was beautiful and strange and yet it had become a new home to her. She wondered if there was a way she could carry some of her drawings with her to her own time.

The thought of leaving hurt her heart. She wasn't just leaving wondrous and strange Caliphorneeah. She would be leaving Drew.

How could she bear it?

She shook the idea aside. She didn't know when or even if she could travel backward in time. It was too soon to know. Drew was right. They needed to learn more.

Drew steered Harley into the yard of his home and turned off the motor. Elinor looked around the yard, frowning.

"Something is not right," she told him as they pulled off their helmets.

He looked about. "I don't see anything different."

She handed him the helmet. "I don't like the feeling. Something's amiss."

She climbed the steps to the back door.

"Sweet my Lord!"

"What is it? Another raccoon break-in?"

She couldn't reply. He came running.

When he looked in through the back door, Drew's hands clamped onto her shoulders so tightly they hurt.

"Don't go in," he said quietly. "Go out by the bike and stay there."

He pushed past her and crossed the kitchen. "Shit."

"Is it all—?"

"Yep," he said, returning. "Let's go."

"But we must clean this—"

"That can wait. I've got to get you out of here."

"No!"

She went past him, gasping at the sight of the front room, with its books and papers torn and scattered.

"Elinor, don't—"

She pressed on through the house.

She thought she was going to be sick.

There, in the bedroom, her clothing had been shredded and flung about as if some wild animal had been turned loose, tusks and teeth free to ravage everything in sight. A pair of her silk underbriefs were twisted around a pillow, as if choking the life from it.

Her clothing alone. Not Drew's.

"Elinor, come on," Drew said, taking her by the arm. "We have to go."

"But your lovely house—this mess—"

"It's just stuff. You're what's important. I've got to get you out of here, now."

Chapter Twenty

Golden lamplight shone out from Lord Curran's house as they drove up. Drew didn't let go of Elinor's arm for a second and she was grateful, for by the time he and Will had seated her in a chair, she realized she hadn't stopped shaking for a moment since she'd witnessed the mess in Drew's bedchamber.

"Just sit tight, Elinor," Will said. "I'm gonna get you a warm drink and a blanket. Ingraham, chafe her hands, get some circulation going. She looks pretty shocky."

"Hang on, princess," Drew said, kneeling before her. "It's going to be all right."

Will returned with down-filled coverlets, a steaming cup of hot ᵗea, as he called it, and a glass of brandy for Drew.

"How you feeling, Elinor?" he asked. He took her wrist in his fingers and stared at the clock on his arm.

"Better, thank you, Sir Doc. But Drew's house—"

"Shh. Drink your tea." Will patted her hand. "Her

pulse is a little fast, but not to worry. So, children, what mischief have you been up to now?"

His tone was light, but Elinor could see the concern in his eyes.

"Somebody tossed my house." Drew cradled the brandy glass between his hands.

"Burglary?"

"Maybe. I didn't wait around to see if anything was missing."

"Well, *mi casa es su casa*," Will said briskly. "Plenty of towels. Hot and cold running water. Regular meals. If you leave your pants outside the door at night, I'll make sure they're altered to fit me by six o'clock the next morning."

"Thanks. Come on, Elinor. You haven't lived till you've had a bath in Casa Loco."

Will showed them to a room in one of the towers. In one corner stood a bed built to accommodate a family of giants. In another corner, a sunken area featured a fireplace and a deep, oval bathing tub. Though it was a warm night, Drew soon had a fire crackling and warm water running in the tub.

"Go ahead and get in," he told her. "Here's a robe to put on when you're done. Help yourself to anything. Anything. Will is rich as Croesus and lives to spoil his friends."

"Drew."

He stopped on his way out the door.

"It was Roger."

"I know, princess. But he won't find you here. Relax and enjoy your bath. I've got to talk to Wild Will."

She stared out the long windows, where the evening was beginning to gather. It was coming true. She'd been hiding the truth from Drew out of fear of ridicule and disbelief, yes, but also out of fear of another sort. Roger's passion for revenge against her family would stretch to include any who aided or sided with the DeCourtenays. Now, that included Drew.

305

Coral Smith Saxe

*   *   *

Will was in the kitchen whipping together a meal for the three of them. Drew took the brandy bottle and poured another glass.

"It's that guy Aston, isn't it?" Will said.

"You were right about him," Drew admitted. "From the looks of what he did to my house today, he's a real sicko."

"Did you call the cops?"

"Uh, it's a little sticky."

"Elinor's in trouble?"

"Not that I know of. Aston's her trouble. He's from her past." *And when I say past, I mean past.*

"Okay. What's the next move? Can we find Aston?"

"What we, white man?"

Will picked up a carving knife, flipped it, then let it fly. It went end over end and sliced into the middle of a cantaloupe resting in the fruit bowl.

Drew gave him a bland smile. "Nice shootin', Tex."

"Damn straight. Now, what's our next move?"

"I need to go back to the house. I need you to look out for Elinor. She looked like she was going to lose her cookies when she saw what he'd done to her clothes. Especially her underwear."

"Sounds like you're working my side of the street."

"You could be right."

"All the more reason for me to go with you. Call Bear to come watch over Elinor and let's ride."

The house looked even worse at night. Most of the lamps had been smashed, even the overheads, so Drew brought an aluminum work-light from the garage. Its white glare added a garish pallor to the mess.

"Anything missing?" Will asked when they'd taken a quick survey of the interior.

Drew shook his head. "Not that I can see. It just looks like he went nuts."

"Any ideas why?"

"He must have come looking for Elinor. When he didn't find her, he went non-linear."

He nudged at a shattered CD with his toe. Sting, "Ten Summoner's Tales." Elinor's favorite.

"I guess he's seriously hung up on her. But from what she's told me, they weren't lovers or anything like that."

Will moved into the hall. "They wouldn't have to be. For some of these guys, just passing her on the street or seeing a picture of her could be enough for them to fixate on her. But you say she does know him?"

"Oh, yeah."

Drew hung back, feeling slightly sick himself at the prospect of reentering the bedroom. There was no blood, no signs of real violence, he knew. Yet the sheer force of the fury that had been unleashed there was stunning. And there was no question it had been aimed at Elinor.

Will went over the room, not touching anything, just looking. He eyed the pillow, choked and sliding off the bed, and for the first time, Drew noticed that the bed itself had been slashed. Long, jagged wounds gaped in the old mattress; its filling protruded. A kitchen knife lay on the floor.

"Well," Will said, putting his hands on his hips. "Believe it or not, I've seen worse." He looked up at Drew. "Not that that's much comfort to you," he added softly. "Obviously Aston has some real problems, a lot of them sexual, but he's not a complete freak."

"How can you tell?"

"With the exception of the bed and the pillow, this looks more like a temper tantrum than a ritual. It's too chaotic, too complete. If you're right and nothing's missing, he didn't take any trophies and he didn't leave any gifts or messages that I can see."

"Man, Doc, but you deal in some ghastly stuff."

"Oh, hey, I don't do this kind of stuff on a regular basis. That's for the forensic shrinks and the FBI guys."

He nodded to the bed. "You might want an expert to look at this."

"I don't think we have the time."

"Okay. You say he wants something she has."

Drew summoned up his courage. They were entering the Twilight Zone.

"He wants that medallion she wears. You know, the one that looks like the sun?" He rubbed the back of his neck. "It's—it's linked to their past somehow."

"Their past? Are we talking about the 1400s, pal?"

Drew winced. "Yeah."

Will crossed the room and rested his back against the stove opposite Drew. He faced him for a long moment, during which Drew stared at him without a plea or an apology. He'd gone too far for that now.

"If Aston's after the medallion, it must hold some sort of power for him."

Drew relaxed. At least Will wasn't getting out his keys to the funny farm.

"So, if it's the medallion he's after," Will continued, "why doesn't Elinor just give it to him?"

"We haven't been able to find him until lately. And, as you can imagine, it took me a long time to believe her."

"Whether you believe her 1400s story or not, you've got to take it all seriously, now. This guy isn't playing pat-a-cake."

Drew nodded. "I hate like hell to do this, but I don't see much choice now. You're right—we've got to get Roger and that damned necklace back together."

"You are correct, of course."

Elinor snuggled deeper into the thick robe she'd found in Will's wardrobe. At least she was no longer trembling like the last autumn leaf in a gale, she thought. But her very bones felt icy at the proposition Drew had just made.

"Are you sure?" he asked, sliding nearer to where she

308

sat, propped on the pillows. "It's your necklace, after all. If you say you just can't part with it, we can try to find some other way."

"Nay. It's—what was it you said?—it's just stuff. I only wish I had had the presence of mind to do this sooner. I could have saved you so much trouble and worry."

"Don't think about it." He reached up and tucked a lock of her hair back behind her ear. "Will says nobody can really predict what nut cases like Aston are going to do. It would have been too dangerous for you to go to him, even if you knew how to find him."

"I suppose." She took his hand and pressed a kiss into the palm. "I still can scarce forgive myself for the danger I've brought to you."

"Let it go, princess," he whispered, pulling her to him. "Will and I have it all planned. This time tomorrow, I think we'll be rid of Roger Aston forever."

Elinor buried her head in the comfort of his shoulder, hiding her face from his keen eyes. She had her own plan.

Yes, by this time tomorrow, Roger Aston would be gone.

And, if her guess was correct, so would she.

Her first obstacle was getting away from Drew. If she hadn't known better, she would have thought he'd guessed her intentions, for even in his sleep he sought to keep her with him. It took her three tries just to extricate herself from his loving embrace without wakening him.

She found her clothes and dressed in the darkness. The sight of Drew sleeping at peace in the big bed almost made her lose courage. Leaving him without a farewell was cruel, she knew, but it could not be helped. She would write a note.

The second challenge she faced was using the phone instrument. The lights from Will's courtyard deck provided just enough illumination for her to read the numbers on Louis's card, but the various noises from the phone made her anxious. At last, after bells rang in her ears for several moments, she heard his voice, sleepy and rasping, coming out of the phone at her.

"Sir Louis?"

"Hello? Who's this? I can hardly hear you."

"It is I, Elinor DeCourtenay." She raised her voice as much as she dared.

"Elinor? It's four o'clock in the morning. What's wrong?"

"I need a great favor."

Her third challenge was convincing Louis, over breakfast in his tiny apartment kitchen, that she should undertake this task at all.

"Elinor, *meydele*, you should listen to your young man. This fellow Aston, he sounds crazier than a bedbug."

"Bagels, you called these?" she asked, holding up the delicious, chewy bread roll he'd given her.

"*Ja, ja*, bagels. Don't try to change the subject. Why do you want to do this alone?"

"Because it is just as you say. Roger is a Bedlam-bug. I cannot permit Drew and Will to risk their lives."

"Why not call in the police?" he asked. "They could at least protect you from him."

"And what would your police say were I to tell them that I desired protection from a man who held part of a necklace that was my only hope of returning to the year 1420?"

She shook her head and spread more creamed cheese on her bagel. "No, I must be alone when I meet with Roger. I need your help in returning to the bridge. If you will do me just that one great kindness, I shall not trouble you again."

"That's what I'm afraid of," he grumbled, hauling out a thick book with yellow pages. "I want you should trouble me again."

*   *   *

"Doc!"

Drew was scrambling into his clothes as he punched the intercom buttons.

"Doc!"

"Speak." Will's voice was groggy with sleep. "And it better be good at this hour."

"Elinor's gone."

"What? Are you sure?"

"Yeah. She left a note."

"Meet you in the kitchen in five."

Drew cursed steadily under his breath as he thrust his feet into his shoes and fumbled with the laces. Fooled again, he told himself. When was he going to learn that the fairer sex was that way for the sole and express purpose of duping boneheaded males like him?

Will had fresh-brewed coffee ready when Drew entered the kitchen, along with a basket of rolls, cheeses and fruits.

"Breakfast elves?" he growled, helping himself to the bounty.

"Automation and obsessive pre-planning. Any other complaints?"

"Sorry. Talk about getting up on the wrong side of the bed. I woke up with this in my face, where my beautiful bed partner should have been."

He shoved the note across the counter.

" 'Dear my lord Drew,' " Will read. " 'I must needs be off today to discover my own way home. I beg you not to pursue me, nor make trouble for yourself upon my behalf. I am sure of my course. A thousand, million thanks for all your kindnesses to Elinor DeCourtenay, Baroness.' "

Will whistled. "If you're thinking what I'm thinking, we need to find her, pronto."

Drew frowned. "I just can't believe she gave us the slip."

"All the vehicles are here, so she must have set out on foot."

"Yeah." Drew's face brightened. "Yeah, she doesn't have any wheels. She can't have gone too far."

"There's something else we need to think about before we get out on the road."

"You don't need to remind me. It's all I can think about. Aston."

"Too right. We have an appointment with Himself today."

Drew drained his coffee cup. "I haven't forgotten," he said grimly. "I intend to keep it. But Elinor comes first, wherever the hell she's gone."

"Or whenever?"

"Don't even think it."

Apple blossoms. That was all Elinor could see as Louis drove down the road to the bridge. Everywhere around them, tender pink buds were turning to creamy white blossoms in the orchards.

New life all about and she felt as if she were going to her death.

Louis stopped the car and turned toward her.

"Well? Is this the place?"

"Aye." She unfastened the belt of the seat. "Roger said that he would be here within the hour." She took hold of his hand. "I shall never forget your kindness. As a father you've been to me."

"As a father I'd be pretty mad with you right now," he said sternly. "But don't worry—we've been over all this already. I understand that you need to go back for your family's sake."

Elinor pressed a kiss on his weathered cheek. "Thank you, my friend. Be well, all your days."

"And you, Elinor DeCourtenay."

She climbed out of his car and closed the door, shooing him off. He made a circle in the road and drove back the way they'd come.

"Now, Lord Lewes," she said aloud, surveying the landscape. "Show yourself."

Roger tapped out a little rhythm on the steering wheel as he drove. His luck was turning. The Fates had simply required a bit of a push, that was all. Paying a visit to Drew Ingraham's house had made Elinor sit up and take notice at last.

He chuckled. Both of them had sat up on their hindquarters and begged like dogs at a banquet, he noted, both Elinor and her motorcycling swain. First, the lover had called and set up a meeting in the town once more, promising the medallion. Then Elinor herself had made a call, arranging to meet him at the bridge.

One way or the other, he'd have his necklace today. And, one way or another, he'd have his revenge on Gerard DeCourtenay's eldest.

Should he take her with him, back to their own time, and make her suffer long, in the presence of her neighbors and peers? Or should he simply take the medallion and vanish into the past, leaving her to fret here in this world, wondering what torments he was visiting upon her precious siblings?

"So many choices," he sang out as he turned onto the bridge road.

He frowned. What if the DeCourtenay bitch decided to betray him? What if she arrived without the other half of the medallion?

Ah, well, he decided, patting the dagger on his belt. He knew where to find the lover. One of them would give him the necklace.

Or he'd simply have to kill them both.

With a broad smile, he pulled up near the bridge. Elinor was there, just as she had said. And glinting from beneath her surcote was the medallion.

He did have the best luck.

* * *

313

Drew wanted to open the throttle and let his bike run full-out. Time seemed to be his worst enemy today.

He reined in his impatience, knowing that getting stopped by a CHP would be an even worse delay. Once he made it to the bridge road, he told himself, he'd open it up and fly.

He and Will had decided that it would be best to divide and conquer. Will would keep the appointment at the restaurant with Roger while Drew played his hunch as to where Elinor might have gone. Will had supplied him with a cell phone—fresh batteries included—so they could contact one another as soon as they knew anything.

Part of him hoped Roger would blow off their meeting, so that Will wouldn't be at risk. Another part of him prayed Aston would show at the meeting and Drew would find Elinor before anything else happened.

He made the turn onto Watertrough Road, picking up the pace a bit as he sailed over its rolling country miles. His heart began to pound as he zipped off onto Venners Creek Road. As the hand of the speedometer climbed, so did his adrenaline level. He had to get a grip, he told himself. If he couldn't stay cool, he might make a costly mistake.

But he couldn't help himself. He fed the Harley more fuel and roared around the last bend before the bridge.

The instant the Jaguar came into view, he knew he'd been right. It didn't cheer him.

He was even less cheered by the sight that greeted him as he slid to a stop beside the Jag.

"Drew, no! Get away!"

Elinor's heart almost failed her as she saw Harley come roaring into the roadway. She had been so careful but it had been for naught. Drew had come after her.

Indeed, he was coming right at them, the motor-beast trained on Roger.

Quicker than thought, Roger jumped sideways and pulled her in front of him. His dagger bit into the skin of her throat.

Drew swerved away. He guided Harley back around and parked him, blocking the entrance onto the bridge. Elinor groaned in frustration as he dismounted and approached.

"What's the deal, Aston?" he asked. "This jewelry thing with you is getting out of hand."

How could he be so calm, she wondered. She felt ready to shriek.

Roger's tone was almost as blithe as Drew's.

"Just eliminating the middle man, as I believe you would say. You weren't about to bring me my medallion, were you, Ingraham?"

"Well, we'll never know, now, will we?" He crooked his hand at Roger. "Okay, Aston. Let her go."

"Whatever for?"

" 'Cause if you don't, I'm gonna rip your miserable little pea-sized heart out and feed it to you."

Elinor heard the lightness in his tone, but she saw the ice-blue steel in his eyes. If she hadn't known him already, she would have been terrified of the coldness— and firmness—of his intent.

Roger only laughed. "Think again, sirrah. You shan't move a step while I have this little piece here in my grasp."

He pressed the blade against her skin. Elinor grim-aced but held still.

"Please, Drew," she pleaded. "Please leave me. I want to do this. I have to."

"You see? No loyalty in women, Ingraham. She might have bedded you last night, but she's begging to go with me today."

Drew seemed unperturbed. "I wouldn't flatter myself if I were you, Aston." He moved closer. "She's told me

315

a lot about you. What's it like to be so hard up you have to extend credit in order to get laid?"

"I wouldn't know," Roger retorted. "Perhaps if you mounted something that wasn't mechanical once in a while, you could find out."

"Ooh, good one, Rog."

Elinor was trembling now. Drew kept coming closer, smiling. Why didn't he keep quiet? Why didn't he get away? He was in danger, yet he seemed to be drawn to it, not repelled by it.

"But hey, Rog, that's enough chit-chat for now. Just let go of the lady and we'll settle this like—*men!*"

In one flashing motion, Drew shoved Elinor out of the way. She stumbled and fell to the muddy grass by the side of the road. When she scrambled to her feet, she saw Drew and Roger struggling on the roadway.

Her heart in her mouth, she watched as Roger struck out with the dagger, missing Drew's face by a hair-breadth. Drew pressed him, they stumbled about. The dagger flashed out once more, but this time Drew raised both his arms. In one scissoring motion, he connected with Roger's arm and the knife skittered across the paving.

Elinor dove for it, claimed it before Roger could move to retrieve it.

"Back off, Elinor," Drew shouted. She obeyed, unthinking.

The two men wrestled, nearer and nearer to Harley and the bridge. Something bright caught the light and sailed into the air. Roger roared as his half of the medallion flew out of Drew's grasp and dropped into the grass.

A mighty shove from Drew sent Roger staggering backward. He came up against Harley, tilting, almost falling.

Thunder cracked. Roger was catapulted backward over the motorcycle.

Elinor held her breath as he rose from behind it, hands clasped to his chest.

Then, in a shimmer of confused light, he disappeared.

Chapter Twenty-one

Elinor stood gaping at the spot where Roger had vanished. She'd heard the shot, seen the bullet enter his body. And yet, he was gone. The bridge stood empty and she could see no stain of blood or sign of the man who had so tormented her and her family.

She turned to look behind her. Delphinium Talcott held a rifle still braced on her shoulder, a look of amazement on her wrinkled features.

Elinor faced Drew. He made a gesture of bewilderment and then opened his arms. She ran to him.

"Forgive me," he muttered between kisses. "Forgive me, please."

"Forgive you for what, love?"

"For not believing you. For being an egotistical, self-centered nut who couldn't accept the truth."

She gave him a wan smile and touched his cheek. "I scarcely believed it myself."

"But I—"

"Hush." She kissed him soundly and slipped out of

his embrace. She looked at Delphinium, who had lowered the rifle but looked pale.

"Come," Elinor said, taking the woman's arm. "Let's get you inside. I know a recipe for a good tisane that will settle the nerves."

"Tisane?" Del snorted. "Honey, I want a good, stiff shot of bourbon. I think I just killed a ghost."

Drew took the rifle from her and quickly began to unload the chamber. "I'm in favor of that. Bourbon all around."

"And chocolate?" Elinor asked, laughing shakily.

He hugged her. "Hershey's, Ghirardelli, Godiva—you name it."

Without speaking, they all turned and looked at the bridge. Drew handed the rifle and ammunition to Del. He walked around Harley and stood for a long moment, just gazing at the stones.

Elinor patted Del's arm and walked toward the bridge to meet him.

"Is it true?" she called softly.

"Like the Wicked Witch of the West, princess. He just plain melted out of the picture."

"You've killed witches before?"

"No. This is my first time—or Del's, maybe—never mind. You're going to want that," he said, pointing at the grass.

She looked and saw the other half of the medallion, partly hidden by some weeds. With a trembling hand, she picked it up and hung it about her neck, where it made a light clanking against its mate. She fingered them hesitantly. Nothing happened.

She looked at Drew and shrugged.

Jangling beeps sounded from Harley. Drew started, then grinned and plucked a small black box from one of the saddlebags.

"Hey, Doc," he said into the box. "I found her."

He listened, laughed. "Yeah, yeah, I owe you. Uh-huh. Uh-huh. Your mouth to God's ear, pal. Look, we're going to be out here for a while. Give Louis a call-back and tell him it's okay, will you? Tell him not to worry."

He pressed a button on the box and slipped it into his shirt pocket. Elinor shuffled a bit at the sharpness of his expression.

"It was the only way," she said. "I could not have reached here without Louis's help. I don't know how to drive Harley or run a car."

He took the bars at Harley's head and began to push it forward.

"She comes through centuries, over an ocean, across a whole continent, and she worries about transportation," he muttered.

She grinned. "I worked the phone-machine, though."

"Great."

An hour or two later, they had eaten and drunk and shadows were beginning to settle in the yard outside Delphinium's house. Del had given Elinor a clean dress to wear in place of her own muddy garments and she felt much better for the change.

Much restored herself, the older woman had telephoned the police in town, complaining that a car had been parked on her property all afternoon and that she expected it to be towed away by the following morning.

"They're gonna wonder what happened to the driver," she told Drew and Elinor when she'd hung up.

Drew nodded. "I know. But it's just going to lead to dead ends. This I know from experience. Old Roger was good at leaving trails that went in circles."

"Boy," Del said to Elinor. "I don't know how the heck you got mixed up with a fella like that. I'm still not sure I believe I saw what I saw out there."

Elinor opened her mouth to speak. Del held up her hands.

"No, no. Don't try to explain it all to me again. I've

320

decided I've seen enough miracles in my lifetime. What's one more?"

She rose from her chair before the fire that Drew had built. "I'm going to turn in, kiddos. I think I've had enough excitement for one day." She pointed around the large old house. "Make yourselves at home, if you want to stay the night. There's plenty of room in this old place."

"Thank you for all you have done for us this day." Elinor escorted her to the stairs. "If you don't mind, we'll stay to see that you are well."

"Fine and dandy. Breakfast's at seven. Be there or be square."

Silence, comforting and peaceful, settled on the house. Elinor looked up at the portraits on the walls. Talcotts of many generations gazed upon them with imperturbable calm. There was even a Talcott portrait whose date proclaimed him to have been alive in her own time. The thought brought her back to events of the day.

"Roger is dead," she said slowly.

"I guess so," Drew said. "Although that final vanishing act makes me wonder."

She shook her head. "No. I can feel it." She touched the amulets at her neck, the new heaviness somehow warm and comforting.

"He died out of his time. Without the amulet, he was lost."

"I hope you're right." He pulled her closer to him on the sofa. "If Del hadn't shot when she did, I would have pulled him apart with my bare hands."

She shivered against him, despite the warmth of the fire.

"Don't say that. I'd never wish for the soul of another to be on your conscience."

"His is on Del's now."

"Aye," she said, feeling a sadness for the peppery old woman rise up within her. "She made light of it, claim-

321

ing he was a trespasser. How she knew I was in danger I shall never know, but I owe her my life."

"I thought I was going to lose it when I saw you with him on the bridge. I'd have been just as happy to mete out the justice today. But, damn, that old lady is quick on the draw!"

They grinned at each other, feeling relief flood in to mingle with their regrets. Drew caressed her back and she buried her face in his neck, feeling the throb of his pulse against her cheek.

She was alive. And she was free of Roger. She had come thousands of miles, hundreds of years, to right the wrongs against her family. She couldn't wait to tell Thomas and Joanna. She raised her head, staring at the portraits once more.

She had to go back.

She'd completed her task, in the most roundabout and fantastical manner to be sure, but completed it nonetheless. She knew the secret of the amulet. Roger was gone, out of their lives forever. There was nothing left to be done here.

Except there was.

She took Drew's face into her hands and kissed him. Her longing for him rose from her aching heart and flooded her being. She couldn't leave without one more chance at sharing the heady magic of their love. Whatever might come after, she knew she would carry the touch of his body on hers, the mingling of their souls, for all time.

Her hunger was indeed a flood tide rising. She nipped gently at Drew's lips and moaned as he captured her mouth with his, delving sweetly with his tongue. Her heart was already racing, her body expanding, contracting, her skin warming here, rising into goosebumps there. The tenderness of his loving lapped around her like the tide, but she could sense a storm of passion gathering between them.

Drew's hand slipped to the hem of her dress, his fingers lightly teasing at her thighs. She murmured her impatience and, taking his hand in hers, guided it to the place where she was already aching for him. Before she could protest, he'd ripped the band of her under-briefs and tossed them away, leaving her deliciously naked beneath the loose, clinging gown.

They built the storm between them with caresses rough and soothing. They fanned the swollen clouds with the gasps and breathy sighs their pleasure elic-ited. The swirling of the waters around them rose still higher, tossing them and catching them like playthings as they played out their own games and fancies. If this was farewell, Elinor felt she could say good-bye to Drew until the end of the ages.

Seeing him loosen the button at the waist of his breeches, she arched and began to lift her dress.

"No," he whispered, stopping her hand. "Come to me this time. I need you."

He caught her under the arms and lifted her up and across his lap. Gently he parted her legs so that she was kneeling on either side of his thighs. Slowly, his eyes never leaving hers, he took her hips and guided her to him, until they were a breath away from joining.

"Come to me, princess," he murmured.

She watched his jewel-blue eyes close as she slowly, slowly lowered herself onto him, savoring the antici-pation that was both torment and satisfaction. When his request was at last fulfilled, she sank against his chest, her breath coming in short, soft gasps. His arms encircling her, he shifted them both to maximize their comfort and then held her still, both of them, she sensed, gratified and shaken just to be so completely joined.

At long last she felt him stir within her, a caress in-timate and sweet, one that could only be shared be-tween lovers. She rose, placed her hands on his shoulders, returning that caress with her own.

The storm that had been held off by their initial joining returned with a rush of hot winds. His hands on her breasts made her lips part, panting with excitement. She arched upward, begging for his lips to taste where his hands now played. And when his mouth closed over her, wetting the silk, and pulled hard on the tender flesh beneath, she felt a sensation of lightning shooting throughout her body.

He urged her to him, one hand behind her neck. As he kissed her, his other hand slipped to where they were joined, probing gently but firmly. The intensity of that first connection almost sent her bucking off of him, but he murmured soothing sounds against her mouth and bade her have patience, to take her pleasure.

She was too enthralled to tell him that she was fair dying of pleasure. But she made the effort to calm herself as he had bidden. She meant to extend this night, this act, for an eternity.

"Princess," he murmured, placing his hands on her thighs, relieving her for a moment. He was gazing into her eyes once more. "What a miracle you are."

"What a miracle is love."

There. She had said it. Or close to it. She waited for his response, but his only reply was to pull her to him for a kiss that seemed like honey and thunder. She threw her fears to the heated winds and poured her love into her answering kiss. He grasped her shoulders, holding hard. His desperation matched hers. She moved against him, fanning her desire to be so close to him that they were lost within one another.

"Sweet Elinor," he groaned. "You feel so good. I can't get enough of you."

She rose above him, rocking her hips, giving him all she knew to give. He added his own efforts by placing his hands on her hips and raising her, then gently pushing her down, then raising her again.

It was too much. She rose and fell with him, his hips rising to meet her downward thrusts, making her dizzy with pleasure. The storm broke over them, urging them to a frenzied pace, their bodies nearly frantic with desire. And then Drew touched her again, in the midst of that storm, touched her in that magical spot that so excited her.

She fell into his arms, heaving and twisting against him. She called his name and heard hers wrung from his lips as he rose fiercely to meet her, pouring himself into her. They collapsed in a tangle of arms, hair and panting kisses.

"My love," she whispered when at last she could speak. Her fingertips caressed his cheek, his lips.

His beautiful eyes studied hers. "Do you mean that?" he asked, his voice soft but serious. "I mean, seriously?"

She nodded, tears starting in her eyes. "I've never loved anyone before as I love you."

He gathered her to him. "God, you don't know how much I've been wanting to hear you say that."

"Even before? Before you believed me?"

"Yes, princess. Even when I couldn't believe in who you were or where you came from, I believed in the fact of you. I fell in love with *you*. Do you think I'd do and say all the weird stuff I've been doing and saying if I didn't love you, yourself?"

She kissed him, long and tenderly.

His words were a balm and a wound. She, too, had longed for declarations of love between them. They were all the sweeter for the wait.

But had they come too late?

She couldn't run away from her responsibility to her brother and sister. She had to go back and face whatever they were facing in that far-off time. She believed with her heart that Roger Aston was dead, but she couldn't be wholly sure that Thomas, Joanna and Oakfield were out of danger until she saw them with her own eyes. Moreover, even if Roger was dead, there were other hardships her siblings faced, with no mother or father to look after their interests.

She had to go back.

"What is it?" Drew asked, brushing a lock of hair from her shoulder. "You look so sad." He cleared his throat. "Do you regret . . . what you just told me? Or what I told you?"

"No," she said quickly. "Not at all." She took one of his hands and pressed it between hers. "It's just that now that Roger is dead . . ."

"Yes?"

"I am free of his hold on me here. I have the rest of the amulet."

A shadow crossed his face. She hated what she was about to say, but she couldn't lie.

"I have to go back."

"I don't want to hear this."

"I did not wish to say it!"

"But Aston's dead, princess." He sat up, punched a cushion. "He won't bother you again."

"But Joanna and Thomas are still in their own time. They are alone and they are but children. I must go back, for their sakes."

He crushed another cushion between his hands. "I hate this. I just got you back, princess. I thought you'd taken off into time with that monster Roger. You don't know how grateful I was to see you on that bridge, still here, even if you were in his hands."

"I know it, aye." She gnawed at her lip. "Perhaps it would have been better if I had gone back with him."

"Don't say that!" He grabbed her, held her to him, his embrace almost crushing her. "I would have gone out of my mind, imagining you with—with—"

"Shh." She touched his lips. "No more. Let us say no more." She slipped out of his hold and stood before him. "Come. We can speak in the morning. Right now, all I want is rest. With you."

He rose and followed her upstairs. They found a room at the end of the west wing of the house with a bathing chamber and a large, canopied bed. With scarcely a word spoken between them, they made up the bed with fresh linens from the cupboard, undressed, and slipped under the covers.

And through that long night, the only words that passed their lips were "yes" and "oh, yes" and "yes, please, my love."

But the end had to come, Drew thought as they stood on the bridge again, two days later. He'd known she was right, that she had to go back to her sister and brother. And he wouldn't have loved her so much if she were someone who could have walked away and abandoned them.

Still, this hurt like hell.

Elinor raised her hand to his face. He took her hand in his and kissed the palm.

"I shall return," she said. "I shall. If there be any possible manner or conveyance, I shall return to you."

"Go care for your brother and sister," he whispered, leaning his forehead to hers. "Take care of yourself."

She wrapped her arms about him. He felt again all the hunger, joy, love and fear they'd shared. With an effort, he sent waves of trust and hope and faith back to her in his own embrace.

"I love you," she whispered.

He could only kiss her, his heart too full to trust his voice.

" 'Tis but a bridge," she murmured. "Naught but a bridge."

She stepped back, out of his embrace, and pulled her blue gown close around her. The wind had risen and caught at her hair. It set up a whistle in his ears.

There was nothing more to say. In a moment, they would know if the medallion was the key or if there was some secret to its magic—a secret that had vanished with Roger Aston.

With one long, last look, Elinor turned and stepped onto the bridge.

"Drew! We've—"

He jumped when he saw it. Or rather, didn't see it. One instant she was there, whole and beautiful, smiling a rueful smile. In less than the blink of an eye, she was gone, melted almost, into the background of rock bridge and apple trees and windswept sky.

"Elinor!" he shouted.

He raced onto the bridge. Yet he knew, even as he ran, that she was gone. She hadn't been snatched up by a helicopter. She hadn't jumped off the bridge. She hadn't used any mirrors or photographic legerdemain.

She had vanished.

Back to another time? Another place? He'd probably never know for certain.

But if he knew anything, he knew she would return.

And if she didn't, he'd move heaven and earth to find her.

Drew had disappeared from her vision like a candle being snuffed out. She had seen it, just as the first sulfurous wind blasted into her and flung her into an instant of such utter darkness that she felt as if the world had ended without a glimmer of hope. Then she fell, as if from the highest battlement of the tallest tower ever built, and the sickening downward rush was too terrifying for her to endure.

Blessedly, she fainted, and for how long she lay, witless, she couldn't say. But at last she felt her feet were her own, her body solidly in place upon the ground, and she opened her eyes.

Her stomach pitched and her head seemed to clang with pain. She groped for the rail of the bridge and leaned over, struggling to keep her dinner. It was a losing battle from the start.

When it was over, she sank to the stones and leaned

her cheek against the cool wall. It was enough, for this moment, just to be alive.

"Linnie?"

She looked up, startled. The sickness of the headache nearly gagged her again, but she drew a deep breath and mustered what she hoped was a smile.

"Joanna?" she whispered.

The young girl squatted down beside her, brown eyes wide. "Are you ill, Linnie?"

"I'll be well in a flash," she said, patting the girl's cheek with a fond hand. She gazed at her sister in joyful astonishment. Miracles had overtaken her once more.

"Just look at you, sweeting. You look so fine."

"But you're crying," Joanna said. "Why did you run away? Are you hurt?"

"I'm not hurt," Elinor said. She put out her hand to the wall and hoisted herself to her feet. "I'm just a bit tired from my . . . travels."

"Well, come along then," her sister said, tugging at her hand. "Papa's going to be so relieved. Mama's angry, of course, but you know Mama, she's just a hen who's all cackle and no beak when it comes to you."

Elinor hung back, stock still, on the bridge.

"Mama?" she said, her throat tight now with tears. "And Papa?" Her eyes were misting. "They are both . . . at home?"

"Of course, ninny. Where else would they be?"

"And Thomas, where is he?"

Joanna giggled again and pulled her along, off the stones of the bridge and onto the path.

"He's here," she said. "You know he thinks he is so much of a man now that he's esquiring for Lord Tristan. But I've fixed him. I've put my largest toads in his bed, so when he lies down tonight, too silly from all the wine, he'll think he's been beset by horrors from beyond the tomb!" Joanna's face was gleefully wicked. "But you must come! You must bathe and dress and let Mama do your hair. Whatever made you put on that old dress?"

Elinor scarcely heard her; she was too busy trying to get her bearings. She glanced about her as her little sister dragged her along the path. No orchards. No paved roads. No motorbeasts. No airplanes overhead.

She was back.

And somehow, all was well. She struggled to grasp it. Her parents were alive! Thomas was fostering in a good lord's home, as he should. Joanna was well and as bloomingly pretty and mischievous as ever. And not much older, by any sign that Elinor could see, than the day that Elinor had kissed her good-bye and set off for Castle Clarisdoune.

She pulled Joanna to a halt once again.

"Jo," she asked, steadying herself with a hand on the girl's shoulder. "What of—where is—is Roger Aston anywhere about?"

"Who?"

"Lord Roger Aston. Lord of Clarisdoune." Elinor gestured to the hilltop where Castle Clarisdoune stood.

She frowned. It was likely some trick of the morning light, she thought. Or the time-travel sickness. Somehow, Clarisdoune seemed different. More welcoming. Fluttering from its keep was a flag that boasted brilliant azure stripes. Roger's banner had borne only a gold fess upon a sable field.

"You mean Sir Toby," Joanna said, her exasperation with her dotty older sister unconcealed.

Elinor shook her head. "Nay, Jo. Roger Aston. Our old enemy."

Joanna shrugged. "Do come home, Linnie. You're talking silly. That's Sir Toby Dunbar's home. Lord Carrowe's friend. You know, the one who used to give me pick-a-back rides upon his big shoulders. He'll be here this noon, too, so come along, you great lazy thing."

Elinor sighed. This was all too much for her to fathom. The nausea was returning and she was suddenly weary to the very marrow. She put her hand into her sister's and allowed herself to be led home.

The sight that greeted her upon entering Oakfield House was enough to make her weep again for joy.

There, before the small fire, her mother paced, looking only slightly older than she had before her death. Hunched over a small table, scribbling away, sat Gerard DeCourtenay, oblivious to any other living being in the world—just as he had done so often in Elinor's memory.

Her heart contracted, then seemed almost to burst with happiness. Tears set the room swimming before her eyes. It was like a dream, this pleasant scene. Everything had changed and yet it was all somehow the same. Time seemed to have passed since she had left, yet her family, her home, had been restored to the state they were in before she had left the abbey to aid her sister and brother against Roger Aston.

Roger. She gasped, even as Joanna tugged on her arm and pulled her into the hall. Had Roger's death changed all this? Had the path of her family's fortunes truly been so dependent upon his will and treachery?

She had no more opportunity to puzzle things out. Her sister loudly proclaimed Elinor's arrival and she was pulled into the center of the family circle with many embraces and questions.

"Linnie's sick," Joanna piped. "I found her on the bridge, green as any reed and talking very silly."

Susannah DeCourtenay felt Elinor's forehead.

"You don't seem feverish," she noted. Then she gave Elinor a gentle shake. "Why in heaven's sweet name ran you away, you foolish girl? Sir Walter was startled in the extreme that you should prove so flighty and irresponsible!"

"Mama," Elinor said wonderingly, clasping her hands on her mother's plump arms. " 'Tis wondrous but true. You are here."

331

Coral Smith Saxe

"Aye, thanks be to grace that I am, Elinor. What a fright you gave us!"

Gerard patted Elinor's shoulder. She turned and saw his familiar bemused smile, as if he wasn't quite sure he understood what was going on about him. A smile that, long ago, had been wiped away by Roger Aston.

She threw her arms about her father. "Oh, Papa. I can't believe it. I'm so happy to see you!"

"It is well, daughter, I'm sure," he murmured, patting her back. " 'Twas but the flutter over the wedding that frighted you. So I told your mother." He gave her a gentle hug and held her out from him at arm's length. "Doubtless you've run your demons to earth, as ever you did as a child."

"I went rather far, indeed," Elinor said, smiling through her tears.

"Now," Susannah announced, all business. "You must go in and be made ready. I'll send some food for you to settle your stomach. Jo may go up with you. And use the back stairs! Your hair is so mussed from your gadabout, Sir Walter would mistake you for a broom, should he see you."

"Sir Walter?"

"Oh, go along with you." Susannah shooed her daughters toward the stairs. "I vow, I should have had all sons, for Thomas is the only one among my children who can keep a sober tongue for the passing of a moment."

Joanna leaned into Elinor as she rushed her from the room.

"That's only because when Thomas speaks his voice breaks first low, then high, like a piper with the staggers!" she whispered.

Elinor swatted her sister gently and they raced up the stairs together, giggling. When they reached Elinor's chamber, Elinor stopped in the center of the room and made a slow turn, taking in everything.

A few things were different than she recalled, but on

332

the whole, it was her childhood room. It was familiar but also a trifle small. How long she had been away.

"Are you ready, m'lady?"

A serving girl that Elinor had never seen poked her head in the door.

"The water is heated for the bath, lady."

"Yes, I suppose I could use a bath," Elinor said. "But can it not wait? I'm so tired and it's been so long since I've been home, in my own room."

"As you say, lady."

The maid withdrew, brow furrowed.

"Goose." Joanna lifted a comb from Elinor's table and pointed to the chair. "Here, I'll tend your hair. 'Can it not wait?' " she mimicked. " 'It's been so long.' As if you weren't here only this morning, when Sir Walter and Papa came to waken you!"

Elinor gazed at her sister in puzzlement and then in horror as realization dawned. Sir Walter and Papa coming to waken her. Get bathed and made ready . . . Sir Toby to be here . . . the flutter over the . . .

Elinor sat down in the chair, her legs having turned to wet straw. She'd been so caught up in the joy of seeing her family and her home restored that she hadn't been listening to what anyone was saying to her.

Saints in heaven, she thought. She'd arrived home just in time for her own wedding.

Chapter Twenty-two

Elinor stood in the center of the room and allowed the maids and Joanna to dress her in her wedding gown. They chattered and giggled and poked one another in high good humor, little noticing how solemn the bride-to-be had become.

In less than an hour, she was to descend from this chamber and be handed to Sir Walter of Brasswell, to become his wife and lady—all because Roger Aston had vanished on a bridge in a faraway land, five hundred years in the future. It was a predicament she never could have dreamed, not even in her wildest childhood fancies.

Drew would be shaking his head and declaring that she was a menace to his mental and physical health. But there was no chance that her Drew could ride Harley into Oakfield Hall and rescue her, right from in front of the priest and all the assembled guests. Delphinium would not come with her odd little cannon. She would have to deal with this herself.

"I need to be alone!" She shooed the women toward the door. "I have prayers to say for my marriage and I would say them in private."

"But, my lady!" one of them gasped, while the others stared, open-mouthed.

"Linnie! Are you going mad?" Joanna looked at her with suspicion. "Are you ill again? Or are you—"

"Heed me, please," Elinor said firmly. "I shan't be long, and the priest and the others will surely not begrudge me my prayers on such an occasion."

"Mama will have my ears if I come down without you!"

"I shall retrieve them for you, imp. Now go!"

Elinor shut the door behind them and listened for the clatter of feet and the last of the echoing, querulous voices fading down the stairs. Then, as silently as she could manage, she slipped the bolt in the door.

She paced the room, straining to think.

She had believed she was free.

Her family was secure. Her parents were alive, something she hadn't dared dream. Her brother was getting his chance to grow into a fine man. Her sister was her usual irrepressible self.

Yet she hadn't thought that their security could threaten her own plans and dreams.

She looked about the old room that seemed so much smaller than she remembered. She loved this place, aye, she thought. And she loved her family. She loved the abbey, as well, though only for the scant protection it offered from unwanted marriage and for the freedom to paint and draw. Yet even if everything were as perfect as a dream, she knew it would not fulfill her deepest desire.

In Drew's world, she would have a chance to do the work she loved, with no limits to her choices save those imposed by her own imagination or skill. But even that was not enough. She could still be an artist if she remained in the abbey.

335

Coral Smith Saxe

'Twas Drew himself made all the difference.

The love she'd shared with him, the love she knew would grow and deepen over time, was what would bring her the deepest joy and satisfaction. Drew was the one who had brought her out into the world again, showed her a different sort of life than one that was rimmed by abbey walls. She couldn't remain in this time and place, even as a sister of the order at Wednesbury. A wider kingdom beckoned.

She smiled. Drew always called her Princess. He'd been right. She'd walled herself inside her own little kingdom believing that no person, no idea, mattered save what she deemed worthy. Even when trying to rescue her family, she'd been adamant that all must proceed on her terms and that no one else could help her or suggest another tactic. And yet the fates had conspired to break down every possible wall—time, distance and her own iron will—so that she might learn to open her heart and her vision.

It was sweet to be reunited with her family once more and to see them all prosperous and healthy. There would be more trials for them, as was the way of all lives in this world. But she had done her part in serving them, succeeding beyond her wildest hope. They must go on without her aid. And she without theirs.

She felt under her gown for the medallion. Its moon was securely attached over the solemn sun; dear Louis Feldon had done his job with a master's skill. But would it take her back to the place, the time, she desired?

She had to try.

Drew, Bear and Will Curran lounged on Curran's deck, taking long, leisurely pulls from misted bottles of cold beer. Cubbie, Tuck and Jennie splashed about in the shallow end of the pool, yipping and laughing, while Rita sat on the edge, dangling her toes in the water. The early summer sun caught the drops that rose above the children's heads and turned them to diamonds in the air. Toys, clothes, towels and sandals were scattered all along the varying levels of decking down to the pool; the remains of a very ordinary lunch of hot dogs, hamburgers and green salad decorated the redwood table.

"The place looks good," Will said, peering about at the cheerful mess. "I've been working on this house for years, looking for the perfect stuff. And you and Rita had it at your place all along."

"We're not movin' in, and it ain't for sale," said Bear. "Get your own, Doc."

"Would that I could. Does Rita have a sister?"

"Yep. Six foot tall, married to an Olympic shot-putter. They live in one of those ashrams down in Los Gatos where they eat raw barley and cashew butter."

"Hmm. Probably no chance there." Will turned to Drew. "What about Elinor? Is there a rosy-cheeked little English maid there for me?"

Drew gave a soft laugh. "Sure. She's nine years old and hell-bent on becoming the next Robin Hood, from what Elinor tells me."

"Hmm, no. Precocious but still too young." Will heaved a dramatic sigh. "Guess I'll just have to put an ad in the classifieds. 'Single white wealthy male psychiatrist seeks demure yet libidinous supermodel with her own Harley for lab research, vacuum-tube radio collecting and marital bliss. Must be over age of consent.' That should cover it."

"Don't worry," said Bear. "She's out there. She just hasn't been referred to your clinic yet. So when's Elinor coming back, man?" he asked, turning to Drew. "The band down at the Fish has been asking about her. Jennie, too."

"No worries, mate," Drew said smoothly. "She'll be back just as soon as she settles her family's affairs in England."

"I can't believe you didn't go with her," Will said. "Were she the least bit interested in me, I'd chain myself to her leg."

"Sounds real healthy, Doc," Bear rumbled.

"Hey, you know my professional motto: It takes one to know one."

Drew listened to the two of them banter as he savored the warmth and peace of the day. He had thought he'd be miserable and desperate, waiting for Elinor's return. And he did miss her, as if he had lost a part of himself. Yet it wasn't a hideous pain, like the pain he'd felt when LeeAnne had died. He felt a peace within himself that he'd never felt before, a peace with his own soul and with life. The place where Elinor alone belonged in his heart would be filled. His faith was as steady as the ancient stars. He didn't know how he knew that—he simply did.

The time was drawing near, in fact. Over the past two weeks, he'd kept himself busier than he'd been in a long time. He visited old friends and renewed old acquaintances. He spent many hours with Delphinium Talcott, helping her with repairs to her ramshackle old house and running errands. He'd had dinner with Louis Feldon and listened with wonder and respect to tales of the world before the war and of the death camp where a young Louis had managed, miraculously, to survive. He'd even volunteered to baby-sit for Bear and Rita, proud to gain a few new coping skills when it came to kids.

He even savored fantasies of a family with Elinor. That is, until he recalled that they had used no protection the night they'd spent in Del's house. Elinor alone in the Middle Ages, pregnant with his child, was one image that did manage to shake his calm. He offered up a prayer or two on that score.

He took on a couple of new jobs, breaking his standing policy of one bike at a time. And just this morning, he and Bear had scouted the area for the perfect place to open a shop—their own Harley shop. Will would provide some of the seed money as an investment and Bear and Drew would run the place. Rita had bitten her lip at the risk they were taking, but she had cheered them on, with the proviso that they begin by soliciting customers in the City, where even bikers had to have high-paying jobs just to afford parking.

Drew had come back to life, just as Will had said. The memories of LeeAnne were actually fresher than they had been, but the first shock was past and the pain was growing duller with each passing day. He was glad he'd told Elinor about his marriage before she'd left. He'd hidden long enough. It was time to not only drive out into the world, but allow the world to drive on in.

His peace was made, with one exception.

He needed Elinor to share it. Elinor and Elinor alone.

It seemed ironic that after his obsession with Lee-Anne, he would be again so totally devoted to one particular woman. But there it was. He was completely in love with and committed to the Lady Elinor Elizabeth Justinia DeCourtenay of the Year of Our Lord Fourteen Hundred and Twenty.

But where his love for LeeAnne had been a smothering, choking emotion—if love was indeed what you'd call it—his feelings for Elinor had somehow pulled him up and shaken him out and opened his eyes to the world. Because of Elinor, he felt alive once more and glad to know it.

Princess Elinor, who cooked with sparrows and believed that the moon governed the politics of nations, had been a refreshing smack on the head, bringing him to his senses and sending him forth to do battle not only with Roger Aston, but with his own inner demons, as well. It had taken a woman from the past to drag him into the present. A woman who was, at least technically, dead had brought him back to life.

"Yo, Ingraham." Bear snapped his fingers in front of

Drew's eyes. "You with us, buddy?"

"Yeah, sure. What's the plan?"

"Got a lead on some Shovelhead parts down in Salinas. You want to ride down there tomorrow and take a look? Rita says she'll take the van."

"No. I trust you to know what we need and what's a good price. I have something else I need to do tomorrow."

"You sure?"

Drew raised his hand and gave the big man a high five. "You best be believin'."

"Okay. Wanna ride with us, Doc? Might be some fine lady waitin' for you down the El Camino Real."

Will nodded. "Yeah. I think you might be right." He gave Drew a quick glance, then asked casually, "Any bridges to cross down Salinas way that you know of?"

Drew raised an eyebrow but said nothing. He wasn't going to rise to Will's bait. Doc would have to find his own pathways into love.

The next morning, he rose early and cleaned and swept the little house. He had ripped out the north wall and was still in the process of placing a large plate-glass window there. He'd wanted it finished before Elinor's return, as a special gift. The prospect of seeing her in that unique light, working away with paint and pens, was enough to spur him on until well into the night. Of course, she'd want to know all the details of how he'd found the glass, carried it to the house, cut the hole and so on, but they'd have a lifetime to satisfy her curiosity.

Without any conscious thought, he finished his cleaning, changed his clothes and donned his jacket. He headed for the garage and mounted up, making certain that he wore one helmet and carried a second.

Body and mind alert and tuned to one thought, one goal, he turned out onto the highway and headed for Venners Creek. In his saddlebags were clothing for Eli-

340

nor, food, spring water, motion sickness patches and an icy bottle of Korbel's best champagne.

He was on his way to reclaim his heart.

Walter Brasswell was a nice-looking man, Elinor decided, peeking into the great hall from the gallery overhead. She hoped he would not be too embarrassed by what she was about to do.

She had coached Joanna in what she was to tell the assembled company, and Joanna, ever the romantic and always up for anything out of the ordinary, was delighted to oblige. Elinor murmured a quick prayer that her sprightly little sister did not embellish the tale overmuch just for the sake of drama.

Now for the journey, she thought, fingering the medallion about her neck. So far, the magic in the golden talisman had served her as she'd guessed it would, bearing her across the ocean to England and across the centuries to her own time. Would it be so obedient in this next endeavor?

She set aside the possibilities, good and bad. She didn't need to consider them. There was only one thing to do: try. Nothing else mattered but returning to Drew.

She crept down the back stairs at Joanna's signal, cloaked and hooded. The spring day that had shone so brightly on her homecoming had turned sullen as she slipped into the pantry and scurried out the pantry door to the yards. Clouds were boiling up overhead, she saw, and the wind was beginning to lash at the trees in the orchards just outside the manor's walls. Though it was but little past noon, the sky was dimming into an early twilight.

She gained the path that led to the outbuildings without encountering a soul. The shops were all dark, the workers sent home with ale and sweetmeats in honor of the occasion. The house-servants were occupied, she imagined, some pressed into service as cooks and some bustling about waiting on the ladies

and lords in attendance at the marriage of Lady De-
Courtenay and Lord Brasswell. She prayed she'd have
time to escape the grounds before Joanna shared her
news. It was entirely possible a search would commence at once, with Susannah DeCourtenay in the
lead.

Elinor made her way along the well-worn path that
wove in and out, connecting the spinning and weaving
shop, the farrier's shop, the tannery, and so on. She
could hear the clamor in the stables before she
rounded the corner of the farrier's shop. Good-natured
shouts and brays of laughter mingled with the snorts
and whinnies of the horses.

The wedding ale was flowing already, she guessed.
So much the better. The attentions of the men would
be on drink and horses and their plans for the night's
revels. She slipped by, head down, heart pounding. She
entered the shadows of the carts and wagons that stood
beyond the stables and sighed her relief.

Now for the gate.

The sky was growing so dark that Elinor wished she
could have lifted one of the torches out of the rough
iron sconces that hung beside the stable doors. As she
scurried in among the low-growing trees and hedges
along the west wall, she wondered how she'd made it
that first time. It had been full dark then, and she'd had
to come all the way down the hill-road from Clarisdoune to reach the bridge, with Roger roaring at her
heels.

The west gate was just ahead. Old Cranham was on
the watch. She hesitated, remaining just inside the
shelter of the hedgerow. It would be impossible to
evade the old fellow. She'd have to confront him. She
backed up several paces.

"Well met, Cranham," she called out, striding forward as if she'd just reached the gate. "And how do you
fare this afternoon?"

The old man, still spry and tanned as good leather,

squinted to see under her hood. He straightened up at once and made a rusty bow, doffing his cap.

"Lady Elinor," he said. "I had no thought of ye comin' out here. Be'n't the wedding about to commence?"

"No, no," Elinor said, waving her fingers airily. "The wedding couldn't start without the bride, now could it?"

"True enow," he said slowly. "But what're ye doing out here? All I been hearin' for days is the lady's gown and the lady's slippers and the lady's hair and all such flutterin's from out the house. I'd thought ye'd be gettin' fussed 'long about this time."

Elinor laughed. "Truth to tell, Cranham, I'm not much of a one for fussings. I slipped out for a moment's breath of air out in the orchards. I see they're starting to blossom." She moved toward the gate.

"Aye." He reached out for the bar over the small entry door, but let it rest there as he worked his lower lip with his teeth. "Ye wouldn't be runnin' away from His Lordship, would ye?"

Elinor almost choked. "No. I scarcely know the man. I have no reason to fear him."

Cranham's head bobbed. "That's the lass, if ye'll pardon my boldness, lady. He's gettin' the finest in two duchies and if he don't know it, ye just send him along to your old Cran and I'll tell him straight, lord or no."

Elinor gave his hand a squeeze. "Thank you," she said, glad for a few wholly honest words to give to this loyal servant. "I won't forget it."

He hoisted the bar with a grunt and pushed the door open for her.

"Don't ye be out too long, lady," he called after her as she hurried out. "There's a storm comin' and ye don't want to be catchin' your death on your weddin' night!"

She waved and nodded and tried not to break into a run until he had closed the gate and she was well out

Coral Smith Saxe

of his line of sight. She moved vaguely in the direction
of the cherry orchard, then, with a backward glance at
the gate, veered left and set a straight course for the
stream and the Oakfield Bridge.

Venners Creek Bridge, she told herself as she broke
into a run. That's what it would be from now on, for
her as it was for Drew.

The clouds dipped low before her, almost reaching
the ground with their fat, dark bellies. She was in for
a wetting, after all. She didn't care. Nothing could stop
her now.

Her feet felt like birds, skimming this way and that,
avoiding rocks and ruts almost before she'd seen them.
Up the hill, she told herself. Over the rise is the little
vale with its gushing stream. Across the stream—the
bridge.

The light was going as she gained the top of the rise.
She stopped. "Dear Lady," she moaned.

Below her, on the plain that stretched to the stream,
bright lights were waving and bobbing. Straining to see
in the gathering dark, she caught glimpses of metal
here and there, and now and then a human form out-
lined by fire.

Thunder rolled, a sound of Armageddon's trumpets
to Elinor's ears. And as the echoes rolled to the far hills,
lightning flashed.

Elinor sank to her knees on the grassy hilltop, partly
because her legs were in rebellion and partly so that
she wouldn't be illuminated by the same flash. She
choked on a cry of despair.

On the banks of the Dunnill Stream, close by the
Oakfield Bridge—her bridge—a host of mailed knights
were making camp for the night. To Elinor's panicked
mind, they looked to be half the royal forces of King
Henry himself.

She would have to go back or take shelter out here
in the storm alone. She twisted about to view the path
behind her.

344

"No," she whispered. Yet she knew it was true. The hunting party was indeed issuing forth from the gates of Oakfield House, torches in hand, despite the breaking storm.

She couldn't go back. She couldn't go forward. She had to find a place to hide.

It was then that she heard the dogs.

Chapter Twenty-three

Drew sat on Delphinium's tree stump munching an apple. He didn't have his watch—what good would it have done? Just tracking the sun sliding slowly across the sky toward the sea was enough to tell him that he'd been here for at least five hours. He couldn't say what he'd expected but he felt a cold uneasiness nipping at the edges of his mind. It had been too long.

He took another bite of the apple. *That's nuts, Ingraham,* he told himself. He didn't really know she would return today, let alone the hour or minute of her arrival.

You don't even know if she is coming back, a bitter voice announced in his mind. *You don't know if she's just a pile of dust somewhere in the fields of England. You don't even know if she ever lived. What if it was all a delusion, Drew, old pal? Kinda like LeeAnne and your marriage?*

He tossed the apple core aside and got up, stretching his legs.

"Go to hell," he told the voice.

Elinor was coming back. His own uneasiness told him that much.

But how? And when?

He couldn't believe that the powerful force that had drawn him out here to this spot, on this day, was a mere whim, or the effects of indigestion or whatever excuse he cared to trot out for the benefit of that snide voice of doubt. He was supposed to be here, just as he'd been on that first night.

He heard a roll of thunder far off. He peered up into the cloudless blue and shrugged. Storm at sea maybe, he thought.

The light was fading around him. He whirled about, squinting. Above the treetops to the west, the sun shone cheerily. It was hours until sunset. Yet he was having trouble seeing.

"I don't like this," he said aloud. "This wasn't supposed to be on the test."

He strode to the bridge and placed the toes of his boots so that they were just off the first stone of the pavement. He didn't know if it would make any difference if he was on the bridge when Elinor returned, but he didn't want to chance it.

Thunder grumbled again, closer this time. Drew ignored it, centering his concentration on the bridge and Elinor.

He didn't like the feeling that was starting to flow over him. It was part electricity, wild and tingling, and part sickening fear. Something was happening. Something was happening on the bridge.

But was it in his time or Elinor's? Hell, he didn't even know if anyone else could travel on this bridge. Could someone else be trying to pass through the centuries contained in these old stones?

The time for pondering was over. A crack of thunder pealed, right over his head, it seemed, followed by a flash so bright that when it passed, Drew saw everything printed on the insides of his eyelids in photo-negative reverse imagery. When he opened his eyes an instant later, night had fallen.

"I've done it again," Elinor muttered to herself. "The whole county riding to hounds and I'm the deer they're chasing."

That was the news from one direction. In the other, a contingent of soldiers was setting up camp on the very stones of her bridge, it seemed.

She could go back and be scolded, railed at, lectured, and then, will her, nil her, she'd be wed to Lord Brasswell. And the very idea of trying to explain her actions to her parents was out of the question.

She could go on and try to steal past armed watchmen and a few dozen knights, many trained to kill without so much as a twitch of the eye let alone the conscience. That was an excellent prospect, to be sure.

She could run now and hope to take shelter among the gorse, praying the dogs would lose her scent in the rain and the fragrant, thorn-laden shrubs.

She could run to a pay phone and dial 911, just the way Rita had showed her.

She could sprout wings and fly.

Think, she told herself, clenching her fists so tightly her nails dug deep into her palms. *I must think before the search party fans out and surrounds me. Before some scouting soldier stumbles across me.*

There was only one thing she wanted more than her life: Drew. And there was no other way to reach him save by the bridge. She'd go on—and take her chances with the army of the king.

The rain was coming now, pouring down. She descended the hill, her hood sheltering her head and face and helping to make her as shapeless as a shadow against the dark hillside. She was running fast by the time she reached the bottom, and her momentum almost pitched her forward into the mud. So much for the lovely violet wedding gown, she thought as she dragged her wet skirts up around her. She staggered a few steps, gained her balance and lit out once more, running and dodging as best she could, making her way toward the left-hand edge of the encampment.

She kept out beyond the reach of the torches that flickered and sputtered in the rain. Meager bonfires flared up here and there and she saw men huddled around them, struggling to cook their suppers. Lights were glowing from inside the tents, where the higher-ranking men rested in relative warmth and comfort. If they stayed well occupied, she might slip by without notice.

Or so she thought. Two men, each Bear-sized and armed with lances and swords, marched to and fro before the entrance to the bridge. Slipping past them was as likely as anyone believing that Elinor needed to use that bridge in order to keep a tryst with her lover five hundred years in the future.

The direct approach had worked with old Cranham at the gate. It might be worth a try with these two. She pulled a long, bracing breath of courage into her lungs and started for the bridge.

"God 'ee good e'en, sirs," she called out while she was still well out of their reach. "Might a gel get across there and go on outta the wet?"

The men stopped. One looked back over his shoulder toward the opposite end of the bridge, on guard against a surprise from the rear. The other one lowered his sword and scowled.

"Ain't no camp-followers allowed," he announced. "Get on wi' ye, gel."

"Oh, I will, sir," Elinor said, mincing a bit as she moved closer. "But your lance is a bit in my way." She grinned. "Me mum was frighted by just such a lance once upon a time, she was."

The second soldier, satisfied that no ambush was coming from across the bridge, gave a grunting chuckle at this. "More like she was frighted by the fella what carried the lance," he said.

"Oh, I wouldn't know," Elinor said, trying to keep up the banter. "I weren't there at the time."

"Right, but I'll wager you was along right smart after, eh?" The first soldier lowered his lance. "Awright. Get on now. If the sergeant finds us cozyin' here wif a bit of skirt it'll be back to muckin' out after the 'orses for us."

Elinor flashed him a genuine smile of gratitude as she passed onto the bridge. " 'Night, then, lads. Stay warm if ye can," she called over her shoulder.

She hadn't gone more than halfway across when a shout from the camp drew the two guards away from their posts. She chuckled and turned back to her path, her hand reaching for the medallion under her dress.

"And who'll keep me warm, then?" a voice asked from out of the dark.

Elinor jumped at the sound. She froze, scanning the darkness for the speaker.

A tall man stepped out of the shadows before her. A distant flare of lightning lit his form for a moment. He was lean and well-muscled, she saw, and he carried himself easily under the weight of his chain mail tabard.

"God 'ee good e'en, sir," she said again. "I'm just goin' across to me old granmam's house to get dry."

"Your granmam, eh?" He came closer, his heavy boots ringing on the stones. "And how much does she charge for a nice piece like you?"

"Oh, sir," Elinor said, forcing a high-pitched giggle from her dry mouth. "Get along wif you. She ain't any such a one."

"No?" He stepped nearer still. "Well, then, if she doesn't charge, I don't have to pay, do I?"

Elinor backed up a step.

"I ain't a whore," she said. "Besides, them two back there said their captain or some such a fellow said there was to be no camp-followers or lightskirts about you lot. You wouldn't want to get in it bad over a stupid country gel, would you?"

"No, I suppose I wouldn't," he said, stepping up again. "Only I'm not too worried. I am their captain."

She caught the stench of sour wine on his breath and felt him move even closer. She knew she should run, but where could she go? He'd catch her, or one of his men, and then she'd be in greater danger than ever before.

"Well," she said, trying with little success to keep her voice from shaking. "So you're the captain what makes the rules, are you? And what do they call you?"

"Sir."

She giggled again. "Not Johnny?" She gave a little jump to the side. "Not Willy?" She gave another little hop, eluding his hands as they reached out to grab her. "Or do they call you Cap'n Willy?"

He reached out again but she managed to dance away. She had to get back to the other end of the bridge. From there, at least, she might scream for help and deflect the man's advances.

He lunged, quicker than the lightning that seemed to set the world aflame to Elinor's terrified mind. He caught her by the elbows, pinning her arms at her sides.

"Not Johnny," he whispered roughly against her ear. "Not Willy." He yanked her against him. "Sir, bitch."

He caught her hands together and raised them over her head in one iron fist. With his other he reached under her cloak and slid his hand down over her body, his fingers roughly probing, pinching. He fastened his mouth to her neck, kissing her roughly, scraping her skin with his beard.

She struggled against him, trying to gain her balance on the slippery stones under her feet.

He raised his head for a moment and gave her a sly, sidelong look.

Coral Smith Saxe

"That's silk you're wearing, my little wet whore. Where did you steal a silk gown? Or was it your pay?" He chuckled. "No matter. I don't care who's tumbled you before. I just want to know if you're worth the price. It ain't gonna cost me a ha'penny."

Elinor opened her mouth to scream. He backhanded her across the mouth. She tasted blood and moaned. He meant to kill her. She could see it in his eyes. If she so much as crossed him, he'd snap her neck.

"Ready then, are you?" he said calmly. "Eager bitch, already screaming and moaning. I like that."

He yanked her arms up painfully and gave her a shove, forcing her back toward the wall of the bridge. Elinor had to scramble to keep upright as he pushed her across the rain-slick stones. When her back came up against the wall, he took a firmer grip on her wrists, braced one hip against her and began to fumble at the hem of her skirt. She struggled, managing to kick him, but he only chuckled, slapped her and went back to pushing up her skirt.

Elinor was awash in panic and pain. She twisted and bit at him, her anger rising. If she died, she was fully prepared to take some of him with her when she went.

What was happening? She was on the bridge with him, she had the medallion. Why were they still in this time? Had the medallion failed after all?

He had her dress up about her hips by now and was fumbling at her undergarments. "What the hell is this?" he grunted, his big fingers ripping at the silk of her briefs. "What kind of—oof!"

Curiosity killed the cat, Elinor wanted to say as her knee connected with his private parts. But she was too busy wrenching herself out of his grasp. She got a hand free and seized the chain at her throat. With a mighty surge, she tore her other hand loose from his grasp and burst forward, heading back down the bridge toward the camp.

She didn't get far. There was a clap of thunder, a

burst of lightning, and she was falling . . .

Thunder rang around and around her head as the captain yanked her up by her hair. But something was wrong. Had he pulled her hair out by the roots? She was falling down again, falling and screaming. The captain was screaming now, too.

Blackness again. And the sound of thunder.

"Holy—"

Elinor repeated dutifully. "Holy Mary, Mother of God—"

There was blackness all around her and echoing, sickening noise. She was trying to stand.

But she should be on her knees. She had penance, did she not?

"Elinor, get back!"

"I can't," she murmured. "It isn't working, Drew. I can't get back—"

"Come no closer! I'll slit her right now if you do!"

Oh, wonderful, she thought giddily. She was dragged up by her hair once more.

"Let her go."

"Who the devil are you?" the captain growled.

"Let go of her, dirtbag, or I'll take you apart like a jigsaw puzzle."

Dirtybag. Another word Elinor didn't know. She'd have to ask—oh, God!

"Drew!" she shrieked, coming to her senses at last. "Drew, get back! He'll kill you!"

Elinor was back and fully awake. She felt hot and clammy. She felt the blade that was pressed against her throat. Not again. She also felt the chain mail that was digging into her shoulder. The captain was armed and ready to do business on his own terms. Drew, she saw, was unarmed.

"Come on," Drew said, his voice soft but taunting. "I don't even have a gun, tin man. You going to just hide behind her skirts?"

Elinor stiffened as the blade pressed a little closer against her throat. Was Drew insane? Taunting the man was an invitation to a funeral—Drew's and hers. This fellow would murder them both for lesser crimes, she sensed.

To her shock, the captain released her, shoving her aside as he lunged for Drew. She stumbled and fell, the nausea rising again. She felt as if all of her bones had been knocked loose. A wretched buzzing filled her ears. She fought against the blackness that was creeping over her. She mustn't swoon, she told herself.

"Nice tunic, big fella," she heard Drew say. "Your mommy knit that for you out of your bottle-cap collection?"

Drew. He'd lost his mind. She had to get to him, make him stop. They had to run.

She scrabbled at the stones with her fingertips and managed to drag herself to the wall. She fought her way up to where she could stand against the wall and turn to look.

She was just in time to see the captain slit Drew's shirtfront. She screamed, but Drew danced backward, twisting away from the blade, a grim little smile playing about his lips.

The soldier slashed again, swinging his sword with the full force of his massive body behind each movement. Drew was backing off the bridge, impossibly light on his feet, still taunting the armored man, daring him to attack. To Elinor's panicky mind, he looked like a fly wading in to do battle with an eagle. She had to help him.

She sucked in air and let it fill her lungs. She exhaled, let it out again, feeling the heaviness in her limbs abate. She took advantage of the momentary restoration of her strength, staggering forward, pursuing the two men over the bridge.

Drew left the bridge first. The soldier came on, sword upraised to split his opponent in half. Drew squatted, spun away, and came up again, a fallen branch in his hands.

Elinor felt hope surge within her. Drew wielded the branch first like a stick used to poke at a trained bear. Then he whirled it somehow between his hands and brought it down with a crack on the soldier's forearm.

With a howl, the man retreated but held onto his sword. Drew waited, legs apart, the branch held out in a line across his torso. The captain attacked, Drew countered. The captain came on like a windmill, his sword swinging from every direction. Drew's staff was always there, always blocking the heavy sword strokes.

But Elinor could see the chips flying from the branch. It wasn't going to hold, she thought, especially if the broadsword hit the same spot twice or thrice. She saw Drew dance in, gasped in horror at the nearness of the blade, then cried aloud in wonder as Drew raised the short end of the branch and dealt the soldier a punishing, backhanded blow to the head. He kept it up, dancing in, delivering a whack, then dancing out of reach.

Then it happened. The soldier made his lucky stroke. With a crack that was as loud as the thunder to Elinor's ears, the sword clove through, breaking the branch into two parts and sending it flying out of Drew's grasp. Elinor's hand flew to her throat, stifling her scream.

She looked down at her hand. She'd found a way to help Drew.

"Dirtybag!" she called to the captain. "Couldn't finish what you started wif me, could you, laddie?" She cocked one hip and tossed her hair back over her shoulder.

"I'll have plenty of time for you later—"

Drew waded in again, this time with his feet. Elinor almost forgot her plan, and the danger, at the sight of him delivering wide, high kicks to the knight's legs, head and middle, never letting the man gain ground. She found herself cheering hoarsely.

But there was a price for such close combat. Drew's rhythm faltered momentarily and the knight regained his stance. The sword flashed out, and this time Elinor saw a crimson stain bloom on Drew's shirt sleeve.

"Bastard!" she shrieked.

She ran at the knight's back and jumped on him, locking her arms around his neck. He roared and slapped at her but she held fast. In an act of pure savage rage, she opened her mouth and bit down on his ear. He screamed and tossed her off of him, staggering back, one hand clapped to his bleeding head.

Elinor dashed for Drew, knocking him backwards with the force of her body in motion. He stumbled back, gained his balance and tried to set her aside.

"No! Drew, stay here!" she cried, pushing him back again. "Wait—"

She scrabbled at the chain around her neck and managed to pull the medallion up. It caught in the tangle of her hair, and she shrieked her frustration through clenched teeth. Her scalp stung as she dragged hard on the heavy gold woven into her long hair.

Drew was on his way back to the bridge when she at last got the medallion free. The knight was staggering, holding his ear and making retching sounds. The time sickness was overtaking him at last, Elinor thought as she raced for Drew once more.

She grabbed for the collar of his shirt and yanked him back with such ferocity that half the buttons popped off and flew about like hailstones. With a yelp, he turned to look at her, his face red with outrage.

"Stay away from the bridge," she cried before he could speak. "Stay here!"

She lifted the medallion and began to swing it in a circle over her head.

"Elinor, no!" Drew lunged and caught her hand. "You won't be able to get back! Your family!"

She gave one last look across the bridge and shook her head. "You're my family."

He stared at her for a moment, but a sound from the bridge brought their attention back to the soldier. Drew released her and stepped aside.

She raised her hand, spun the chain once again and let the necklace fly. She watched it arc away, a glint of stars sailing across the cloud-dimmed sky. It made a perfect connection, winding itself around the soldier's neck with a hiss and a solid thunk. The knight's hands flew to his neck in surprise.

Then he disappeared.

Elinor dropped to the ground, crying and laughing in hysterical relief. All at once, Drew was with her, holding her. They knelt there in the road for a long time.

Drew sat on the ground beneath the leafing apple trees, munching another apple while Elinor gathered herbs and mixed them with Evian to make a poultice for his injured arm.

"Just to be sure," she said as she tied off the bandage she'd made from the edge of her undershirt, "you'd best put some of your anti-ointment on it when we reach home."

"Antibiotic," he said automatically. "How come you're not sick? Last time you traveled, you were so wiped out you could hardly walk."

She sat back on her heels. "I'm not sure. Roger had also drugged me last time, you know. That may have added to it. Yet I was green as yon apple leaves when that knave and I returned on the bridge today. I believe much of it went away when he disappeared."

"Or when the medallion disappeared?"

Drew's eyes were tender. "Elinor," he said, touching her cheek. "I'm sorry you can't go home again. If you hadn't gotten involved with me, you'd—"

She pushed his hand away.

"Such pride!" she said, shaking her head. "And I suppose you wish for me to bow down and thank you for letting the sun rise this day?"

"Now what are you on about? I'm not proud that you can't go home." He groaned. "Look who's lecturing me about royal pride!"

She folded her hands in her lap and looked at him in her best thin-lipped imitation of Mother Agnes.

"The sin of pride is not limited to vanity over one's good works," she intoned. "One may also suffer a fancy that he is all-powerful in doing damage where he truly has no influence."

"Okay, Sister Elinor," he drawled. "Just what am I so sinfully proud about?"

"Me."

"You?"

"Aye. Was it you who dragged me through time to this place?"

"No, but—"

"Were you the author of the medallion?"

"No. I—"

"Did you drag a villainous knight with you to endanger us both on this bridge?"

"Elinor!"

She shook her head. "Nay, your argument is all straws, sir. You may not take honor for my flight from the wedding my happy, healthy parents did arrange for me."

"Your parents are alive?" he cried, his face alight. He scowled. "What do you mean, wedding?"

She gave him a prim nod. "See? You do not know all, sir. I arrived at Oakfield to find family, bridegroom, priest and wedding guests awaiting my entrance for the ceremony. Needless to say, I did not wish to be married to Walter of Brasswell at this time, so I—"

Drew grabbed her by the shoulders and kissed her soundly. She kissed him back with rising joy. Suddenly he set her back and stared.

"Your parents were going to make you marry that

tin-plated thug?" He gestured toward the bridge.

"Nay. That was not he. Walter is a good man. But his horse lacks style. I prefer Harley. Walter is simply not my typing."

"Type. But who was that goon, then?"

"I know not. When I ran from home, I was pursued by my family, riding out with dogs and horns and all good intentions to save me from my own folly. Ahead of me, a score of king's soldiers were camped at the bridge. I knew, somehow, that I must return to you this day. I don't know why. Still, I ran through the storm till I gained the bridge and was granted permission to cross. The moment I started across, my family and friends arrived at the camp and the bridge was deserted, save for Sir Captain Goon."

Drew swore a good, round oath.

"Elinor," he said, seizing her by the shoulders and giving her a shake. "You might have been killed or—"

"I know," she whispered. The fresh realization of how close she'd come to being raped and murdered in another time caused her heart to contract.

She shook for a moment, letting the fear and shock run its course through her system. Drew took her hands in his firm grasp, anchoring her firmly to him, to now, to here.

"I could not comprehend why the medallion was failing," she went on. "Sir Goon and I should have been transported by then. I managed to give the villain a kick in a place that would give him pause for consideration—"

Drew broke into a cheer. "Mother Agnes would be proud!"

"—and in that moment I was able to fetch the necklace from inside my gown. Once it was in my hand, we . . . arrived here."

"It has—had—to be in your hands in order to work?"

"I imagine so."

His eyes narrowed. "Did you know that when you did that slingshot business?"

She shook her head, raised her shoulders. "In truth, I only came to understood it now, as I spoke. I wasn't thinking when I threw it at him—I simply threw. I was blessed lucky to have it land so well, but I think now it was his hand upon the thing that sent him away. Just as it had worked once more when I took it into mine own hand."

Drew kissed her again.

"You never do anything small, do you?" he asked in amused wonder. "What am I going to do with you? How am I going to protect you from yourself?"

"Your pride is showing again, sir," she said, smiling. "But you did protect me marvelous well, my love. As soon as we get home I want you to teach me to do those dancing kicks. You fairly flew about Sir Goon!" She made several jabbing motions with her hands.

"Whoa," he said, chuckling and holding up his hands. "That was just something I picked up from Will. Besides, we aren't home yet."

He leaned toward her, light flickering from the depths of his eyes. "Do you want to go now?"

She laid her arms on his shoulders, clasping her hands at the back of his neck.

"Mmm, let me consider," she said, gazing about.

The sky was clearing, showing a sunset of peach and aqua, with broad golden rays piercing the remaining clouds. The last of the apple blossoms drifted down like minute angels, coming to land on the lush grass beneath the trees, adding more blessings to the fragrant snowfall of blooms already heaped there.

Elinor thought of the storm and the troubles she had left behind in her old world, and how miraculous this one appeared to her, this place where Drew Ingraham's light blue eyes were smiling at her in the most plainly inviting way. She was a foreigner in this place, to be sure, but the longer she stayed here, the more fond she'd grown of that notion.

Everything was new in this world. There was so much more to learn, to try. So many pictures to paint, new foods to taste, new skills to master.

But most of all, here was love. She'd crossed the bridge for the last time. It was love that turned any hut, cave, country, place or time into a home. And she'd found her love here and now.

"I think I am home," she murmured, rising and reaching for his hand.

He stood and followed her into the orchard, to a spot where the branches of several trees reached almost to the ground, forming a canopy of bountiful green leaves, accented here and there with the sparkling white stars of the last blossoms.

She drew him into the grassy bower and released his hand. "You are my home," she murmured, kissing him tenderly. "For all time."

The sun slipped behind the trees and into the ocean, quenching itself. The stars winked into their assigned places. The moon peered in through the roof-branches of their leafy room and poured its night-silver over them, setting the blossoms aglow against the darkness of the grass. They fell asleep in the soothing light, bodies entwined like the branches over their heads.

At least, the sun woke them. With the languor of love soaked into their bones and spirits, they rose, dressed, and let the Master of All Beasts carry them to their new home: the future.

THE END

A Stolen Rose

CORAL SMITH SAXE

Bestselling Author Of *Enchantment*

Feared by all Englishmen and known only as the Blackbird, the infamous highwayman is really the stunning Morgana Bracewell. And though she is an aristocrat who has lost her name and family, nothing has prepared the well-bred thief for her most charming victim. Even as she robs Lord Phillip Greyfriars blind, she knows his roving eye has seen through her rogue's disguise—and into her heart. Now, the wickedly handsome peer will stop at nothing to possess her, and it will take all Morgana's cunning not to surrender to a man who will accept no ransom for her love.

__3843-9 $5.50 US/$7.50 CAN

BITTERROOT

TIMESWEPT

VICTORIA CHANCELLOR

Bestselling Author Of *Forever & A Day*

In the Wyoming Territory—a land both breathtaking and brutal—bitterroots grow every summer for a brief time. Therapist Rebecca Hartford has never seen such a plant—until she is swept back to the days of Indian medicine men, feuding ranchers, and her pioneer forebears. Nor has she ever known a man as dark, menacing, and devastatingly handsome as Sloan Travers. Sloan hides a tormented past, and Rebecca vows to use her professional skills to help the former Union soldier, even though she longs to succumb to personal desire. But when a mysterious shaman warns Rebecca that her sojourn in the Old West will last only as long as the bitterroot blooms, she can only pray that her love for Sloan is strong enough to span the ages....

_52087-7 $5.50 US/$7.50 CAN

Dorchester Publishing Co., Inc.
65 Commerce Road
Stamford, CT 06902

Please add $1.75 for shipping and handling for the first book and $.50 for each book thereafter. NY, NYC, PA and CT residents, please add appropriate sales tax. No cash, stamps, or C.O.D.s. All orders shipped within 6 weeks via postal service book rate. Canadian orders require $2.00 extra postage and must be paid in U.S. dollars through a U.S. banking facility.

Name _____

Address _____

City _____ State _____ Zip _____

I have enclosed $_____ in payment for the checked book(s).

Payment <u>must</u> accompany all orders. ☐ Please send a free catalog.

Rejar

DARA JOY

Lord Byron thinks he's a scream, the fashionable matrons titter behind their fans at a glimpse of his hard form, and nobody knows where he came from. His startling eyes—one gold, one blue—promise a wicked passion, and his voice almost seems to purr. There is only one thing a woman thinks of when looking at a man like that. *Sex.* And there is only one woman he seems to want. *Lilac.* In her wildest dreams she never guesses that bringing a stray cat into her home will soon have her stroking the most wanted man in 1811 London....

_52178-4 $5.99 US/$6.99 CAN